Good Old Anna

By

Marie Belloc Lowndes

Double9
BOOKS

Good Old Anna
by Marie Belloc Lowndes

Copyright © 2024

All Rights reserved.

ISBN: 978-93-61420-00-9

Published by

DOUBLE 9 BOOKS

2/13-B, Ansari Road
Daryaganj, New Delhi – 110002
info@double9books.com
www.double9books.com
Tel. 011-40042856

This book is under public domain

ABOUT THE AUTHOR

Marie Adelaide Elizabeth Rayner Lowndes (5 August 1868 – 14 November 1947), who wrote as Marie Belloc Lowndes, was an English author who wrote a lot of books. She was the sister of the author Hilaire Belloc. She was active from 1898 until her death, and her writing was known for mixing exciting events with psychological ones. Four of her books were made into movies: The Chink in the Armour (1912; adapted in 1922), The Lodger (1913; adapted several times), Letty Lynton (1931; adapted in 1932), and The Story of Ivy (1927; adapted in 1947). The Lodger was also turned into a radio play in 1940 and an opera in 1960. Belloc was born in London's Marylebone on George Street and grew up in La Celle-Saint-Cloud, France. She was the only child of French lawyer Louis Belloc and English feminist Bessie Parkes. Hilaire Belloc was her younger brother. In her last book, The Young Hilaire Belloc, which came out after she died in 1956, she wrote about him. The French painter Jean-Hilaire Belloc was Belloc's grandfather, and the philosopher and priest Joseph Priestley was her great-great-grandfather. It was 53 years after her father died that her mother passed away in 1925.

CONTENTS

CHAPTER I

And now," asked Miss Forsyth thoughtfully, "and now, my dear Mary, what, may I ask, are you going to do about your good old Anna?"

"Do about Anna?" repeated the other. "I don't quite understand what you mean."

In her heart Mrs. Otway thought she understood very well what her old friend, Miss Forsyth, meant by the question. For it was Wednesday, the 5th of August, 1914. England had just declared war on Germany, and Anna was Mrs. Otway's faithful, highly valued German servant.

Miss Forsyth was one of those rare people who always require an answer to a question, and who also (which is rarer still) seldom speak without having first thought out what they are about to say. It was this quality of mind, far more than the fact that she had been born, sixty years ago, in the Palace at Witanbury, which gave her the position she held in the society of the cathedral town.

But this time she herself went on speaking: "In your place I should think very seriously of sending Anna back to Germany." There was an unusual note of hesitation and of doubt in her voice. As a rule Miss Forsyth knew exactly what she thought about everything, and what she herself would be minded to do in any particular case.

But the other lady, incensed at what she considered uncalled-for, even rather impertinent advice, replied sharply, "I shouldn't think of doing anything so unkind and so unjust! Why, because the powers of evil have conquered—I mean by that the dreadful German military party—should I behave unjustly to a faithful old German woman who has been with me—let me see—why, who has been with me exactly eighteen years? With the exception of a married niece with whom she went and stayed in Berlin three autumns ago, my poor old Anna hasn't a relation left in Germany. Her whole life is centred in me—or perhaps I ought to say in Rose. She was the only nurse Rose ever had."

"And yet she has remained typically German," observed Miss Forsyth irrelevantly.

"Of course she has!" cried Mrs. Otway quickly. "And that is why we are both so much attached to her. Anna has all the virtues of the German woman; she is faithful, kindly, industrious, and thrifty."

"But, Mary, has it not occurred to you that you will find it very awkward sometimes?" Again without waiting for an answer, Miss Forsyth went on: "Our working people have long felt it very hard that there should be so many Germans in England, taking away their jobs."

"They have only themselves to thank for that," said Mrs. Otway, with more sharpness than was usual with an exceptionally kindly and amiable nature. "Germans are much more industrious than our people are, and they are content with less wages. Also you must forgive me if I say, dear Miss Forsyth, that I don't quite see what the jealousy of the average working-man, or, for the matter of that, of the average mechanic, has to do with my good old Anna, especially at such a time as this."

"Don't you really?" Miss Forsyth looked curiously into the other's flushed and still fair, delicately tinted face. She had always thought Mary Otway a rather foolish, if also a lovable, generous-hearted woman. But this was one of the few opinions Miss Forsyth always managed to keep to herself.

"I suppose you mean," said the other reluctantly, "that if I had not had Anna as a servant all these years I should have been compelled to have an Englishwoman?"

"Yes, Mary, that is exactly what I do mean! But of course I should never have spoken to you about the matter were it not for to-day's news. My maid, Pusey, you know, spoke to me about it this morning, and said that if you should be thinking of parting with her—if your good old Anna should be thinking, for instance, of going back to Germany—she knew some one who she thought would suit you admirably. It's a woman who was cook in a very good London place, and whose health has rather given way."

Miss Forsyth spoke with what was for her unusual animation.

As is always the way with your active, intelligent philanthropist, she was much given to vicarious deeds of charity. At the same time she never spared herself. Her own comfortable house always contained one or more of the odd-come-shorts whom she had not managed to place out in good situations.

Again a wave of resentment swept over Mrs. Otway. This was really too much!

"How would such a woman as you describe—a cook who has been in a good London place, and who has lost her health—work into our—mine and Rose's—ways? Why, we should both be afraid of such a woman! She would impose on us at every turn. If you only knew, dear Miss Forsyth, how often, in the last twenty years, I have thanked God—I say it in all reverence—for having sent me my good old Anna! Think what it has been to me"—she spoke with a good deal of emotion—"to have in my tiny household a woman so absolutely trustworthy that I could always go away and leave my child with her, happy in the knowledge that Rose was as safe with Anna as she was with me——"

Her voice broke, a lump came into her throat, but she hurried on: "Don't think that it has all been perfect—that I have lain entirely on a bed of roses! Anna has been very tiresome sometimes; and, as you know, her daughter, to whom I was really attached, and whom I regarded more or less as Rose's foster-sister, made that unfortunate marriage to a worthless London tradesman. That's the black spot in Anna's life—I don't mind telling you that it's been a blacker spot in mine than I've ever cared to admit, even to myself. The man's always getting into scrapes, and having to be got out of them! Why, *you* once helped me about him, didn't you? and since then James Hayley actually had to go to the police about the man."

"Mr. Hayley will be busier than ever now."

"Yes, I suppose he will."

And then the two ladies, looking at one another, smiled one of those funny little smiles which may mean a great deal, or nothing at all.

James Hayley, the son of one of Mrs. Otway's first cousins, was in the Foreign Office; and if he had an inordinate opinion of himself and of his value to his country, he was still a very good, steady fellow. Lately he had fallen into the way of coming down to Witanbury exceedingly often; but when doing so he did not stay with the Otways, in their pretty house in the Close, as would have been natural and as would also naturally have made his visits rather less frequent; instead, he stayed in lodgings close to the gateway which divided the Close from the town, and thus was able to be at the Trellis House as much or as little as he liked. It was generally much. Mrs. Otway wondered whether the war would so far affect his work as to keep him away from Witanbury this summer. She rather hoped it would.

"I'm even more sorry than usual for Jervis Blake to-day!" and this time there was a note of real kindness in Miss Forsyth's voice. "I shouldn't be surprised if he enlisted."

"Oh, I hope he won't do *that!*" Mrs. Otway was shocked at the suggestion. Jervis Blake was a person for whom she had a good deal of tolerant affection. He was quite an ordinary young man, and he had had the quite ordinary bad luck of failing to pass successive Army examinations. The news that he had failed again had just become known to his friends, and unluckily it was his last chance, as he was now past the age limit. The exceptional feature in his very common case was that he happened to be the only son of a distinguished soldier.

"I should certainly enlist if I were he," continued Miss Forsyth thoughtfully. "He wouldn't have long to wait for promotion from the ranks."

"His father would never forgive him!"

"The England of to-day is a different England from the England of yesterday," observed Miss Forsyth drily; and as the other stared at her, genuinely astonished by the strange words, "Don't you agree that that is so, Mary?"

"No, I can't say that I do." Mrs. Otway spoke with greater decision than was her wont. Miss Forsyth was far too fond of setting the world to rights.

"Ah! well, I think it is. And I only wish I was a young man instead of an old woman! I'm sorry for every Englishman who is too old to take up arms in this just cause. What must be Major Guthrie's feelings to-day! How he must regret having left the Army to please his selfish old mother! It's the more hard on him as he always believed this war would come. He really *knows* Germany."

"Major Guthrie only knows *military* Germany," said Mrs. Otway slowly.

"It's only what you call military Germany which counts to-day," observed Miss Forsyth quickly; and then, seeing that her friend looked hurt, and even, what she so very seldom was, angry too, she held out her hand with the words: "And now I must be moving on, for before going to the cathedral I have to see Mrs. Haworth for a minute. By the way, I hear that the Dean intends to give a little address about the war." She added, in a different and a kindlier tone: "You must forgive me, Mary, for saying what I did about your good old Anna! But you know I'm really fond of you, and I'm even fonder of your sweet Rose than I am of you. I always feel that there is a great deal in Rose—more than in any other girl I know. And then—well,

Mary, she is so very pretty! prettier than you even were, though you had a way of making every one think you lovely!"

Mrs. Otway laughed. She was quite mollified. "I know how fond you are of Rose," she said gratefully, "and, of course, I don't mind your having spoken to me about Anna. But as to parting with her—that would mean the end of the world to us, to your young friend Rose even more than to me. Why, it would be worse—far worse—than the war!"

CHAPTER II

As Mrs. Otway walked slowly on, she could not help telling herself that dear old Miss Forsyth had been more interfering and tiresome than she usually was this morning.

She felt ruffled by the little talk they two had just had—so ruffled and upset that, instead of turning into the gate of the house where she had been bound—for she, too, had meant to pay a call in the Close on her way to the cathedral—she walked slowly on the now deserted stretch of road running through and under the avenue of elm trees which are so beautiful and distinctive a feature of Witanbury Close.

Again a lump rose to her throat, and this time the tears started into her eyes and rolled down her cheeks. In sheer astonishment at her own emotion, she stopped short, and taking out her handkerchief dabbed her eyes hurriedly. How strange that this interchange of words with one whose peculiarities she had known, and, yes, suffered under and smiled at for so many years, should make her feel so—so—so upset!

Mrs. Otway was a typical Englishwoman of her age, which was forty-three, and of her class, which was that from which are drawn most of the women from whom the clergy of the Established Church choose their wives. There are thousands such, living in serene girlhood, wifehood, or widowhood, to be found in the villages and country towns of dear old England. With but very few exceptions, they are kindly-natured, unimaginative, imbued with a shrinking dislike of any exaggerated display of emotion; in some ways amazingly broad-minded, in others curiously limited in their outlook on life. Such women, as a rule, present few points of interest to students of human nature, for they are almost invariably true to type, their virtues and their defects being cast in the same moulds.

But Mrs. Otway was much more original and more impulsive, thus far less "groovy," than the people among whom her lot was cast. There were even censorious folk in Witanbury who called her eccentric. She was generous-hearted, easily moved to enthusiasm, tenacious of her opinions and prejudices. She had remained young of heart, and her fair, curling hair, her slight, active figure, and delicately-tinted skin, gave her sometimes an almost girlish look. Those who met her for the first time were always surprised to find that Mrs. Otway had a grown-up daughter.

As a girl she had spent two very happy years in Germany, at Weimar, and she had kept from those far-off days a very warm and affectionate feeling towards the Fatherland, as also a rather exceptionally good knowledge both of the German language and of old-fashioned German literature. Then had come a short engagement, followed by five years of placid, happy marriage with a minor canon of Witanbury Cathedral. And then, at the end of those five years, which had slipped by so easily and so quickly, she had found herself alone, with one little daughter, and woefully restricted means. It had seemed, and indeed it had been, a godsend to come across, in Anna Bauer, a German widow who, for a miraculously low wage, had settled down into her little household, to become and to remain, not only an almost perfect servant, but as time went on a most valued and trusted friend.

The fact that Mrs. Otway had been left a legacy by a distant relation, while making her far more comfortable, had not caused her to alter very materially her way of life. She had raised Anna's modest wage, and she was no longer compelled to look quite so closely after every penny. Also, mother and daughter were now able to take delightful holidays together. They had planned one such for this very autumn to Germany—Germany, the country still so dear to Mrs. Otway, which she had always longed to show her daughter.

It was natural that the news which had burst upon England to-day should have unsealed the fountain of deep emotion in her nature. Mrs. Otway, like almost every one she knew, had not believed that there would or could be a great Continental war, and when that had become, with stunning suddenness, an accomplished fact, she had felt sure that her country would remain out of the awful maelstrom.

Send their good old Anna back to Germany? Why, the idea was unthinkable! What would she, Mary Otway, what would her daughter, Rose, do without Anna? Anna had become—Mrs. Otway realised it to-day as she had never realised it before—the corner-stone of their modest, happy House of Life.

Miss Forsyth had, however, said one thing which was unfortunately true. It is strange how often these positive, rather managing people hit the right nail on the head! The fact that England and Germany were now at war *would* sometimes make things a little awkward with regard to poor old Anna. Something of the kind had, indeed, happened on this very morning, less than two hours ago. And at the time it had been very painful, very disagreeable....

Mrs. Otway and her daughter, each opening a newspaper before beginning breakfast, had looked up, and in awe-struck tones simultaneously exclaimed, "Why, we are at war!" and "War has been declared!" And then Mrs. Otway, as was her wont, had fallen into eager, impulsive talk. But she had to stop abruptly when the dining-room door opened—for it revealed the short, stumpy figure of Anna, smiling, indeed beaming even more than usual, as she brought in the coffee she made so well. Mother and daughter had looked at one another across the table, an unspoken question in each pair of kind eyes. That question was: *Did poor old Anna know?*

The answer came with dramatic swiftness, and in the negative. Anna approached her mistress, still with that curious look of beaming happiness in her round, fat, plain face, and after she had put down the coffee-jug she held out her work-worn hand. On it was a pink card, and in her excitement she broke into eager German.

"The child has come!" she exclaimed. "Look! This is what I have received, gracious lady," and she put the card on her mistress's plate.

What was written, or rather printed, on that fancy-looking card, ran, when Englished, as follows:

The Joyous Birth of a Large-Eyed Sunday Maiden
is announced, ultra-jubilantly, by
WILHELM WARSHAUER, Sub-Inspector of Police in
Berlin, and Wife MINNA, born BROCKMANN.

Of course they both congratulated their good old Anna very heartily on the birth of the little great-niece in Berlin—indeed Rose, jumping up from the table, had surprised her mother by giving her old nurse a hug. "I'm so glad, dear Anna! How happy they seem to be!"

But when Anna had returned to her kitchen the two ladies had gone on silently and rather sadly with their breakfasts and their papers; and after she had finished, Mrs. Otway, with a heavy heart, had walked across the hall, to her pretty kitchen, to tell Anna the great and tragic news.

The kitchen of the Trellis House was oddly situated just opposite Mrs. Otway's sitting-room and at right angles to the dining-room. Thus the two long Georgian windows of Anna's domain commanded the wide green of the Cathedral Close, and the kitchen door was immediately on your right as you walked through the front door into the arched hall of the house.

On this momentous morning Anna's mistress found the old German woman sitting at her large wooden table writing a letter. When Mrs. Otway came in, Anna looked up and smiled; but she did not rise, as an English servant would have done.

Mrs. Otway walked across to her, and very kindly she laid her hand on the older woman's shoulder.

"I have something sad to tell you," she said gently. "England, my poor Anna, is at war! England has declared war on Germany! But I have come to tell you, also, that the fact that our countries are at war will make no difference to you and to me, Anna—will it?"

Anna had looked up, and for a moment she had seemed bewildered, stunned by the news. Then all the colour had receded from her round face; it became discomposed, covered with red streaks. She broke into convulsive sobs as, shaking her head violently, she exclaimed, "Nein! Nein!"

If only poor old Anna had left it there! But she had gone on, amid her sobs, to speak wildly, disconnectedly, and yes—yes, rather arrogantly too, of the old war with France in 1870—of her father, and of her long-dead brother; how both of them had fought, how gloriously they had conquered!

Mrs. Otway had begun by listening in silence to this uncalled-for outburst. But at last, with a touch of impatience, she broke across these ill-timed reminiscences with the words, "But now, Anna? *Now* there is surely no one belonging to your family likely to fight? No one, I mean, likely to fight against England?"

The old woman stared at her stupidly, as if scarcely understanding the sense of what was being said to her; and Mrs. Otway, with a touch of decision in her voice, had gone on—"How fortunate it is that your Louisa married an Englishman!"

But on that Anna had again shaken her head violently. "No, no!" she cried. "Would that a German married she had—an honest, heart-good German, not a man like that bad, worthless George!"

To this surely unnecessary remark Mrs. Otway had made no answer. It was unluckily true that Anna's English son-in-law lacked every virtue dear to a German heart. He was lazy, pleasure-loving, dishonest in small petty ways, and contemptuous of his thrifty wife's anxious efforts to save money. Still, though it was not perhaps wise to say so just now, it would certainly have been a terrible complication if "little Louisa," as they called her in that household, had married a German—a German who would have had to go back to the Fatherland to take up arms, perhaps, against his adopted country! Anna ought surely to see the truth of that to-day, however unpalatable that truth might be.

But, sad to say, good old Anna had been strangely lacking in her usual good sense, and sturdy good-humour, this morning. Not content with that uncalled-for remark concerning her English son-in-law, she had wailed out something about "Willi"—for so she always called Wilhelm Warshauer—the nephew by marriage to whom she had become devotedly attached during the pleasant holiday she had spent in Germany three years ago.

"I do not think Willi is in the least likely to go to the war and be killed," said Mrs. Otway at last, a little sharply. "Why, he is in the police—a sub-inspector! They would never dream of sending him away. And then— — Anna? I wish you would listen to me quietly for a moment— —"

Anna fixed her glazed, china-blue eyes anxiously on her mistress.

"If you go on in this way you will make yourself quite ill; and that wouldn't do at all! I am quite sure that you will soon hear from your niece that Willi is quite safe, that he is remaining on in Berlin. England and Germany are civilised nations after all! There need not be any unreasonable bitterness between them. Only the soldiers and sailors, not our two nations, will be at war, Anna."

Yes, the recollection of what had happened this morning left an aftermath of bitterness in Mrs. Otway's kind heart. It was only too true that it would sometimes be awkward; in saying so downright Miss Forsyth had been right! She told herself, however, that after a few days they surely would all get accustomed to this strange, unpleasant, new state of things. Why, during the long Napoleonic wars Witanbury had always been on the *qui vive*, expecting a French landing on the coast—that beautiful coast which was as lonely now as it had been then, and which, thanks to motors and splendid roads, seemed much nearer now than then. England had gone on much as usual a hundred years ago. Mrs. Otway even reminded herself that Jane Austen, during those years of stress and danger, had been writing her delightful, her humorous, her placid studies of life as though there were no war!

And then, perhaps because of her invocation of that dear, shrewd mistress of the average British human heart, Mrs. Otway, feeling far more comfortable than she had yet felt since her talk with Miss Forsyth, began retracing her steps towards the cathedral.

She was glad to know that the Dean was going to give a little address this morning. It was sure to be kindly, wise, benignant—for he was himself all these three things. Many delightful German thinkers, theologians and professors, came and went to the Deanery, and Mrs. Otway was always asked to meet these distinguished folk, partly because of her excellent knowledge of German, and also because the Dean knew that, like himself, she loved Germany.

And now she turned sick at heart, as she suddenly realised that for a time, at any rate, these pleasant meetings would take place no more. But soon—or so she hoped with all her soul—this strange unnatural war would be over. Even now the bubble of Prussian militarism was pricked, for the German Army was not doing well at Liége. During the last two or three days she had read the news with increasing amazement and—but she hardly admitted it to herself—with dismay. She did not like to think of Germans breaking and running away! It had hurt her, made her angry, to hear the exultation with which some of her neighbours had spoken of the news. It was all very well to praise the gallant little Belgians, but why should that be done at the expense of the Germans?

Mrs. Otway suddenly told herself that she hoped Major Guthrie would not be at the cathedral this morning. Considering that they disagreed about almost everything, it was odd what friends he and she were! But about Germany they had never agreed, and that was the more strange inasmuch as Major Guthrie had spent quite a long time in Stuttgart. He thought the Germans of to-day entirely unlike the Germans of the past. He honestly believed them to be unprincipled, untrustworthy, and unscrupulous; and, strangest thing of all—or so Mrs. Otway had thought till within the last few days—he had long been convinced that they intended to conquer Europe by force of arms! So strong was this conviction of his that he had given time, and yes, money too, to the propaganda carried on by Lord Roberts in favour of National Service.

It was odd that a man whose suspicions of the country which was to her so dear almost amounted to a monomania, should have become her friend. But so it was. In fact, Major Guthrie was her only man friend. He advised her about all the things concerning which men are supposed to know more than women—such as investments, for instance. Of course she did not always take his advice, but it was often a comfort to talk things out with him, and she had come instinctively to turn to him when in any little trouble. Few days passed without Major Guthrie's calling, either by chance or in response to a special invitation, at the Trellis House.

Unfortunately, or was it fortunately? the handsome old mother, for whose sake Major Guthrie had left the Army three years ago, didn't care for clerical society. She only liked country people and Londoners. As far as Mrs. Otway could dislike any one, she disliked Mrs. Guthrie; but the two ladies seldom had occasion to meet—the Guthries lived in a pretty old house in Dorycote, a village two miles from Witanbury. Also Mrs. Guthrie was more or less chair-ridden, and Mrs. Otway had no carriage.

The bells of the cathedral suddenly broke across her troublesome, disconnected thoughts. Mrs. Otway never heard those chimes without a wave of remembrance, sometimes very slight, sometimes like to-day quite strong and insistent, of past joys and sorrows. Those bells were interwoven with the whole of her wifehood, motherhood, and widowhood; they had rung for her wedding, they had mustered the tiny congregation who had been present at Rose's christening; the great bell had tolled the day her husband had died, and again to bid the kindly folk of Witanbury to his simple funeral. Some day, perhaps, the bells would ring a joyful peal in honour of Rose's wedding.

As she walked up the path which leads from the road encircling the Close to the cathedral, she tried to compose and attune her mind to solemn, peaceful thoughts.

There was a small congregation, perhaps thirty in all, gathered together in the choir, but the atmosphere of that tiny gathering of people was slightly electric and charged with emotion. The wife of the Dean, a short, bustling lady, who had never been so popular in Witanbury and its neighbourhood as was her husband, came forward and beckoned to Mrs. Otway. "If no one else comes in," she whispered, "I think we might all come up a little nearer. The Dean is going to say a few words about the war."

And though a few more people did come in during the five minutes that followed, the whole of the little congregation finally collected in the stalls nearest the altar. And it was not from the ornate white stone pulpit, but from the steps of the altar, that the Dean, after the short service was over, delivered his address.

For what seemed a long time—it was really only a very few moments—Dr. Haworth stood there, looking thoughtfully at this little gathering of his fellow-countrymen and countrywomen. Then he began speaking. With great simplicity and directness he alluded to the awesome news which this morning had brought to them, to England. England's declaration of war against their great neighbour, Germany—their great neighbour, and they should never forget, the only other great European nation which shared with them the blessings, he was willing to admit the perhaps in some ways doubtful blessings, brought about by the Reformation.

On hearing these words, three or four of his hearers moved a little restlessly in their seats, but soon even they settled themselves down to take in, and to approve, what he had to say.

England was going to war, however, in a just cause, to make good her promise to a small and weak nation. She had often drawn her sword on behalf of the oppressed, and never more rightly than now. But it would be wrong indeed for England to allow her heart to be filled with bitterness. It was probable that even at this moment a large number of Germans were ashamed of what had happened last Monday—he alluded to the Invasion of Belgium. Frederick the Great had once said that God was always on the side of the big battalions; in so saying he had been wrong. Even in the last two or three days they had seen how wrong. Belgium was putting up a splendid defence, and the time might come—he, the speaker, hoped it would be very soon—when Germany would realise that Might is not Right, when she would confess, with the large-hearted chivalry possible to a great and powerful nation, that she had been wrong.

Meanwhile the Dean wished to impress on his hearers the need for a generous broad-mindedness in their attitude towards the foe. England was a great civilised nation, and so was Germany. The war would be fought in an honourable, straightforward manner, as between high-souled enemies. Christian charity enjoined on us to be especially kind and considerate to those Germans who happened to be caught by this sad state of things, in our midst. He had heard these people spoken of that morning as "alien enemies." For his part he would not care to describe by any such offensive terms those Germans who were settled in England in peaceful avocations. The war was not of their making, and those poor foreigners were caught up in a terrible web of tragic circumstance. He himself had many dear and valued friends in Germany, professors whose only aim in life was the spread of "Kultur," not perhaps quite the same thing as we meant by the word culture, for the German "Kultur" meant something with a wider, more universal significance. He hoped the time would come, sooner perhaps than many pessimists thought possible, when those friends would acknowledge that England had drawn her sword in a righteous cause and that Germany had been wrong to provoke her.

CHAPTER III

While Mrs. Otway had been thinking over the now rather painful problem of her good old Anna, the subject of her meditations, that is Anna herself, from behind the pretty muslin curtain which hid her kitchen from the passers-by, was peeping out anxiously on the lawn-like stretch of green grass, bordered on two sides by high elms, which is so pleasant a feature of Witanbury Close.

Her knitting was in her hands, for Anna's fingers were never idle, but just now the needles were still.

When your kitchen happens to be one of the best rooms on the ground floor, and one commanding not only the gate of your domain but the road beyond, it becomes important that it should not be quite like other people's kitchens. It was Mrs. Otway's pride, as well as Anna's, that at any moment of the day a visitor who, after walking into the hall, opened by mistake the kitchen door, would have found everything there in exquisite order. The shelves, indeed, were worth going some way to see, for each shelf was edged with a beautiful "Kante" or border of crochet-work almost as fine as point lace. In fact, the kitchen of the Trellis House was more like a stage kitchen than a kitchen in an ordinary house, and the way in which it was kept was the more meritorious inasmuch as Anna, even now, when she had become an old woman, would have nothing of what is in England called "help." She had no wish to see a charwoman in *her* kitchen. Fortunately for her, there lay, just off and behind the kitchen, a roomy scullery, where most of the dirty, and what may be called the smelly, work connected with cooking was done.

To the left of the low-ceilinged, spacious, rather dark scullery was Anna's own bedroom. Both the scullery and the servant's room were much older than the rest of the house, for the picturesque gabled bit of brown and red brick building which projected into the garden, at the back of the Trellis House, belonged to Tudor days, to those spacious times when the great cathedral just across the green was a new pride and joy to the good folk of Witanbury.

As Anna stood at one of the kitchen windows, peeping out at the quiet scene outside, but not drawing aside the curtain—for that she knew was forbidden to her, and Anna very seldom consciously did anything she knew to be forbidden—she felt far more unhappy and far more disturbed than did Mrs. Otway herself.

This morning's news had stirred poor old Anna—stirred her more profoundly than even her kind mistress guessed. Mrs. Otway would have been surprised indeed had it been revealed to her that ever since breakfast Anna had spent a very anxious time thinking over her own immediate future, wondering with painful indecision as to whether it were not her duty to go back to Germany. But whereas Mrs. Otway had the inestimable advantage of being quite sure that she knew what it was best for Anna to do, the old German woman herself was cruelly torn between what was due to her mistress, to her married daughter, and, yes, to herself.

How unutterably amazed Mrs. Otway would have been this morning had she known that more than a month ago Anna had received a word of warning from Berlin. But so it was: her niece had written to her, "It is believed that war this summer there is to be. Willi has been warned that something shortly will happen."

And now, as Anna stood there anxiously peeping out at the figure of her mistress pacing up and down under the avenue of high elms across the green, she did not give more than a glancing thought to England's part in the conflict, for her whole heart was absorbed in the dread knowledge that Germany was at war with terrible, barbarous Russia, and with prosperous, perfidious France.

England, so Anna firmly believed, had no army to speak of—no *real* army. She remembered the day when France had declared war on Germany in 1870. How at once every street of the little town in which she had lived had become full of soldiers—splendid, lion-hearted soldiers going off to fight for their beloved Fatherland. Nothing of the sort had taken place here, though Witanbury was a garrison town. The usual tradesmen, strong, lusty young men, had called for orders that morning. They had laughed and joked as usual. Not one of them seemed aware his country was at war. The old German woman's lip curled disdainfully.

For the British, as a people, Anna Bauer cherished a tolerant affection and kindly contempt. It was true that, all unknowing to herself, she also had a great belief in British generosity and British justice. The idea that this war, or rather the joining in of England with France against Germany, could affect her own position or condition in England would have seemed to her absurd.

Germany and England? A contrast indeed! In Germany her son-in-law, that idle scamp George Pollit, would by now be marching on his way to the French or Russian frontier. But George, being English, was quite safe—unfortunately. The only difference the war would make to him would be that it would provide him with an excuse for trying to get at some of Anna's carefully-hoarded savings.

If good old Anna had a fault—and curiously enough it was one of which her mistress was quite unaware, though Rose had sometimes uncomfortably suspected the fact—it was a love of money.

Anna, in spite of her low wages, had saved far more than an English servant earning twice as much would have done. Her low wage? Yes, still low, though she had been raised four pounds a year when her mistress had come into a better income. Before then Anna had been content with sixteen pounds a year. She now received twenty pounds, but she was ruefully aware that she was worth half as much again. In fact thirty pounds a year had actually been offered to her, in a roundabout way, by a lady who had come as a visitor to a house in the Close. But the lady, like Anna herself, was a German; and, apart altogether from every other consideration, including Anna's passionate love of Miss Rose, nothing would have made her take service with a mistress of her own nationality.

"This Mrs. Hirsch me to save her money wants. Her kind I know," she observed to the emissary who had been sent to sound her. "You can say that Anna Bauer a good mistress has, and knows when she well suited is."

She had said nothing of the matter to Mrs. Otway, but even so she sometimes thought of that offer, and she often felt a little sore when she reflected on the wages some of the easy-going servants who formed part of the larger households in the Close received from their employers.

Yet, in this all-important matter of money a stroke of extraordinary good luck had befallen Anna—one of those things that very seldom come to pass in our work-a-day world. It had happened, or perhaps it would be truer to say it had begun—for, unlike most pieces of good fortune, it was continuous—just three years ago, in the autumn of 1911, shortly after her return from that glorious holiday at Berlin. This secret stroke of luck, for she kept it jealously to herself, though there was nothing about it at all to her discredit, had now lasted for over thirty months, and it had had the agreeable effect of greatly increasing her powers of saving. Of saving, that is, against the day when she would go back to Germany, and live with her niece.

Mrs. Otway would have been surprised indeed had she known that Anna not only meant to leave the Trellis House, but that, in a quiet, reflective kind of way, she actually looked forward to doing so. Miss Rose would surely marry, for a good many pleasant-mannered gentlemen came and went to the Trellis House (though none of them were as rich as Anna would have liked one of them to be), and she herself would get past her work. When that had come to pass she would go and live with her niece in Berlin. She had not told her daughter of this arrangement, and it had been spoken of by Willi and her niece more as a joke than anything else; still, Anna generally managed to carry through what she had made up her mind to accomplish.

But on this August morning, standing there by the kitchen window of the Trellis House, the future was far from good old Anna's mind. Her mind was fixed on the present. How tiresome, how foolish of England to have mixed up with a quarrel which did not concern her! How strange that she, Anna Bauer, in spite of that word of warning from Berlin, had suspected nothing!

As a matter of fact Mrs. Otway had said something to her about Servia and Austria—something, too, more in sorrow than in anger, of Germany "rattling her sword." But she, Anna, had only heard with half an ear. Politics were out of woman's province. But there! English ladies were like that.

Many a time had Anna laughed aloud over the antics of the Suffragettes. About a month ago the boy who brought the meat had given her a long account of a riot—it had been a very little one—provoked by one such lady madwoman in the market-place of Witanbury itself. In wise masculine Germany the lady's relatives (for, strange to say, the Suffragette in question had been a high-born lady) would have put her in the only proper place for her, an idiot asylum.

Anna had been genuinely shocked and distressed on learning that her beloved nursling, Miss Rose, secretly rather sympathised with this mad female wish for a vote. Why, in Germany only some of the *men* had votes, and yet Germany was the most glorious, prosperous, and much-to-be-feared nation in the world. "Church, Kitchen, and Children"—that should be, and in the Fatherland still was, every true woman's motto and province.

Anna's mind came back with a sudden jerk to this morning's surprising, almost incredible news. Since her two ladies had gone out, she had opened the newspapers on her kitchen table and read the words for herself— "England Declares War on Germany." But how could England do such a thing, when England had no Army? True, she had ships—but then so now had Germany!

During that blissful holiday in Berlin, Anna had been persuaded to join the German Navy League. She had not meant to keep up her subscription, small though it was, after her return to England, but rather to her disgust she had found that one of the few Germans she knew in Witanbury represented the League, and that her name had been sent to him as that of a new member. Twice he had called at the tradesmen's entrance to the Trellis House, and had demanded the sum of one shilling from her.

To-day Anna remembered with satisfaction those payments she had grudged. Thanks to her patriotism, and that of millions like her, Germany had now a splendid fleet with which to withstand her enemies. She wondered if that fleet (for which she had helped to pay) would ensure the safe delivery of parcels and letters. Probably yes.

With a relieved look on her face, the old woman dropped the curtains, and went back to the table and to her knitting.

Suddenly, with what seemed uncanny suddenness, the telephone bell rang in the hall.

Now Anna had never got used to the telephone. She had not opposed its introduction into the Trellis House, because it had been done by Miss Rose's wish, but once it was installed, Anna had bitterly regretted its being there. It was the one part of her work that she carried out badly, and she knew that this was so. Not only did she find it most difficult to understand what was said through the horrible instrument, but her mistress's friends found even more difficulty in hearing her, Anna. Sometimes—but she was very much ashamed of this—she actually allowed the telephone bell to go on ringing, and never answered it at all! She only did this, however, when her two ladies were away from Witanbury, and when, therefore, the message, whatever it might happen to be, could not possibly be delivered.

She waited now, hoping that the instrument would grow weary, and leave off ringing. But no; on it went, ping, ping, ping, ping—so at last very reluctantly Anna opened the kitchen door and went out into the hall.

Taking up the receiver, she said in a grumpy tone, "Ach! What is it? Yes?" And then her face cleared, and she even smiled into the telephone receiver.

To her great surprise—but the things that had happened to-day were so extraordinary that there was no real reason why she should be surprised at anything now—she had heard the voice of the one German in Witanbury—and there were a good many Germans in Witanbury—with whom she was on really friendly terms.

This was a certain Fritz Fröhling, a pleasant elderly man who, like herself, had been in England a long time—in fact in his case nearer forty than twenty years. He was a barber and hairdresser, and did a very flourishing business with the military gentlemen of the garrison. So Anglicised had he and his wife become that their son was in the British Army, where he had got on very well, and had been promoted to sergeant. Even among themselves, when Anna spent an evening with them, the Fröhlings generally talked English. Still, Fröhling was a German of the good old sort; that is, he had never become naturalised. But he was a Socialist; he did not share Anna's enthusiasm for the Kaiser, the Kaiserine, and their stalwart sons.

This was the first time he had ever telephoned to her. "Is it Frau Bauer that I am addressing?"

And Anna, slightly thrilled by the unusual appellation, answered, "Yes, yes—it is, Herr Fröhling."

"With you a talk I should like to have," said the friendly familiar voice. "Could I this afternoon you see?"

"Not this afternoon," answered Anna, "but this evening, I think yes. My mistress will I ask if I an evening free have can."

"Is it necessary her to ask?" The question was put doubtfully.

"Yes, yes! But mind she will not. To me she is goodness itself—never more good than this morning she was," shouted back Anna loyally.

"Fortunate you are," the voice became rather sharp and dry. "I notice already have to quit—told I must skip."

"Never!" cried Anna indignantly. "Who has that you told?"

"The police."

"A bad business," wailed Anna. She was shocked at what her old acquaintance told her. "I will Mrs. Otway ask you to help," she shouted back.

He muttered a word or two and then, "Unless before eight you communicate, Jane and I expect you this evening."

"Certainly, Herr Fröhling."

CHAPTER IV

As Mrs. Otway left the cathedral, certain remarks made to her by members of the little congregation jarred on her, and made her feel, almost for the first time in her life, thoroughly out of touch with her friends and neighbours.

Some one whom Mrs. Otway really liked and respected came up to her and exclaimed, "I couldn't help feeling sorry the Dean did not mention France and the French! Any one listening to him just now would have thought that only Germany and ourselves and Belgium were involved in this awful business." And then the speaker, seeing that her words were not very acceptable, added quietly, "But of course the Dean, with so many German friends, is in a difficult position just now." In fact, almost every one said something that hurt and annoyed her, and that though it was often only a word of satisfaction that at last England had gone in, as more than one of them put it, "on the right side."

Passing through the arch of the square gateway which separates the town from the Close, Mrs. Otway hurried down the pretty, quiet street which leads in a rather roundabout way, and past one of the most beautiful grey stone crosses in England, into the great market square which is one of the glories of the famous cathedral city. Once there, she crossed the wide space, part cobbled, part paved, and made her way into a large building of stucco and red brick which bore above its plate-glass windows the inscription in huge gilt letters, "The Witanbury Stores."

The Monday Bank Holiday had been prolonged, and so the Stores were only, so to speak, half open. But as Mrs. Otway stepped through into the shadowed shop, the owner of the Stores, Manfred Hegner by name, came forward to take her orders himself.

Manfred Hegner was quite a considerable person in Witanbury. Not only was he the biggest retail tradesman in the place, and an active member of the Witanbury City Council, but he was known to have all sorts of profitable irons in the fire. A man to keep in with, obviously, and one who was always willing to meet one half-way. Because of his German birth—he had been naturalised some years ago—and even more because of certain facial and hirsute peculiarities, he went by the nickname of "The Kaiser."

Mrs. Otway took out of her bag a piece of paper on which she had written down, at her old Anna's dictation, a list of groceries and other things needed at the Trellis House. And then she looked round, instinctively, towards the corner of the large shop where all that remained of what had once been the mainstay of Manfred Hegner's business was always temptingly set forth. This was a counter of *Delicatessen*. Glancing at the familiar corner, Mr. Hegner's customer told herself that her eyes must be playing her false. In the place of the familiar sausages, herrings, the pretty coloured basins of sauerkraut, and other savoury dainties, there now stood nothing but a row of large uninteresting Dutch cheeses!

The man who was waiting attentively by her side, a pencil and block of paper in his hand, saw the surprised, regretful look on his valued customer's face.

"I have had to put away all my nice, fresh *Delicatessen*," he said in a low voice. "It seemed wiser to do so, gracious lady." He spoke in German, and it was in German that she answered.

"Did you really think it necessary to do such a thing? I think you are unfair on your adopted country, Mr. Hegner! English people are not so unreasonable as that."

He was about to answer, when an odd-looking man, rather like a sailor, came in, and Mr. Hegner, with a hurried "Please excuse me one minute, ma'am," in English, went off to attend to the new comer.

As Mr. Hegner went across his shop, Mrs. Otway was struck by his curious resemblance to the German Emperor; in spite of the fact that he was wearing a long white apron, he had quite a martial air. He certainly deserved his nickname. There were the same piercing, rather prominent eyes, the same look of energy and decision in his face; also the same peculiar turned-up moustache. But whereas the resemblance last week would have brought a smile, now it brought a furrow of pain to the English lady's kindly face.

Poor Manfred Hegner! What must he and thousands of others like him — excellent, industrious, civil-spoken Germans — feel all through England to-day? Mrs. Otway, who had always liked the man, and who enjoyed her little chats with him, knew perhaps rather more about this prosperous tradesman than most of the Witanbury people knew. She was aware that he had been something of a rolling stone; he had, for instance, been for quite a long time in America, and it was there that he had shed most of his Germanisms of language. He was older than he looked, and his son by a first marriage lived in Germany — where, however, the young man was buyer for a group of English firms who did a great deal of business in cheap German-made goods.

His conversation with the odd-looking stranger over, Mr. Hegner hurried back to where his valued customer was standing. "Every one on the City Council is being most kind," he said suavely. "And last night I had the honour of meeting the Dean. At his suggestion I am calling a little meeting this evening, here in my Stores, of the non-naturalised Germans of this town. There are a good many in Witanbury."

And then Mrs. Otway suddenly remembered that the man now standing opposite to her was a member of the City Council. She remembered that some time ago, three or four years back at least, some disagreeable person had expressed indignation that an ex-German, one only just naturalised, should be elected to such a body. She had thought the speaker narrow-minded and ill-natured. An infusion of German thoroughness and thrift would do the City Council good, and perhaps keep down the rates!

"But you, Mr. Hegner, have been naturalised quite a long time," she said sympathetically.

"Yes, indeed, gracious lady!" Mr. Hegner seemed surprised, perhaps a thought disturbed, by her natural remark. "I took out my certificate before I built the Stores, and just after I had married my excellent little English wife. Glad indeed am I now that I did so!"

"I am very glad too," said Mrs. Otway. And yet—and yet she felt a slight quiver of discomfort. The man standing there was so *very* German after all—German not only in his appearance, but in all his little ways! If nothing else had proved it, his rather absurd nickname was clear proof that so he was even now regarded in Witanbury.

"And how about your son, Mr. Hegner?" she asked. "I suppose he is in Germany now? You must feel rather anxious about him."

He hesitated oddly, and looked round him before he spoke. Then, vanquished, maybe, by the obvious sincerity and kindness of the speaker, he answered, in German, and almost in a whisper. "He is, I fear, by now on his way to the frontier. But may I ask a favour of the gracious lady? Do not speak of my son to the people of Witanbury."

"Then *he* was never naturalised?" Mrs. Otway also spoke in a low voice—a voice full of pity and concern.

"No, no," said Mr. Hegner hastily. "There was no necessity for him to be. His work was mostly, you see, over there."

"Still he was educated here, surely?"

"That is so, gracious lady. He talks English better even than I do. He and I did consider the question of his taking out a certificate. Then we decided that, as he would be so much in Germany, it was better he should remain German. But his wife is an English girl."

"How sorry you must be now that he did not naturalise!" she exclaimed.

An odd look came over Manfred Hegner's face. "Yes, it is very regretful—the more so that it would do me harm if it were known in the town that I had a son in the German Army. But he will not fight against the English," he added hastily. "No one will do that but the German sailors—is not that so, madam?"

"I really don't know."

"If at any time the gracious lady should hear anything of the sort, I should be grateful—nay, far more than grateful if she will let me know it!" He had lapsed back into German, and Mrs. Otway smiled very kindly at him.

"Yes, I will certainly let you know anything I hear. I know how very anxious you must be about this sad state of things."

Mrs. Otway had left the shop, and she was already some way back across the Market Place, when there came the rather raucous sound of an urgent voice in her ear. Startled, she turned round. The owner of the Witanbury Stores stood by her side.

"Pardon, pardon!" he said breathlessly. "But would you, gracious lady, ask your servant" (he used the German word "Stütze") "if she could make it convenient to join our gathering this evening at nine o'clock? Frau Anna Bauer is so very highly respected among the Germans here that we should like her to be present."

"Certainly I will arrange for Anna to come," answered Mrs. Otway. "But you may not be aware, Mr. Hegner, that my cook has become to all intents and purposes quite English—without, of course," she hastily corrected herself, "giving up her love for the Fatherland. She has only one relation left in Germany, a married niece in Berlin. Her own daughter is the wife of an Englishman, a tradesman in London."

"That makes no difference," said Manfred Hegner; "she will be welcome, most heartily welcome, to-night! This is the moment, as the Reverend Mr. Dean so well put it to me, when all Germans should stick together, and consult as to the wisest and best thing to do in their own interests."

"Yes, indeed, Mr. Hegner. I quite agree with the Dean. But do not do anything to upset my poor old Anna. She really is not involved in the question at all. She has lived with me nearly twenty years, and my daughter and I regard her far more as a friend than as a servant. The fact that she is German is an accident—the merest accident! Nothing in her life, thank God, will be changed for the worse. And, Mr. Hegner? I should like to say one more thing." She looked earnestly into his face, but even she could see that his eyes were wandering, and that there was a slight look of apprehension in the prominent eyes now fixed on a group of farmers who stood a few yards off staring at him and at Mrs. Otway.

"Yes, gracious lady," he said mechanically, "I am attending."

"Do not think that English people bear any ill-feeling to you and your great country! We feel that Germany, by breaking her word to Belgium, has put herself in the wrong. It is England's duty to fight, not her pleasure, Mr. Hegner. And we hope with all our hearts that the war will soon be over."

He murmured a word of respectful assent. And then, choosing a rather devious route, skirting the fine old Council House, which is the most distinctive feature of Witanbury Market Place, he hurried back to his big stores.

Mrs. Otway opened the wrought-iron gate of the Trellis House with a feeling of restful satisfaction; but there, in her own pretty, peaceful home, a not very pleasant surprise awaited her. Good old Anna, hurrying out into the black and white hall to meet her gracious lady, did not receive Mr. Hegner's kind invitation as her mistress had supposed she would do. A look of indecision and annoyance crossed her pink face.

"Ach, but to go to Mr. Fröhling promised have I," she muttered.

And then Mrs. Otway exclaimed, "But the Fröhlings are Germans! They will certainly be there themselves. Mr. Fröhling cannot have known of this meeting when he and his wife asked you to supper. I think, Anna, that it is your duty to attend this gathering. The Dean not only approves of it, but, from what I could make out, he actually suggested that it should take place. Of course I know it makes no real difference to you; but still, Anna," she spoke reprovingly, "you should not forget at such a time as this that you are German-born."

The old woman looked up quickly at her mistress. Forget she was German-born! Mrs. Otway was a most good lady, a most kind employer, but she was sometimes foolish, very very foolish, in what she said! She, Anna Bauer, had often noticed it. Still, averse as she was from the thought, the old German woman was ruefully aware that she would have to accept

Mr. Hegner's invitation. When it came to a tussle of will between the two, herself and her mistress, Mrs. Otway generally won, partly because she was, after all, Anna's employer, and also because she always knew exactly what it was she wanted Anna to do. Anna was emotional, easily touched, highly excitable; she also generally knew what she wanted, but she did not find it easy to force her will on others, least of all on her beloved if not exactly admired mistress.

Grumbling under her breath, she retreated into her kitchen; while Mrs. Otway, feeling tired and rather dispirited, went upstairs.

The back-door bell rang, and Anna went and opened it. A boy stood there, bearing on a tray not only the various little things Mrs. Otway had ordered at the Witanbury Stores half an hour before, but also an envelope addressed to "Frau Bauer." Anna brought the things into the kitchen, then she opened with interest the envelope addressed to herself. It contained a card, elegantly headed:

"THE WITANBURY STORES.
Proprietor: Manfred Hegner."

Across it were written in German the words: "You are bidden to a meeting at the above address to-night at nine o'clock. There will be cakes and coffee served before the meeting begins. Entrance by Market Row."

Anna read the words again and again. This was treating her at last as she ought always to have been treated! Anna did not like her erst fellow-country-man, and she considered that she had good reason for her dislike. Resentment against ingratitude is not confined to any one nationality.

When Manfred Hegner had first come to Witanbury, Anna had been delighted to make his acquaintance, and she had spent many happy half-hours chatting with him in the little *Delicatessen* shop he had established in Bridge Street, close to the Market Place.

Starting with only the good-will of a bankrupt confectioner, he had very soon built up a wonderfully prosperous business. But his early success had been in a measure undoubtedly owing to Mrs. Otway and her German cook. Mrs. Otway had told all her friends of this amusing little German shop, and of the good things which were to be bought there. *Delicatessen* had become quite the fashion, not only among the good people of Witanbury itself, but among the county gentry who made the cathedral town their shopping headquarters, and who enjoyed motoring in there to spend an idly busy morning.

Then had come the erection of the big Stores. Over that matter quite a storm had arisen, and local feeling had been very mixed. A petition originated by those who called themselves the Art Society of Witanbury, pointed out that a large modern building of the kind proposed would ruin the old-world, picturesque appearance of the Market Place. But the big local builder, the man who later promoted the election of Manfred Hegner on to the City Council, bore down all opposition, and a group of charming old gabled houses—houses that were little more than cottages, and therefore perhaps hardly in keeping with the Market Place of so prosperous a town as was Witanbury—had been pulled down, and the large Stores had risen on their site.

And then one day—which happened to be a day when Mrs. Otway and her daughter were away on a visit—Manfred Hegner himself walked along into the Close, and so to the Trellis House, in order to make Anna a proposal. It was a simple thing that he asked Anna to do—namely that she should persuade her mistress to remove her custom from the long-established tradesmen where she had always dealt, and transfer it entirely to his Stores. His things, so he said, were better as well as cheaper than those sold by the smaller people, also he would be pleased to pay Anna a handsome commission on every bill paid by her mistress.

Anna had willingly fallen in with this plan. It had taken some time and some trouble, but in the end Mrs. Otway found it very convenient to get everything at the same place. For a while all had gone well for Manfred Hegner—well for him and well for Anna. At the end of a year, however, he had arbitrarily halved Anna's commission, and that she felt to be (as indeed it was) most unfair, and not in the bond. She had no longer the power to retaliate, for her mistress had fallen into the way of going into the Stores herself. Mrs. Otway enjoyed rubbing up her German with Mr. Hegner, and the really intelligent zeal with which he always treated her, and her comparatively small orders, was very pleasant. Twice he had taken great trouble to procure for her a local Weimar delicacy which she remembered enjoying as a girl.

But when Anna, following her mistress's example, walked along to the Stores to enjoy a little chat in her native language, Mr. Hegner would be short with her, very short indeed! In fact it was now a long time since the old woman had cared to set foot there. For another thing she did not like Mrs. Hegner, the pretty English girl Manfred Hegner had married five years before; she thought her a very frivolous, silly little woman, not at all what the wife of a big commercial man should be. Anna's Louisa would have been a perfect helpmate for Manfred Hegner, and there had been a time, a certain three months, when Anna had thought the already prosperous widower was considering Louisa. His marriage to pretty Polly Brown had been a disappointment.

But now this politely-worded card of invitation certainly made a difference. Old Anna, who was not lacking in a certain simple shrewdness, had not expected Manfred Hegner to show any kindness to his ex-compatriots. She was touched to find him a better man than she expected. Most certainly would she attend this meeting!

As soon as her mistress had gone out to lunch, Anna telephoned to Mr. Fröhling and explained why she could not come to him that evening.

"We too asked to Hegner's have been. As you are going, we your example will follow," shouted the barber.

CHAPTER V

Rose Otway sat in the garden of the Trellis House, under the wide-branched cedar of Lebanon which was, to the thinking of most people in the Close, that garden's only beauty. For it was just a wide lawn, surrounded on three sides by a very high old brick wall, under which ran an herbaceous border to which Rose devoted some thought and a good deal of time.

The great cedar rose majestically far above its surroundings; and when you stood at one of the windows of the Trellis House, and saw how wide the branches of the tree spread, you realised that the garden was a good deal bigger than it appeared at first sight.

Rose sat near a low wicker table on which in an hour or so Anna would come out and place the tea-tray. Spread out across the girl's knee was a square of canvas, a section of a bed-spread, on which was traced an intricate and beautiful Jacobean design. Rose had already been working at it for six months, and she hoped to have finished it by the 14th of December, her mother's birthday. She enjoyed doing this beautiful work, of which the pattern had been lent to her by a country neighbour who collected such things.

How surprised Rose would have been on this early August afternoon could she have foreseen that this cherished piece of work, on which she had already lavished so many hours of close and pleasant toil, would soon be put away for an indefinite stretch of time; and that knitting, which she had always disliked doing, would take its place!

But no such thought, no such vision of the future, came into her mind as she bent her pretty head over her work.

She felt rather excited, a thought more restless than usual. England at war, and with Germany! Dear old Anna's Fatherland—the great country to which Rose had always been taught by her mother to look with peculiar affection, as well as respect and admiration.

Rose and Mrs. Otway had hoped to go to Germany this very autumn. They had saved up their pennies—as Mrs. Otway would have put it—for a considerable time, in order that they might enjoy in comfort, and even in luxury, what promised to be a delightful tour. Rose could hardly realise even yet that their journey, so carefully planned out, so often discussed, would now have to be postponed. They were first to have gone to Weimar, where Mrs. Otway had spent such a happy year in her girlhood, and then to Munich, to Dresden, to Nuremberg—to all those dear old towns with whose names Rose had always been familiar. It seemed such a pity that now they would have to wait till after the war to go to Germany.

After the war? Fortunately the people she had seen that day—and there had been a good deal of coming and going in the Close—all seemed to think that the war would be over very soon, and this pleasant view had been confirmed in a rather odd way.

Rose's cousin, James Hayley, had rung her up on the telephone from London. She had been very much surprised, for a telephone message from London to Witanbury costs one-and-threepence, and James was careful about such things. When he did telephone, which was very seldom, he always waited to do so till the evening, when the fee was halved. But to-day James had rung up just before luncheon, and she had heard his voice almost as though he were standing by her side.

"Who's there? Oh, it's you, is it, Rose? I just wanted to say that I shall probably be down Saturday night. I shan't be able to be away more than one night, worse luck. I suppose you've heard what's happened?"

And then, as she had laughed—she had really not been able to help it (how very odd James was! He evidently thought Witanbury *quite* out of the world), he had gone on, "It's a great bore, for it upsets everything horribly. The one good point about it is that it won't last long."

"How long?" she had called out.

And he had answered rather quickly, "You needn't speak so loud. I hear you perfectly. How long? Oh, I think it'll be over by October—may be a little before, but I should say October."

"Mother thinks there'll be a sort of Trafalgar!"

And then he had answered, speaking a little impatiently for he was very overworked just then, "Nothing of the sort! The people who will win this war, and will win it quickly, are the Russians. We have information that they will mobilise quickly—much more quickly than most people think. You see, my dear Rose,"—he was generally rather old-fashioned in his phraseology— "the Russians are like a steam roller"; she always remembered that she had heard that phrase from him first. "We have reason to believe that they can put ten million men into their fighting line every year for fifty years!"

Rose, in answer, said the first silly thing she had said that day: "Oh, I do *hope* the war won't last as long as that!"

And then she had heard, uttered in a strange voice, the words, "Another three minutes, sir?" and the hasty answer at the other end, "No, certainly not! I've quite done." And she had hung up the receiver with a smile.

And yet Rose, if well aware of his little foibles, liked her cousin well enough to be generally glad of his company. During the last three months he had spent almost every week-end at Witanbury. And though it was true, as her mother often observed, that James was both narrow-minded and self-opinionated, yet even so he brought with him a breath of larger air, and he often told the ladies at the Trellis House interesting things.

While Rose Otway sat musing over her beautiful work in the garden, good old Anna came and went in her kitchen. She too still felt restless and anxious, she too wondered how long this unexpected war would last. But whereas Rose couldn't have told why she was restless and anxious, her one-time nurse knew quite well what ailed herself this afternoon.

Anna had a very good reason for feeling worried and depressed, but it was one she preferred to keep to herself. For the last two days she had been expecting some money from Germany, and since this morning she had been wondering, with keen anxiety, whether that money would be stopped in the post.

What made this possibility very real to her was the fact that an uncle of Anna's, just forty-four years ago, that is, in the August of 1870, had been ruined owing to the very simple fact that a sum of money owing him from France had not been able to get through! It was true that she, Anna, would not be ruined if the sum due to her, which in English money came to fifty shillings exactly, were not to arrive. Still, it would be very disagreeable, and the more disagreeable because she had foolishly given her son-in-law five pounds a month ago. She knew it would have to be a gift, though he had pretended at the time that it was only a loan.

Anna wondered how she could find out whether money orders were still likely to come through from Germany. She did not like to ask at the Post Office, for her Berlin nephew, who transmitted the money to her half-yearly, always had the order made out to some neighbouring town or village, not to Witanbury. In vain Anna had pointed out that this was quite unnecessary, and indeed very inconvenient; and that when she had said she did not wish her mistress to know, she had not meant *that*. In spite of her protests Willi had persisted in so sending it.

Suddenly her face brightened. How easy it would be to find out all that sort of thing at the meeting to-night! Such a man as Manfred Hegner would be sure to know.

There came a ring at the front door of the Trellis House, and Anna got up reluctantly from her easy chair and laid down her crochet. She was beginning to feel old, so she often told herself regretfully—older than the Englishwomen of her own age seemed to be. But none of them had worked as hard as she had always worked. Englishwomen, especially English servants, were lazy good-for-nothings!

Poor old Anna; she did not feel happy or placid to-day, and she hated the thought of opening the door to some one who, maybe, would condole with her on to-day's news. All Mrs. Otway's friends knew Anna, and treated her as a highly respected institution. Those who knew a little German were fond of trying it on her.

It was rather curious, considering how long Anna had been in England, that she still kept certain little habits acquired in the far-off days when she had been the young cook of a Herr Privy Councillor. Thus never did she open the front door with a cheerful, pleasant manner. Also, unless they were very intimately known to her and to her mistress, she always kept visitors waiting in the hall. She would forget, that is, to show them straight into the pretty sitting-room which lay just opposite her kitchen. She often found herself regretting that the heavy old mahogany door of the Trellis House lacked the tiny aperture which in Berlin is so well named a "stare-hole," and which enables the person inside the front door to command, as it were, the position outside.

But to-day, when she saw who it was who stood on the threshold, her face cleared a little, for she was well acquainted with the tall young man who was looking at her with so pleasant a smile. His name was Jervis Blake, and he came very often to the Trellis House. For two years he had been at "Robey's," the Army coaching establishment which was, in a minor degree, one of the glories of Witanbury, and which consisted of a group of beautiful old Georgian houses spreading across the whole of one of the wide corners of the Close.

Some of the inhabitants of the Close resented the fact of "Robey's." But Mr. Robey was the son of a former Bishop of Witanbury, the Bishop who had followed Miss Forsyth's father.

Bishop Robey had had twin sons, who, unlike most twins, were very different. The elder, whom some of the oldest inhabitants remembered as an ugly, eccentric little boy, with a taste for cutting up dead animals, had insisted on becoming a surgeon. To the surprise of his father's old friends, he had made a considerable reputation, which had been, so to speak, officially certified with a knighthood. The professional life of a great surgeon is limited, and Sir Jacques Robey, though not much over fifty and still a bachelor, had now retired.

The younger twin, Orlando, was the Army coach. He had been, even as a little boy, a great contrast to his brother, being both good looking and anything but eccentric. The brothers were only alike in the success they had achieved in their several professions, but they had for one another in full measure that curiously understanding sympathy and affection which seem to be the special privilege of twins.

Mr. Robey was popular and respected, and those dwellers in the Close who had daughters were pleased with the life and animation which the presence of so many young men gave to the place. The more thoughtful were also glad to think that the shadow of their beloved cathedral rested benignantly over the temporary home of those future officers and administrators of the Empire. And of all those who had been coached at "Robey's" during the last two years, there was none better liked, though there had been many more popular, than the young man who now stood smiling at old Anna.

During the first three months of his sojourn in the Close, Jervis Blake had counted very little, for it had naturally been supposed that he would soon go off to Sandhurst or Woolwich. Then he had failed to pass the Army Entrance Examination, not once, as so many did, but again and again, and the good folk of Witanbury, both gentle and simple, had grown accustomed to see him coming and going in their midst.

Unfortunately for Jervis Blake, his father, though a distinguished soldier, was a very peculiar man, one who had owed nothing in his hard laborious youth to influence; and he had early determined that his only son should tread the path he had himself trod.

And now poor young Blake had reached the age limit, and failed for the last time. Every one had been sorry, but no one had been surprised in Witanbury Close, when the result of the May Army Exam. had been published in July.

One person, Mr. Robey himself, had been deeply concerned. Indeed, the famous coach muttered to one or two of his old friends, "It's a pity, you know! Although I make my living by it, I often think there's a good deal to be said against a system which passes in—well, some boys whose names I could give you, and which keeps out of the Army a lad like Jervis Blake! He'd make a splendid company officer—conscientious, honest, unselfish, keen about his work, and brave—well, brave as only a man——"

And one of those to whom he said it, seeing him hesitate, had broken in, with a slight smile, "Brave as only a man totally lacking in imagination can be, eh, Robey?"

"No, no, I won't have you say that! Even an idiot has enough imagination to be afraid of danger! There's something fine about poor Jervis."

They'd gradually all got to call young Blake "Jervis" in that household. Perhaps Mrs. Robey alone of them all knew how much they would miss him. He was such a thoroughly good fellow, he was so useful to her husband in keeping order among the wilder spirits, and that without having about him a touch of the prig!

Rose looked up and smiled as the tall young man came forward and shook hands with her, saying as he did so, "I hope I'm not too early? The truth is, I've a good many calls to pay this afternoon. I've come to say good-bye."

"I'm sorry. I thought you weren't going away till Saturday." Rose really did feel sorry—in fact, she was herself surprised at her rather keen sensation of regret. She had always liked Jervis Blake very much—liked him from the first day she had seen him. He had a certain claim on the kindness of the ladies of the Trellis House, for his mother had been a girl friend of Mrs. Otway's.

Most people, as Rose was well aware, found his conversation boring. But it always interested her. In fact Rose Otway was the one person in Witanbury who listened with real pleasure to what Jervis Blake had to say. Oddly enough, his talk almost always ran on military matters. Most soldiers—and Rose knew a good many officers, for Witanbury is a garrison town—would discuss, before the Great War, every kind of topic except those connected with what they would have described as "shop." But Jervis Blake, who, owing to his bad luck, seemed fated never to be a soldier, thought and talked of nothing else. It was thanks to him that Rose knew so much about the great Napoleonic campaigns, and was so well "up" in the Indian Mutiny.

And now, on this 4th of August, 1914, Jervis Blake sat down by Rose Otway, and began tracing imaginary patterns on the grass with his stick.

"I'm not going to tell any one else, but there's something I want to tell you." He spoke in a rather hard, set voice, and he did not look up, as he spoke, at the girl by his side.

"Yes," she said. "Yes, Jervis? What is it?" There was something very kind, truly sympathetic, in her accents.

"I'm going to enlist."

Rose Otway was startled—startled and sorry.

"Oh, no, you mustn't do that!"

"I've always thought I should *like* to do it, if—if I failed this last time. But of course I knew it was out of the question—because of my father. But now—everything's different! Even father will see that I have no other course open to me."

"I—I don't understand what you mean," she answered, and to her surprise there came a queer lump in her throat. "Why is everything different now?"

He looked round at her with an air of genuine surprise, and, yes, of indignation, in his steady grey eyes. And under that surprised and indignant look, so unlike anything there had ever been before from him to her, the colour flushed all over her face.

"You mean," she faltered, "you mean because—because England is at war?"

He nodded.

"But I thought—of course I don't know anything about it, Jervis, and I daresay you'll think me very ignorant—but from what the Dean said this morning I thought that only our fleet is to fight the Germans."

"The Dean is an old——" and then they both laughed. Jervis Blake went on: "If we don't go to the help of the French and the Belgians, then England's disgraced. But of course we're going to fight!"

Rose Otway was thinking—thinking hard. She knew a good deal about Jervis, and his relations with the father he both loved and feared.

"Look here," she said earnestly. "We've always been friends, you and I, haven't we, Jervis?"

And again he simply nodded in answer to the question.

"Well, I want you to promise me something!"

"I can't promise you I won't enlist."

"I don't want you to promise me that. I only want you to promise me to wait just a few days—say a week. Of course I don't know anything about how one becomes a soldier, but you'd be rather sold, wouldn't you, if you enlisted and then if your regiment took no part in the fighting—if there's really going to be fighting?"

Rose Otway stopped short. She felt a most curious sensation of fatigue; it was as though she had been speaking an hour instead of a few moments. But she had put her whole heart, her whole soul, into those few simple words.

There was a long, long pause, and her eyes filled with tears. Those who knew her would have told you that Rose Otway was quite singularly self-possessed and unemotional. In fact she could not remember when she had cried last, it was so long ago. But now there came over her a childish, irresistible desire to have her way—to save poor, poor Jervis from himself. And suddenly the face of the young man looking at her became transfigured.

"Rose," he cried—"Rose, do you really care, a little, what happens to me? Oh, if you only knew what a difference that would make!"

And then she pulled herself together. Jervis mustn't become what she in her own mind called "silly." Young men, ay, and older men too, had a way of becoming "silly" about Rose Otway. And up to now she had disliked it very much. But this afternoon she was touched rather than displeased.

"I care very much," she said quietly. She knew the battle was won, and it was very collectedly that she added the words, "Now, I have your promise, Jervis? You're not to do anything foolish——" Then she saw she had made a mistake. "No, no!" she cried hastily; "I don't mean that—I don't mean that a man who becomes a soldier in time of war is doing anything foolish! But I do think that you ought to wait just a few days. Everything is different now." For the first time she felt that everything was indeed different in England—in this new strange England which was at war. It was odd that Jervis Blake should have brought that knowledge home to her.

"Very well," he said slowly. "I'll wait. I can't wait a whole week, but I'll wait till after Sunday."

"The Robeys are going to the seaside on Monday, aren't they?" She was speaking now quite composedly, quite like herself.

"Yes, and they kindly asked me to stay on till then."

He got up. "Well," he said, looking down at her—and she couldn't help telling herself what a big, manly fellow he looked, and what a fine soldier he would make—"well, Rose, so it isn't good-bye, after all?"

"No, I'm glad to say it isn't." She gave him a frank, kindly smile. "Surely you'll stay and have some tea?"

"No, thank you. Jack Robey is feeling a little above himself to-day. You see it's the fourth day of the holidays. I think I'll just go straight back, and take him out for a walk. I rather want to think over things."

As he made his way across the lawn and through the house, feeling somehow that the whole world had changed for the better, though he could not have told you exactly why, Jervis Blake met Mrs. Otway.

"Won't you stay and have some tea?" she asked, but she said it in a very different voice from that Rose had used—Rose had meant what she said.

"Thanks very much, but I've got to get back. I promised Mrs. Robey I'd be in to tea; the boys are back from school, you know."

"Oh, yes, of course! I suppose they are. Well, you must come in some other day before you leave Witanbury."

She hurried through into the garden.

"I hope Jervis Blake hasn't been here very long, darling," she said fondly. "Of course I know he's your friend, and that you've always liked him. But I'm afraid he would rather jar on one to-day. He's always *so* disliked the Germans! Poor fellow, how he must feel out of it, now that the war he's always been talking about has actually come!"

"Well, mother, Jervis was right after all. The Germans *were* preparing for war."

But Mrs. Otway went on as if she had not heard the interruption. It was a way she had, and sometimes both Rose and old Anna found it rather trying. "This morning Miss Forsyth was saying she thought young Blake would enlist—that she'd enlist if she were in his place! It's odd what nonsense she sometimes talks."

Rose remained silent and her mother continued. "I've so many things to tell you I hardly know where to begin. It was a very interesting committee, more lively than usual. There seemed a notion among some of the people there that there will be war work of some kind for us to do. Lady Bethune thought so—though I can't see how the war can affect any of *us*, here, in Witanbury. But just as we were breaking up, Lady Bethune told us some interesting things. There are, she says, two parties in the Government—one party wants us to send out troops to help Belgium, the other party thinks we ought to be content with letting the fleet help the French. I must say I agree with the Blue Water school."

"I don't," said Rose rather decidedly. "If we really owe so much to Belgium that we have gone to war for her sake, then it seems to me we ought to send soldiers to help her."

"But then we have such a small army," objected Mrs. Otway.

"It may grow bigger," observed her daughter quietly, "especially if people like Jervis Blake think of enlisting."

"But it wasn't Jervis Blake, darling child—it was Miss Forsyth who said that to me."

"So it was! How stupid I am!" Rose turned a little pink. She did not wish to deceive her mother. But Mrs. Otway was so confiding, so sure that every one was as honourable as herself, that she could not always be trusted to keep secrets.

CHAPTER VI

Mr. and Mrs. Hegner stood together in their brilliantly lighted but now empty front shop. In a few minutes their guests would begin to arrive. Mrs. Hegner looked tired, and rather cross, for the shop had not been transformed into its present state without a good deal of hard work on the part of all of them, her husband, their German assistants, and herself—their English shopman had been told that to-night his services would not be required. But Mrs. Hegner, though her pretty face was tired and peevish-looking, yet looked far pleasanter than she had done half an hour ago, for her husband had just presented her with a long gold chain.

In a very, very quiet way, quite under the rose, so to speak, Mr. Hegner sometimes went in for small money-lending transactions. He would give loans on jewellery, and even on "curios" and good furniture; always, however, in connection with an account which had, maybe, run a little too long—never as a separate transaction. The old-fashioned chain of 18-carat gold, which he had just hung with a joking word round his pretty wife's slender neck, had been the outcome of one of these minor activities.

It was now a quarter to nine; and suddenly there came the sound of loud, rather impatient knocking on the locked and barred front door of the shop. A frown gathered over Mr. Hegner's face; it transformed his good-looking, generally genial, countenance into something which was, for the moment, very disagreeable.

"What can that be?" he said to his wife. "Did you not put plainly on every card 'Entrance by Market Row,' Polly?"

"Yes," she said, a little frightened by his look. "It was most carefully put in every case, Manfred."

The knocking had stopped now, as if the person outside expected the door to open. Husband and wife went forward.

"Who can it be?" said Mrs. Hegner uneasily.

And then her question was answered.

The voice was clear and silvery. "It's Miss Haworth! Can I come in and speak to you a moment, Mr. Hegner, or has the meeting already begun?"

"Why, it's the young lady from the Deanery!" exclaimed Manfred Hegner in a relieved voice; and both he and his wife began hastily unlocking and unbarring the great plate-glass doors.

The unbidden, unexpected visitor stepped forward into the shop, and Mrs. Hegner eagerly noted the cut and shape of the prettily draped pale blue silk evening coat, and tried to gain some notion of the evening gown beneath.

"I'm so glad to be in time—I mean before your meeting has begun. How very nice it all looks!" The speaker cast an approving glance on the rout chairs, on the table at the top of the room, on the counter where steamed, even now, the fragrant coffee. "The Dean has asked me to bring a message—of course quite an informal message, Mr. Hegner. He wants you to tell everybody that he is quite at their service if they want anything done."

"That is very, very good of Mr. Dean. Polly, d'you hear that? Is not the Reverend gentleman truly good?"

"Yes, indeed," said Mrs. Hegner, a trifle mechanically.

She felt a touch of sharp envy as she looked at the beautiful girl standing there. Though Edith Haworth knew very little of Mrs. Hegner, except that Mrs. Hegner's sister was her maid, Mrs. Hegner knew a great deal about Miss Haworth. How she had gone up to London just for one month of the season, and how during that one month she had become engaged to a rich young gentleman, a baronet. He was in the Army, too, but he couldn't be much of a soldier, for he seemed to be a great deal in Witanbury—at least he had been here a great deal during the last three weeks. The two often walked about the town together; once they had stood for quite a long time just opposite the open doors of the Stores, and Mrs. Hegner on that occasion had looked at the handsome couple with sympathetic interest and excitement.

But now, to-night, nothing but sharp envy filled her soul. It was her fate, poor, pretty Polly's fate, to sit behind that horrid glass partition over there, taking money, paying out endless small change, compelled always to look pleasant, or Manfred, if he caught her looking anything else, even when giving a farthing change out of a penny, would soon know the reason why! The young lady who stood smiling just within the door was not half as "fetching" as she, Polly, had been in her maiden days—and yet she was going to have everything the heart of woman could desire, a rich, handsome, young husband, and plenty of money!

As her eyes strayed out to the moonlit space outside where stood waiting, under the quaint little leafy mall which gives the Market Square of Witanbury such a foreign look, a gentleman in evening dress, Mrs. Hegner repeated mechanically, "Very kind, I'm sure, miss. They'll appreciate it— that they will."

"Well, that was all I came to say—only that my father will be very glad indeed to do anything he can. Oh, I did forget one more thing——" She lowered her voice a little. "The Dean thinks it probable, Mr. Hegner, that after to-day no German of military age will be allowed to leave England. You ought to tell everybody that this evening, otherwise some of them, without knowing it, might get into trouble."

And then Mrs. Hegner, perhaps because she had become nervously aware that her husband had looked at her rather crossly a moment ago, blurted out, "There's no fear of that, miss. We sent off a lot this morning to Harwich. I expect they'll have been able to get a boat there all right——" She stopped suddenly, for her husband had just made a terrible face at her—a face full of indignation and wrath.

But Miss Haworth did not seem to have noticed anything.

"Oh, well," she said, "perhaps it was a mistake to do that, but I don't suppose it matters much, one way or the other. I must go now. The meeting is due to begin, isn't it? And—and Sir Hugh is leaving to-night. He expects to find his marching orders when he gets back to town." A little colour came into her charming face; she sighed, but not very heavily. "War is an awful thing!" she said; "but every soldier, of course, wants to see *something* of the fighting. I expect the feeling is just as strong in France and Germany as it is here."

She shook hands warmly with Mr. and Mrs. Hegner, then she turned and tripped out into the dimly lighted and solitary Market Square. They watched her cross the road and take her lover's arm.

"Fool!" said Mr. Hegner harshly. "Pretty, silly fool!" He mimicked what he thought to be her mincing accents. "Wants to see something of war, does he? I can tell him he will be satisfied before he has done!" There was a scowl on his face. "And you"—he turned on his wife furiously—"what business had you to say that about those young German men? I was waiting—yes, with curiosity—to hear what else you were going to tell her—whether you would tell her that I had paid their fares!"

"Oh, no, Manfred. You know I would never have done that after what you said to me yesterday."

"Take it from me now, once for all," he said fiercely, "that you say nothing—*nothing*, mark you—about this cursed, blasted war—this war which, if we are not very careful, is going to make us poor, to bring us to the gutter, to the workhouse, you and I!"

And then Hegner's brow cleared as if by enchantment, for the first of their visitors were coming through from the back of the shop.

It was the manager of a big boot factory and his wife. They were both German-born, and the man had obtained his present excellent position owing to the good offices of Mr. Hegner. Taking his friend's wise advice, he had become naturalised a year ago. But a nephew, who had joined him in business, had not followed his example, and he had been one of the young men who had been speeded off to Harwich, through Mr. Hegner's exertions, early that morning.

While Mrs. Hegner tried to make herself pleasant to Mrs. Liebert, Mr. Hegner took Mr. Liebert aside.

"I have just learnt," he said, in a quick whisper, "that the military gentlemen here *are* expecting marching orders to the Continent—I presume to Belgium."

"That is bad," muttered the other.

But Mr. Hegner smiled. "No, no," he said, "not bad! It might have been disagreeable if they could have been got there last week. But by the time the fifty thousand, even the hundred thousand, English soldiers are in Belgium, there will be a million of our fellows there to meet them."

"What are you going to say at this meeting?" asked the other curiously; he used the English word, though they still spoke German.

Mr. Hegner shrugged his shoulders. "This is not going to be a meeting," he said laughingly. "It's going to be a Kaffeeklatch! Those people to whom I have to say a word I shall see by myself, in our little parlour. I trust to you, friend Max, to make everything go well and lively. As to measures, it is far too early to think of any measures. So far all goes very well with me. I have had many tokens of sympathy and of friendship this morning. Just two or three, perhaps, would have liked to be disagreeable, but they did not dare."

He hurried away, for his guests were arriving thick and fast.

It was a strange and, or so Mrs. Otway would have thought, a rather pathetic little company of men and women, who gathered together at Manfred Hegner's Stores at nine o'clock on that fine August night. The blinds had been drawn down, and behind the blinds the shutters had been put up.

As to the people there, they all looked prosperous and respectable, but each one wore a slight air of apprehension and discomfort. Strange to say, not one of the Germans present really liked or trusted their host, and that was odd, for Manfred Hegner, apart from certain outstanding exceptions, had managed to make himself quite popular among the English inhabitants of Witanbury.

The men and the women had instinctively parted into two companies, but Mrs. Hegner went to and fro among both sets, pressing hospitably on all her guests the coffee, the creamy milk, and the many cakes, to say nothing of the large sandwiches she had been ordered to make that afternoon.

She felt oppressed and rather bewildered, for the people about her were all talking German, and she had never taken the trouble to learn even half a dozen words of her husband's difficult nasal language. She kept wondering when the meeting would begin. Time was going on. They always got up very early in the morning, and already she was tired, very, very tired in fact, for it had been a long and rather an exciting day.

She had never before seen her husband quite so pleasant and jovial, and as she moved about she heard continually his loud, hearty laugh. He was cheering up the people round him—so much was clear. All of them had looked gloomy, preoccupied, and troubled when they came in, but now they seemed quite merry and bright.

There was one exception. Poor Mr. Fröhling looked very miserable. Mrs. Hegner felt very sorry for Mr. and Mrs. Fröhling. When her husband had heard of what had befallen the unfortunate barber, and how he had been ordered to pack up and leave his shop within a few hours, he had said roughly: "Fröhling is a fool! I told him to take out his certificate. He refused to do it, so now of course he will have to go. Witanbury has no use for that man!"

And now Mr. and Mrs. Fröhling, alone of the company there, sat together apart, with lowering brows.

Mrs. Hegner went up to them, rather timidly. "I want to tell you how sorry I am, Mr. Fröhling," she said conciliatingly. Polly had a kind heart, if a pettish manner. "What a pity you didn't take out your certificate when Manfred advised you to do so!"

Mr. Fröhling remained silent. But his wife said wistfully, "Ach, yes, Mrs. Hegner. It is a pity now; but still, the officers they have been kind to us, really very kind. One of them even said it would not have made much difference— —"

Her husband interrupted her. "He nothing, Jane, said of the kind! That it *ought* not any difference to have made was what say he did. I, who have in England lived since the year 1874; I, who England love; I, whose son will soon for England be fighting!"

"My husband said," began Mrs. Hegner— — And again Mr. Fröhling interrupted rather rudely: "You need not tell me what your husband say," he remarked. "I know for myself exactly what Mr. Hegner say. If everything could be foreseen in this life we should all be very wise. Mr. Hegner, he does foresee more than most people, and wise he is."

Mrs. Fröhling drew her hostess a little aside. "Don't mind him," she whispered. "He is so unhappy. And yet we should be thankful, for the gentlemen officers are getting up a little testimonial fund for poor Fröhling."

"I suppose you've saved a good bit, too?" said Mrs. Hegner with curiosity.

"Not much—not much! Only lately have we turned the corner— —" Mrs. Fröhling sighed. Then her face brightened, and Mrs. Hegner looking round saw that Anna Bauer, Mrs. Otway's servant, was pushing her way through the crowd towards them.

Now pretty Polly disliked the old woman. Frau Bauer was not a person of any account, yet Manfred had ordered that she should be treated this evening with special consideration, and so Mrs. Hegner walked forward and stiffly shook hands with her latest guest.

CHAPTER VII

Sit down, Fröhling, sit down!"

The old barber, rather to his surprise, had been invited to follow his host into the Hegners' private parlour, a little square room situated behind the big front shop.

The floor of the parlour was covered with a large-patterned oilcloth. There was a round mahogany pedestal table, too large for the room, and four substantial cane-backed armchairs. Till to-day there had always hung over the piano a large engraving of the German Emperor, and on the opposite wall a smaller oleograph picture of Queen Victoria with her little great-grandson, the Prince of Wales, at her knee. The German Emperor had now been taken down, and there was a patch of clean paper marking where the frame had hung.

As answer to Mr. Hegner's invitation, the older man sat down heavily in a chair near the table.

Both men remained silent for a moment, and a student of Germany, one who really knew and understood that amazing country, might well, had he seen the two sitting there, have regarded the one as epitomising the old Germany, and the other—naturalised Englishman though he now was—epitomising the new. Manfred Hegner was slim, active, and prosperous-looking; he appeared years younger than his age. Ludwig Fröhling was stout and rather stumpy; he seemed older than he really was, and although he was a barber, his hair was long and untidy. He looked intelligent and thoughtful, but it was the intelligence and the thoughtfulness of the student and of the dreamer, not of the man of action.

"Well, Mr. Fröhling, the International haven't done much the last few days, eh? I'm afraid you must have been disappointed." He of course spoke in German.

"Yes, I *have* been disappointed," said the other stoutly, "very much disappointed indeed! But still, from this great crime good may come, even now. It has occurred to me that, owing to this war made by the great rulers, the people in Russia, as well as in my beloved Fatherland, may arise and cut their bonds."

A light came into the speaker's eyes, and Manfred Hegner looked at him in mingled pity and contempt. It was not his intention, however, to waste much time this evening listening to a foolish old man. In fact, he had hesitated as to whether he should include the Fröhlings in his invitations—then he had thought that if he omitted to do so the fact might possibly come to the ears of the Dean. Fröhling and the Dean had long been pleasantly acquainted. Then, again, it was just possible—not likely, but possible—that he might be able to get out of the ex-barber of the Witanbury garrison some interesting and just now valuable information.

"What are you going to do now?" he asked. "Have you made any plans yet?"

"We are thinking of going to London, and of making a fresh start there. We have friends in Red Lion Square." Fröhling spoke as if the words were being dragged out of him. He longed to tell the other man to mind his own business.

"You haven't a chance of being allowed to do that! Why, already, on the very first day, every German barber is suspected." The speaker gave a short, unpleasant laugh.

"I am not suspected. So!" exclaimed Fröhling heatedly. "Not one single person has spoken as if he suspected me in this town! On the contrary, England is not harsh, Mr. Hegner. English people are too sensible and broad-minded to suspect harm where there is none. Indeed, they are not suspecting enough."

Strange to say, old Fröhling's last sentence found an agreeable, even a comforting, echo in Mr. Hegner's heart. He looked up, and for the first time the expression on his face was really cordial. "Maybe you are right, Mr. Fröhling. Most heartily do I desire it may be so! And yet—well, one cannot say people would be altogether wrong in suspecting barbers, for barbers hear a great deal of interesting conversation, is it not so?"

"That depends on their customers," said the other coldly. "I cannot say that I ever found the conversation of the young English officers here in Witanbury very illuminating."

"Not exactly illuminating," said the other cautiously. "But take the last few days? You must have heard a good deal of information as to coming plans."

"Not one word did I hear," said the other man quickly—"not one word, Mr. Hegner! Far more from my own intelligent, level-headed German assistant. He knew and guessed what none of these young gentlemen did—

to what all the wicked intrigues of Berlin, Petersburg and Vienna, of the last ten days were tending."

"I have heard to-night—in fact it was the daughter of the Dean who mentioned it—that the British Army is going to Belgium," said Mr. Hegner casually. "Is your son going to Belgium, Mr. Fröhling?"

"Not that I know of," said the other. But a troubled look came over his face. He opened his mouth as if to add something, and then tightly shut it again.

Mr. Hegner had the immediate impression that old Fröhling could have told him something worth hearing had he been willing to do so.

"Well, that is all," said the host with a dismissory air, as he got up from his seat. "I have many to see, many to advise to-night. One thing I *do* tell you, Mr. Fröhling. You may take it from me that if you wish to leave this place you should clear out quickly. They will be making very tiresome regulations soon—but not now, not for a few days. Fortunately for you, and for all those who have not taken out their certificates, there is no organisation in this country. As for thoroughness, they do not know the meaning of the word."

"I have sometimes wondered," observed Mr. Fröhling mildly, "why you, who dislike England so much, should have taken out your certificate, Mr. Hegner. In your place I should have gone back to America."

"You have no right, no business, to say that I dislike England!" cried his host vehemently. "It is a wicked thing to say to me on such a day as this! It is a thing that might do me great harm in this city of which I am a Councillor."

"It is not a thing that I should say to any one but you," returned the old man. "But nevertheless it is true. We have not very often met—but every time we have met you have spoken in a disagreeable, a derogatory, a jeering way of what is now your country."

"And you," said Mr. Hegner, his eyes flashing, "have often spoken to me in a derogatory, a jeering, a disagreeable way of Germany—of the country where we were each born, of our *real* Fatherland."

"It is not of Germany that I speak ill," said the older man wearily; "it is of what a few people have made of my beloved country. To-day we see the outcome of their evil doings. But all that is transitory. I am an old man, and yet I hope to see a free Germany rise up."

He walked through into the shop, and beckoned to his wife. Then they both turned towards the door through which they had gained admittance earlier in the evening.

Mr. Hegner smoothed out his brow, and a mechanical smile came to his lips. He was glad the old Socialist had cleared out early. It is not too much to say that Manfred Hegner hated Fröhling. He wondered who would get the German barber's job. He knew a man, a sharp, clever fellow, who like himself had lived for a long time in America—who was, in fact, an American citizen, though he had been born in Hamburg—who would be the very man for it. Perhaps now was scarcely the moment to try and get yet another foreigner, even if only this time an American, into the neighbourhood of the barracks.

The owner of the Witanbury Stores went over to the place where Anna Bauer was sitting talking to the mother of one of Mr. Hegner's German employés. To call that young man German is, however, wrong, for some six weeks ago he had become naturalised. Well for him that he had done so, otherwise he would have had now to go back to the Fatherland and fight. His mother was the one really happy person in the gathering to-night, for the poor woman kept thanking God and Mr. Hegner in her heart for having saved her son from an awful fate. Treating the mother of his shopman as if she had not been there, Mr. Hegner bent towards the other woman.

"Frau Bauer," he said graciously, "come into our parlour for a few moments. I should like a little chat with you."

Anna got up and followed him through the crowd. What was it Mr. Hegner wanted to say to her? She felt slightly apprehensive. Surely he was going to tell her that now, owing to the war, he would have to stop the half-commission he was still giving her on Mrs. Otway's modest orders? Her heart rose in revolt. An Englishman belonging to the type and class of Anna Bauer would have determined "to have it out" with him, but she knew well that she would not have the courage to say anything at all if he did this mean thing.

To her great surprise, after she had followed him into the parlour, Mr. Hegner turned the key in the lock.

"I have but a very little to say," he exclaimed jovially, "but, while I say it, I do not care to be interrupted! It is more cosy so. Sit down, Frau Bauer, sit down!"

Still surprised, and still believing that her host was going to "best" her in some way, Anna did sit down. She fixed her light-blue, short-sighted eyes watchfully on his face. What a pity it was that he so greatly resembled her adored Kaiser!

"You are very kind," she said mechanically.

"I believe that last Sunday, August 1st, there was owing to you this sum." So saying, he pushed towards her across the table five half-sovereigns.

Anna Bauer uttered an exclamation of profound astonishment. She stared down at the money lying now close to her fat red hand.

"Is not that so?" he said, looking at her fixedly.

And at last she stammered out, "Yes, that is so. But—but——do you then know Willi, Mr. Hegner?"

The man sitting opposite to her remained silent for a moment. He hadn't the slightest idea who "Willi" was. "Ach, yes! It is from him that you generally receive this money every six months—I had forgotten that! Willi is a good fellow. Have you known him long?" He wisely waited for a reply, for on his tongue had been the words, "I suppose he lives in London?"

"I have only known him three years," said Anna, "and that though he married my niece seven years ago. Yes, Willi is indeed an excellent fellow!"

And then she suddenly bethought herself of what Mrs. Otway had said that very morning. Mr. Hegner would certainly be able to tell her the truth—he was the sort of man who knew everything of a practical, business nature. "Perhaps you will be able to tell me," she asked eagerly, "if my nephew will have to fight—to go to the frontier. Mrs. Otway, she says that the police are always the last to be called out—is that true, Mr. Hegner?"

"Yes, I think I may assure you, Frau Bauer, that it is a fact." He looked at her curiously. "You are very fond, then, of your niece's husband, of the excellent Willi?"

"I am indeed," she said eagerly, "and grateful to him too, for this money he sends me is very welcome, Mr. Hegner. I was so afraid it might not come this time."

"And you were right to be afraid! It will become more and more difficult to get money from Germany to England," said her host, and there was a touch of grimness in his voice. "Still, there are ways of getting over every difficulty. Should the war last as long, I will certainly see that you, Frau Bauer, receive what is your due on the 1st of next January. But many strange things may happen before then. Long before Christmas you may no longer be earning this money."

"Oh! I hope that will not be the case!" She looked very much disturbed. £5 a year was about a fifth of good old Anna's total income.

"Well, we shall see. I will do my best for you, Frau Bauer."

"Thank you, thank you! I am very grateful to you, Mr. Hegner."

Indeed old Anna's feelings towards the man who sat there, playing with a pen in his hand, had undergone an extraordinary transformation. She had come into the room disliking him, fearing him, feeling sure that he was going to take some advantage of her. Now she stared at his moody, rather flushed face, full of wondering gratitude.

How strange that he had never taken the trouble to tell her that he knew Willi! She was sorry to remember how often she had dissuaded her mistress from getting something at the Stores that could be got elsewhere, some little thing on which the tiny commission she received would have been practically nil, or, worse still, overlooked. Her commission had been often overlooked of late unless she kept a very sharp look-out on the bills, which Mrs. Otway had a tiresome habit of locking away when receipted.

She took the five precious gold pieces off the table, and moved, as if to rise from her chair.

But Mr. Hegner waved his hand. "Sit down, sit down, Frau Bauer," he said. "There is no hurry. I enjoy the thought of a little chat with you." He waited a moment. "And are you thinking of staying on in your present position? You are—let me see—with Mrs. Otway?"

"Oh yes," she said, brightening. "I shall certainly stay where I am. I am very happy there. They are very kind to me, Mr. Hegner. I love my young lady as much as I do my own child."

"It is a quiet house,"rdquo; he went on, "a quiet house, with very little coming and going, Frau Bauer. Is not that so?"

"There is a good deal of visiting," she said quickly. "It is a hospitable house."

"Not often gentlemen of the garrison, I suppose?"

"Indeed, yes," cried Anna eagerly. "You know how it is in England? It is not like in our country. Here everybody is much more associated. In some ways it is pleasanter."

"Very true. And had any of these officers who came and called on your two ladies reason to suppose that the war was coming?"

Anna stared at him, surprised. "No, indeed!" she cried. "English officers never talk of warlike subjects. I have never even seen one of them wearing his uniform."

"It looks to me as if I shall have to add a new line of officers' kit to the Stores," said Mr. Hegner thoughtfully. "And any information you give me about officers just now might be very useful in my business. I know, Frau Bauer, that you were annoyed, disappointed about that little matter of the commission being halved."

"Oh no," murmured Anna, rather confusedly.

"Yes, and I understand your point of view. Well, from to-day, Frau Bauer, I restore the old scale! And if at any time you can say anything about the Stores to the visitors who come to see your ladies—anything, you understand, that may lead to an order—I will be generous, I will recognise your help in the widest sense."

Anna got up again, and so did her host. "Well, we have had a pleasant gossip," he said. "And one word more, Frau Bauer. You have not told *any one*, not even your daughter, of—of——" he hesitated, for he did not wish to put in plain words the question he wished to convey—"of that other matter—of that in which your nephew is concerned?"

"I gave my solemn promise to Willi to say nothing," said Anna, "and I am not one who ever breaks my word, Mr. Hegner."

"That I am sure you are not! And Frau Bauer? Do not attempt to write to the Fatherland henceforth. Your letters would be opened, your business all spied out, and then the letters destroyed! I am at your disposal for any information you require. Come in and see us sometimes," he said cordially. "Let me see—to-day is Wednesday. How about Sunday? Come in on Sunday night, if you can do so, and have a little supper. You may have news of interest to my business to give me, and in any case it is pleasant to chat among friends."

CHAPTER VIII

It was now the morning of Friday, the third day of war, and Mrs. Otway allowed the newspaper she had been holding in her hands to slip on to the floor at her feet with an impatient sigh.

From where she sat, close to the window in her charming sitting-room, her eyes straying down to the ground read in huge characters at the top of one of the newspaper columns the words:

"THE FLEET MOBILISED."

"MOTOR RUSH FOR VOLUNTEERS."

"HOW THE NAVAL RESERVE RECEIVED THEIR NOTICES."

"OUR SAILORS' GOOD-BYE."

Then, at the top of another column, in rather smaller characters, as though that news was after all not really so important as the home news:

"Defeat of the Germans at Liége."

"Complete Rout."

"Germans Repulsed at All Points."

Finally, in considerably smaller characters:

"ALLEGED GERMAN CRUELTIES IN BELGIUM."

She raised her eyes and looked out, over the Close, to where the Cathedral rose like a diamond set in emeralds. What a beautiful day— and how quiet, how much more quiet than usual, was the dear, familiar, peaceful scene! All this week, thanks in a great measure to the prolonged Bank Holiday, Witanbury had been bathed in a sabbatical calm.

Oddly enough, this had not been as pleasant as it ought to have been. In fact, it had been rather unpleasant to find nearly all the shops shut day after day, and it had become really awkward and annoying not to be able to get money as one required it. At this very moment Rose was out in the town, trying to cash a cheque, for they were quite out of petty cash.

During the last three days Major Guthrie, who so seldom allowed more than a day and a half to slip by without coming to the Trellis House, had not called, neither had he written. Mrs. Otway was surprised, and rather annoyed with herself, to find how much she missed him. She realised that it was the more unreasonable of her, as at first, say all last Wednesday, she had shrunk from the thought of seeing him, the one person among her acquaintances, with the insignificant exception of young Jervis Blake, who had believed in the possibility of an Anglo-German conflict. But when the whole of that long day, the first day of war, had gone by, and the next day also, without bringing with it even the note which, during his infrequent absences, she had grown accustomed to receive from Major Guthrie, she felt hurt and injured.

Major Guthrie was one of those rather inarticulate Englishmen who can express themselves better in writing than in speech. When he and Mrs. Otway were together, she could always, and generally did, out-talk him; but often, after some discussion of theirs, he would go home and write her quite a good letter. And then, after reading it, and perhaps smiling over it a little, she would tear it up and put the pieces in the waste-paper basket.

Yes, her rather odd, unconventional friendship with Major Guthrie was a pleasant feature of her placid, agreeably busy life, and it was strange that he had neither come, nor written and explained what kept him away.

And while Mrs. Otway sat there, waiting she knew not quite for what, old Anna sat knitting in her kitchen on the other side of the hall, also restlessly longing for something, anything, to happen, which would give her news of what was really going on in the Fatherland. All her heart, during these last three days, had been with Minna and Willi in far-off Berlin.

A few moments ago a picture paper had been spread out on the table before Anna. She always enjoyed herself over that paper. It was Miss Rose's daily gift to her old nurse, and was paid for out of her small allowance. The two morning papers read by her ladies were in due course used to light the fires; but Anna kept her own *Daily Pictorials* most carefully, and there was an ever-growing neat pile of them in a corner of the scullery.

But to-day's *Daily Pictorial* lay in a crumpled heap, tossed to one side on the floor of the kitchen, for poor old Anna had just read out the words:

"FRENCH FRONTIER SUCCESSES."

"GERMAN DRAGOON REGIMENT ANNIHILATED."

"ONE THOUSAND GERMAN PRISONERS IN ALSACE."

Up to this strange, sinister week, Anna had contented herself with looking at the pictures. She had hardly ever glanced at the rest of the paper. She did not like the look of English print, and she read English with difficulty. But this morning the boy who had brought the fish had said, not disagreeably, but as if he was giving her a rather amusing bit of information, "Your friends have been catching it hot, Mrs. Bauer; and from what I can make out, they deserves it!" She had not quite understood what he meant, but it had made her uneasy; and after she had cleared away breakfast, and washed up, she had sat down with her paper spread before her.

She had looked long at a touching picture of a big sailor saying good-bye to the tiny baby in his arms. He was kissing the child, and Anna had contemplated him with a good deal of sympathy. That big bearded British sailor would soon be face to face with the German Navy. Thus he was surely doomed. His babe would soon be fatherless. Kind old Anna wiped her eyes at the thought.

And then? And then she had slowly spelled out the incredible, the dreadful news about the German Dragoon Regiment. Her father, forty-four years ago, had been a non-commissioned officer in a Dragoon Regiment.

Yes, both mistress and maid felt wretched on this, the third day of the war, which no one, in England at least, yet thought of as the Great War.

Mrs. Otway was restless, quite unlike herself. She wondered, uneasily, why she felt so depressed. Friday was the day when she always paid her few household books, but to-day, as it was still Bank Holiday, the books had not come in. Instead, she had had three letters, marked in each case "Private," from humble folk in the town, asking her most urgently to pay at once the small sum she owed to each of them. In every case the writer expressed the intention of calling in person for the money. It was partly to try and get the cash with which to pay these accounts that Rose had gone out with a cheque. It was so odd, so disagreeable, to find oneself without the power of getting any ready money. Such a thing had never happened to Mrs. Otway before! It would be really very disagreeable if Rose, after all, failed to cash that cheque.

Then it suddenly occurred to her that James Hayley might bring her down some money to-morrow. Nothing would be easier, or so she supposed, than for *him* to get it. She went over to her writing-table by the window and hurriedly wrote a note. Then she made out a cheque for twenty pounds.

Oh yes, it would be quite easy for James, who was in a Government office, to get her the money!

Mrs. Otway, like most English people, had a limitless belief in the powers of any one connected with the Government. Twenty pounds? It was a good deal of money. She had never had so much cash in the house before. But what was happening now had taught her a lesson. The Dean had said that all the banks would be open again on Monday. But the Dean was not quite infallible. How often had he and she agreed that Germany would never, *never* dream of going to war with any of her peaceful neighbours!

She read over the letter she had written:

"Dear James,—I enclose a cheque for twenty pounds. Would you kindly get it cashed for me, and would you bring down the money to-morrow when you come? Of course I should like the money, if possible, in gold, but still it will do if you can get me two five-pound notes and the rest in gold and silver. I find that several people to whom I owe small amounts are anxious to be paid, and they do not seem to care about taking cheques. What strange times we live in! Both Rose and I long to see you and hear all the news.

"Your affectionate aunt,
"Mary Otway."

James Hayley always called her "Aunt Mary," though as a matter of fact he was the child of a first cousin.

She got up from her table, and began folding up the sheets of newspaper lying on the floor. She did not want poor old Anna to see the great staring headlines telling of the defeat of the Germans. Having folded the paper, and put it away in an unobtrusive corner, she went upstairs for her hat. She felt that it would do her good to go out into the air, and post the letter herself.

And then, as she came downstairs, she heard the gate of the Trellis House open and swing to. Rose coming back, no doubt. But no, it was not Rose, for instead of the handle of the door turning, there was a ring and a knock.

It was a ring and a knock which sounded pleasantly familiar. Mrs. Otway smiled as she turned into her sitting-room. It was the first time she had smiled that day.

Major Guthrie at last! It was half-past eleven now; they could have a good long, comfortable talk, and perhaps he would stop to lunch. Of course she would have to eat humble pie about the war, but he was the last man to say "I told you so!"

There were so many things she wanted to know, which now she could ask him, secure of a sensible, true answer. Major Guthrie, whatever his prejudices, was a professional soldier. He really did know something of military matters. He was not like the people who lived in the Close, and who were already talking such nonsense about the war. Mrs. Otway was too intelligent not to realise the fact that they, whatever their boasts, knew nothing which could throw real light on the great adventure which was beginning, only beginning, to fill all her thoughts.

Suddenly the door opened, and Anna announced, in a grumpy tone, "Major Guthrie."

"I thought I was never going to see you again!"

There was an eagerness, a warmth of welcome in Mrs. Otway's manner of which she was unconscious, but which gave a sudden shock of pleasure, aye, and perhaps even more than pleasure, to her visitor. He had expected to find her anxious, depressed, troubled—above all, deeply saddened by the dreadful thing having come to pass which she had so often vehemently declared would never, never happen.

They shook hands, but before she could go on to utter one of the many questions which were on her lips, Major Guthrie spoke. "I've come to say good-bye," he said abruptly. "I've had my marching orders!" There was a strange light in the dark blue eyes which were the one beautiful feature he had acquired from his very handsome mother.

"I—I don't understand——" And she really didn't.

What could he mean? His marching orders? But he had left the Army four or five years ago. Besides, the Dean had told her only that morning that no portion of the British Army was going to the Continent—that on England's part this was only going to be a naval war. The Dean had heard this fact from a friend in London, a distinguished German professor of Natural Theology, who was a very frequent visitor to the Deanery.

Major Guthrie slightly lowered his voice: "I had the telegram an hour ago," he explained. "I thought you knew that I was in the Reserve, that I form part of what is called the Expeditionary Force."

"The Expeditionary Force?" she repeated in a bewildered tone. "I didn't know there was such a thing! You never told me about it."

"Well, you've never been interested in such matters." Major Guthrie smiled at her indulgently, and suddenly she realised that when they were together she generally talked of her own concerns, very, very seldom of his.

But what was this he was now saying? "Besides, it's by way of being a secret. That's the real reason I haven't been out the last few days. I didn't feel I could leave home for even five minutes. I've been on tenterhooks—in fact it will take me two or three days to get fit again. You see, I couldn't say anything to anybody! And one heard such absurd rumours—rumours that the Government didn't mean to send any troops to the Continent—that they had been caught napping—that the transport arrangements had broken down, and so on. However, it's all right now! I report myself to-night; rejoin my old regiment to-morrow; and—well, in three or four days, please God, I shall be in France, and in a week at latest in Belgium."

Mrs. Otway looked at him silently. She was too much surprised to speak. She felt moved, oppressed, excited. A British Army going to France—to Belgium? It seemed incredible!

And Major Guthrie also felt moved and excited, but *he* was not oppressed—he was triumphant, overjoyed. "I thought you'd understand," he said, and there was a little break in his voice. "It's made me feel a young man again—that's what it's done!"

"How does your mother take it?" asked Mrs. Otway slowly.

And then for the first time a troubled look came over his kind, honest face. "I haven't told my mother," he answered. "I've thought a good deal about it; and I don't mean to say good-bye to her—I shall simply write her a note saying I've had to go up to town on business. She'll have it when I'm gone. Then, when the news is allowed to be made public, I'll write and tell her the truth. She felt my going to South Africa so much. You see, the man to whom she was engaged as a girl was killed in the Crimea."

There was a moment's silence between them, and then he asked, "And Miss Rose?—I should like to say good-bye to her. Is she at home?"

"No, she's out in the town, doing some business for me—or rather trying to do it! Have *you* found any difficulty in getting cheques changed the last few days, Major Guthrie?"

"No; for I've always kept money in the house," he said quickly. "And glad I am now that I did. It used to annoy my mother—it used to make her afraid that we should be burgled. But of course I never told any one else." He looked at her rather oddly. "I've quite a lot of money here, with me now."

"I wonder if you would be so kind as to cash me a cheque?" She grew a little pink. She was not used to asking even small favours from her friends. Impulsive, easy-going as she seemed, there was yet a very proud and reticent streak in Mary Otway's nature.

"Of course I will. In fact——" and then he stopped abruptly, for she had gone up to her table, and was opening the letter she had just written to James Hayley.

"Could you really conveniently let me have as much as twenty pounds?" and she held him out the cheque.

"Certainly. Then you're not expecting Miss Rose back for a minute or two?"

"Oh, no! She only went out twenty minutes ago."

He was still standing, and Mrs. Otway suddenly felt herself to be inhospitable.

"Do sit down," she said hurriedly. Somehow in the last few minutes her point of view, her attitude to her friend, her kind, considerate, courteous friend, had altered. She no longer looked at him with indulgent half-contempt as an idle man, a man who, though he was very good to his mother, and sometimes very useful to herself, had always led, excepting during the South African War (and that was a long time ago), an idle, useless kind of life. He was going now to face real danger, perchance—but her mind shrank from *that* thought, from that dread possibility—death itself. Somehow the fact that Major Guthrie was going with his regiment to France brought the War perceptibly nearer to Mrs. Otway, and made it for the first time real.

He quietly took the easy chair she had motioned him to take, and she sat down too.

"Well, I have to confess that you were right and I wrong! You always thought we should fight the Germans." She tried to speak playfully, but there was a certain pain in the admission, for she had always scorned his quiet prophecies and declared him to be, in this one matter, prejudiced and unfair.

"Yes," he said, "that's quite true! But, Mrs. Otway? I'm very, very sorry to have been proved right. And I fear that you must feel it very much, as you have so many German friends."

"I haven't many German friends now," she said quickly. "I had as a girl, and of course I've kept up with two or three of them, as you know. But it's true that the whole thing is a great shock and—and a great pain to me. Unlike you, I've always thought very well of Germans."

He said quietly, "So have I."

"Ah, but not in my sense!" She could not help smiling a little ruefully. "You know I never thought of them in your sense at all—I mean not as soldiers."

There was a pause, a long and rather painful pause, between them.

CHAPTER IX

Major Guthrie looked at Mrs. Otway meditatively.

Apart from his instinctive attraction for her—an attraction which had sprung into being the very first time they had met, at a dinner party at the Deanery—he had always regarded her as an exceptionally clever woman. She was able to do so much more than most of the ladies he had known. To his simple soldier mind there was something interesting and, well, yes, rather extraordinary, in a woman who sat on committees, who could hold her own so well in argument, and who yet remained very feminine, sometimes—so he secretly thought—quite delightfully absurd and inconsequent, with it all.

Major Guthrie had always been sorry that Mrs. Otway and his mother didn't exactly hit it off. His mother had once been a beauty, and was now a rather shrewish, sharp-tongued old lady, who had outlived most of the people and most of the things she had cared for in life. Mrs. Otway irritated Mrs. Guthrie. The old lady despised the still pretty widow's eager, interested, enthusiastic outlook on life.

Suddenly Major Guthrie took a large pocket-book out of his right breast pocket. He opened it, and Mrs. Otway saw that it contained a packet of bank-notes held together by an india-rubber band. There was also an empty white envelope in the pocket-book. Slipping off the band, he began counting the notes. When he had counted four, she called out, "Stop! Stop! I am only giving you a twenty-pound cheque." And then she saw that they were not five-pound notes, as she had supposed, but ten-pound notes.

He went on counting, and mechanically, hardly knowing that she was doing so, she counted with him up to ten. He then took the envelope he had brought with him, put the ten notes inside, and getting up from his chair he laid the envelope on Mrs. Otway's writing-table by the window.

"I want you to keep this by you in case of need. I know you will forgive me if I say that I shall go away feeling much happier if you will oblige me by doing what I ask in this matter." Under the tan his face had got very red, and there was a deprecating expression in his dark blue eyes.

"I don't understand," she said, and the colour also rushed into her face.

"I beg of you not to be angry with me— —" Major Guthrie stood up and looked down at her so humbly, so wistfully, that she felt touched instead of angry. "You see, I don't like the thought of your being caught, as you've been caught this week apparently, without any money in the house."

But if Mrs. Otway felt touched by the kind thought which had prompted the offer of this uncalled-for loan, she also felt just a little vexed. Major Guthrie was treating her just like a child!

"I'm not in the least likely to be short of money," she cried, "once the banks are open again. The Dean says that everything will be as usual by Monday, and I have quite a lot of money coming in towards the end of this month. In fact, as we can't now go abroad, I shall be even richer than usual. Still, please don't think I'm not grateful!"

She got up too, and looked at him frankly. The colour had now gone from his face, and he looked tired and grey. She told herself that it *had* been very kind of him to have thought of this—the act of a true friend. And so, a little shyly, she put out her hand for a moment, naturally supposing that he would grasp it in friendship. But he did nothing of the sort, so she quietly let her hand fall again by her side, and feeling rather foolish sat down again by her writing-table.

"With regard to the money you are expecting at the end of this month—do you mean the dividends due on the amount you put in that Six Per Cent. Hamburg Loan?" he asked, quietly going back to his armchair.

"Yes, it is six per cent. on four thousand pounds—quite a lot of money!" She spoke in a playful tone, but she was beginning to feel embarrassed and awkward. It was, after all, an odd thing for Major Guthrie to have done—to bring her the considerable sum of a hundred pounds in bank-notes without even first asking her permission to do so.

The envelope containing the notes was still lying there, close to her elbow.

"I'm afraid, Mrs. Otway, that you're not likely to have those dividends paid you this August. All money payments from Germany to England, or from England to Germany, have of course stopped since Wednesday."

And then, when he saw the look of utter dismay deepening into horrified surprise come over her face, he added hastily, "Of course we must hope that these moneys will be kept intact till the end of the war. Still, I doubt very much whether your bankers would allow you to draw on that probability, even if you were willing to pay a high rate of interest. German credit is likely to suffer greatly before this war is over."

"But Major Guthrie? I don't suppose you know what this means to me and to Rose. Why, more than half of everything we have in the world is invested in Germany!"

"I know that," he said feelingly. "In fact, that was among the first things, Mrs. Otway, which occurred to me when I learnt that war had been declared. I expected to find you very much upset about it."

"I never gave it a thought; I didn't know a war could affect that sort of thing. What a fool I've been! Oh, if only I'd followed your advice—I mean two years ago!" She spoke with a great deal of painful agitation, and Major Guthrie felt very much distressed indeed. It was hard that he should have had to be the bearer of such ill tidings.

"I blame myself very, very much," he said sombrely, "for not having insisted on your putting that money into English or Colonial securities."

"Oh, but you did insist!" Even now, in the midst of her keen distress, the woman's native honesty and generosity of nature asserted itself. "You couldn't have said more! Don't you remember that we nearly quarrelled over it? Short of forging my name and stealing my money and investing it properly for me, you couldn't have done anything more than you did do, Major Guthrie."

"That you should say that is a great comfort to me," he said in a low voice. "But even so, I don't feel as if I'd really done enough. You see, I was as sure—as sure as ever man was of anything—that this war was going to come either this year or next! As a matter of fact I thought it would be next year—I thought the Germans would wish to be even more ready than they are."

"But do you really think they are ready?" she said doubtfully. "Look how badly they've been doing at Liége." It was strange how Mrs. Otway's mind had veered round in the last few minutes. She now wanted the Germans to be beaten, and beaten quickly.

He shook his head impatiently. "Wait till they get into their stride!" And then, in a different, a more diffident voice, "Then you'll consent to relieve my mind by keeping the contents of that envelope—I mean of course by spending them? As a matter of fact I've a confession to make to you." He looked at her deprecatingly. "I've just arranged with my London banker to make up those Hamburg dividends. He'll send you the money in notes. He understands——" and then he got rather red. "He understands that I'm practically your trustee, Mrs. Otway."

"But, Major Guthrie—it isn't *true*! How could you say such a thing?"

She felt confused, unhappy, surprised, awkward, grateful. Of course she couldn't take this man's money! He was a friend, in some ways a very close friend of hers, but she hadn't known him more than four years. If she *should* run short of money, why there must be a dozen people or more on whose friendship she had a greater claim, and who could, and would, help her.

And then Mary Otway suddenly ran over in secret review her large circle of old friends and acquaintances, and she realised, with a shock of pain and astonishment, that there was not one of them to whom she would wish to go for help in that kind of trouble. Of her wide circle—and like most people of her class she had a very wide circle—there was only one person, and that was the man who was now sitting looking at her with so much concern in his eyes, to whom it would even have occurred to her to confess that her income had failed through her foolish belief in the stability, and the peaceful intentions, of Germany.

Far, far quicker than it would have taken for her to utter her thoughts aloud, these painful thoughts and realisations flashed through her brain. If she had been content to put into this Hamburg Loan only the amount of the legacy she had inherited three years ago! But she had done more than that—she had sold out sound English railway stock after that interview she had had with a pleasant-speaking German business man in the big London Hamburg Loan office. He had said to her, "Madam, this is the opportunity of a lifetime!" And she had believed him. The kind German friend who had written to her about the matter had certainly acted in good faith. Of that she could rest assured. But this was very small consolation now.

"So you see, Mrs. Otway, that it's all settled—been settled over your head, as it were. And you'll oblige me, you'll make me feel that you're really treating me as a friend, if you say nothing more about it."

And then, as she still remained silent, and as Major Guthrie could see by the expression of her face that she meant to refuse what he so generously and delicately offered her, he went on:

"I feel now that I ought to tell you something which I had meant to keep to myself." He cleared his throat—and hum'd and hum'd a little. "I'm sure you'll understand that every sensible man, when going on active service, makes a fresh will. I've already written out my instructions to my solicitor, and he will prepare a will for me to sign to-morrow." He waited a moment, and then added, as lightly as he could: "I've left you a thousand pounds, which I've arranged you should receive immediately on my death. You see, I'm a lonely man, and all my relations are well off. I think you know, without my telling out, that I've become very much attached to you—to you and to Miss Rose."

And still Mrs. Otway was too much surprised, and yes, too much moved, to speak. Major Guthrie was indeed proving himself a true friend.

"Under ordinary circumstances," he went on slowly, "this clause in my will would be of very little practical interest to you, for I am a healthy man. But we're up against a very big thing, Mrs. Otway——" He did not like to add that it was quite possible she would receive his legacy before she had had time to dip very far into the money he was leaving with her.

She looked at him with a troubled look. And yet? And yet, though it was not perhaps very reasonable that it should be so, somehow she did feel that the fact that Major Guthrie was leaving her—and Rose—the legacy of which he spoke, made a difference. It would make it easier, that is, to accept the money that lay there on her table. Though Major Guthrie was not, in the technical sense, a clever man, he had a far more intimate knowledge of human character than had his friend.

"I don't know how to thank you," she said at last.

He answered rather sharply, "I don't want you to thank me. And Mrs. Otway? I can say now what I've never had the opportunity of saying, that is, how much I've felt honoured by your friendship—what a lot it's meant to me."

He said the words in a rather hard, formal voice, and she answered, with far more emotion than he had betrayed, "And it's been a very, very great thing for me, too, Major Guthrie. Do please believe that!"

He bowed his head gravely. "Well, I must be going now," he said, a little heavily and sadly. "Oh, and one thing more—I should be very grateful if you'd go and see my mother sometimes. During the last few days hardly a soul's been near her. Of course I know how different you are the one from the other, but all the same——" he hesitated a moment. "My mother has fine qualities, once you get under that—well, shall I call it that London veneer? She saw a great deal of the world after she became a widow, while she was keeping house for a brother—when I was in India. She'd like to see Rose, too"—unconsciously he dropped the "Miss." "She likes young people, especially pretty girls."

"Of course I'll go and see her, and so will Rose! You know I've always liked Mrs. Guthrie better than she liked me. I'm not 'smart' enough for her." Mrs. Otway laughed without a trace of bitterness. And then with sudden seriousness she asked him a curious question: "How long d'you think you'll be away?"

"D'you mean how long do I think the War will last?"

Somehow she had not thought of her question quite in that sense. "Yes: I suppose that is what I do mean."

"I think it will be a long war. It will certainly last a year—perhaps a good deal longer."

He walked over to the window nearest the door. Standing there, he told himself that he was looking perhaps for the last time on the dear, familiar scene before him: on the green across which high elms now flung their short morning shadows; on the encompassing houses, some of exceeding stateliness and beauty, others of a simpler, less distinguished character, yet each instinct with a dignity and seemliness which exquisitely harmonised it with its finer fellows; and finally on the slender Gothic loveliness of the Cathedral.

"I'm trying to learn this view by heart," said Major Guthrie, in a queer, muffled voice. "I've always thought it the most beautiful view in England— the one that stands for all a man cares for, all he would fight for."

Mrs. Otway was touched—touched and pleased too. She knew that her friend was baring to her a very secret chamber of his heart.

"It *is* a beautiful, peaceful outlook," she said quietly. "I was thinking so not long before you came in—when I was sitting here, reading the strange, dreadful news in to-day's paper."

He turned away from the window and looked at her. She saw in the shadow that his face looked grey and strained. "Major Guthrie?" she began, a little shyly.

"Yes?" he said rather quickly. "Yes, Mrs. Otway?"

"I only want to ask if you would like me to write to you regularly with news of Mrs. Guthrie?"

"Will you really? How good of you; I didn't like to ask you to do that! I know how busy you always are." But he still lingered, as if loth to go away. Perhaps he was waiting on in the hope that Rose would come in.

"Do you know where you will land in France?" she asked, more to say something than for any real reason, for she knew very little of France.

"I am not sure," he answered hesitatingly. And then, "Still, I have a very shrewd idea of where they are going to fix the British base. I think it will be Boulogne. But, Mrs. Otway? Perhaps I ought to tell you again that all I've told you to-day is private. I may count on your discretion, may I not?" He looked at her a little anxiously.

"Of course I won't tell any one," she said quickly. "You really do mean not any one—not even the Dean?"

"Yes," he said. "I really do mean not any one. In fact I should prefer your not telling even Miss Rose."

"Oh, let me tell Rose," she said eagerly. "I always tell her everything. She is far more discreet than I am!" And this was true.

"Well, tell Miss Rose and no one else," he said. "I don't even know myself when I am going, where I am going, or how I am going."

They were now standing in the hall.

"Then you don't expect to be long in London?" she said.

"No. I should think I shall only be there two or three days. Of course I've got to get my kit, and to see people at the War Office, and so on." He added in a low voice, "There's not going to be any repetition of the things that went on at the time of the Boer War—no leave-takings, no regiments marching through the streets. It's our object, so I understand, to take the Germans by surprise. Everything is going to be done to keep the fact that the Expeditionary Force is going to France a secret for the present. I had that news by the second post; an old friend of mine at the War Office wrote to me."

He gripped her hand in so tight a clasp that it hurt. Then he turned the handle of the front door, opened it, and was gone.

Mrs. Otway felt a sudden longing for sympathy. She went straight into the kitchen. "Anna!" she exclaimed, "Major Guthrie is going back into the Army! England is sending troops over to the Continent to help the Belgians!"

"Ach!" exclaimed Anna. "To Ostend?" She had once spent a summer at Ostend in a boarding-house, where she had been hard-worked and starved. Since then she had always hated the Belgians.

"No, no," said Mrs. Otway quickly. "Not to Ostend. To Boulogne, in France."

CHAPTER X

In the early morning sunshine—for it was only a quarter-past seven—Rose Otway stood just within the wrought-iron gate of the Trellis House.

It was Saturday in the first week of war. She had got up very early, almost as early as old Anna herself, for, waking at five, she had found it impossible to go to sleep again.

For the first time almost in her life, Rose felt heavy-hearted. The sudden, mysterious departure of Major Guthrie had brought the War very near; and so, in quite another way, had done Lord Kitchener's sudden, trumpet-like call, for a hundred thousand men. She knew that, in response to that call, Jervis Blake would certainly enlist, if not with the approval, at any rate with the reluctant consent, of his father; and Rose believed that this would mean the passing of Jervis out of her life.

To Rose Otway's mind there was something slightly disgraceful in any young man's enlistment in the British Army. The poorer mothers of Witanbury, those among whom the girl and her kind mother did a good deal of visiting and helping during the winter months, were apt to remain silent concerning the son who was a soldier. She could not help knowing that it was too often the bad boy of the family, the ne'er-do-weel, who enlisted. There were, of course, certain exceptions—such, for instance, as when a lad came of a fighting family, with father, uncles, and brothers all in the Army. As for the gentleman ranker, he was *always* a scapegrace.

Lord Kitchener's Hundred Thousand would probably be drawn from a different class, for they were being directly asked to defend their country. But even so, at the thought of Jervis Blake becoming a private, Rose Otway's heart contracted with pain, and, yes, with vicarious shame. Still, she made up her mind, there and then, that she would not give him up, that she would write to him regularly, and that as far as was possible they would remain friends.

How comforted she would have been could an angel have come and told her with what eyes England was henceforth to regard her "common soldiers."

Rose Otway was very young, and, like most young things, very ignorant of life. But there was, as Miss Forsyth had shrewdly said, a great deal in the girl. Even now she faced life steadily, unhelped by the many pleasant illusions cherished by her mother. Rose was as naturally reserved as her mother was naturally confiding, and Mrs. Otway was therefore far more popular in their little world than her daughter.

Rose, however, was very pretty, with a finished, delicately fresh and aloof type of beauty which was singularly attractive to the intelligent and fastidious. And so there had already appeared, striking across the current of their placid lives, more than one acute observer who, divining certain hidden depths of feeling in the girl's nature, longed to probe and rouse them. But so far such attempts, generally undertaken by men who were a good deal older than Rose Otway, had failed to inspire anything but shrinking repugnance in their object.

But Jervis Blake was different. Jervis she had known more or less always, owing to that early girlish friendship between his mother and her mother. When he had come to "Robey's" to be coached, Mrs. Otway had made him free of her house, and though she herself, not unnaturally, did not find him an interesting companion, he soon had become part of the warp and woof of Rose's young life. Like most only children, she had always longed for a brother or a sister; and Jervis was the nearest possession of the kind to which she had ever attained.

Yes, the War was coming very near to Rose Otway, and for more than one reason. As soon as she got up she sat down and wrote a long letter to a girl friend who was engaged to a naval officer. She had suddenly realised with a pang that this girl, of whom she was really fond, must now be feeling very miserable and very anxious. Every one seemed to think there would soon be a tremendous battle between the British and the German fleets. And the Dean, who had been to Kiel last year, believed that the German sailors would give a very good account of themselves.

The daily papers were delivered very early in Witanbury Close. And after she had helped old Anna as far as Anna would allow herself to be helped in the light housework with which she began each day, Rose went out and stood by the gate. She longed to know what news, if any, there was.

But the moments went slowly by, and with the exception of a milk cart which clattered gaily along, the Close remained deserted. Half-past seven in the morning, even on a fine August day, saw a good many people still in bed in an English country town. To-day Rose Otway, having herself risen so early, was inclined to agree with Anna that English people are very lazy, and lose some of the best part of each morning.

And then, as she stood out there in the sunshine, her mind reverted to Major Guthrie and to his sudden disappearance. Rose liked Major Guthrie, and she was sorry she had missed him yesterday morning, when out on her fruitless quest for money.

Rose had been surprised at the way her mother had spoken of Major Guthrie's departure. Mrs. Otway had declared the fact to be a secret—a secret that must at all costs be kept. As a matter of fact the girl had already heard the news from Anna, and she had observed, smiling, "But, mother, you seem to have told Anna all about it?" And Mrs. Otway, her gentle temper for once ruffled, had answered sharply, "I don't count Anna! Major Guthrie particularly mentioned the Dean. He did not wish the Dean to know. He said his going was to be kept secret. So I beg you, Rose, to do as I ask."

Anna came out of the front door, and began polishing the brass knob. "Ach!" she exclaimed. "Come in, child—do! You a chill will take. If it is the postman you want, he gone by already has."

Rose smiled. Dear old Anna had never acquired the British love of fresh air. "I'm waiting for the papers," she said. "I can't think why the man doesn't begin with us, instead of going all round the other way first! But I'm going to catch him this morning."

And Anna, grumbling, went back into the house again.

All at once Rose heard the sound of quick footsteps to her right, on the path outside. She moved back into the paved court in front of the Trellis House, and stood, a charming vision of youth and freshness, in her pale mauve cotton frock, by a huge stone jar filled with pink geraniums.

And then, a moment later, the tall figure of Jervis Blake suddenly swung into view. He was very pale, and there was an eager, absorbed, strained look on his face. In his hand was a white telegraph form.

Rose ran forward, and once more opened the gate. "Jervis!" she cried. "What is it? What's the matter? Have you had bad news from home?"

He shook his head, and she saw that he was trying to smile. But there was still that on his face which she had never seen before—a rapt, transfigured look which made her feel—and she both disliked and resented the feeling— as if he were, for the moment, remote from herself. But he stayed his steps, and came through the gate.

For a moment he stood opposite to her without speaking. Then he took out of his breast pocket a large sheet of notepaper folded in four. He opened it, and held it out to her. It was headed "War Office, Whitehall, London," and in it Jervis Blake, Esquire, was curtly informed that, if he still desired to enter the Army, he was at liberty to apply for a commission. But in that case he was asked to report himself as soon as possible.

Rose read the cold, formal sentences again and again, and a lump rose to her throat. How glad she was! How very, very glad! Indeed, her gladness, her joy in Jervis's joy, surprised herself.

"And it's all owing to you," he exclaimed in a low voice, "that I didn't go and make an ass of myself on Wednesday. If it hadn't been for you, Rose, I should have enlisted. This would have come too late. It *is* luck to have seen you now, like this. You're the very first I've told." He was wringing her hand, his face now as flushed as it had been pale.

And as they stood there together, Rose suddenly became aware that Anna, at the kitchen window, was looking out at them both with a rather peculiar expression on her emotional German face.

A feeling of annoyance swept over the girl; she knew that to her old nurse every young man who ever came to the Trellis House was a potential lover. But even Anna might have left Jervis Blake out of the category. There was nothing silly or—or sentimental, in the real, deep friendship they two felt for one another.

And then Rose did something which surprised herself. Withdrawing her hand from his, she exclaimed, "I'll walk with you to the corner"—and led the way out, through the gate, and so along the empty roadway.

They walked along in silence for a few moments. The Close was still deserted. Across the green, to their right, rose the noble grey mass of the Cathedral. In many of the houses the blinds were even now only beginning to be pulled up.

"I rather expected yesterday that you would come in and tell me that you were going off to be one of the hundred thousand men Lord Kitchener has asked for," she said at last.

"Of course I meant to be, but Mr. Robey thought I ought to communicate with my father before actually joining," he answered. "In fact, I had already written home. That's one reason why I'm going to get this wire off so early."

"I suppose you'll be at Sandhurst this time next week?"

And he frowned, for the first time that morning.

"Oh no, I hope not! Mr. Robey heard last night from one of our fellows— one of those who passed last time—and he said he was being drafted at once into a regiment! You mustn't forget how long I was in the O.T.C. It seems they're sending all those who were in the O.T.C. straight into regiments."

"Then by next week you'll be second lieutenant in the Wessex Light Infantry!" she exclaimed. She knew that it was in that famous regiment that General Blake had won his early spurs, and that it had been settled, in the days when no one had doubted Jervis Blake's ability to pass the Army Exam., that he would join his father's old regiment, now commanded by one of that father's very few intimates.

"Yes, I suppose I shall," he said, flushing. "Oh, Rose, I can't believe in my luck. It's so much—much too good to be true!"

They had come to the corner, to the parting of their ways. To the left, through the grey stone gateway, was the street leading into the town; on the right, within a few moments' walk, the Cathedral.

Rose suddenly felt very much moved, carried out of her reserved self. A lump rose to her throat. She knew that this was their real parting, and that she was not likely to see him again, save in the presence of her mother for a few minutes.

"I wonder," said Jervis Blake hoarsely, "I wonder, Rose, if you would do me a great kindness? Would you go on into the Cathedral with me, just for three or four minutes? I should like to go there for the last time with you."

"Yes," she said; "of course I will." Rose had inherited something of her mother's generosity of nature. If she gave at all, she gave freely and gladly. "I do hope the door will be open," she said, trying to regain her usual staid composure. She was surprised and disturbed by the pain which seemed to be rising, brimming over, in her heart.

They walked on in silence. Jervis Blake was looking straight before him, his face set and grim. He was telling himself that a fellow would be a cur to take advantage of such a moment to say anything, and that especially was that the case with one who might so soon be exposed to something much worse than death—such as the being blinded, the being maimed, for life. War was a very real thing to Jervis, more real certainly than to any other one of the young men who had been his comrades at Robey's during the last two years.

But the most insidious of all tempters, Nature herself, whispered in his ear, "Why not simply tell her that you love her? No woman minds being told that she is loved! It can do no harm, and it will make her think of you kindly when you are far away. This strange, secret meeting is yet another piece of good fortune to-day—this glorious day—has brought you! Do not throw away your chance. Look again down into her face. See her dear eyes full of tears. She has never been moved as she is moved to-day, and it is you who have moved her."

And then another, sterner voice spoke: "*You* have not moved her—presumptuous fool! Nay, it is the thought of England, of her country, of all you stand for to-day, that has moved her. And the next few minutes will show the stuff of which you are made—if you have the discipline, the self-restraint, essential to the man who has to lead others, or if—if you only have the other thing. You are being given now what you could never have hoped for, a quiet, intimate time with her alone; you might have had to say good-bye to her in her mother's presence—that mother who has never really liked you, and whom you have never really liked."

He held open the little wicket gate for her to pass through. They walked up the stone path to the wide, hospitable-looking porch which is the only part of Witanbury Cathedral that has remained much as it was in pre-Reformation days.

To Jervis Blake, suffused with poignant emotion, every perception sharpened by mingling triumph and pain, the "faire Doore" of Witanbury Cathedral had never seemed so lovely as on this still August morning. As they stepped through the exquisite outer doorway, with its deep mouldings, both dog-toothed and foliated, marking the transition from Norman to Gothic, a deep, intense joy in their dual solitude suddenly rose up in his heart like a white flame.

The interior of the porch was little larger than an ordinary room, but it was wonderfully perfect in the harmony of its proportions; and even Rose, less perceptive than her companion, and troubled and disturbed, rather than uplifted, by an emotion to which she had no clue, was moved by the delicate, shadowed beauty of the grey walls and vaulted roof now encompassing her.

For a moment they both lingered there, irresolute; and then Jervis, stepping forward, lifted the great iron handle of the black oak, nail-studded door. But the door remained shut, and he turned round with the words, "It's still closed. We shan't be able to get in. I'm sorry." He looked indeed so disappointed that there came over Rose the eager determination that he should not go away baulked of his wish.

"I'm sure it opens at eight," she exclaimed; "and it can't be very far from eight now. Let's wait here the few minutes! I'm in no hurry, if you can spare the time?" Rose spoke rather quickly and breathlessly. She was trying hard to behave as if this little adventure of theirs was a very conventional, commonplace happening.

He said something—she was not sure whether it was "All right" or "Very well."

On each side of the porch ran a low and deep stone bench, from which sprang the slender columns which seemed to climb eagerly upwards to the carved ribs of the vaulted roof. But they both went on standing close to one another, companioned only by the strange sculptured creatures which grinned down from the spandrels of the arches above.

And then, after waiting for what seemed an eternity—it was really hardly more than a minute—in the deep, brooding silence which seemed to enwrap the Close, the Cathedral, and their own two selves in a mantle of stillness, Rose Otway, bursting into sobs, made a little swaying movement. A moment later she found herself in Jervis Blake's arms, listening with a strange mingling of joy, surprise, shame, and, yes, triumph, to his broken, hoarsely-whispered words of love.

He, being a man, could only feel—she, being a woman, could also think, aye, and even question her own heart as to this amazing thing which was happening, and which had suddenly made her free of the wonderful kingdom of romance of which she had so often heard, but the existence of which she had always secretly doubted. Whence came her instinctive response to his pleading: "Oh, Rose, let me kiss you! Oh, Rose, my darling little love, this may be the last time I shall see you!"

Was it at the end of a moment, or of an æon of time, that there fell athwart their beating hearts a dull, rasping sound, that of the two great inner bolts of the huge oak door being pushed back into their rusty sockets?

They parted, reluctantly, lingeringly, the one from the other; but whoever had drawn back the bolts did not open the door, and soon they heard the sounds of heavy, shuffling feet moving slowly away.

"I expect it's Mrs. Bent, the verger's wife," said Rose, in a low, trembling voice.

Jervis looked at her. There was a mute, and at once imperious and imploring demand in his eyes. But Rose had stepped across the magic barrier, she was half-way back to the work-a-day world—not very far, but still far enough to know how she would feel if Bent or Mrs. Bent surprised her in Jervis's arms. A few moments ago she would hardly have cared.

"Let's go into the Cathedral now," she said, and, to break the cruelty of her silent refusal of what he asked, she held out her hand. To her surprise, and yes, her disappointment, he did not seem to see it. Instead, he stepped forward to the door, and turning the weighty iron handle, pushed it widely open.

Together, side by side, they passed through into the great, still, peaceful place, and with a delicious feeling of joy they saw that they were alone—that Mrs. Bent, having done her duty in unbolting the great door, had slipt out of a side door, and gone back to her cottage, behind the Cathedral.

Rose led the way into the nave; there she knelt down, and Jervis Blake knelt down by her, and this time, when she put out her hand, he took it in his and clasped it closely.

Rose tried to collect her thoughts. She even tried to pray. But she could only feel,—she could not utter the supplications which filled her troubled heart. And yet she felt as though they two were encompassed by holy presences, by happy spirits, who understood and sympathised in her mingled joy and grief.

If Jervis came back, if he and she both lived till the end of the War, it was here that their marriage would take place. But the girl had a strange presentiment that they two would never stand over there, where so many brides and bridegrooms had stood together, even within her short memory. It was not that she felt Jervis was going to be killed—she was mercifully spared those dread imaginings which were to come on her later. But just now, for these few moments only perhaps, Rose Otway was "fey"; she seemed to know that to-day was her cathedral marriage day, and that an invisible choir was singing her epithalamium.

The quarter past the hour chimed. She released her hand from his, and touched him on the arm with a lingering, caressing touch. He was so big and strong, so gentle too—all hers. And now, just as they had found one another, she was going to lose him. It seemed so unnatural and so cruel. "Jervis," she whispered, and the tears ran down her face, "I think you had better go now. I'd rather we said good-bye here."

_ He got up at once. "Do you mean to tell your mother?" he asked. And then, as he thought she was hesitating: "I only want to know because, if so, I will tell them at home."

She shook her head. "No," she said brokenly. "I'd rather we said nothing now—if you don't mind."

She lifted up her face to him as a child might have done; and, putting his arm round her, he bent down and kissed her, very simply and gravely. Suddenly, he took her two hands and kissed their soft palms; and then he stooped very low, and lifting the hem of her cotton frock kissed that too.

"Rose?" he cried out suddenly. "Oh, Rose, I do love you so!" And then, before she could speak he had turned and was gone.

CHAPTER XI

Rather more than an hour and a half later, Rose Otway, with bursting heart, but with dry, gleaming eyes—for she had a nervous fear of her mother's affectionate questioning, and she had already endured Anna's well-meant, fussy, though still unspoken sympathy—stood at the spare-room window of the Trellis House. From there she could watch, undisturbed, the signs of departure now going busily on before the big gates of the group of three Georgian houses known as "Robey's."

Piles of luggage, bags, suit-cases, golf sticks, and so on, were being put outside and inside the mid-Victorian fly, which was still patronised by the young gentlemen of "Robey's," in their goings and comings from the station. And then, even before the old cab-horse had started his ambling trot townwards, Mr. and Mrs. Robey, their two little girls, and their three boys not long back from school, all appeared together at the gate.

In their midst stood Jervis Blake, his tall figure towering above them all.

Most young men would have felt, and perhaps a little resented the fact, that the whole party looked slightly ridiculous. Not so this young man. There had never been much of the schoolboy in Jervis Blake. Now he felt very much a man, and he was grateful for the affectionate kindness which made these good people anxious to give him what one of the little girls had called "a grand send-off."

Rose saw that there was a moment of confusion, of hesitation at the gate, and she divined that it was Jervis who suggested that they should take the rather longer way round, that which led under the elm trees and past the Cathedral. He did not wish to pass close by the Trellis House.

The girl standing by the window felt a sudden rush of understanding tenderness. How strangely, how wonderfully their minds worked the one in with the other! It would have been as intolerable to her as to him, to have seen her mother run out and stop the little party—to have been perchance summoned from upstairs "to wish good luck to Jervis Blake."

From where she stood Rose Otway commanded the whole Close, and during the minutes which followed she saw the group of people walking with quick, steady steps, stopped by passers-by three or four times, before they disappeared out of her sight.

It had seemed to her, but that might have been only her fancy, that the pace, obviously set by Jervis, quickened rather as they swept past the little gate through which he and she had gone on their way to the porch, on their way to—to Paradise.

Half-way through the morning there came an uncertain knock at the front door of the Trellis House. It presaged a note brought by one of the young Robeys for Mrs. Otway—a note written by Jervis Blake, telling her of his good fortune, and explaining that he had not time to come and thank her in person for all her many kindnesses to him. One sentence ran: "The War Office order is that I come and report myself as soon as possible—so of course I had to take the ten-twenty-five train." And he signed himself, as he had never done before, "Your affectionate Jervis Blake."

Mrs. Otway felt mildly excited, and really pleased. "Rose will be very glad to hear this!" she said to herself, and at once sought out her daughter.

Rose was still upstairs, in the roomy, rather dark old linen cupboard which was the pride of Anna's German heart.

"A most extraordinary thing has happened. Jervis Blake is to have a commission after all, darling! He had a letter from the War Office this morning. I suppose it's due to his father's influence." And as Rose answered, in what seemed an indifferent voice, "I should think, mother, that it's due to the War," Mrs. Otway exclaimed, "Oh no. I don't think so! What could the War have to do with it? But whatever it's due to, I'm very, very pleased that the poor boy has attained the wish of his heart. He's written me such a very nice note, apologising for not coming to say good-bye to us. He doesn't mention you in his letter, but I expect you'll hear from him in a day or two. He generally does write during the holidays, doesn't he, Rose?"

"Yes," said Rose quietly. "Jervis has always written to me during the holidays, up to now."

As she spoke, the girl turned again to the shelves laden with the linen, much of which had been beautifully embroidered and trimmed with crochet lace by good old Anna's clever hands. Mrs. Otway had a curious sensation, one she very, very seldom had—that of being dismissed. Somehow it was clear that Rose was not as interested in the piece of good news as her mother had thought she would be. And so Mrs. Otway went downstairs again, grieving a little at her child's curious, cold indifference to the lot of one who had been so much in and out of their house during the last two years.

Eager for sympathy, she went into the kitchen. "Oh, Anna," she exclaimed, "Mr. Blake is going into the Army after all! I'm so pleased. He is so happy!"

"Far more than Major Guthrie young Mr. Blake the figure of a good officer has," observed Anna thoughtfully. Anna had always liked Jervis Blake. In the old days that now seemed so long ago he would sometimes come with Miss Rose into her kitchen, and talk his poor, indifferent German. Then they all three used to laugh heartily at the absurd mistakes he made.

And now, to her mistress's astonishment, old Anna suddenly burst into loud, noisy sobs.

"Anna, what *is* the matter?"

"Afflicted I am——" sobbed the old woman. And then she stopped, and began again: "Afflicted I am to think, gracious lady, of that young gentleman, who to me kind has been, killing the soldiers of my country."

"I don't suppose he will have the chance of killing any of them," said Mrs. Otway hastily. "You really mustn't be so silly, Anna! Why, the War will be over long before Mr. Blake is ready to go out. They always keep the young men two years at Sandhurst. That's the name of the officers' training college, you know."

Anna wiped her eyes with her apron. She was now ashamed of having cried. But it had come over her "all of a heap," as an English person would have said.

She had had a sort of vision of that nice young gentleman, Mr. Jervis Blake, in the thick of battle, cutting down German men and youths with a sword. He was so big and strong—it made her turn sick to think of it. But her good mistress, Mrs. Otway, had of course told the truth. The War would be over long before Mr. Jervis Blake and his kind would be fit to fight.

Fighting, as old Anna knew well, though most of the people about her were ignorant of the fact, requires a certain apprenticeship, an apprenticeship of which these pleasant-spoken, strong, straight-limbed young Englishmen knew nothing. The splendidly trained soldiers of the Fatherland would have fought and conquered long before peaceful, sleepy England knew what war really meant. There was great comfort in that thought.

As that second Saturday of August wore itself away, it is not too much to say that the most interesting thing connected with the War which had happened in Witanbury Close was the fact that Jervis Blake was now going to be a soldier. When people met that day, coming and going about their business, across the lawn-like green, and along the well-kept road which ran round it, they did not discuss the little news there was in that morning's papers. Instead they at once informed one another, and with a most congratulatory air, "Jervis Blake has heard from the War Office! He is going into the Army after all. Mr. and Mrs. Robey are *so* pleased. The whole family went to the station with him this morning!"

And it was quite true that the Robeys were pleased. Mr. Robey was positively triumphant. "I can't tell you how glad I am!" he said, first to one, and then to the other, of his neighbours. "Young Blake will make a splendid company officer. It's for the sake of the country, quite as much as for his sake, and for that of his unpleasant father, that I'm glad. What sort of book-learning had Napoleon's marshals? Or, for the matter of that, Wellington's officers in the Peninsula, and at Waterloo?"

As the day went on, and he began receiving telegrams from those of his young men—they were not so very many after all—who had failed to pass, containing the joyful news that now they were accepted, his wife, instead of rejoicing, began to look grave. "It seems to me, my dear, that our occupation in life will now be gone," she said soberly. And he answered lightly enough, "Sufficient unto the day is the good thereof!" And being the high-minded, sensible fellow that he was, he would allow no selfish fear of the future to cloud his satisfaction in the present.

The only jarring note that day came from James Hayley. He had had to take a later train than he had thought to do, and he only arrived at the Trellis House, duly dressed for dinner, just before eight.

"Witanbury is certainly a most amusing place," he observed, as he shook hands with his pretty cousin. "I met two of your neighbours as I came along. Each of them informed me, with an air of extreme delight, that young Jervis Blake had heard from the War Office that, in spite of his many failures, his services will now be welcomed by a grateful country. I didn't like to make the obvious answer——"

"And what is the obvious answer?" asked Rose, wrenching her hand away from his. She told herself that she hated the feel of James's cold, hard hand.

"That we must be jolly short of officers if they're already writing round to those boys! But then, of course" —he lowered his voice, though there was no one there to hear, "we are short—short of everything, worse luck!"

But that was the only thing Cousin James said of any interest, and it did not specially interest Rose. She did not connect this sinister little piece of information with the matter that filled her heart for the moment to the exclusion of everything else. It was not Jervis who was short of anything—only Jervis's (and her) country.

After Mrs. Otway had come down and joined them, though James talked a great deal, he yet said very little, and as the evening went on, his kind hostess could not help feeling that the War had not improved James Hayley. He seemed more supercilious, more dogmatic than usual, and at one moment he threatened to offend her gravely by an unfortunate allusion to her good old Anna's nationality.

By that time they were sitting out in the garden, enjoying the excellent coffee Anna made so well, and as it was rather chilly, Rose had run into the house to get her mother a shawl.

"I never realised how very German your maid is," he observed suddenly. "It made me feel quite uncomfortable while we were talking at dinner! Do you intend to keep her?"

"Yes, of course I do." Mrs. Otway felt hurt and angry. "I shouldn't dream of sending her away! Anna has lived in England over twenty years, and her only child is married to an Englishman." She waited a moment, and as he said nothing, she went on: "My good old Anna is devoted to England, though of course she loves her Fatherland too."

"I should have thought the two loves quite incompatible at the present time," he objected drily.

Mrs. Otway flushed in the half darkness. "I find them quite compatible, James," she exclaimed. "Of course I'm sorry that the military party should triumph in Germany—that, we all must feel, and probably many Germans do too. But, after all, you may hate the sin and love the sinner!"

"Will you feel the same when Germans have killed Englishmen?" he asked idly. He was watching the door through which Rose had vanished a few moments ago, longing with a restrained, controlled longing for her return.

As a matter of fact he himself had never had any feeling of dislike of the Germans; on the contrary, he had struck up an acquaintance which had almost become friendship with one of the younger members of the German Embassy. And suddenly Mrs. Otway remembered it.

"Why, you yourself," she cried, "you yourself, James, have a German friend—I mean that young Von Lissing. I liked him so much that week-end you brought him down. What's happened to him? I suppose he's gone?"

"Gone?" He turned and looked at her in the twilight. Really, Aunt Mary was sometimes very silly. "Of course, he's gone! As a matter of fact he left London ten days before his chief." And then he added reflectively, perhaps with more a wish to tease her than anything else, "I've rather wondered this last week whether Von Lissing's friendship with me was regarded by him as a business matter. He sometimes asked me such odd questions. Of course one has always known that Germans are singularly inquisitive—that they are always wanting to find out things. I confess it never struck me at the time that his questions meant anything more than that sort of insatiable wish *to know* that all Germans have."

"What sort of things did he ask you, James?" asked Mrs. Otway curiously.

"Well, I'll tell you one thing he said, and it astonished me very much indeed. He asked me what attitude I thought our colonies would take if we became embroiled in a European war! I reminded him of what they'd done in South Africa fourteen years ago, and he said he thought the world had altered a good deal since then, and that people had become more selfish. But he never asked me any question concerning my own special department. In those ways he quite played the game—not that it would have been of any use, because of course I shouldn't have told him anything. But he was certainly oddly inquiring about other departments."

Then Rose came out again, and James Hayley tried to make himself pleasant. Fortunately for himself he did not know how little he succeeded. Rose found his patronising, tutor-like manner intolerable.

CHAPTER XII

Mrs. Hegner leant her woe-begone, tear-stained little face against the centre window-pane of one of the two windows in her bedroom.

The room was a very large room. But she had never liked it, large, spacious, and airy though it was. You see, it was furnished entirely like a German bedroom, not like a nice cosy English room. Thus the place where a fireplace would naturally have been was taken up by a large china stove; and instead of a big brass double bed there were two low narrow box beds. On her husband's bed was a huge eiderdown, and under that only a sheet— no blankets at all! Polly hoped that this horrid fact would never be known in Witanbury. It would make quite a talk.

There was linoleum on the floor instead of a carpet, and there was very little ease about the one armchair which her husband had grudgingly allowed her to have up here.

Close to his bed, at right angles to it, was a huge black and green safe. That safe, as Polly well knew, had cost a very great deal of money, enough money to have furnished this room in really first-class style, with good Wilton pile carpet all complete.

But Manfred had chosen to furnish the room in his own style, and it was a style to which Polly could never grow accustomed. It outraged all the instinctive prejudices and conventions inherited from her respectable, lower middle-class forbears. Instead of being good substantial mahogany or walnut, it was some queerly veined light-coloured wood, and decorated with the strangest coloured rectangular designs, and painted—well, with nightmare oddities, that's what she called them! And she was not far wrong, for all down one side of the wardrobe waddled a procession of bright green ducks.

Polly could never make her husband out. He was so careful, so—so miserly in some ways, so wildly extravagant in others. All this furniture had come from Germany, and must have cost a pretty penny. It was true that he had got it, or so he assured her, with very heavy discount off—and that no doubt was correct.

The only ornaments in the room, if ornaments they could be called, were faded photographs and two oleographs in gilt frames. One of the photographs was the portrait of Manfred's first wife, a very plain, fat woman. Then there were tiny cartes of Manfred's father and mother—regular horrors they must have been, so Polly thought resentfully. The oleographs were views of Heidelberg and of the Kiel Canal.

Poor Polly! She had been sent up here, just as if she was a little girl in disgrace, about half an hour ago—simply for having told her own sister Jenny, who was useful maid to Miss Haworth at the Deanery, that Manfred had spent yesterday at Southampton. He had gone on smiling quite affably as long as Jenny was there, but the door had hardly closed on her before he had turned round on *her*, Polly, in furious anger.

"Blab! Blab! Blab!" he had snapped out. "You'll end by hanging me before you've done! It won't be any good then saying 'Oh, I didn't know,' 'Oh, I didn't mean to!'" He mimicked with savage irony her frightened accents. And then, as she had burst into tears, he had ordered her up here, out of his sight.

Yes, Manfred had an awful temper, and since Wednesday evening he hadn't given her one kind word or look. In fact, during the last few days Polly had felt as if she must run away from him. Not to do anything wicked, you understand—good gracious, no! She had had enough of men.

And now, resentfully, she asked herself why Manfred bothered so much about this war. After all, he had taken out his certificate; he was an Englishman now. She told herself that it was all the Dean's fault. Stupid, interfering old gentleman—that's what the Dean was! Manfred had gone up to the Deanery last Wednesday, and the Dean told him it was his duty to look after the Germans in Witanbury—as if Germans couldn't look after themselves. Of course they could! They were far cleverer at that sort of thing than English people were. Polly could have told the Dean that.

As to business—business-had been just as brisk, or very nearly as brisk, during the last few days as ever before, and that though they had only been able to keep the shop, so to speak, half open. It was clear this silly war wasn't going to make any difference to *them*.

At first she had tried to make allowances; no doubt Manfred did feel unhappy about his son, Fritz, who was now on his way to fight the Russians. But he had hardly mentioned Fritz after the first minute. Instead of that, he had only exclaimed, at frequent intervals, that this war would ruin them. He really did believe it, too, for he had even said it in his sleep.

Why, they were made of money. Polly had the best of reasons for knowing *that*. They didn't owe a penny to anybody, excepting to the builder. And no one could have acted better than that builder had done.

He had hurried round the very first thing on Wednesday to tell them not to worry. In fact, even Manfred, who seldom had a good word for anybody, agreed that Mr. Smith had behaved very handsomely.

People were now beginning to walk across the Market Place, and rather more were going to evening service in the Cathedral than usual.

Polly didn't want any one to look up and see she had been crying. So she retreated a little way into the room. Then she went over and poured some water from the queer-shaped jug into the narrow, deep basin, which was so unlike a nice big wide English basin. After that she washed her face, and dabbed her eyes with eau-de-Cologne.

Manfred, who was so economical about most things, and who even grudged her spending more than a certain sum on necessary household cleaning implements, was very fond of scent, and he had quite a row of scent-bottles and pomades on his side of the washhand-stand....

While Polly was dabbing her eyes and face she looked meditatively at the big safe in the corner.

With that safe was connected her one real bit of deceit. Manfred thought she didn't know what was in the safe, but as a matter of fact she knew what was safely put away there as well as he did. Amazing to relate, she actually had a key to the safe of which he, her husband, knew nothing.

It had fallen out in this wise. The gentleman who had come from London to superintend the fixing of the safe had left an envelope for Manfred, or rather he had asked for an envelope, then he had popped inside it a piece of paper and something else.

"Look here, Mrs. Hegner!" he had exclaimed. "I can't wait to see your husband, for I've got to get my train back to town. Will you just give him this? Many people only provide two keys to a safe, but our firm always provides three."

She had waited till the man had gone, and then she had at once gone upstairs and locked herself into her bedroom with the new safe and the open envelope containing the receipted bill and the three keys. One of these keys she had put in her purse, and then she had placed the bill, and the two remaining keys, in a fresh envelope.

Polly didn't consider husbands and wives ought to have any secrets from one another. But from the very first, even when Manfred was still very much in love with her—aye, and very jealous of her too, for the matter of that—he had never told her anything.

For a long time she hadn't known just where to keep her key of the safe, and it had lain on her mind like a great big load of worry; she had felt obliged to be always changing the place where she hid it.

Then, suddenly, Manfred had presented her with an old-fashioned rosewood dressing-case he had taken from some one in part payment of a small debt. And in this dressing-case, so a friend had shown her, there was a secret place for letters. You pushed back an innocent-looking little brass inlaid knob, and the blue velvet back fell forward, leaving a space behind.

From the day she had been shown this dear little secret space, the key of the safe had lain there, excepting on the very rare occasions when she was able to take it out and use it. Of course she never did this unless she knew that Manfred was to be away for the whole day from Witanbury, and even then she trembled and shook with fright lest he should suddenly come in and surprise her. But what she had learnt made her tremors worth while.

It was pleasant, indeed, to know that a lot of money—nice golden sovereigns and crisp five-pound notes—was lying there, and that Manfred must be always adding to the store. Last time she had looked into the safe there was eight hundred pounds! Two-thirds in gold, one-third in five-pound notes. She had sometimes thought it odd that Manfred kept such a lot of gold, but that was his business, not hers.

It was very unkind of him not to have told her of all this money. After all, she helped to earn it! But she knew he believed her to be extravagant.

What sillies men were! As if the fact that he had this money put away, no doubt accumulating in order that they might pay off the mortgage quicker, would make her spend more. Why, it had actually had the effect of making her more careful.

In addition to the money in the safe, there were one or two deeds connected with little bits of house property Manfred had acquired in Witanbury during the last six years. And then, on the top shelf of the safe, there were a lot of letters—letters written in German, of which of course she could make neither head nor tail. Once a month a registered letter arrived, sometimes from Holland, sometimes from Brussels, for Manfred; and it had gradually become clear to her that it was these letters which he kept in the safe.

There came a loud impatient knock at the door. She started guiltily.

"Open!" cried her husband imperiously. "Open, Polly, at once! I have already forbidden you to lock the door."

But she knew by the tone of his voice that he was no longer really angry with her. So, walking rather slowly, she went across and unlocked the door.

She stepped back quickly—the door opened, and a moment later she was in her husband's arms, and he was kissing her.

"Well, little one! You're good now, eh? Does my little sugar lamb want a treat?"

Polly knew that when he called her his little sugar lamb it meant that he was in high good-humour.

"It won't be much of a treat to stay at home and do the civil to that old Mrs. Bauer," she said, and looked up at him coquettishly.

There were good points about Manfred. When he was good-tempered, as he seemed to be just now, it generally meant that there would be a present for her coming along. And sure enough he pulled a little box out of one of his bulging pockets.

"Here's a present for my little lollipop," he said.

Eagerly she opened the box; but though she exclaimed "It's very pretty!" she really felt a good deal disappointed. For it was only a queer, old-fashioned light gold locket. In tiny diamonds—they were real diamonds, but Polly did not know that—were set the words "*Rule Britannia*," and below the words was a funny little enamel picture of a sailing-ship. Not the sort of thing she would care to wear, excepting just to please Manfred.

"You can put that on the chain I gave you," he said. "It looks nice and patriotic. And about this evening—well, I've changed my mind. You need not stop in for Mrs. Bauer. Just say how-d'ye-do to her, and then go out—to the Deanery if you like. You see that I trust you, Polly;" his face stiffened, a frown came over it. "I have written a letter to the Dean for you to take; you may read it if you like."

She drew the bit of paper out of the envelope with a good deal of curiosity. Whatever could Manfred have to write to the Dean about? True, he was fond of writing letters, and he expressed himself far better than most Englishmen of his station. Polly had quite a nice packet of his love-letters, which, at the time she had received them, had delighted her by their flowery appropriateness of language, and quaint, out-of-the-way expressions.

"Most Reverend Sir"—so ran Manfred Hegner's letter to the Dean. "I wish to thank you for your kindness to me during the last few eventful days. I have endeavoured to deserve it in every way possible. I trust you will approve of a step I propose taking on Monday. That is, to change my name to

Alfred Head. As you impressed upon me, Reverend Sir, in the interview you were good enough to grant me, I am now an Englishman, with all the duties as well as the privileges of this great nation. So it is best I have a British name. I am taking steps to have my new name painted up outside the Stores, and I am informing by circular all those whom it may concern. Your interest in me, Reverend Sir, has made me venture to tell you, before any one else, of the proposed alteration. I therefore sign myself, most Reverend Sir,

"Yours very faithfully,

"Alfred Head."

"I think Head is a horrid name!" said his wife imprudently. "I don't think 'Polly Head' is half as nice as 'Polly Hegner.' Why, mother used to know a horrid old man called Head. He was a scavenger, and he only cleaned himself once a year—on Christmas Day!"

Then, as she saw the thunderclouds gathering, she exclaimed in a rather frightened tone, "But don't mind what *I* say, Manfred. You know best. I daresay I'll get used to it soon!"

As they went downstairs Polly had been thinking.

"I fancy you've had this in your mind for some time."

"What makes you fancy that?" he asked.

"Because we've so near got to the end of our stock of cards and bill-heads," she said, "and you wouldn't let me order any more last week."

"You're a sharp girl"—he laughed. "Well, yes! I have been thinking of it some time. And what's happened now has just tipped the bucket—see?"

"Yes, I see that."

"I've already written out the order for new bill-heads and new cards! and I've sent round the order about Monday," he went on. "But if this dratted Bank Holiday goes on, there won't be much work done in Witanbury on Monday! Hush! Here she comes."

There had come a ring at the back door. Polly went out, and a moment later brought back the old German woman.

Anna was surprised to find the husband and wife alone. She had thought that the Fröhlings at least would be there.

"Well, Mrs. Bauer"—her host spoke in German—"a friend or two who were coming have failed, and you will have to put up with me, for my wife has to go up to the Deanery to see her sister. But you and I will have plenty to talk about at such a time as this. And I have got some papers from Berlin for you. I do not know how much longer they will be coming to England."

The old woman's face lighted up. Yes, it would be very nice to see one or two of the grand German picture papers which had been lately started in the Fatherland in imitation of those which were so popular in England.

"Do not trouble to look at them now," he added hastily. "You can take them home with you. Mrs. Otway, she is too broad-minded a lady to mind, is she not?"

"Ach! Yes indeed," said Anna. "Mrs. Otway, she loves the Fatherland. This foolish trouble makes not the slightest difference to her."

Polly had been standing by rather impatiently. "Sometimes I'm quite sorry I haven't taken the trouble to learn German," she said.

Her husband chucked her under the chin. "How would Frau Bauer and I ever be able to talk our secrets together if you understood what we said, little woman?"

And Anna joined in the laugh with which this sally was greeted.

"So long!" said Polly brightly. "I expect I'll be back before you've gone, Mrs. Bauer."

CHAPTER XIII

There is good news!" exclaimed Anna's host, as soon as the door was shut behind his wife. "The British have sunk one of our little steamers, but we have blown up one of theirs—a very big, important war-vessel, Frau Bauer!"

Good old Anna's face beamed. It was not that she disliked England—indeed, she was very fond of England. But she naturally felt that in this great game of war it was only right and fair that the Fatherland should win. It did not occur to her, and well he knew it would not occur to her, that the man who had just spoken was at any rate nominally an Englishman. She, quite as much as he did himself, regarded the naturalisation certificate as a mere matter of business. It had never made any difference to any of the Germans Anna had known in England—in fact the only German-Englishman she knew was old Fröhling, who had never taken out his certificate at all. Fröhling really did adore England, and this had sometimes made old Anna feel very impatient. To Fröhling everything English was perfect, and he had been quite pleased, instead of sorry, when his son had joined the British Army.

"So? That is good!" she exclaimed. "Very good! But we must not seem too pleased, must we, Herr Hegner?"

And he shook his head. "No, to be *too* pleased would not be grateful," he said, "to good old England!" And he spoke with no sarcasm, he really meant what he said.

"It makes me sad to think of all the deaths, whether they are German or English," went on Anna sadly. "I do not feel the same about the Russians or the French naturally."

"Ach! How much I agree with you," he said feelingly. "The poor English! Truly do I pity them. I am quite of your mind, Frau Bauer; though every Russian and most Frenchmen are a good riddance, I do not rejoice to think of any Englishman, however lazy, tiresome, and pigheaded, being killed."

They both ate steadily for a few minutes, then Manfred Hegner began again. "But very few Englishmen will be killed by our brave fellows. You will have to shed no tears for any one you know in Witanbury, Frau Bauer.

The English are not a fighting people. Most of their sailors will be drowned, no doubt, but at that one must not after all repine."

"Yet the English are sending an army to Belgium," observed Anna, thoughtfully.

"What makes you think that?" He stopped in the work on which he was engaged, that of cutting a large sausage into slices. "Have you learnt it on good authority, Frau Bauer? Has this news been told you by the young gentleman official from London who is connected with the Government—I mean he who is courting your young lady?"

Anna drew back stiffly. "How they do gossip in this town!" she exclaimed, frowning. "Courting my young lady, indeed! No, Mr. Hegner, it was not Mr. Hayley who told this. Mr. Hayley is one of those who talk a great deal without saying anything."

"Then on whose authority do you speak?" He spoke with a certain rough directness.

"I know because Major Guthrie started for Belgium on Friday last, at two o'clock. By now he must be there, fighting our folk."

"Major Guthrie?" He looked puzzled. "Is he a gentleman of the garrison?—surely not?"

"No, no. He has nothing to do with the garrison!" exclaimed Anna. "But you must have very often seen him, for he is constantly in the town. And he speaks German, Mr. Hegner. I should have thought he would have been in to see you."

"You mean the son of the old lady who lives at Dorycote? They have never dealt at my Stores"—there was a tone of disappointment, of contempt, in Mr. Hegner's voice. "But that gentleman has retired from the Army, Frau Bauer; it is not he, surely, whom they would call out to fight?"

"Still, all the same, he is going to Belgium. To France first, and then to Belgium." She spoke very positively, annoyed at being doubted.

Mr. Hegner hesitated for a moment. He stroked his moustache. "I daresay this Major has gone back to his old regiment, for the English have mobilised their army—such as it is. But that does not mean that they are sending troops to the Continent."

"But I even know where the Major is going to land in France."

Mr. Hegner drew in his breath. "Ach!" he said. "That is *really* interesting! Do you indeed? And what is the name of the place?"

"Boulogne," she said readily.

"But how do you know all this?" he asked slowly.

"Mrs. Otway told me. This Major is a great friend of my ladies. But though it was she who told me about Boulogne, I heard the good-byes said in the hall. Everything can be heard from my kitchen, you see."

"Try and remember exactly what it was that this Major said. It may be of special interest to me."

"He said"—she hesitated a moment, and then, in English, quoted the words: "He said, 'I shall be very busy seeing about my kit before I leave England.'"

"Before I leave England?" he repeated meditatively. "Yes, if you did indeed hear him say those words they are proof positive, Frau Bauer."

"Of course they are!" she said triumphantly.

They had a long and pleasant meal, and old Anna enjoyed every moment of it. Not since she had spent that delightful holiday in Berlin had she drunk so much beer at one sitting. And it was such nice light beer, too! Mrs. Otway, so understanding as to most things connected with Germany, had sometimes expressed her astonishment at the Germans' love of beer; she thought it, strange to say, unhealthy, as well as unpalatable.

To this day Anna could remember the resentful pain with which she had learnt, some time after she had arrived at the Trellis House, that many English ladies allowed their servants "beer money." Had she made a stand at the first, she too might have had "beer money." But, alas! Mrs. Otway, when engaging her, had observed that in her household coffee and milk took the place of alcohol. Poor Anna, at that time in deep trouble, finding her eight-year-old child an almost insuperable bar to employment, would have accepted any conditions, however hard, to find a respectable roof once more over her head and that of her little Louisa.

But, as time had gone on, she had naturally resented Mrs. Otway's peculiar rule concerning beer, and she had so far broken it as to enjoy a jug of beer—of course at her own expense—once a week. But she had only begun doing that after Mrs. Otway had raised her wages.

Host and guest talked on and on. Mr. Hegner confided to Anna his coming change of name, and he seemed pleased to know that she thought it quite a good plan.

Then suddenly he began to cross-question her about Mr. James Hayley. But unluckily she could tell him very little beyond at last admitting that he was, without doubt, in love with her young lady. There was, however, nothing very interesting in that.

Yes, Mr. Hayley was fond of talking, but, as Anna had said just now, he talked without saying anything, and she was too busy to pay much heed to what he did say. He had come to dinner yesterday, that is, Saturday, but he had had to leave Witanbury early this morning. The one thing Anna *did* remember having heard him remark, for he said it more than once, was that up to the last moment they had all thought, in *his* office, that there would be no war.

"He is not the only one. I, too, believed that the war would only come next year," observed Anna's host ruefully.

The old woman thought these questions quite natural, for all Germans have an insatiable curiosity concerning what may be called the gossip side of life.

At last Manfred Hegner pushed back his chair.

"Will you look at the pictures in these papers, Frau Bauer? I have to go upstairs for something. I shall not be gone for more than two or three minutes." He opened wide a sheet showing the Kaiser presiding at fire drill on board his yacht.

Then, leaving his visitor quite happy, he hurried upstairs, and going into his bedroom, locked the door and turned on the electric light. With one of the twin tiny keys he always carried on his watch-chain he opened his safe, and in a very few moments had found what he wanted. Polly would indeed have been surprised had she seen what it was. From the back of the pile of letters she had never disturbed, he drew out a shabby little black book. It was a book of addresses written in alphabetical order, and there were the names of people, and of places, all over the Continent. This little book had been forwarded, registered, by one of its present possessor's business friends in Holland some ten days ago, together with a covering letter explaining the value, in a grocery business, of these addresses. Mr. Hegner was not yet familiar with its contents, but he found fairly quickly the address he wanted—that of a Spanish merchant at Seville.

Taking out the block, which he always carried about with him, from his pocket, he carefully copied on it the address in question. Then he turned over the thin pages of the little black book till he came to another address. This time it was the name of a Frenchman, Jules Boutet, who lived in the Haute Ville, Boulogne. He put this name down, too, but he did not trouble about Boutet's address. Finally he placed the book back in the safe, among the private papers which Polly never disturbed. Then, tearing off the top sheet of the block, he wrote the Spanish address out, and under it, "Father can come back on or about August 19. Boutet is expecting him."

He hesitated for some time over the signature. And then, at last, he put the English Christian name of "Emily."

He pushed the book back, well out of sight, then shutting the safe hastened downstairs again.

At any moment Polly might return home; they were early folk at the Deanery.

Anna had already got up. "I think I must be going home," she observed. "My ladies will soon be back. I do not like them to find the house empty—though Mrs. Otway knows that I am here."

"Do you ever have occasion to go to the Post Office?" he said thoughtfully.

And she answered, "Yes; I have a Savings Bank account. Do you advise me, Mr. Hegner, to take my money out of the Savings Bank just now? Will they not be taking all the money for the war?"

"I think I should take it out. Have you much in?" As he spoke, he was filling up a foreign telegraph form, printing the words in.

"Not very much," she said cautiously. "But a little sum—yes."

"How much?"

She hesitated uncomfortably. "I have forty pounds in the English Savings Bank," she said.

"If I were you"—he looked at her fixedly—"I should take it all out. Make them give it you in sovereigns. And then, if you will bring it to me here, I shall be able to give you for that—let me see——" he waited a moment. "Yes, if you do not mind taking bank-notes and silver, I will give you for that gold of yours forty pounds and five shillings. Gold is useful to me in my business. Oh—and, Frau Bauer? When you do go to the Post Office I should be glad if you would send off this telegram for me. It is a business telegram, as you can see, in fact a code telegram."

She took the piece of paper in her hand, then looked at it and at him, uncomprehendingly.

"It concerns a consignment of bitter oranges. I do not want the Witanbury Post Office to know my business."

"Yes, I understand what you mean."

"It is, as you see, a Spanish telegram, and it will cost"—he made a rapid calculation, then went to the sideboard and took out some silver. "It will cost five-and-sixpence. I therefore give you seven-and-sixpence, Frau Bauer.

That is two shillings for your trouble. If possible, I should prefer that no one sees this telegram being despatched. Do I make myself clear?"

"Yes, yes. I quite understand."

"And if you are asked who gave it you to despatch, say it is a Mrs. Smith, slightly known to you, whom you just met, and who was in too great a hurry to catch her train to come into the Post Office."

Anna took a large purse out of her capacious pocket. In it she put the telegram and the money. "I will send it off to-morrow morning," she exclaimed. "You may count on me."

"Frau Bauer?"

She turned back.

"Only to wish you again a cordial good-night, and to say I hope you will come again soon!"

"Indeed, that I will," she called out gratefully.

As he was shutting the back door, he saw his wife hurrying along across the quiet little back street.

"Hullo, Polly!" he cried, and she came quickly across. "They are in great trouble at the Deanery," she observed, "at least, Miss Edith is in great trouble. She has been crying all to-day. They say her face is all swelled out—that she looks an awful sight! Her lover is going away to fight, and some one has told her that Lord Kitchener says none of the lot now going out will ever come back! There is even talk of their being married before he starts. But as her trousseau is not ready, my sister thinks it would be a very stupid thing to do."

"Did the Dean get my letter?" he asked abruptly.

"Oh yes, I forgot to tell you that. I gave it to Mr. Dunstan, the butler. He says that the Dean opened it and read it. And then what d'you think the silly old thing said, Manfred?"

"You will have to get into the way of calling me Alfred," he said calmly.

"Oh, bother!"

"Well, what did the reverend gentleman say?"

"Mr. Dunstan says that he just exclaimed, 'I'm sorry the good fellow thinks it necessary to do that.' So you needn't have troubled after all. All the way to the Deanery I was saying to myself, 'Mrs. Head—Polly Head. Polly

Head—Mrs. Head.' And no, it's no good pretending that I like it, for I just don't!"

"Then you'll just have to do the other thing," he said roughly. Still, though he spoke so disagreeably, he was yet in high good-humour. Two hours ago this information concerning Miss Haworth's lover would have been of the utmost interest to him, and even now it was of value, as corroborating what Anna had already told him. Frau Bauer was going to be very useful to him. Alfred Head, for already he was thinking of himself by that name, felt that he had had a well-spent, as well as a pleasant, evening.

CHAPTER XIV

Had it not been for the contents of the envelope which she kept in the right-hand drawer of her writing-table, and which she sometimes took out surreptitiously, when neither her daughter nor old Anna were about, Mrs. Otway, as those early August days slipped by, might well have thought her farewell interview with Major Guthrie a dream.

For one thing there was nothing, positively nothing, in any of the daily papers over which she wasted so much time each morning, concerning the despatch of an Expeditionary Force to the Continent! Could Major Guthrie have been mistaken?

Once, when with the Dean, she got very near the subject. In fact, she ventured to say a word expressive of her belief that British troops *were* to be sent to France. But he snubbed her with a sharpness very unlike his urbane self. "Nonsense!" he cried. "There isn't the slightest thought of such a thing. Any small force we could send to the Continent would be useless—in fact, only in the way!"

"Then why does Lord Kitchener ask for a hundred thousand men?"

"For home defence," said the Dean quickly, "only for home defence, Mrs. Otway. The War Office is said to regard it as within the bounds of possibility that England may be invaded. But I fancy the Kaiser is far too truly attached to his mother's country to think of doing anything *really* to injure us! I am sure that so intelligent and enlightened a sovereign understands our point of view—I mean about Belgium. The Kaiser, without doubt, was overruled by the military party. As to our sending our Army abroad—why, millions are already being engaged in this war! So where would be the good of our small army?"

That had been on Sunday, only two days after Major Guthrie had gone. And now, it being Wednesday, Mrs. Otway bethought herself that she ought to fulfil her promise with regard to his mother. Somehow she had a curious feeling that she now owed a duty to the old lady, and also—though that perhaps was rather absurd—that she would be quite glad to see any one who would remind her of her kind friend—the friend whom she missed more than she was willing to admit to herself.

But of course her friend's surprising kindness and thought for her had made a difference to her point of view, and had brought them, in a sense, very much nearer the one to the other. In fact Mrs. Otway was surprised, and even a little hurt, that Major Guthrie had not written to her once since he went away. It was the more odd as he very often *had* written to her during former visits of his to London. Sometimes they had been quite amusing letters.

She put on a cool, dark-grey linen coat and skirt, and a shady hat, and then she started off for the mile walk to Dorycote.

It was a very warm afternoon. Old Mrs. Guthrie, after she had had her pleasant little after-luncheon nap, established herself, with the help of her maid, under a great beech tree in the beautiful garden which had been one of the principal reasons why Major Guthrie had chosen this house at Dorycote for his mother. The old lady was wearing a pale lavender satin gown, with a lace scarf wound about her white hair and framing her still pretty pink and white face.

During the last few days the people who composed Mrs. Guthrie's little circle had been too busy and too excited to come and see her. But she thought it likely that to-day some one would drop in to tea. Any one would be welcome, for she was feeling a little mopish.

No, it was not this surprising, utterly unexpected, War that troubled her. Mrs. Guthrie belonged by birth to the fighting caste; her father had been a soldier in his time, and so had her husband.

As for her only son, he had made the Army his profession, and she knew that he had hoped to live and die in it. He had been through the Boer War, and was wounded at Spion Kop, so he had done his duty by his country; this being so, she could not help being glad now that Alick had retired when he had. But she had wisely kept that gladness to herself as long as he was with her. To Mrs. Guthrie's thinking, this War was France's war, and Russia's war; only in an incidental sense England's quarrel too.

Russia? Mrs. Guthrie had always been taught to mistrust Russia, and to believe that the Tsar had his eye on India. She could remember, too, and that with even now painful vividness, the Crimean War, for a man whom she had cared for as a girl, whom indeed she had hoped to marry, had been killed at the storming of the Redan. To her it seemed strange that England and Russia were now allies.

As a matter of fact, the one moment of excitement the War had brought her was in connection with Russia. An old gentleman she knew, a tiresome neighbour whose calls usually bored rather than pleased her, had hobbled in yesterday and told her, as a tremendous secret, that Russia was sending a big army to Flanders *via* England, through a place called Archangel of which she had vaguely heard. He had had the news from Scotland, where a nephew of his had actually seen and spoken to some Russian officers, the advance guard, as it were, of these legions!

Mrs. Guthrie was glad this war had come after the London season was over. Her great pleasure each day was reading the *Morning Post*, and during this last week that paper had been a great deal too full of war news. It had annoyed her, too, to learn that the Cowes Week had been given up. Of course no German yachts could have competed, but apart from that, why should not the regatta have gone on just the same? It looked as if the King (God bless him!) was taking this war too seriously. Queen Victoria and King Edward would have had a better sense of proportion. The old lady kept these thoughts to herself, but they were there, all the same.

Yes, it was a great pity Cowes had been given up. Mrs. Guthrie missed the lists of names—names which in the majority of cases, unless of course they were those of Americans and of uninteresting *nouveaux riches*, recalled pleasant associations, and that even if the people actually mentioned were only the children or the grandchildren of those whom she had known in the delightful days when she had kept house for her widower brother in Mayfair.

As she turned her old head stiffly round, and saw how charming her well-kept lawn and belt of high trees beyond looked to-day, she felt sorry that she had not written one or two little notes and bidden some of her Witanbury Close acquaintances come out and have tea. The Dean, for instance, might have come. Even Mrs. Otway, Alick's friend, would have been better than nobody!

Considering that she did not like her, it was curious that Mrs. Guthrie was one of the very few women in that neighbourhood who realised that the mistress of the Trellis House was an exceptionally attractive person. More than once—in fact almost always after chance had brought the two ladies in contact, Mrs. Guthrie would observe briskly to her son, "It's rather odd that your Mrs. Otway has never married again!" And it always amused her to notice that it irritated Alick to hear her say this. It was the Scotch bit of him which made Alick at once so shy and so sentimental where women were concerned.

Mrs. Guthrie had no idea how very often her son went to the Trellis House, but even had she known it she would only have smiled satirically. She had but little sympathy with platonic friendships, and she recognised, with that shrewd mother-sense so many women acquire late in life, that Mrs. Otway was a most undesigning widow.

Not that it would have *really* mattered if she had been the other sort. Major Guthrie's own private means were small. It was true that after his mother's death he would be quite well off, but Mrs. Guthrie, even if she had a weak heart, did not think herself likely to die for a long, long time.... And yet, as time went on, and as the old lady became, perhaps, a thought less selfish, she began to wish that her son would fancy some girl with money, and marrying, settle down. If that could come to pass, then she, Mrs. Guthrie, would be content to live on by herself, in the house which she had made so pretty, and where she had gathered about her quite a pleasant circle of admiring and appreciative, if rather dull, country friends.

But when she had said a word in that sense to Alick, he had tried to turn the suggestion off as a joke. And as she had persisted in talking about it, he had shown annoyance, even anger. At last, one day, he had exclaimed, "I'm too old to marry a girl, mother! Somehow—I don't know how it is—I don't seem to care very much for girls."

"There are plenty of widows you could marry," she said quickly. "A widow is more likely to have money than a girl." He had answered, "But you see I don't care for money." And then she had observed, "I don't see how you could marry without money, Alick." And he had said quietly, "I quite agree. I don't think I could." And it may be doubted if in his loyal heart there had even followed the unspoken thought, "So long as you are alive, mother."

Yes, Alick was a very good son, and Mrs. Guthrie did not grudge him his curious friendship with Mrs. Otway.

And then, just as she was saying this to herself, not for the first time, she heard the sound of doors opening and closing, and she saw, advancing towards her over the bright green lawn, the woman of whom she had just been thinking with condescending good-nature.

Mrs. Otway looked hot and a little tired—not quite as attractive as usual. This perhaps made Mrs. Guthrie all the more glad to see her.

"How kind of you to come!" exclaimed the old lady. "But I'm sorry you find me alone. I rather hoped my son might be back to-day. He had to go up to London unexpectedly last Friday. He has an old friend in the War Office, and I think it very likely that this man may have wanted to consult him. I don't know if you are aware that Alick once spent a long leave in Germany. Although I miss him, I should be glad to think he is doing something useful just now. But of course I shouldn't at all have liked the thought of his beginning again to fight—and at his time of life!"

"I suppose a soldier is never too old to want to fight,"—but even while she spoke, Mrs. Otway felt as if she were saying something rather trite and foolish. She was a little bit afraid of the old lady, and as she sat down her cheeks grew even hotter than the walking had made them, for she suddenly remembered Major Guthrie's legacy.

"Yes, that's true, of course! And for the first two or three days of last week I could see that Alick was very much upset, in fact horribly depressed, by this War. But I pretended to take no notice of it—it's always better to do that with a man! It's never the slightest use being sympathetic—it only makes people more miserable. However, last Friday, after getting a telegram, he became quite cheerful and like his old self again. He wouldn't admit, even to me, that he had heard from the War Office. But I put two and two together! Of course, as he is in the Reserve, he may find himself employed on some form of home defence. I could see that Alick thinks that the Germans will probably try and land in England—invade it, in fact, as the Normans did." The old lady smiled. "It's an amusing idea, isn't it?"

"But surely the fleet's there to prevent that!" said Mrs. Otway. She was surprised that so sensible a man as Major Guthrie—her opinion of him had gone up very much this last week—should imagine such a thing as that a landing by the Germans on the English coast was possible.

"Oh, but he says there are at least a dozen schemes of English invasion pigeonholed in the German War Office, and by now they've doubtless had them all out and examined them. He has always said there is a very good landing-place within twenty miles of here—a place Napoleon selected!"

A pleasant interlude was provided by tea, and as Mrs. Guthrie, her old hand shaking a little, poured out a delicious cup for her visitor, and pressed on her a specially nice home-made cake, Mrs. Otway began to think that in the past she had perhaps misjudged Major Guthrie's agreeable, lively mother.

Suddenly Mrs. Guthrie fixed on her visitor the penetrating blue eyes which were so like those of her son, and which were indeed the only feature of her very handsome face she had transmitted to her only child.

"I think you know my son very well?" she observed suavely.

Rather to her own surprise, Mrs. Otway grew a little pink. "Yes," she said. "Major Guthrie and I are very good friends. He has sometimes been most kind in giving me advice about my money matters."

"Ah, well, he does that to a good many people. You'd be amused to know how often he's asked to be trustee to a marriage settlement, and so on. But I've lately supposed, Mrs. Otway, that Alick has made a kind of—well, what shall I say?—a kind of sister of you. He seems so fond of your girl, too; he always *has* liked young people."

"Yes, that's very true," said Mrs. Otway eagerly. "Major Guthrie has always been most kind to Rose." And then she smiled happily, and added, as if to herself, "Most people are."

Somehow this irritated the old lady. "I don't want to pry into anybody's secrets," she said—"least of all, my son's. But I *should* like to be so far frank with you as to ask you if Alick has ever talked to you of the Trepells?"

"The Trepells?" repeated Mrs. Otway slowly. "No, I don't think so. But wait a moment—are they the people with whom he sometimes goes and stays in Sussex?"

"Yes; he stayed with them just after Christmas. Then he *has* talked to you of them?"

"I don't think he's ever exactly talked of them," answered Mrs. Otway. She was trying to remember what it was that Major Guthrie had said. Wasn't it something implying that he was going there to please his mother—that he would far rather stay at home? But she naturally did not put into words this vague recollection of what he had said about these—yes, these Trepells. "It's an odd name, and yet it seems familiar to me," she said hesitatingly.

"It's familiar to you because they are the owners of the celebrated 'Trepell's Polish,'" said the old lady rather sharply. "But they're exceedingly nice people. And it's my impression that Alick is thinking very seriously of the elder daughter. There are only two daughters—nice, old-fashioned girls, brought up by a nice, old-fashioned mother. The mother was the younger daughter of Lord Dunsmuir, and the Dunsmuirs were friends of the Guthries—I mean of my husband's people—since the year one. Their London house is in Grosvenor Square. When I call Maisie Trepell a girl, I do not mean that she is so very much younger than my son as to make the thought of such a marriage absurd. She is nearer thirty than twenty, and he is forty-six."

"Is she the young lady who came to stay with you some time ago?" asked Mrs. Otway.

She was so much surprised, in a sense so much disturbed, by this unexpected confidence that she really hardly knew what she was saying. She had never thought of Major Guthrie as a marrying man. For one thing, she had frequently had occasion to see him, not only with her own daughter, but with other girls, and he had certainly never paid them any special attention. But now she did remember vividly the fact that a young lady had come and paid quite a long visit here before Easter. But she remembered also that Major Guthrie had been away at the time.

"Yes, Maisie came for ten days. Unfortunately, Alick had to go away before she left, for he had taken an early spring fishing with a friend. But I thought—in fact, I rather hoped at the time—that he was very much disappointed."

"Yes, he naturally must have been, if what you say is——" and then she stopped short, for she did not like to say "if what you say is true," so "if what you say is likely to come to pass," she ended vaguely.

"I hope it will come to pass." Mrs. Guthrie spoke very seriously, and once more she fixed her deep blue eyes on her visitor's face. "I'm seventy-one, not very old as people count age nowadays, but still I've never been a strong woman, and I have a weak heart. I should not like to leave my son to a lonely life and to a lonely old age. He's very reserved—he hasn't made many friends in his long life. And I thought it possible he might have confided to you rather than to me."

"No, he never spoke of the matter to me at all; in fact, we have never even discussed the idea of his marrying," said Mrs. Otway slowly.

"Well, forget what I've said!"

But Mrs. Guthrie's visitor went on, a little breathlessly and impulsively: "I quite understand how you feel about Major Guthrie, and I daresay he would be happier married. Most people are, I think."

She got up; it was nearly six—time for her to be starting on her walk back to Witanbury.

Obeying a sudden impulse, she bent down and kissed the old lady good-bye. There was no guile, no taint of suspiciousness, in Mary Otway's nature.

Mrs. Guthrie had the grace to feel a little ashamed.

"I hope you'll come again soon, my dear." She was surprised to feel how smooth and how young was the texture of Mrs. Otway's soft, generously-lipped mouth and rounded cheek.

There rose a feeling of real regret in her cynical old heart. "She likes him better than she knows, and far better than I thought she did!" she said to herself, as she watched the still light, still singularly graceful-looking figure hurrying away towards the house.

As for Mrs. Otway, she felt oppressed, and yes, a little pained, by the old lady's confidence. That what she had just been told might not be true did not occur to her. What more natural than that Major Guthrie should like a nice girl—one, too, who was, it seemed, half Scotch? The Trepells were probably in London even now—she had seen it mentioned in a paper that every one was still staying on in town. If so, Major Guthrie was doubtless constantly in their company; and the letter she had so—well, not exactly longed for, but certainly expected, might even now be lying on the table in the hall of the Trellis House, informing her of his engagement!

She remembered now what she had heard of the Trepells. It concerned the great, the almost limitless, wealth brought in by their wonderful polish. She found it difficult to think of Major Guthrie as a very rich man. Of course, he would always remain, what he was now, a quiet, unassuming gentleman; but all the same, she, Mary Otway, did feel that somehow this piece of news made it impossible for her to accept the loan he had so kindly and so delicately forced on her.

Mrs. Otway had a lively, a too lively, imagination, and it seemed to her as if it was Miss Trepell's money which lay in the envelope now locked away in her writing-table drawer. Indeed, had she known exactly where Major Guthrie was just now, she would have returned it to him. But supposing he had already started for France, and the registered letter came back and was opened by his mother—how dreadful that would be!

When she reached home, and walked through into her cool, quiet house, Mrs. Otway was quite surprised to find that there was no letter from Major Guthrie lying for her on the hall table.

CHAPTER XV

Rose Otway ran up to her room and locked the door. She had fled there to read her first love-letter.

"My Darling Rose,—This is only to tell you that I love you. I have been writing letters to you in my heart ever since I went away. But this is the first moment I have been able to put one down on paper. Father and mother never leave me—that sounds absurd, but it's true. If father isn't there, then mother is. Mother comes into my room after I am in bed, and tucks me up, just as she used to do when I was a little boy.

"It's a great rush, for what I have so longed for is going to happen, so you must not be surprised if you do not have another letter from me for some time. But you will know, my darling love, that I am thinking of you all the time. I am so happy, Rose—I feel as if God has given me everything I ever wanted all at once.

"Your own devoted
"Jervis."

And then there was a funny little postscript, which made her smile through her tears: "You will think this letter all my—'I.' But that doesn't really matter now, as you and I are one!"

Rose soon learnt her first love-letter by heart. She made a little silk envelope for it, and wore it on her heart. It was like a bit of Jervis himself—direct, simple, telling her all she wanted to know, yet leaving much unsaid. Rose had once been shown a love-letter in which the word "kiss" occurred thirty-four times. She was glad that there was nothing of that sort in Jervis's letter, and yet she longed with a piteous, aching longing to feel once more his arms clasping her close, his lips trembling on hers....

At last her mother asked her casually, "Has Jervis Blake written to you, my darling?" And she said, "Yes, mother; once. I think he's busy, getting his outfit."

"Ah, well, they won't think of sending out a boy as young as that, even if Major Guthrie was right in thinking our Army is going to France." And

Rose to that had made no answer. She was convinced that Jervis was going on active service. There was one sentence in his letter which could mean nothing else.

Life in Witanbury, after that first week of war, settled down much as before. There was a general impression that everything was going very well. The brave little Belgians were defending their country with skill and tenacity, and the German Army was being "held up."

The Close was full of mild amateur strategists, headed by the Dean himself. Great as had been, and was still, his admiration for Germany, Dr. Haworth was of course an Englishman first; and every day, when opening his morning paper, he expected to learn that there had been another Trafalgar. He felt certain that the German Fleet was sure to make, as he expressed it, "a dash for it." Germany was too gallant a nation, and the Germans were too proud of their fleet, to keep their fighting ships in harbour. The Dean of Witanbury, like the vast majority of his countrymen and countrywomen, still regarded War as a great game governed by certain well-known rules which both sides, as a matter of course, would follow and abide by.

The famous cathedral city was doing "quite nicely" in the matter of recruiting. And the largest local employer of labour, a man who owned a group of ladies' high-grade boot and shoe factories, generously decided that he would permit ten per cent. of those of his men who were of military age to enlist; he actually promised as well to keep their places open, and to give their wives, or their mothers, as the case might be, half wages for the first six months of war.

A good many people felt aggrieved when it became known that Lady Bethune was not going to give her usual August garden party. She evidently did not hold with the excellent suggestion that England should now take as her motto "Business as Usual." True, a garden-party is not exactly business—still, it is one of those pleasures which the great ladies of a country neighbourhood find it hard to distinguish from duties.

Yes, life went on quite curiously as usual during the second week of the Great War, and to many of the more well-to-do people of Witanbury, only brought in its wake a series of agreeable "thrills" and mild excitements.

Of course this was not quite the case with the inmates of the Trellis House. Poor old Anna, for instance, very much disliked the process of Registration. Still, it was made as easy and pleasant to her as possible, and Mrs. Otway and Rose both accompanied her to the police station. There, nothing could have been more kindly than the manner of the police inspector who handed

Anna Bauer her "permit." He went to some trouble in order to explain to her exactly what it was she might and might not do.

As Anna seldom had any occasion to travel as far as five miles from Witanbury Close, her registration brought with it no hardship at all. Still, she was surprised and hurt to find herself described as "an enemy alien." She could assure herself, even now, that she had no bad feelings against England—no, none at all!

Though neither her good faithful servant nor her daughter guessed the fact, Mrs. Otway was the one inmate of the Trellis House to whom the War, so far, brought real unease. She felt jarred and upset—anxious, too, as she had never yet been, about her money matters.

More and more she missed Major Guthrie, and yet the thought of him brought discomfort, almost pain, in its train. With every allowance made, he was surely treating her in a very cavalier manner. How odd of him not to have written! Whenever he had been away before, he had always written to her, generally more than once; and now, when she felt that their friendship had suddenly come closer, he left her without a line.

Her only comfort, during those strange days of restless waiting for news which never came, were her daily talks with the Dean. Their mutual love and knowledge of Germany had always been a strong link between them, and it was stronger now than ever.

Alone of all the people she saw, Dr. Haworth managed to make her feel at charity with Germany while yet quite confident with regard to her country's part in the War. He did not say so in so many words, but it became increasingly clear to his old friend and neighbour, that the Dean believed that the Germans would soon be conquered, on land by Russia and by France, while the British, following their good old rule, would defeat them at sea.

Many a time, during those early days of war, Mrs. Otway felt a thrill of genuine pity for Germany. True, the Militarist Party there deserved the swift defeat that was coming on them; they deserved it now, just as the French Empire had deserved it in 1870, though Mrs. Otway could not believe that modern Germany was as arrogant and confident as had been the France of the Second Empire.

Much as she missed Major Guthrie, she was sometimes glad that he was not there to—no, not to crow over her, he was incapable of doing that, but to be proved right.

There was a great deal of talk of the mysterious passage of Russians through the country. Some said there were twenty thousand, some a hundred thousand, and the stories concerning this secret army of avengers grew more and more circumstantial. They reached Witanbury Close from every quarter. And though for a long time the Dean held out, he at last had to admit that, yes, he did believe that a Russian army was being swiftly, secretly transferred, *via* Archangel and Scotland, to the Continent! More than one person declared that they had actually *seen* Cossacks peeping out of the windows of the trains which, with blinds down, were certainly rushing through Witanbury station, one every ten minutes, through each short summer night.

All the people the Otways knew took great glory and comfort in these rumours, but Mrs. Otway heard the news with very mixed feelings. It seemed to her scarcely fair that a Russian army should come, as it were, on the sly, to attack the Germans in France—and she did not like to feel that England would for ever and for aye have to be grateful to Russia for having sent an army to her help.

It was the morning of the 18th of August—exactly a fortnight, that is, since England's declaration of war on Germany. Coming down to breakfast, Mrs. Otway suddenly realised what a very, very long fortnight this had been—the longest fortnight in her life as a grown-up woman. She felt what she very seldom was, depressed, and as she went into the dining-room she was sorry to see that there was a sullen look on old Anna's face.

"Good morning!" she said genially in German. And in reply the old servant, after a muttered "Good morning, gracious lady," went on, in a tone of suppressed anger, "Did you not tell me that the English were not going to fight my people? That it was all a mistake?"

Mrs. Otway looked surprised. "Yes, I feel sure that no soldiers are going abroad," she said quietly. "The Dean says that our Army is to be kept at home, to defend our shores, Anna."

She spoke rather coldly; there was a growing impression in Witanbury that the Germans might try to invade England, and behave here as they were behaving in Belgium. Though Mrs. Otway and Rose tried to believe that the horrible stories of burning and murder then taking place in Flanders were exaggerated, still some of them were very circumstantial and, in fact, obviously true.

Languidly, for there never seemed any real news nowadays, she opened wide her newspaper. And then her heart gave a leap! Printed right across the page, in huge black letters, ran the words:

"BRITISH EXPEDITIONARY FORCE IN FRANCE."

And underneath, in smaller type:

"Landed at Boulogne without a Single Casualty."

Then Major Guthrie had been right and the Dean wrong? And this was why Anna had spoken as she had done just now, in that rather rude and injured tone?

Later in the morning, when she met the Dean, he showed himself, as might have been expected, very frank and genial about the matter.

"I have to admit that I was wrong," he observed; "quite wrong. I certainly thought it impossible that any British troops could cross the Channel till a decisive fleet action had been fought. And, well—I don't mind saying to *you*, Mrs. Otway, I still think it a pity that we have sent our Army abroad."

Three days later Rose and her mother each received a quaint-looking postcard from "Somewhere in France." There was neither postmark nor date. The first four words were printed, but what was really *very* strange was the fact that the sentences written in were almost similar in each case. But whereas Jervis Blake wrote his few words in English, Major Guthrie's few words were written in French.

Jervis Blake's postcard ran:

"I am quite well and very happy. This is a glorious country. I will write a letter soon." And then "J. B."

That of Major Guthrie:

"I am quite well." Then, in queer archaic French, "and all goes well with me. I trust it is the same with thee. Will write soon."

But he, mindful of the fact that it was an open postcard, with your Scotchman's true caution, had not even added his initials.

Mrs. Otway's only comment on hearing that Jervis Blake had written Rose a postcard from France, had been the words, said feelingly, and with a sigh, "Ah, well! So he has gone out too? He is very young to see something of real war. But I expect that it will make a man of him, poor boy."

For a moment Rose had longed to throw herself in her mother's arms and tell her the truth; then she had reminded herself that to do so would not be fair to Jervis. Jervis would have told his people of their engagement if she had allowed him to do so. It was she who had prevented it. And then—and then—Rose also knew, deep in her heart, that if anything happened to Jervis, she would far rather bear the agony alone. She loved her mother dearly, but she told herself, with the curious egoism of youth, that her mother would not understand.

Rose had been four years old when her father died; she thought she could remember him, but it was a very dim, shadowy memory. She did not realise, even now, that her mother had once loved, once lost, once suffered. She did not believe that her mother knew anything of love—of real love, of true love, of such love as now bound herself to Jervis Blake.

Her mother no doubt supposed Rose's friendship with Jervis Blake to be like her own friendship with Major Guthrie—a cold, sensible, placid affair. In fact, she had said, with a smile, "It's rather amusing, isn't it, that Jervis should write to you, and Major Guthrie to me, by the same post?"

But neither mother nor daughter had offered to show her postcard to the other. There was so little on them that it had not seemed necessary. Of the two, it was Mrs. Otway who felt a little shy. The wording of Major Guthrie's postcard was so peculiar! Of course he did not know French well, or he would have put what he wanted to say differently. He would have said "you" instead of "thee." She was rather glad that her dear little Rose had not asked to see it. Still, its arrival mollified her sore, hurt feeling that he might have written before. Instead of tearing it up, as she had always done the letters Major Guthrie had written to her in the old days that now seemed so very long ago, she slipped that curious war postcard inside the envelope in which were placed his bank-notes.

CHAPTER XVI

August 23, 1914! A date which will be imprinted on the heart, and on the tablets of memory, of every Englishman and Englishwoman of our generation. To the majority of thinking folk, that was the last Sunday we any of us spent in the old, prosperous, happy, confiding England—the England who considered that might as a matter of course follows right—the England whose grand old motto was "Victory as Usual," and to whom the word defeat was without significance.

Almost the whole population of Witanbury seemed to have felt a common impulse to attend the evening service in the cathedral. They streamed in until the stately black-gowned vergers were quite worried to find seats for the late comers. In that great congregation there was already a certain leaven of anxious hearts—not over-anxious, you understand, but naturally uneasy because those near and dear to them had gone away to a foreign country, to fight an unknown foe.

It was known that the minor canon who was on the rota to preach this evening had gracefully yielded the privilege to the Dean, and this accounted, in part at least, for the crowds who filled the great building.

When Dr. Haworth mounted the pulpit and prepared to begin his sermon, which he had striven to make worthy of the occasion, he felt a thrill of satisfaction as his eyes suddenly lighted on the man whom he still instinctively thought of by his old name of "Manfred Hegner."

Yes, there they were, Hegner and his wife, at the end of a row of chairs, a long way down; she looking very pretty and graceful, instinctively well-dressed in her grey muslin Sunday gown and wide floppy hat—looking, indeed, "quite the lady," as more than one of her envious neighbours had said to themselves when seeing her go by on her husband's arm.

Because of the presence of this man who, though German-born, had elected to become an Englishman, and devote his very considerable intelligence—the Dean prided himself on his knowledge of human nature, and on his quickness in detecting humble talent—to the service of his adopted country, the sermon was perhaps a thought more fair, even cordial, to Britain's formidable enemy, than it would otherwise have been.

The messages of the King and of Lord Kitchener to the Expeditionary Force gave the Dean a fine text for his discourse, and he paid a very moving and eloquent tribute to the Silence of the People. He reminded his hearers that even if they, in quiet Witanbury, knew nothing of the great and stirring things which were happening elsewhere, there must have been thousands—it might truly be said tens of thousands—of men and women who had known that our soldiers were leaving their country for France. And yet not a word had been said, not a hint conveyed, either privately or in the press. He himself had one who was very dear and near to his own dearest and nearest, in that Expeditionary Force, and yet not a word had been breathed, even to him.

Then he went on to a sadder and yet in its way an even more glorious theme—the loss of His Majesty's good ship *Amphion*. He described the splendid discipline of the men, the magnificent courage of the captain, who, when recovering from a shock which had stretched him insensible, had rushed to stop the engines. He told with what composure the men had fallen in, and how everything had been done, without hurry or confusion, in the good old British sea way; and how, thanks to that, twenty minutes after the *Amphion* had struck a mine, men, officers, and captain had left the ship.

And after he had finished his address—he kept it quite short, for Dr. Haworth was one of those rare and wise men who never preach a long sermon—the whole congregation rose to their feet and sang "God Save the King."

This golden feeling of security, of happy belief that all was, and must be, well, lasted till the following afternoon. And the first of the dwellers in Witanbury Close to have that comfortable feeling shattered—shattered for ever—was Mrs. Otway.

She was about to pay a late call on Mrs. Robey, who, after all, had not taken her children to the seaside. Rather to the amusement of his neighbours, Mr. Robey, who was moving heaven and earth to get some kind of War Office job, had bluntly declared that, however much people might believe in "business as usual," he was not going to practice "pleasure as usual" while his country was at war.

Mrs. Otway stepped out of her gate, and before turning to the right she looked to the left, as people will. The Dean was at the corner, apparently on his way back from the town. He held an open paper in his hand, and though that was not in itself a strange thing, there suddenly came over the woman who stood looking at him a curious feeling of unreasoning fear, a queer prevision of evil. She began walking towards him, and he, after hesitating for a moment, came forward to meet her.

"There's serious news!" he cried. "Namur has fallen!"

Now, only that morning Mrs. Otway had read in a leading article the words, "Namur is impregnable, or, if not impregnable, will certainly hold out for months. That this is so is fortunate, for we cannot disguise from ourselves that Namur is the key to France."

"Are you sure that the news is true?" she asked quietly, and, disturbed as he was himself, the Dean was surprised to see the change which had come over his neighbour's face; it suddenly looked aged and grey.

"Yes, I'm afraid it's true—in fact, it's official. Still, I don't know that the falling of a fortress should really affect our Expeditionary Force."

Mary Otway did not pay her proposed call on Mrs. Robey. Instead, she retraced her steps into the Trellis House, and looked eagerly through the papers of the last few days. She no longer trusted the Dean and his easy-going optimism. The fall of Namur without effect on the Expeditionary Force? As she read on, even she saw that it was bound to have—perhaps it had already had—an overwhelming effect on the fortunes of the little British Army.

From that hour onwards a heavy cloud of suspense and of fear hung over Witanbury Close: over the Deanery, where the cherished youngest daughter tried in vain to be "brave," and to conceal her miserable state of suspense from her father and mother; over "Robey's," all of whose young men were in the Expeditionary Force; and very loweringly over the Trellis House.

What was now happening over there, in France, or in Flanders? People asked each other the question with growing uneasiness.

The next day, that is, on the Tuesday, sinister rumours swept over Witanbury—rumours that the British had suffered a terrible defeat at a place called Mons.

In her restlessness and eager longing for news, Mrs. Otway after tea went into the town. She had an excuse, an order to give in at the Stores, and there the newly-named Alfred Head came forward, and attended on her, as usual, himself.

"There seems to be serious news," he said respectfully. "I am told that the English Army has been encircled, much as was the French Army at Sedan in 1870."

As he spoke, fixing his prominent eyes on her face, Mr. Head's customer now suddenly felt an inexplicable shrinking from this smooth-tongued German-born man.

"Oh, we must hope it is not as bad as that," she exclaimed hastily. "Have you any real reason for believing such a thing to be true, Mr. Heg—I mean, Mr. Head?"

And he answered regretfully, "One of my customers has just told me so, ma'am. He said the news had come from London—that is my only reason for believing it. We will hope it is a mistake."

After leaving the Stores, Mrs. Otway, following a sudden impulse, began walking rather quickly down the long street which led out of Witanbury towards the village where the Guthries lived. Why should she not go out and pay a late call on the old lady? If any of these dreadful rumours had reached Dorycote House, Mrs. Guthrie must surely be very much upset.

Her kind thought was rewarded by a sight of the letter Major Guthrie had left to be posted to his mother on the 18th of August, that is, on the day when was to be published the news that the Expeditionary Force had landed safely in France.

The letter was, like its writer, kind, thoughtful, considerate; and as she read it Mrs. Otway felt a little pang of jealous pain. She wished that he had written *her* a letter like that, instead of a rather ridiculous postcard. Still, as she read the measured, reassuring sentences, she felt soothed and comforted. She knew that she was not reasonable, yet—yet it seemed impossible that the man who had written that letter, and the many like him who were out there, could allow themselves to be surrounded and captured—by Germans!

"He has also sent me a rather absurd postcard," observed the old lady casually. "I say absurd because it is not dated, and because he also forgot to put the name of the place where he wrote it. It simply says that he is quite well, and that I shall hear from him as soon as he can find time to write a proper letter."

She waited a few moments, and then went on: "Of course I felt a little upset when I realised that Alick had really gone on active service. But I know how he would have felt being left behind."

Then, rather to her visitor's discomfiture, Mrs. Guthrie turned the subject away from her son, and from what was going on in France. She talked determinedly of quite other things—though even then she could not help going very near the subject.

"I understand," she exclaimed, "that Lady Bethune is giving up her garden-party to-morrow! I'm told she feels that it would be wrong to be merrymaking while some of our men and officers may be fighting and dying. But I quite disagree, and I'm sure, my dear, that you do too. Of course it is the duty of the women of England, at such a time as this, to carry on their social duties exactly as usual."

"I can't quite make up my mind about that," replied her visitor slowly.

When Mrs. Otway rose to go, the old lady suddenly softened. "You'll come again soon, won't you?" she said eagerly. "Though I never saw two people more unlike, still, in a curious kind of way, you remind me of Alick! That must be because you and he are such friends. I suppose he wrote to you before leaving England?" She looked rather sharply out of her still bright blue eyes at the woman now standing before her.

Mrs. Otway shook her head. "No, Major Guthrie did not write to me before leaving England."

"Ah, well, he was very busy, and my son's the sort of man who always chooses to do his duty before he takes his pleasure. He can write quite a good letter when he takes the trouble."

"Yes, indeed he can," said Mrs. Otway simply, and Mrs. Guthrie smiled.

As she walked home, Mary Otway pondered a little over the last words of her talk with Mrs. Guthrie. It was true, truer than Mrs. Guthrie knew, that she and Major Guthrie were friends. A man does not press an unsolicited loan of a hundred pounds on a woman unless he has a kindly feeling for her; still less does he leave her a legacy in his will.

And then there swept a feeling of pain over her burdened heart. That legacy, which she had only considered as a token of the testator's present friendly feeling, had become in the last few hours an ominous possibility. She suddenly realised that Major Guthrie, before leaving England, had made what Jervis Blake had once called "a steeplechase will."

Rumours soon grew into certainties. It was only too true that the British Army was now falling back, back, back, fighting a series of what were called by the unfamiliar name of rearguard actions; and at last there came the official statement, "Our casualties have been very heavy, but the exact numbers are not yet known."

After that, as the days went on, Rose Otway began to wear a most ungirlish look of strain and of suspense; but no one, to her secret relief, perceived that she looked any different—all the sympathy of the Close was concentrated on Edith Haworth, for it was known that the cavalry had been terribly cut up. Still, towards the end of that dreadful week, Rose's mother suddenly woke up to the fact that Rose had fallen into the way of walking to the station in order to get the evening paper from London half an hour before it could reach the Close.

It was their good old Anna who consoled and sustained the girl during those first days of strain and of suspense. Anna was never tired of repeating in her comfortable, cosy, easy-going way, that after all very few soldiers *really* get killed in battle. She, Anna, had had a brother, and many of her relations, fighting in 1870, and only one of them all had been killed.

The old woman kept her own personal feelings entirely to herself—and indeed those feelings were very mixed. Of course she did not share the now universal suspense, surprise, and grief, for to her mind it was quite right and natural that the Germans should beat the English. What would have been really most disturbing and unnatural would have been if the English had beaten the Germans!

But even so she was taken aback by the secret, fierce exultation which Manfred Hegner—she could not yet bring herself to call him Alfred Head—displayed, when he and she were left for three or four minutes alone by his wife, Polly.

Since that pleasant evening they had spent together—it now seemed a long time ago, yet it was barely a fortnight—Anna had fallen into the way of going to the Stores twice, and even three times, a week, to supper. Her host flattered her greatly by pointing out that the information she had given him concerning Major Guthrie and the Expeditionary Force, as it was oddly called, had been sound. Frankly he had exclaimed, "As the days went on and nothing was known, I thought you must have been mistaken, Frau Bauer. But you did me a good turn, and one I shall not forget! I have already sold some of the goods ordered with a view to soldier customers, for they were goods which can be useful abroad, and I hear a great many parcels will soon be sent out. For that I shall open a special department!"

To her pleased surprise, he had pressed half a crown on her; and after a little persuasion she had accepted it. After all, she had a right, under their old agreement, to a percentage on any profit she brought him! That news about Major Guthrie had thus procured a very easily earned half-crown, even more easily earned than the money she had received for sending off the telegram to Spain. Anna hoped that similar opportunities of doing Mr. Hegner a good turn would often come her way. But still, she hated this war, and with the whole of her warm, sentimental German heart she hoped that Mr. Jervis Blake would soon be back home safe and sound. He was a rich, generous young gentleman, the very bridegroom for her beloved Miss Rose.

CHAPTER XVII

Sunday, the 30th of August. But oh, what a different Sunday from that of a week ago! The morning congregation in Witanbury Cathedral was larger than it had ever been before, and over every man and woman there hung an awful pall of suspense, and yes, of fear, as to what the morrow might bring forth.

Both the post and the Sunday papers were late. They had not even been delivered by church time, and that added greatly, with some of those who were gathered there, to the general feeling of anxiety and unease.

In the sermon that he preached that day the Dean struck a stern and feeling note. He told his hearers that now not only their beloved country, but each man and woman before him, must have a heart for every fate. He, the speaker, would not claim any special knowledge, but they all knew that the situation was very serious. Even so, it would be a great mistake, and a great wrong, to give way to despair. He would go further, and say that even despondency was out of place.

Only a day or two ago he had been offered, and he had purchased, the diary of a citizen of Witanbury written over a hundred years ago, and from a feeling of natural curiosity he had looked up the entries in the August of that year. Moved and interested indeed had he been to find that Witanbury just then had been expecting a descent on the town by the French, and on one night it was rumoured that a strong force had actually landed, and was marching on the city! Yet the writer of that diary—he was only a humble blacksmith—had put in simple and yet very noble language his conviction that old England would never go down, *if only she remained true to herself.*

It was this fine message from the past which the Dean brought to the people of Witanbury that day. What had been true when we had been fighting a far greater man than any of those we were fighting to-day—he meant of course Napoleon—was even truer now than then. All would be, must be, ultimately well, if England to herself would stay but true.

A few of those who listened with uplifted hearts to the really inspiriting discourse, noted with satisfaction that, for the first time since the declaration of war, Dr. Haworth paid no tribute to the enemy. The word "Germany" did not even pass his lips.

And then, when at the end of the service Mrs. Otway and Rose were passing through the porch, Mrs. Otway felt herself touched on the arm. She turned round quickly to find Mrs. Haworth close to her.

"I've been wondering if Rose would come back with me and see Edith? I'm sorry to say the poor child isn't at all well to-day. And so we persuaded her to stay in bed. You see"—she lowered her voice, and that though there was no one listening to them—"you see, we hear privately that the cavalry were very heavily engaged last Wednesday, and that the casualties have been terribly heavy. My poor child says very little, but it's evident that she's so miserably anxious that she can think of nothing else. Her father thinks she's fretting because we would not allow—or perhaps I ought to say we discouraged the idea of—a hasty marriage. I feel sure it would do Edith good to see some one, especially a dear little friend like Rose, who has no connection with the Army, and who can look at things in a sensible, normal manner."

And so mother and daughter, for an hour, went their different ways, and Mrs. Otway, as she walked home alone, told herself that anxiety became Mrs. Haworth, that it rendered the Dean's wife less brusque, and made her pleasanter and kindlier in manner. Poor Edith was her ewe lamb, the prettiest of the daughters whom she had started so successfully out into the world, and the one who was going to make, from a worldly point of view, the best marriage. Yes, it would indeed be a dreadful thing if anything happened to Sir Hugh Severn.

Casualties? What an odd, sinister word! One with which it was difficult to become familiar. But it was evidently the official word. Not for the first time she reminded herself of the exact words the Prime Minister in the House of Commons had used. They had been "Our casualties are very heavy, though the exact numbers are not yet known." Mrs. Otway wondered uneasily when they would become known—how soon, that is, a mother, a sister, a lover, and yes, a friend, would learn that the man who was beloved, cherished, or close and dear as a friend may be, had become—what was the horrible word?—a casualty.

She walked through into her peaceful, pretty house. Unless the household were all out, the front door was never locked, for there was nothing to steal, and no secrets to pry out, in the Trellis House. And then, on the hall table, she saw the belated evening paper which she had missed this morning, and two or three letters. Taking up the paper and the letters, she went straight through into the garden. It would be pleasanter to read out there than indoors.

With a restful feeling that no one was likely to come in and disturb her yet awhile, she sat down in the basket-chair which had already been put out by her thoughtful old Anna. And then, quite suddenly, she caught sight of the middle letter of the three she had gathered up in such careless haste. It was an odd-looking envelope, of thin, common paper covered with pale blue lines; but it bore her address written in Major Guthrie's clear, small, familiar handwriting, and on the right-hand corner was the usual familiar penny stamp. That stamp was, of course, a positive proof that he was home again.

For quite a minute she simply held the envelope in her hand. She felt so relieved, and yes, so ridiculously happy, that after the first moment of heartfelt joy there came a pang of compunction. It was wrong, it was unnatural, that the safety of *one* human being should so affect her. She was glad that this curious revulsion of feeling, this passing from gloom and despondency to unreasoning peace and joy, should have taken place when she was by herself. She would have been ashamed that Rose should have witnessed it.

And then, with a certain deliberation, she opened the envelope, and drew out the oddly-shaped piece of paper it contained.

This is what she read:

"France, "
Wednesday morning.

"Every letter sent by the usual channel is read and, very properly, censored. I do not choose that this letter should be seen by any eyes but mine and yours. I have therefore asked, and received, permission to send this by an old friend who is leaving for England with despatches.

"The work has been rather heavy. I have had very little sleep since Sunday, so you must forgive any confusion of thought or unsuitable expressions used by me to you. Unfortunately I have lost my kit, but the old woman in whose cottage I am resting for an hour has good-naturedly provided me with paper and envelopes. Luckily I managed to keep my fountain-pen.

"I wish to tell you now what I have long desired to tell you — that I love you — that it has long been my greatest, nay, my only wish, that you should become my wife. Sometimes, lately, I have thought that I might persuade you to let me love you.

"In so thinking I may have been a presumptuous fool. Be that as it may, I want to tell you that our friendship has meant a very great deal to me; that without it I should have been, during the last four years, a most unhappy man.

"And now I must close this hurriedly written and poorly expressed letter. It does not say a tenth—nay, it does not say a thousandth part of what I would fain say. But let me, for the first, and perhaps for the last time, call you my dearest."

Then followed his initials "A. G.," and a postscript: "As to what has been happening here, I will only quote to you Napier's grand words: 'Then was seen with what majesty the British soldier fights.'"

Mrs. Otway read the letter right through twice. Then, slowly, deliberately, she folded it up and put it back in its envelope. Uncertainly she looked at her little silk handbag. No, she could not put it there, where she kept her purse, her engagement book, her handkerchief. For the moment, at any rate, it would be safest elsewhere. With a quick furtive movement she thrust it into her bodice, close to her beating heart.

Mrs. Otway looked up to a sudden sight of Rose—of Rose unusually agitated.

"Oh, mother," she cried, "such a strange, dreadful, extraordinary thing has happened! Old Mrs. Guthrie is dead. The butler telephoned to the Deanery, and he seems in a dreadful state of mind. Mrs. Haworth says she can't possibly go out there this morning, and they were wondering whether you would mind going. The Dean says he was out there only yesterday, and that Mrs. Guthrie spoke as if you were one of her dearest friends. Wasn't that strange?"

Rose looked very much shocked and distressed—curiously so, considering how little she had known Mrs. Guthrie. But there is something awe-inspiring to a young girl in the sudden death of even an old person. Only three days ago Mrs. Guthrie had entertained Rose with an amusing account of her first ball—a ball given at the Irish Viceregal Court in the days when, as the speaker had significantly put it, it really *was* a Court in Dublin. And when Rose and her mother had said good-bye, she had pressed them to come again soon; while to the girl: "I don't often see anything so fresh and pretty as you are, my dear!" she had exclaimed.

Mrs. Otway heard Rose's news with no sense of surprise. She felt as if she were living in a dream—a dream which was at once poignantly sad and yet exquisitely, unbelievably happy. "I have been there several times lately," she said, in a low voice, "and I had grown quite fond of her. Of course I'll go. Will you telephone for a fly? I'd rather be alone there, my dear."

Rose lingered on in the garden for a moment. Then she said slowly, reluctantly: "And mother? I'm afraid there's rather bad news of Major Guthrie. It came last night, before Mrs. Guthrie went to bed. The butler says she took it very bravely and quietly, but I suppose it was that which—which brought about her death."

"What *is* the news?"

Mrs. Otway's dream-impression vanished. She got up from the basket-chair in which she had been sitting, and her voice to herself sounded strangely loud and unregulated.

"What is it, Rose? Why don't you tell me? Has he been killed?"

"Oh, no—it's not as bad as that! Oh! mother, don't look so unhappy—it's only that he's 'wounded and missing.'"

CHAPTER XVIII

No, ma'am, there was nothing, ma'am, to act, so to speak, in the nature of a warning. Mrs. Guthrie had much enjoyed your visit, and, if I may say so, ma'am, the visit of your young lady, last Thursday. Yesterday she was more cheerful-like than usual, talking a good bit about the Russians. She said that their coming to our help just now in the way they had done had quite reconciled her to them."

Howse, Major Guthrie's butler, his one-time soldier-servant, was speaking. By his side was Mrs. Guthrie's elderly maid, Ponting. Mrs. Otway was standing opposite to them, and they were all three in the middle of the pretty, cheerful morning-room, where it seemed but a few hours ago since she and her daughter had sat with the old lady.

With the mingled pomp, enjoyment, and grief which the presence of death creates in a certain type of mind, Howse went on speaking: "She made quite a hearty tea for her—two bits of bread and butter, and a little piece of tea-cake. And then for her supper she had a sweetbread—a sweetbread and bacon. It's a comfort to Cook now, ma'am, to remember as how Mrs. Guthrie sent her a message, saying how nicely she thought the bacon had been done. Mrs. Guthrie always liked the bacon to be very dry and curly, ma'am."

He stopped for a moment, and Mrs. Otway's eyes filled with tears for the first time.

On entering the house, she had at once been shown the War Office telegram stating that Major Guthrie was wounded and missing, and she had glanced over it with shuddering distress and pain, while her brain kept repeating "wounded and missing—wounded and missing." What exactly did those sinister words signify? How, if he was missing, could they know he was wounded? How, if he had been wounded, could he be missing?

But soon she had been forced to command her thoughts, and to listen, with an outward air of calmness and interest, to this detailed account of the poor old lady's last hours.

With unconscious gusto, Howse again took up the sad tale, while the maid stood by, with reddened eyelids, ready to echo and to supplement his narrative.

"Perhaps Mrs. Guthrie was not quite as well as she seemed to be, ma'am for she wouldn't take any dessert, and after she had finished her dinner she didn't seem to want to sit up for a while, as she sometimes did. When she became so infirm, a matter of two years ago, the Major arranged that his study should be turned into a bedroom for her, ma'am, so we wheeled her in there after dinner."

After a pause, he went on with an added touch of gloom: "She gazed her last upon the dining-room, and on this 'ere little room, which was, so to speak, ma'am, her favourite sitting-room. Isn't that so, Ponting?" The maid nodded, and Howse said sadly: "Ponting will now tell you what happened after that, ma'am."

Ponting waited a moment, and then began: "My mistress didn't seem inclined to go to bed at once, so I settled her down nicely and comfortably with her reading-lamp and a copy of *The World* newspaper. She found the papers very dull lately, poor old lady, for you see, ma'am, there was nothing in them but things about the war, and she didn't much care for that. But she can't have been reading more than five minutes when there came the telegram."

Howse held up his hand, for it was here that he again came on the scene.

"The minute the messenger boy handed me the envelope," he exclaimed, "I says to myself, 'That's bad news—bad news of the Major!' I sorely felt tempted to open it. But there! I knew if I did so it would anger Mrs. Guthrie. She was a lady, ma'am, who always knew her own mind. It wasn't even addressed 'Guthrie,' you see, but 'Mrs. Guthrie,' as plain as plain could be. The boy 'ad brought it to the front door, and as we was having our supper I didn't want to disturb Ponting. So I just walked along to Mrs. Guthrie's bedroom, and knocked. She calls out, 'Come in!' And I answers, 'There's a telegram for you, ma'am. Would you like me to send Ponting in with it?' And she calls out, 'No, Howse. Bring it in yourself.'

"I shall never forget seeing her open it, poor old lady. She did it quite deliberate-like; then, after just reading it over, she looked up straight at me. 'I know you'll be sorry to hear, Howse, as how Major Guthrie is wounded and missing,' she said, and then, 'I need not tell you, who are an old soldier, Howse, that such are the fortunes of war.' Those, ma'am, were her exact words. Of course I explained how sorry I was, and I did my very best to hide from her how bad I took the news to be. 'I think I would like to be alone now, Howse,' she says, 'just for a little while.' And then, 'We must hope for better news in the morning.' I asked her, 'Would you like me to send Ponting up to you, ma'am?' But she shook her head: 'No, Howse, I would rather be by myself. I will ring when I require Ponting. I do not feel as if I should care to go to bed just yet,' she says quite firmly.

"Well, ma'am, we had of course to obey her orders, but we all felt very uncomfortable. And as a matter of fact in about half an hour Ponting did make an excuse to go into the room"—he looked at the woman by his side. "You just tell Mrs. Otway what happened," he said, in a tone of command.

Ponting meekly obeyed.

"I just opened the door very quietly, and Mrs. Guthrie did not turn round. Without being at all deaf, my mistress had got a little hard of hearing, lately. I went a step forward, and then I saw that she was reading the Bible. I was very much surprised, madam, for it was the first time I had ever seen her do such a thing—though of course there was always a Bible and a Prayer Book close to her hand. She was wheeled into church each Sunday—when it was fine, that is. The Major saw to that.... I couldn't help feeling sorry she hadn't rung and asked me to move the Book for her, for it is a big Bible, with very clear print. She was following the words with her finger, and that was a thing I had never seen her do before with any book. As she did not turn round, I said to myself that it was better not to disturb her. So I just backed very quietly out of the door again. I shall always be glad," she said, in a lower tone, "that I saw her like that."

"And then," interposed Howse, "quite a long time went on, ma'am, and we all got to feel very uneasy. We none of us liked to go up—not one of us. But at last three of us went up together—Cook, me, and Ponting—and listened at the door. But try our hardest, as we did, we could hear nothing. It was the stillness of death!"

"Yes," said Ponting, her voice sinking to a whisper, "that's what it was. For when at last I opened the door, there lay my poor mistress all huddled up in the chair, just as she had fallen back. We sent for the doctor at once, but he said there was nothing to be done—that her heart had just stopped. He said it might have happened any time in the last two years, or she might have lived on for quite a long time, if all had gone on quiet and serene."

"We've left the Bible just as it was," said Howse slowly. "It's just covered over, so that the Major, if ever he *should* come home again, though I fear that's very unlikely"—he dolefully shook his head—"may see what it was her eyes last rested on. Major Guthrie, if you would excuse me for saying so, ma'am, has always been a far more religious gentleman than his mother was a religious lady. I feel sure it would comfort him to know that just before her end she was reading the Book."

"It was open at the twenty-second Psalm," added Ponting, "and when I came in that time and saw her without her seeing me, she must have been just reading the verse about the dog."

"The dog?" said Mrs. Otway, surprised.

"Yes, madam. 'Deliver my soul from the sword: my darling from the power of the dog.'"

Howse here chimed in, "Her darling, that's the Major, and the dog is the enemy, ma'am."

He paused, and then went on, in a brisker, more cheerful tone:

"I telegraphed the very first thing to Mr. Allen—that's Major Guthrie's lawyer, ma'am. The Major told me I was to do that, if anything awkward happened. Then it just occurred to me that I would telephone to the Deanery. The Dean was out here yesterday afternoon, ma'am, and Mrs. Guthrie liked him very much. Long ago, when she lived in London, she used to know the parents of the young gentleman to whom Miss Haworth is engaged to be married. They had quite a long pleasant talk about it all. I had meant, ma'am, if you'll excuse my telling you, to telephone to you next, and then I heard as how you were coming here. The Major did tell me the morning he went away that if Mrs. Guthrie seemed really ailing, I was to ask you to be kind enough to come and see her. Of course I knew where he was going, and that he'd be away for a long time, though he didn't say anything to me about it. But he knew that I knew, right enough!"

"Had Mrs. Guthrie no near relation at all—no sister, no nieces?" asked Mrs. Otway, in a low voice. Again she felt she was living in a dreamland of secret, poignant emotions shadowed by a great suspense and fear.

"No. Nothing of the kind," said Howse confidently. "And on Major Guthrie's side there was only distant cousins. It's a peculiar kind of situation altogether, ma'am, if I may say so. Quite a long time may pass before we know whether the Major is alive or dead. 'Wounded and missing'? We all knows as how there is only one thing worse that could be than that—don't we, ma'am?"

"I don't quite know what you mean, Howse."

"Why, the finding and identifying of the Major's body, ma'am."

Through the still, silent house there came a loud, long, insistent ringing—that produced by an old-fashioned front door bell.

"I expect it's Mr. Allen," exclaimed Howse. "He wired as how he'd be down by two o'clock." And a few moments later a tall, dark, clean-shaven man was shaking hands, with the words, "I think you must be Mrs. Otway?"

There was little business doing just then among London solicitors, and so Mr. Allen had come down himself. He had a very friendly regard for his wounded and missing client, and his recollection of the interview which had taken place on the day before Major Guthrie had sailed with the First Division of the Expeditionary Force was still very vivid in his mind.

His client had surprised him very much. He had thought he knew everything about Major Guthrie and Major Guthrie's business, but before receiving the latter's instructions about his new will he had never heard of Mrs. Otway and her daughter. Yet, if Major Guthrie outlived his mother, as it was of course reasonable, even under the circumstances, to suppose that he would do, a considerable sum of money was to pass under his will to Mrs. Otway, and, failing her, to her only child, Rose Otway.

Strange confidences are very often made to lawyers, quite as often as to doctors. But Major Guthrie, when he came to sign his will, the will for which he had sent such precise and detailed instructions a few days before, made no confidences at all.

Even so, the solicitor, putting two and two together, had very little doubt as to the relations of his client and of the lady whom he had made his residuary legatee. He felt sure that there was an understanding between them that either after the war, or after Mrs. Guthrie's death—he could not of course tell which—they intended to make one of those middle-aged marriages which often, strange to say, turn out more happily than earlier marriages are sometimes apt to do.

The lawyer naturally kept his views to himself during the afternoon he spent at Dorycote House, and he simply treated Mrs. Otway as though she had been a near relation of the deceased lady. What, however, increased his belief that his original theory was correct, was the fact that there was no mention of Mrs. Otway's name in Mrs. Guthrie's will. The old lady, like so many women, had preferred to keep her will in her own possession. It had been made many years before, and in it she had left everything to her son, with the exception of a few trinkets which were to be distributed among certain old friends and acquaintances, fully half of whom, it was found on reference to Ponting, had predeceased the testator.

As the hours went on, Mr. Allen could not help wondering if Mrs. Otway was aware of the contents of Major Guthrie's will. He watched her with considerable curiosity. She was certainly attractive, and yes, quite intelligent; but she hardly spoke at all, and there was a kind of numbness in her manner which he found rather trying. She did not once mention Major Guthrie of her own accord. She always left such mention to him. He told himself that doubtless it was this quietude of manner which had attracted his reserved client.

"I suppose," he said at last, "that we must presume that Major Guthrie is alive till we have an official statement to the contrary?" And then he was startled to see the vivid expression of pain, almost of anguish, which quivered over her eyes and mouth. Then she did care, after all.

"Howse tells me," she said slowly, "that Major Guthrie is probably a prisoner. He says, he says——" and then she stopped abruptly—it was as if she could not go on with her sentence, and Mr. Allen exclaimed, "I heard what he said, Mrs. Otway. Of course he is right in stating that an effort is always made to find and bring in the bodies of dead officers. But I fear that this war is not at all like the only war of which Howse has had any first-hand knowledge. This last week has been a very bad business. Still, I quite agree that we must not give up hope. I have been wondering whether you would like me to make inquiries at the War Office, or whether you have any better and quicker—I mean of course by that any private—means of procuring information?"

"No," she said hopelessly; "I have no way of finding out anything. And I should be very grateful indeed, Mr. Allen, if you would do what you can." For the first time she spoke as if she had a direct interest in Major Guthrie's fate. "Perhaps"—she fixed her eyes on him appealingly, and he saw them slowly fill up and brim over with tears—"Perhaps if you *should* hear anything, you would not mind telegraphing to me direct? I think you have my address."

And then, bursting into bitter sobs, she suddenly got up and ran out of the room.

So she did know about Major Guthrie's will. In what other way could he, the man to whom she was speaking, know her address? Mr. Allen also told himself, with some surprise, that he had been mistaken—that Mrs. Otway, after all, was not the quiet, passionless woman he had supposed her to be.

When she reached the Trellis House late that Sunday afternoon, Mrs. Otway was met at the door by Rose, and the girl, with face full of mingled awe and pain, told her that the blow on the Deanery had fallen. Edith Haworth had received the news that Sir Hugh Severn was dead—killed at the head of his men in a great cavalry charge.

CHAPTER XIX

There are times in life when everything is out of focus, when events take on the measure, not of what they really are, but of the mental state of the people affected by them. Such a time had now come to the mistress of the Trellis House. For a while Mrs. Otway saw everything, heard everything, read everything, through a mist of aching pain and of that worst misery of all—the misery of suspense.

The passion of love, so hedged about with curious and unreal conventions, is a strangely protean thing. The dear old proverb, "Absence makes the heart grow fonder," is far truer than those who believe its many cynical counterparts would have us think, and especially is this true of an impulsive and imaginative nature.

It was the sudden, dramatic withdrawal of Major Guthrie from her life which first made the woman he had dumbly loved realise all that his constant, helpful presence had meant to her. And then his worldly old mother's confidences had added just that touch of jealousy which often sharpens love. Lastly, his letter, so simple, so direct, and yet, to one who knew his quiet, reserved nature, so deeply charged with feeling, had brought the first small seed to a blossoming which quickened every pulse of her nature into ardent, sentient life. This woman, who had always been singularly selfless, far more interested in the lives of those about her than in her own, suddenly became self-absorbed.

She looked back with a kind of wonder to her old happy, satisfied, and yes, unawakened life. She had believed herself to be a woman of many friends, and yet there was now not one human being to whom she felt even tempted to tell her wonderful secret.

Busily occupied with the hundred and one trifles, and the eager, generally successful little excursions into philanthropy—for she was an exceptionally kind, warm-hearted woman—which had filled her placid widowhood, she had yet never made any real intimate. The only exception had been Major Guthrie; it was he who had drawn her into what had seemed for so long their pleasant, quiet garden of friendship.

And now she realised that were she to tell any of the people about her of the marvellous change which had taken place in her heart, they would regard her with great surprise, and yes, even with amusement. All the world loves a young lover, but there is not much sympathy to spare in the kind of world to which Mary Otway belonged by birth, position, and long association, for the love which appears, and sometimes only attains full fruition, later in life.

As the days went on, each bringing its tale of exciting and momentous events, there came over Mrs. Otway a curious apathy with regard to the war, for to her the one figure which had counted in the awful drama now being enacted in France and Flanders had disappeared from the vast stage where, as she now recognised, she had seen only him. True, she glanced over a paper each day, but she only sufficiently mastered its contents to be able to reply intelligently to those with whom her daily round brought her in contact.

And soon, to her surprise, and ever-growing discomfort, Anna Bauer— her good, faithful old Anna, for whom she had always had such feelings of affection, and yes, of gratitude—began to get on her nerves. It was not that she associated Anna with the War, and with all that the War had brought to her personally of joy and of grief. Rather was it the sudden perception that her own secret ideals of life and those of the woman near whom she had lived for close on eighteen years, were utterly different, and, in a deep sense, irreconcilable.

Mrs. Otway grew to dislike, with a nervous, sharp distaste, the very sight of Anna's favourite motto, "*Arbeit macht das Leben süss, und die Welt zum Paradies*" ("Work makes life sweet and the world a paradise"). Was it possible that in the old days she had admired that lying sentiment? Lying? Yes, indeed! Work did *not* make life sweet, or she, Mary Otway, would now be happier than ever, for she had never worked as hard as she was now working—working to destroy thought—working to dull the dreadful aching at her heart, throwing herself, with a feverish eagerness which surprised those about her, into the various war activities which were now, largely owing to the intelligence and thoroughness of Miss Forsyth, being organised in Witanbury.

Mrs. Otway also began to hate the other German mottoes which Anna had put all about the Trellis House, especially in those rooms which might be regarded as her own domain—the kitchen, the old nursery, and Rose's bedroom. There was something of the kind embroidered on every single article which would take a *Spruch*, and Anna's mistress sometimes felt as if she would like to make a bonfire of them all!

Every time she went into her kitchen she also longed to tear down, with violent hands, the borders of fine crochet work, the *Kante*, with which each wooden shelf was edged, and of which she had been almost as proud as had been Anna. This crochet work seemed to haunt her, for wherever it could be utilised, Anna, during those long years of willing service, had sewn it proudly on, in narrow edgings and in broad bands.

Not only were all Mrs. Otway's and Rose's under-clothing trimmed with it, but it served as insertion for curtains, ran along the valance of each bed, and edged each pillow and cushion. Anna had worked miles of it since she first came to the Trellis House, for there were balls of crochet work rolled up in all her drawers, and when she was not occupied in doing some form of housework she was either knitting or crocheting. The old German woman never stirred without her little bag, itself gaily embroidered, to hold her *Hand Arbeit*; and very heartily, as Mrs. Otway knew well, did she despise the average Englishwoman for being able to talk without a crochet-hook or a pair of knitting-needles in her hands.

Something—not much, but just a little—of what her mistress was feeling with regard to Major Guthrie gradually reached Anna's perceptions, and made her feel at once uncomfortable, scornful, and angry.

Anna felt the deepest sympathy for her darling nursling, Miss Rose; for it was natural, warming-to-the-heart, that a young girl should feel miserable about a young man. In fact, Rose's lack of interest in marriage and in the domesticities had disturbed and puzzled good old Anna, and to her mind had been a woeful lack in the girl.

So she had welcomed, with great sympathy, the sudden and surprising change. Anna shrewdly suspected the truth, namely, that Rose was Jervis Blake's secret betrothed. She felt sure that something had happened on the morning young Mr. Blake had gone away, during the long half-hour the two young people had spent together. On that morning, immediately after her return home, Rose had gone up to her room, declaring that she had had breakfast—though she, Anna, knew well that the child had only had an early cup of tea....

But if Anna sympathised with and understood the feelings of the younger of her two ladies, she had but scant toleration for Mrs. Otway's restless, ill-concealed unhappiness. Even in the old days Anna had disapproved of Major Guthrie, and she had thought it very strange indeed that he came so often to the Trellis House. To her mind such conduct was unfitting. What on earth could a middle-aged man have to say to the mother of a grown-up daughter?

Of course Anna knew that marriages between such people are sometimes arranged; but to her mind they are always marriages of convenience, and in this case such a marriage would be very inconvenient to everybody, and would thoroughly upset all her, Anna's, pleasant, easy way of life. A widower with children has naturally to find a woman to look after his house; and a poor widow is as a rule only too pleased to meet with some one who will marry her, especially if the some one be better off than herself. But on any betrayal of sentiment between two people past early youth Anna had very scant mercy.

She had also noticed lately, with mingled regret and contempt, that Mrs. Otway now had a few grey threads in her fair, curling hair. If the gracious lady were not careful, she would look quite old and ugly by the time Major Guthrie came back!

At intervals, indeed every few days, Rose received a short, and of course read-by-the-censor letter from Jervis Blake. He had missed the first onrush of the German Army and the Great Retreat, for he had been what they called "in reserve," kept for nearly three full weeks close to the French port where he had landed. Then there came a long, trying silence, till a letter written by his mother to Mrs. Otway revealed the fact that he was at last in the fighting-line, on the river Aisne.

"You have always been so kind to my dear boy that I know you will be interested to learn that lately he has been in one or two very dangerous 'scraps,' as they seem to be called. They are not supposed to tell one anything in their letters, and Jervis as a matter of fact no longer even writes postcards. But my husband knows exactly where he is, and we can but hope and pray, from day to day, that he is safe."

It was on the very day that Mrs. Otway read to Rose this letter from Lady Blake that there arrived at the Trellis House a telegram signed Robert Allen: "Have ascertained that Major Guthrie is alive and prisoner in Germany. Letter follows."

But when the letter came it told tantalisingly little, for it merely conveyed the fact that the name of Major Guthrie had come through in a list of wounded prisoners supplied to the Geneva Red Cross. There was no clue as to where he was, or as to his condition, and Mr. Allen ended with the words: "I am trying to get in touch with the American Embassy in Berlin. I am told that it is the best, in fact the only, medium for getting authentic news of wounded prisoners."

"The gracious lady sees that I was right. Never did I believe the Major to be dead! Officers are always behind their soldiers. They are in the safe place." Such were the words, uttered of course in German, with which Anna greeted the great news.

As Mrs. Otway turned away, and silently left the kitchen, the old woman shook her head with an impatient gesture. Why make all that fuss over the fact that Major Guthrie was a prisoner in Germany? Anna could imagine no happier fate just now than that of being in the Fatherland—even as a prisoner. She could remember the generous way in which the French prisoners, or at least some of them, had been treated in 1870. Why, the then Crown Princess—she who was later known as "the Englishwoman"—had always visited those wards containing the French prisoners first, before she went and saw the German wounded. Anna could remember very clearly the angry remarks which had been provoked by that royal lady's action, as also by her strange notion that the wounded required plenty of fresh air.

Some time ago Anna had seen in an English paper, in fact it had been pointed out to her by Mrs. Otway herself, that the German Government had had to restrain the daughters and wives of the Fatherland from over-kindness to the French.

Still, when all was said and done, good old Anna was genuinely glad that Major Guthrie was safe. It would make her gracious lady more cheerful, and it also provided herself with a little bit of gossip wherewith to secure a warmer welcome from Alfred Head when she went along to supper with him and his Polly this very evening.

"That sort of letter may be very valuable in our business—I know best its worth to me."

The owner of the Witanbury Stores was speaking English, and addressing his pretty wife.

Anna, just arrived, had at once become aware that the atmosphere was electric, that something very like a quarrel was going on between Alfred Head and Polly. Mrs. Head looked very angry, and there was a red spot on each of her delicately tinted cheeks.

Only half the table had been laid for supper under the bright pendant lamp; on the other half were spread out some dirty-looking letters. In each letter a number of lines had been heavily blacked out—on one indeed there was very little left of the original writing.

"It's such rubbish!" Polly said crossly. "Why, by spending a penny each Sunday on *The News of the World* or on *Reynolds's*, you'd see a lot more letters than you've got there, and all nicely printed, too!"

She turned to the visitor: "Alfred can't spare me half a sovereign for something I want really badly, but he can give seven-and-sixpence to a dirty old woman for a sight of all that muck!" Snatching one of the letters off the table, she began reading aloud: "My dear Mum, I hope that this finds you as well as it does me. We are giving it to the Allemans, as they call them out here, right in the neck." She waved the sheet she was reading and exclaimed, "And then comes four lines so scrubbed about that even the Old Gentleman himself couldn't read them! Still, it's for that Alfred here is willing to pay——"

Her husband interrupted her furiously: "Put that down at once! D'you hear, Polly? I'm the best judge of what a thing's worth to me in my business. If I give Mrs. Tippins seven-and-sixpence for her letters, they're worth seven-and-sixpence to me and a bit over. See? I shouldn't 'a thought it was necessary to tell *you* that!"

He turned to Anna, and said rapidly in German: "The man who wrote these letters is a sergeant. He's a very intelligent fellow. As you see, he writes quite long letters, and there are a lot of little things that I find it well worth my while to make a note of. In fact, as I told you before, Frau Bauer, I am willing to pay for the sight of any good long letter from the British Front. I should much like to see some from officers, and I prefer those that are censored—I mean blacked out like these. The military censors so far are simple folk." He laughed, and Anna laughed too, without quite knowing why. "I should have expected that Major whose mother died just after the war broke out, to be writing to your ladies. Has he not done so yet?"

"The news has just come this very day, that he is a prisoner; but they do not yet know where he is imprisoned," said Anna eagerly.

"That is good news," observed her host genially. "In spite of all my efforts, I could never obtain that dratted Major's custom. But do not any of the younger officers write to your young lady, in that strange English way?" and he fixed his prominent eyes on her face, as if he would fain look Anna through and through. "I had hoped that we should be able to do so much business together," he said.

"I have told you of the postcards——" She spoke in an embarrassed tone.

"Ach! Yes. And I did pay you a trifle for a sight of them. But that was really politeness, for, as you know, there was nothing in the postcards of the slightest use to me."

Anna remained silent. She was of course well aware that her young lady often received letters, short, censored letters, from Mr. Jervis Blake. But Rose kept them in some secret place; also nothing would have tempted good old Anna to show one of her darling nursling's love-letters to unsympathetic eyes.

Alfred Head turned to his wife. "Now, Polly," he said conciliatingly, "you asked me for what I am paying." He took up the longest of the letters off the table. "See here, my dear. This man gives a list of what he would like his mother to send him every ten days. As a matter of fact that is how I first knew Mrs. Tippins had these letters. She brought one along to show me, to see if I could get her something special. Part of the letter has been blacked out, but of course I found it very easy to take that blacking out," he chuckled. "And what had been blacked out was as a matter of fact very useful to me!"

Seeing that his wife still looked very angry and lowering, he took a big five-shilling piece out of his pocket and threw it across at her. "There!" he cried good-naturedly—"catch! Perhaps I will make it up to the ten shillings in a day or two—if, thanks to these letters, I am able to do a good stroke of business!"

Anna looked at him with fascinated eyes. The man seemed made of money. He was always jingling silver in his pocket. Gold was rather scarce just then in Witanbury, but whenever Anna saw a half-sovereign, she always managed somehow to get hold of it. In fact she kept a store of silver and of paper money for that purpose, for she knew that Mr. Head, as he was now universally called, would give her threepence over its face value if it was ten shillings, and fivepence if it was a sovereign. She had already made several shillings in this very easy way.

As she walked home, after having enjoyed a frugal supper, she told herself that it was indeed unfortunate that Major Guthrie was wounded and missing. Had he still been with his regiment, he would certainly have written to Mrs. Otway frequently. Anna, in the past, had occasionally found long letters from him torn up in the waste-paper basket, and she had also seen, in the days that now seemed so long ago, letters in the same hand lying about on Mrs. Otway's writing-table.

CHAPTER XX

October and November wore themselves away, and the days went by, the one very like the other. Mrs. Otway, after her long hours of work, or of official visiting among the soldiers' and sailors' wives and mothers, fell into the way of going out late in the afternoon for a walk by herself. She had grown to dread with a nervous dislike the constant meeting with acquaintances and neighbours, the usual rather futile exchange of remarks about the War, or about the local forms of war and charitable work in which she and they were now all engaged. The stillness and the solitariness of the evening walk soothed her sore and burdened heart.

Often she would walk to Dorycote and back, feeling that the darkened streets—for Witanbury had followed the example of London—and, even more, the country roads beyond, were haunted, in a peaceful sense, by the presence of the man who had so often taken that same way from his house to hers.

It was during one of these evening walks that there came to her a gleam of hope and light, and from a source from which she would never have expected it to come.

She was walking swiftly along on her way home, going across the edge of the Market Square, when she heard herself eagerly hailed with "Is it Mrs. Otway?" She stopped, and answered, not very graciously, "Yes, I'm Mrs. Otway—who is it?"

There came a bubble of laughter, and she knew that this was a very old acquaintance indeed, a Mrs. Riddick, whom she had not seen for some time.

"I don't wonder you didn't know me! It's impossible to see anything by this light. I've been having such an adventure! I only came back from Holland yesterday. I went to meet a young niece of mine there—you know, the girl who was in Germany so long."

"In Germany?" Mrs. Otway turned round eagerly. "Is she with you now? How I should like to see her!"

"I'm afraid you can't do that. She's gone to Scotland. I sent her off there last night. Her parents have been nearly frantic about her!"

"Did she see—did she hear anything of the English prisoners while she was in Germany?" Mrs. Otway's voice sounded strangely pleading in the darkness, and the other felt a little surprised.

"Oh, no! She was virtually a prisoner herself. But I hear a good deal of information is coming through—I mean unofficial information about our prisoners. My sister—you know, Mrs. Vereker—is working at that place they've opened in London to help people whose friends are prisoners in Germany. She says they sometimes obtain wonderful results. They work in with the Geneva Red Cross, and from what I can make out, it's really better to go there than to write to the Foreign Office. I went and saw my sister yesterday, when I was coming through London. I was really most interested in all she told me—such pathetic, strange stories, such heart-breaking episodes, and then now and again something so splendid and happy! A girl came to them a fortnight ago in dreadful trouble, every one round her saying her lover had been killed at Mons, though she herself hoped against hope. Well, only yesterday morning they were able to wire to her that he was safe and well, being kindly treated too, in a fortress, far away, close to the borders of Prussia and Poland! Wasn't that splendid?"

"What is the address of the place," asked Mrs. Otway in a low tone, "where Mrs. Vereker works?"

"It's in Arlington Street—No. 20, I think."

Mrs. Otway hastened on, her heart filled with a new, eager hope. Oh, if she could only go up now, this evening, to London! Then she might be at 20, Arlington Street, the first thing in the morning.

Alas, she knew that this was not possible; every hour of the next morning was filled up.

There was no one to whom she could delegate her morning round among those soldiers' mothers and wives with whom she now felt in such close touch and sympathy. But she might possibly escape the afternoon committee meeting, at which she was due, if Miss Forsyth would only let her off. The ladies of Witanbury were very much under the bondage of Miss Forsyth, and subject to her will; none more so than the good-tempered, yielding Mary Otway.

Unluckily one of those absurd little difficulties which are always cropping up at committees was on the agenda for to-morrow afternoon, and Miss Forsyth was counting on her help to quell a certain troublesome person. Still, she might go now, on her way home, and see if Miss Forsyth would relent.

Miss Forsyth lived in a beautiful old house which, though its approach was in a narrow street, yet directly overlooked at the back the great green lawns surrounding the cathedral.

The house had been left to her many years ago, but she had never done anything to it. Unaffected by the many artistic and other crazes which had swept over the country since then, it remained a strange mixture of beauty and ugliness. Miss Forsyth loved the beauty of her house, and she put up with what ugliness there was because of the major part of her income, which was not very large, had to be spent, according to her theory of life, on those less fortunate than herself.

At the present moment all her best rooms, those rooms which overlooked her beloved cathedral, had been given up by her to a rather fretful-natured and very dissatisfied Belgian family, and so she had taken up her quarters on the darker and colder side of her house, that which overlooked the street.

It was there, in a severe-looking study on the ground floor, that Mrs. Otway found her this evening.

As her visitor was ushered in by the cross-looking old servant who was popularly supposed to be the only person of whom Miss Forsyth stood in fear, she got up and came forward, a very kindly, welcoming look on her plain face.

"Well, Mary," she said, "what's the matter now? Mrs. Purlock drunk again, eh?"

"Well, yes—as a matter of fact the poor woman was quite drunk this morning! But I've really come to know if you can spare me to-morrow afternoon. I want to go to London on business. I was also wondering if you know of any nice quiet hotel or lodging near Piccadilly—I should prefer a lodging—where I could spent two nights?"

"Near Piccadilly? Yes, of course I do—in Half-Moon Street. I'll engage two rooms for you. And as for to-morrow, I can spare you quite well. In fact I shall probably manage better alone. Can't you go up by that nice early morning train, my dear?"

Mrs. Otway shook her head. "No, I can't possibly get away before the afternoon. You see I must look after Mrs. Purlock. She got into rather bad trouble this morning. And oh, Miss Forsyth, I'm so *sorry* for her! She believes her two boys are being starved to death in Germany. Unfortunately she knows that woman whose husband signed his letter 'Your loving Jack Starving.' It's thoroughly upset Mrs. Purlock, and if, as they all say, drink drowns thought and makes one feel happy, can we wonder at all the drinking that goes on just now? But I'm going to try to-morrow morning to arrange for her to go away to a sister—a very sensible, nice woman she seems, who certainly won't let her do anything of the sort."

"Surely you're rather inconsistent?" said Miss Forsyth briskly. "You spoke only a minute ago as if you almost approved of drunkenness," but there was an intelligent twinkle in her eye.

Mrs. Otway smiled, but it was a very sad smile. "You know quite well, dear Miss Forsyth, that I didn't mean *that*! Of course I don't approve, I only meant that—that I understand." She waited a moment, and then added, quietly, and with a little sigh, "So you see I can't go up to town to-morrow morning. What I want to do there will wait quite well till the afternoon."

Miss Forsyth accompanied her visitor into the hall—the old eighteenth-century hall which was so exquisitely proportioned, but the walls of which were covered with the monstrously ugly mid-Victorian marble paper she much disliked, but never felt she could afford to change as long as it still looked so irritatingly "good" and clean. She opened the front door on to the empty, darkened street; and then, to Mrs. Otway's great surprise, she suddenly bent forward and kissed her warmly.

"Well, my dear," she exclaimed, "I'm glad to have seen you even for a moment, and I hope your business, whatever it be, will be successful. I want to tell you something, here and now, which I've never said to you yet, long as we've known one another!"

"Yes, Miss Forsyth?" Mrs. Otway looked up surprised—perhaps a little apprehensive as to what was coming.

"I want to tell you, Mary, that to my mind you belong to the very small number of people, of my acquaintance at any rate, who shall see God."

Mrs. Otway was startled and touched by the other's words, and yet, "I don't quite know what you mean?" she faltered—and she really didn't.

"Don't you?" said Miss Forsyth drily. "Well, I think Mrs. Purlock, and a good many other unhappy women in Witanbury, could tell you."

Late in the next afternoon, after leaving the little luggage she had brought with her at the old-fashioned lodgings where she found that Miss Forsyth had made careful arrangements for her comfort, even to ordering what she should have for dinner, Mrs. Otway made her way, on foot, into Piccadilly, and thence into quiet Arlington Street.

There it was very dark—too dark to see the numbers on the doors of the great houses which loomed up to her right.

Bewildered and oppressed, she touched a passer-by on the arm. "Could you tell me," she said, "which is No. 20?" And he, with the curious inability of the average Londoner to tell the truth or to acknowledge ignorance in such a case, at once promptly answered, "Yes, miss. It's that big house standing back here, in the courtyard."

She walked through the gate nearest to her, and so up to a portico. Then, after waiting for a moment, she rang the bell.

The moments slipped by. She waited full five minutes, and then rang again. At last the door opened.

"Is this the place," she said falteringly, "where one can make inquiries as to the prisoners of war in Germany?" And the person who opened the door replied curtly, "No, it's next door to the right. A lot of people makes that mistake. Luckily the family are away just now—or it would be even a greater botheration than it is!"

Sick at heart, she turned and walked around the paved courtyard till she reached the street. Then she turned to her right. A door flush on the street was hospitably open, throwing out bright shafts of light into the darkness. Could it be—she hoped it was—here?

For a moment she stood hesitating in the threshold. The large hall was brilliantly lit up, and at a table there sat a happy-faced, busy-looking little Boy Scout. He, surely, would not repulse her? Gathering courage she walked up to him.

"Is this the place," she asked, "where one makes inquiries about prisoners of war?"

He jumped up and saluted. "Yes, madam," he said civilly. "You've only got to go up those stairs and then round the top, straight along. There are plenty of ladies up there to show you the way."

As she walked towards the great staircase, and as her eyes fell on a large panoramic oil painting of a review held in a historic English park a hundred years before, she remembered that it was here, in this very house, that she had come to a great political reception more than twenty years ago—in fact just after her return from Germany. She had been taken to it by James Hayley's parents, and she, the happy, eager girl, had enjoyed every moment of what she had heard with indignant surprise some one describe as a boring function.

As she began walking up the staircase, there rose before her a vision of what had been to her so delightful and brilliant a scene—the women in evening dress and splendid jewels; the men, many of them in uniform or court dress; all talking and smiling to one another as they slowly made their way up the wide, easy steps.

She remembered with what curiosity and admiration she had looked at the figure of her host. There he had stood, a commanding, powerful, slightly stooping figure, welcoming his guests. For a moment she had looked up into his bearded face, and met his heavy-lidded eyes resting on her bright young face, with a half-smile of indulgent amusement at her look of radiant interest and happiness.

This vivid recollection of that long-forgotten Victorian "crush" had a good effect on Mary Otway. It calmed her nervous tremor, and made her feel, in a curious sense, at home in that great London house.

Running round the top of the staircase was a narrow way where girls sitting at typewriters were busily working. But they had all kind, intelligent faces, and they all seemed anxious to help and speed her on her way.

"Mrs. Vereker? Oh yes, you'll find her at once if you go along that gallery and open the door at the end."

She walked through into a vast room where a domed and painted ceiling now looked down on a very curious scene. With the exception of some large straight settees, all the furniture which had once been in this great reception-room had been cleared away. In its place were large office tables, plain wooden chairs, and wire baskets piled high with letters and memoranda. The dozen or so people there were all intent on work of some sort, and though now and again some one got up and walked across to ask a question of a colleague, there was very little coming or going. Personal inquirers generally came early in the day.

As she stood just inside the door, Mary Otway knew that it was here, twenty years ago, that she had seen the principal guests gathered together. She recalled the intense interest, the awe, the sympathy with which she had looked at one figure in that vanished throng. It had been the figure of a woman dressed in the deep mourning of a German widow, the severity of the costume lightened only by the beautiful Orders pinned on the breast.

At the time she, the girl of that far-off day, had only just come back from Germany, and the Imperial tragedy, which had as central figure one so noble and so selfless, had moved her eager young heart very deeply. She remembered how hurt she had felt at hearing her cousin mutter to his wife, "I'm sorry she is here. She oughtn't to have come to this kind of thing. Royalties, especially foreign Royalties, should have no politics." And with what satisfaction she had heard Mrs. Hayley's spirited rejoinder: "What nonsense! She hasn't come because it's political, but because it's English. She loves England, and everything to do with England!"

The vision faded, and she walked forward into the strangely changed room.

"Can I speak to Mrs. Vereker?" she asked, timidly addressing one of the ladies nearest the door. Yet it was with unacknowledged relief that she received the answer: "I'm so sorry, but Mrs. Vereker isn't here. She left early this afternoon. Is there anything I can do for you? Do you want to make inquiries about a prisoner?"

And then, as Mrs. Otway said, "Yes," the speaker went on quickly, "I think I shall do just as well if you will kindly give me the particulars. Let us come over here and sit down; then we shan't be disturbed."

Mrs. Otway looked up gratefully into the kind face of the woman speaking to her. It was a comfort to know that she was going to tell her private concerns to a stranger, and not to the sister of an acquaintance living at Witanbury.

The few meagre facts were soon told, and then she gave her own name and address as the person to whom the particulars, if any came through, were to be forwarded.

"I'll see that the inquiries are sent on to Geneva to-night. But you mustn't be disappointed if you get no news for a while. Sometimes news is a very long time coming through, especially if the prisoner was wounded, and is still in hospital." The stranger added, with real sympathy in her voice, "I'm afraid you're very anxious, Mrs. Otway. I suppose Major Guthrie is your brother?"

And then the other answered quietly, "No, he's not my brother. Major Guthrie and I are engaged to be married."

The kind, sweet face, itself a sad and anxious face, changed a little—it became even fuller of sympathy than it had been before. "You must try and keep up courage," she exclaimed. "And remember one thing—if Major Guthrie was really severely wounded, he's probably being very well looked after." She waited a moment, and then went on, "In any case, you haven't the anguish of knowing that he's in perpetual danger; my boy is out there, so I know what it feels like to realize that."

There was a moment of silence, and then, "I wonder," said Mrs. Otway, "if you would mind having the inquiries telegraphed to-night?" She opened her bag. "I brought a five-pound note——"

But the other shook her head. "Oh, no. You needn't pay anything," she said. "We're always quite willing to telegraph if there's any good reason for doing so. But you know it's very important that the name should be correctly spelt, and the particulars rightly transmitted. That's why it's really better to write. But of course I'll ask them to telegraph to you at once if they get any news here on a day or at a time I happen to be away."

Together they walked to the door of the great room, and the woman whose name she was not to know for a long time, and who was the first human being to whom she had told her secret, pressed her hand warmly.

Quietly Mrs. Otway walked through into the gallery, and then she burst out crying like a child. It was with her handkerchief pressed to her face that she walked down the gallery, and so round to the great staircase. No one looked at her as she passed so woefully by; they were all only too well used to such sights. But before she reached the front door she managed to pull herself together, and was able to give the jolly little Boy Scout a friendly farewell nod.

CHAPTER XXI

Early that afternoon, after her mother had left the Trellis House, Rose went upstairs to her own room. She had been working very hard all that morning, helping to give some last touches of prettiness and comfort to the fine, airy rooms at "Robey's," which had now been transformed into Sir Jacques Robey's Red Cross Hospital. As a matter of fact, everything had been ready for the wounded who, after having been awaited with anxious impatience for weeks, were now announced as being due to arrive to-morrow.

Meanwhile Anna, her hands idle for once, sat at her kitchen table. She was wearing her best black silk apron, and open in front of her was her *Gesangbuch*, or hymnbook.

Thus was Anna celebrating the anniversary of her husband's death. Gustav Bauer had been a very unsatisfactory helpmeet, but his widow only chose to remember now the little in him that had been good.

Calmly she began reading the contents of her hymnbook to herself. All the verses were printed as if in prose, which of course made it easier as well as pleasanter to read.

As she spoke the words to herself, her eyes filled with tears, and she longed, with an intense, wordless longing, to be in the Fatherland, especially now, during this strange and terrible time. She keenly resented not being able to write to her niece, Minna, in Berlin. Since her happy visit there three years before, that little household had been very near her heart, nearer far than that of her own daughter, Louisa. But Louisa was now to all intents and purposes an Englishwoman.

It was too true that the many years she had been in England had not made good old Anna think better of English people, and, as was natural, her prejudices had lately become much intensified. She lived in a chronic state of wonder over the laziness, the thriftlessness, and the dirt of Englishwomen. She had described those among whom she dwelt to her niece Minna in the following words: "They wash themselves from head to foot each day, but more never. Their houses are dreadful, and linen have they not!"

Those words had represented her exact opinion three years ago, and she had had no reason to change it since.

On this dull, sad, November afternoon she suddenly remembered the delightful *Ausflug*, or "fly out," as it is so happily called, when she had accompanied Willi and his Minna to Wannsee, on the blue Havel.

How happy they had all been that day! The little party had brought their own coffee and sugar, but they had had many a delicious glass of beer as well. All had been joy and merriment.

It was bitter to know that some people heard from Germany even now. There was little doubt in her mind that Manfred Hegner, or rather Alfred Head, as she was learning to call him at his very particular request, was in communication with the Fatherland. He had as good as said so the last time she had seen him; adding the unnecessary warning that she must be careful not to tell any one so in Witanbury, as it might do him harm.

Anna was naturally a prudent woman, and she had become quite proud of Alfred Head's friendship and confidence. She much enjoyed the evenings she now so often spent in the stuffy little parlour behind the large, airy shop. Somehow she always left there feeling happy and cheerful. The news that he gave her of the Fatherland, and of what was happening on the various fighting fronts, was invariably glorious and comforting. He smiled with good-natured contempt at the "Kitcheners" who were beginning to flood the old cathedral city with an ever-growing tide of khaki, and who brought him and all his fellow-tradesmen in Witanbury such increased prosperity.

"Fine cannon-fodder!" Mr. Head would exclaim, of course in German. "But no good without the rifles, the ammunition, and above all the guns, which I hear they have not!"

Every one was still very kind to Anna, and her ladies' friends made no difference in their manner—in fact they were perhaps a shade more cordial and kindly. Nevertheless the old woman realised that feeling towards Germany and the Germans had undergone a surprising change during the last few weeks. No, it was not the War—not even the fact that so many Englishmen had already been killed by German guns and shells. The change was owing—amazing and almost incredible fact—to the behaviour of the German Army in Belgium!

Anna hated Belgium and the Belgians. She could not forget how unhappy and ill-used she had been in Ostend; and yet now English people of all classes hailed the Belgians as heroes, and were treating them as honoured guests! She, Anna, knew that the women of Belgium had put out the eyes of wounded German soldiers; she had read the fact in one of the German newspapers Mr. Head had managed to smuggle through. The paper had said, very truly, as she thought, that no punishment for such conduct could be too severe.

And as she sat there, on this melancholy anniversary afternoon, thinking sad, bitter thoughts, her dear young lady opened the door.

"I had a letter from Mr. Blake this morning, and I think you'll like to read it, Anna! He speaks in it so kindly of some German soldiers who gave themselves up. I haven't time to stop and read it to you now. But I think you can read it, for he writes very, very clearly. This is where it begins——" she pointed half-way down the first sheet. "I shan't be back till eight o'clock. There's a great deal to do if, as Sir Jacques believes, some wounded are really likely to arrive to-morrow." Her face shadowed, and that of the old woman looking fondly up at her, softened.

"There's a little piece of beautiful cold mutton," exclaimed Anna in German. "Would my darling child like that for her supper—with a nice little potato salad as well?"

But Rose shook her head. "No, I don't feel as if I want any meat. I'll have anything else there is, and some fruit."

A moment later she was gone, and Anna turned to the closely-written sheets of paper with great interest. She read English writing with difficulty, but, as her beloved young lady had said truly, Mr. Blake's handwriting was very clear. And this is what she spelled out:

"A great big motor lorry came up, full of prisoners, and our fellows soon crowded round it. They were fine, upstanding, fair men, and looked very tired and depressed—as well they might, for we hear they've had hardly anything to eat this last week! I offered one of them, who had his arm bound up, a cigarette. He took it rather eagerly. I thought I'd smoke one too, to put him at his ease, but I had no matches, so the poor chap hooked out some from his pocket and offered me one. This is a funny world, Rose! Fancy those thirteen German prisoners in that motor lorry, and that they were once—in fact only an hour or so ago—doing their best to kill us, while now we are doing our best to cheer them up. Then to-morrow we shall go out and have a good try at killing their comrades. Mind you, they look quite ordinary people. Not one of them has a terrible or a brutal face. They look just like our men— in fact rather less soldierly than our men; the sort of chaps you might see walking along a street in Witanbury any day. One of them looked so rosy and sunburnt, so *English*, that we mentioned it to the interpreter. He translated it to the man, and I couldn't help being amused to see that he looked rather sick at being told he looked like an Englishman. Another man, who I'm bound to say did not look English at all, had actually lived sixteen years in London, and he talked in quite a Cockney way."

Anna read on:

"I have at last got into a very comfortable billet. As a matter of fact it's a pill factory belonging to an eccentric old man called Puteau. All over the house, inside and out, he has had painted two huge P's, signifying *Pilules Puteau*. For a long time no use was made of the building, as it was thought too good a mark. But for some reason or other the Boches have left it alone. Be that as it may, one of our fellows discovered a very easy way of reaching it from the back, and now no one could tell the place is occupied, in fact packed, with our fellows. The best point about it is that there is a huge sink, as large as a bath. You can imagine what a comfort — —"

And then the letter broke off. Rose had only left that part of it she thought would interest her old nurse. The beginning and the end were not there.

Anna looked at the sheets of closely-written paper in front of her consideringly. There was not a word about food or kit—not a word, that is, which by any stretch of the imagination could be of any use to a man like Mr. Head in his business. On the other hand, there was not a word in the letter which Miss Rose could dislike any one reading. The old woman was shrewd enough to know that. She would like Mr. Head to see that letter, for it would prove to him that her ladies did receive letters from officers. And the next one might after all contain something useful.

She looked up at the kitchen clock. It was now four o'clock. And then a sudden thought made up good old Anna's mind for her.

Miss Rose had said she did not want any meat for her supper; but she was fond of macaroni cheese. Anna would never have thought of making that dish with any cheese but Parmesan, and she had no Parmesan left in the house. That fact gave her an excellent excuse for going off now to the Stores, and taking Mr. Blake's letter with her. If she got an opportunity of showing it, it would make clear to Mr. Head what a good fellow was Miss Rose's betrothed, and what a kind heart he had.

And so, but for Rose's remark as to her distaste for meat, Jervis Blake's letter would not have been taken by old Anna out of the Trellis House, for it was the lack of Parmesan cheese in the store cupboard which finally decided the matter.

After putting on her green velvet bonnet and her thick, warm brown jacket, she folded up the sheets of French notepaper and put them in an inside pocket.

The fact that it was early closing day did not disturb Anna, for though most of the Witanbury tradespeople were so ungracious that when their shops were shut they would never put themselves out to oblige an old customer, the owner of the Stores, if he was in—and he nearly always did stay indoors on early closing day—was always willing to go into the closed shop and get anything that was wanted. He was not one to turn good custom away.

The back door was opened by Alfred Head himself. "Ah, Frau Bauer! Come into the passage." He spoke in German, but in spite of his cordial words she felt the lack of welcome in his voice. "Is there anything I can do for you?"

"Yes," she said. "I want half a pound of Parmesan cheese, and you might also give me a pound of butter."

"Oh, certainly. Come through into the shop." He turned on the light. "I do not ask you into the parlour, for the simple reason that I have some one there who has come to see me on business—it is business about one of my little mortgages. Polly is out, up at the Deanery. Her sister is not going to stay on there; she has found some excuse to go away. It makes her so sad and mopish to be always with Miss Haworth. Even now, after all this time, the young lady will hardly speak at all. She does not glory in her loss, as a German betrothed would do!"

"Poor thing!" said old Anna feelingly. "Women are not like men, Herr Hegner. They have tender hearts. She thinks of her dead lover as her beloved one—not as a hero. For my part, my heart aches for the dear young lady, when I see her walking about, all dressed in black."

They were now standing in the big empty shop. Alfred Head turned to the right and took off a generous half-pound from the Parmesan cheese which, as Anna knew well, was of a very much better quality, if of rather higher price, than were any of the other Parmesan cheeses sold in Witanbury. But she was rather shocked to note that the butter had not been put away in the refrigerator. That, of course, was Mrs. Head's fault. A German housewife would have seen to that. There the butter lay, ready for the next morning's sale, put up in half-pounds and pounds. Mr. Head took up one of the pounds, and deftly began making a neat parcel of the cheese and of the butter. She felt that he was in a hurry to get rid of her, and yet she was burning to show him young Mr. Blake's letter.

She coughed, and then, a little nervously, she observed: "You were saying some days ago that you would like to see some officers' letters from the Front. That being so, I have brought part of a letter from Mr. Jervis Blake to show you. There is nothing in it concerning food or kit, but still it is very long, and shows that the young man is a good fellow. If you are busy, however, it may not be worth your while to look at it now."

Alfred Head stopped in what he was doing. "Could you leave it with me?" he asked.

Anna shook her head. "No, that I cannot do. My young lady left it for me to read, and though she said she would not be back till eight, she might run in any moment, for she is only over at Robey's, helping with the hospital. They are expecting some wounded to-morrow. They have waited long enough, poor ladies!"

The old woman was standing just under the electric light; there was an anxious, embarrassed look on her face.

The man opposite to her hesitated a moment, then he said quickly, "Very well, show it me! It will not take a moment. I will tell you at once if it is of any use. Perhaps it will be."

She fumbled a moment in her inside pocket, and brought out Jervis Blake's letter.

He took up the sheets, and put them close to his prominent eyes. Quickly he glanced through the account of the German prisoners, and then he began to read more slowly. "Wait you here one moment," he said at last. "I will go and tell my visitor that I am engaged for another minute or two. Then I will come back to you, and read the letter through properly, though the writer is but a silly fellow!"

Still holding the letter in his hand, he hurried away.

Anna was in no hurry. But even so, she began to grow a little fidgety when the moment of which he had spoken grew into something like five minutes. She felt sorry she had brought her dear child's letter. — "*Dummer Kerl*" indeed! Mr. Jervis Blake was nothing of the sort — he was a very kind, sensible young fellow! She was glad when at last she heard Mr. Head's quick, active steps coming down the short passage.

"Here!" he exclaimed, coming towards her. "Here is the letter, Frau Bauer! And though it is true that there is nothing in it of any value to me, yet I recognise your good intention. The next time there may be something excellent. I therefore give you a florin, with best thanks for having brought it. Instead of all that gossip concerning our poor prisoners, it would have been better if he had said what it was that he liked to eat as a relish to the bully beef on which, it seems, the British are universally fed."

Anna's point of view changed with lightning quickness. What a good thing she had brought the letter! Two shillings was two shillings, after all.

"Thanks many," she said gratefully, as he hurried her along the passage and unlocked the back door. But, as so often happens, it was a case of more haste less speed—the door slammed-to before the visitor could slip out, and at the same moment that of the parlour opened, and Anna, to her great surprise, heard the words, uttered in German, "Look here, Hegner! I really can't stay any longer. You forget that I've a long way to go." She could not see the speaker, though she did her best to do so, as her host thrust her, with small ceremony, out of the now reopened door.

Anna felt consumed with curiosity. She crossed over the little street, and hid herself in the shadow of a passage leading to a mews. There she waited, determined to see Alfred Head's mysterious visitor.

She had not time to feel cold before the door through which she had lately been pushed so quickly opened again, letting out a short, thin man, dressed in a comfortable motoring coat. She heard very plainly the good-nights exchanged in a low voice.

As soon as the door shut behind him, the prosperous-looking stranger began walking quickly along. Anna, at a safe distance, followed him. He turned down a side street, where, drawn up before a house inscribed "to let," stood a small, low motor-car. In it sat a Boy Scout. She knew he was a Boy Scout by his hat, for the lad's uniform was covered by a big cape.

She walked quietly on, and so passed the car. As she went by, she heard Hegner's friend say in a kindly voice, and in excellent English, albeit there was a twang in it, "I hope you've not been cold, my boy. My business took a little longer than I thought it would." And the shrill, piping answer, "Oh no, sir! I have been quite all right, sir!" And then the motor gave a kind of snort, and off they went, at a sharp pace, towards the Southampton road.

Anna smiled to herself. Manfred Hegner was a very secretive person—she had always known that. But why tell her such a silly lie? Hegner was getting quite a big business man; he had many irons in the fire—some one had once observed to Anna that he would probably end by becoming a millionaire. It is always well to be in with such lucky folk.

As she opened the gate of the Trellis House, she saw that her mistress's sitting-room was lit up, and before she could put the key in the lock of the front door, it opened, and Rose exclaimed in an anxious tone, "Oh, Anna! Where have you been? Where is my letter? I looked all over the kitchen, but I couldn't find it."

Old Anna smilingly drew it out from the inside pocket of her jacket. "There, there!" she said soothingly. "Here it is, dearest child. I thought it safer to take it along with me than to leave it in the house."

"Oh, thank you—yes, that was quite right!" the girl looked greatly relieved. "Mr. Robey said he would very much like to read it, so I came back for it. And Anna?"

"Yes, my gracious miss."

"I am going to stay there to supper after all. Mr. and Mrs. Robey, and even Sir Jacques, seem anxious that I should do so."

"And I have gone out and got you such a nice supper," said the old woman regretfully.

"I'll have it for lunch to-morrow!" Rose looked very happy and excited. There was a bright colour in her cheeks. "Mr. Robey thinks that Mr. Blake will soon be getting ninety hours' leave." Her heart was so full of joy she felt she must tell the delightful news.

"That is good—very good!" said Anna cordially. "And then, my darling little one, there will be a proper betrothal, will there not?"

Rose nodded. "Yes, I suppose there will," she said in German.

"And perhaps a war wedding," went on Anna, her face beaming. "There are many such just now in Witanbury. In my country they began the first day of the War."

"I know." Rose smiled. "One of the Kaiser's sons was married in that way. Don't you remember my bringing you an account of it, Anna?" She did not wait for an answer. "Well, I must hurry back now."

The old woman went off into her kitchen, and so through the scullery into her cosy bedroom.

The walls of that quaint, low-roofed apartment were gay with oleographs, several being scenes from *Faust,* and one, which Anna had had given to her nearly forty years ago, showed the immortal Charlotte, still cutting bread and butter.

On the dressing-table, one at each end, were a pair of white china busts of Bismarck and von Moltke. Anna had brought these back from Berlin three years before. Of late she had sometimes wondered whether it would be well to put them away in one of the three large, roomy cupboards built into the wall behind her bed. One of these cupboards already contained several securely packed parcels which, as had been particularly impressed on Anna, must on no account be disturbed, but there was plenty of room in the two others. Still, no one ever came into her oddly situated bedroom, and so she left her heroes where they were.

After taking off her things, she extracted the two-shilling piece out of the pocket where it had lain loosely, and added it to the growing store of silver in the old-fashioned tin box where she kept her money. Then she put on her apron and hurried out, with the cheese and the butter in her hands, to the beautifully arranged, exquisitely clean meat safe, which had been cleverly fixed to one of the windows of the scullery soon after her arrival at the Trellis House.

The next morning Mrs. Otway came home, and within an hour of her arrival the mother and daughter had told one another their respective secrets. The revelation came about as such things have a way of coming about when two people, while caring deeply for one another, are yet for the moment out of touch with each other's deepest feelings. It came about, that is to say, by a chance word uttered in entire ignorance of the real state of the case.

Rose, on hearing of her mother's expedition to Arlington Street, had shown surprise, even a little vexation: "You've gone and tired yourself out for nothing—a letter would have done quite as well!"

And, as her mother made no answer, the girl, seeing as if for the first time how sad, how worn, that same dear mother's face now looked, came close up to her and whispered, "I think, mother—forgive me if I'm wrong—that you care for Major Guthrie as I care for Jervis Blake."

CHAPTER XXII

The days that followed Mrs. Otway's journey to London, the easy earning by good old Anna of a florin for Alfred Head's brief sight of Jervis Blake's letter, and the exchange of confidences between the mother and daughter, were comparatively happy, peaceful days at the Trellis House.

Her visit to 20, Arlington Street, had greatly soothed and comforted Mrs. Otway. She felt sure somehow that those kind, capable people, and especially the unknown woman who had been so very good and—and so very understanding, would soon send her the tidings for which she longed. For the first time, too, since she had received Major Guthrie's letter she forgot herself, and in a measure even the man she loved, in thought for another. Rose's confession had moved her greatly, stirred all that was maternal in her heart. But she was far more surprised than she would have cared to admit, for she had always thought that Rose, if she married at all, would marry a man considerably older than herself. With a smile and a sigh, she told herself that the child must be in love with love!

Jervis and the girl were both still so very young—though Rose was in a sense much the older of the two, or so the mother thought. She was secretly glad that there could be no talk of marriage till the end of the War. Even then they would probably have to wait two or three years. True, General Blake was a wealthy man, but Jervis was entirely dependent on his father, and his father might not like him to marry yet.

The fact that Rose had told her mother of her engagement had had another happy effect. It had restored, in a measure, the good relations between Mrs. Otway and her faithful old servant, Anna Bauer. Anna kept to herself the fact that she had guessed the great news long before it had become known to the mother, and so she and her mistress rejoiced together in the beloved child's happiness.

And Rose was happy too—far happier than she had yet been since the beginning of the War. Twice in recent letters to her Jervis had written, "I wish you would allow me to tell my people—you know what!" and now she was very, very glad to release him from secrecy. She was too modest to suppose that General and Lady Blake would be pleased with the news of their only son's engagement. But she felt it their due that they should know how matters stood betwixt her and Jervis. If they did not wish him to marry soon, she and Jervis, so she assured herself, would be quite content to wait.

Towards the end of that peaceful week there came quite an affectionate telegram from Lady Blake, explaining that the great news had been sent to her and to her husband by their son. The telegram was followed by a long loving letter from the mother, inviting Rose to stay with them.

Mrs. Otway would not acknowledge even to herself how relieved she felt. She had been afraid that General Blake would regard his son's engagement as absurd, and she was surprised, knowing him slightly and not much liking what little she knew of him, at the kindness and warmth with which he wrote to her.

"Under ordinary circumstances I should not have approved of my son's making so early a marriage, but everything is now changed. And though I suppose it would not be reasonable to expect such a thing, I should be, for my part, quite content were they to be married during the leave to which I understand he will shortly be entitled."

But on reading these words, Mrs. Otway had shaken her head very decidedly. What an odd, *very* odd, man General Blake must be! She felt sure that neither Jervis nor Rose would think of doing such a thing. It was, however, quite natural that Jervis's parents should wish to have Rose on a visit; and of course Rose must go soon, and try to make good friends with them both—not an over-easy matter, for they were very different and, as Mrs. Otway knew, not on really happy terms the one with the other.

There was some little discussion as to who in Witanbury should be told of Rose's engagement. It seemed hopeless to keep the affair a secret. For one thing, the officials at the Post Office knew—they had almost shown it by their funny, smiling manner when Rose had gone in to send her answer to Lady Blake's telegram. But the first to be informed officially, so to speak, must of course be the Dean and the Robeys.

Dr. Haworth had aged sadly during the last few weeks. Edith was going to nurse in a French hospital, and she and her mother had gone away for a little change first. And so, as was natural, the Dean came very often to the Trellis House; and though, when he was told of Rose's engagement, he sighed wearily, still he was most kind and sympathetic—though he could not help saying, in an aside to Mrs. Otway, "I should never have thought Rose would become the heroine of a Romeo and Juliet affair! They both seem to me so very young. Luckily there's no hurry. It looks as if this war was going to be a long, long war— —" and he had shaken his head very mournfully.

Poor Dr. Haworth! An imprudent passage uttered in the first sermon he had delivered after the declaration of war had been dragged out of its context, and had figured, weeks later, in the London papers. As a result he had had many cruel anonymous letters, and, what had been harder to bear, reproaches from old and tried friends.

But what was far, far worse to the Dean than these mosquito bites was the fact that his own darling child, Edith, could not forgive him for having had so many German friends in the old days. Her great loss, which in theory should have softened her, had had just the opposite effect. It had made her bitter, bitter; and during the weeks which had followed the receipt of the fatal news she had hardly spoken to her father. This was the more unreasonable—nay, the more cruel—of her inasmuch as it had been her mother, to whom she now clung, who had so decidedly set her face against the hasty marriage which poor Edith was now always regretting had not taken place.

But if the Dean's congratulations were saddened by his own melancholy situation, those of the Robeys were clear and sunshiny. They knew Jervis Blake, and they regarded Rose as a very lucky girl. They also knew Rose, and they regarded Jervis Blake as a very lucky man.

True, Mrs. Robey, when alone with her husband after first hearing the news, had said, rather nervously, "I hope more than ever *now* that nothing will happen to dear Jervis!" And he had turned on her almost with ferocity: "Happen to Jervis? Of course nothing will happen to Jervis! As I've often told you, it's the impulsive, reckless boys who get killed—not born soldiers, like Jervis. He knows that his life is now valuable to his country, and you may be sure that he takes all reasonable precautions to preserve it."

And as she did not answer at once, he had gone on hurriedly: "Of course one can't tell; we may see his name in the list of casualties to-morrow morning! But if I were you, my dear, I should not build a bridge to meet trouble!"

As a matter of fact Mrs. Robey had no time to waste on such an unprofitable occupation. Her brother-in-law, the great surgeon, Sir Jacques Robey, and all his best nurses had been now waiting for quite a long time for wounded who never came; and it required a good deal of diplomacy and tact on Mrs. Robey's part to keep them all in a good humour, and on fairly pleasant terms with her own original household.

Rose's engagement was now ten days old, and she was about to start for her visit to her future parents-in-law, when early one afternoon the Dean, who had been lunching with Mr. and Mrs. Robey, rang the bell of the Trellis House.

"Die Herrschaft ist nicht zu Hause" ("The family are not at home."). Anna was smiling in the friendliest way at the Dean. He had always been in a very special sense kind to her, and never kinder than during the last fourteen weeks.

"Do you expect them back soon? It is very urgent," he exclaimed, of course speaking German; and the smile on Anna's face faded, so sad did he look, and so concerned.

"Oh, most reverend Doctor!" she cried, joining her hands together, "do not say that anything has happened to the Betrothed of my young lady?"

"Yes," he said sadly. "Something has happened, Anna, but it might be much worse. The Betrothed of your young lady has been severely wounded. But reflect on the wonderful organisation of our Red Cross! Mr. Blake was wounded, I believe, yesterday afternoon, and it is expected that he will be here, in Sir Jacques Robey's care, in a few hours from now!"

Even as he was speaking, a telegraph boy hurried up to the door.

"This is evidently to tell your ladies that which I had hoped to be able to break to them. So I will not stop now." And as Anna stared at him with woe-begone eyes, he said kindly:

"It might have been, as I said just now, infinitely worse. I am told that there is a great difference between the words *severely* and *dangerously*. Had he been dangerously wounded, he could not possibly have been moved to England. And consider what a comfort it will be to the poor girl to have him here, within a stone's throw. Why, she will be able to be with him all the time. Yes, yes, it might be worse—a great deal worse!" He added feelingly, "It is a very sad time that we are *all* living through."

He held out his hand and grasped the old woman's hard, work-worn fingers very warmly in his. Dr. Haworth, as the good people of Witanbury were fond of reminding one another—generally in a commendatory, though sometimes in a complaining, tone—was a real gentleman.

There followed hours of that merciful rush and bustle which at such moments go a long way to deaden suspense and pain. General and Lady Blake were arriving this evening, and the spare room of the Trellis House had to be got ready for them, and Rose's room—a lengthier matter this—transformed into a dressing-room.

But at last everything was ready, and then Rose went off, alone, to the station, to meet the London express.

The train was very late, and as she paced up and down the long platform she began wondering, with a kind of weary, confused wonder, whether there had been an accident, for now everything startling and dreadful seemed within the bounds of possibility. Yesterday with what eagerness would she have bought two or three evening papers—but now the thought of doing so did not even occur to her.

Yesterday—nay, to-day, up to three hours ago—she had been so happy, lacking even that latent anxiety which had been with her for so long, for she had supposed Jervis to be out of the trenches, resting. In fact, for the first time she had not been thinking much of Jervis, for her mind had been filled with her coming visit to London.

She was but very slightly acquainted with Sir John Blake, and she felt rather frightened of him—of the father whom Jervis loved and feared. True, he had written her a very kind, if a very short, note; but she had been afraid that she would not please him—that he would not approve of Jervis's choice....

At last the train came in. There was a great crowd of people, and her eyes sought in vain for the tall, still active figure she vaguely remembered. Then suddenly she saw Lady Blake—Lady Blake looking about her with an anxious, bewildered face, which changed to eager relief when the girl grasped her hand.

"Is this Rose? Dear little Rose! I am alone, dear child. I have not brought a maid. My husband went down to Southampton early this morning to wait for the hospital ship. I was so grateful for your mother's kind telegram. It will be an infinite comfort to stay with you both. But I think Sir John may find it more convenient to stay at an hotel." She grew a little pink, and Rose Otway, whose perceptions as to a great deal that is sad or strange in human nature, had grown of late, felt a little rush of anger against Sir John Blake.

As they left the station, Rose was able to ask the questions she was longing to ask. But Lady Blake knew nothing. "No, we have had no details at all. Only just the telegram telling us that he has been severely wounded—severely, you know, is much less serious than dangerously—and that he was being sent to Sir Jacques Robey's hospital at Witanbury. It seems so strange that Jervis should be coming *here*—so strange, but, my dear, so very happy too! My husband says that they probably show the wounded officers a list of hospitals, and perhaps give them a certain measure of choice."

They did not say much during the short drive to the Close; they simply held each other's hands. And Rose's feeling of indignation against Jervis's father grew and grew. How could he be impatient, still less unkind, to this sweet, gentle woman?

There followed a time of anxious waiting at the Trellis House, and, reluctantly, Rose began to understand why Sir John Blake was impatient with his wife. Lady Blake could not sit still; and she made no effort to command her nerves. In her gentle voice she suggested every painful possibility, from the torpedoing of the hospital ship in the Channel to a bad break down, or even a worse accident, to the motor ambulances which were to convey Jervis and four other wounded officers to Witanbury.

But at last, when even Sir Jacques himself had quite given them up for that night, three motor ambulances drove into the Close, and round to the temporary hospital.

And then such a curious, pathetic scene took place in the courtyard of "Robey's." Improvised flares and two electric reading-lamps, brought hurriedly through the windows of the drawing-room, shone on the group of waiting people—nurses ready to step forward when wanted; Sir Jacques Robey and a young surgeon who had come up from the Witanbury Cottage Hospital; Lady Blake trembling with cold and excitement close to Mrs. Otway and Rose; and a number of others who had less reason and excuse for being there.

From a seat by one of the drivers there jumped down Sir John Blake. He looked round him with a keen glance, and then made his way straight to where his wife was standing. Taking no notice of her, he addressed the girl standing by her side. "Is this Rose," he said—"Rose Otway?" and taking her hand gripped it hard. "He's borne the journey very well," he said quickly, reassuringly; and then, at last, he looked at his wife. She was gazing at him with imploring, anxious eyes. "Well," he said impatiently, "well, my dear, what is it you want to say to me?"

She murmured something nervously, and Rose hurriedly said, "Lady Blake wants to know where Jervis was wounded."

"A fragment of shell struck his left arm—but the real mischief was done to his right leg. When the building in which he and his company were resting was shelled, a beam fell on it. I should have thought myself that it would have been better to have kept him, for at any rate a while, at Boulogne. But they now think it wiser, if it be in any way possible, to bring them straight back."

Rose hardly heard what he said. She was absorbed in wondering which of the stretchers now being brought out of the ambulances bore the form of Jervis Blake; but she accepted, with a quiet submission which increased the great surgeon's already good opinion of her, his decree that no one excepting himself and his nurses was to see or speak to any of the wounded that night.

CHAPTER XXIII

Time and the weather run through the roughest day." It may be doubted if Rose Otway knew that consoling old proverb, but with her time, even in the shape of a very few days, and perhaps, too, the weather, which was remarkably fine and mild for the time of year, soon wrought a wonderful change.

And as she sat by Jervis Blake's bedside, on a bright, sunny day in late November, it seemed to her as if she had nothing left to wish for. The two nurses who attended on him so kindly and so skilfully told her that he was going on well—far better, in fact, than they could have expected. And though Sir Jacques Robey did not say much, she had no reason to suppose him other than satisfied. True, Jervis's face looked strained and thin, and there was a cradle over his right foot, showing where the worst injury had been. But the wound in his shoulder was healing nicely, and once or twice he had spoken of when he would be able to go back; but now he had left off doing that, for he saw that it troubled her.

Yesterday something very pleasant had happened, and something which, to Jervis Blake himself, was quite unexpected. He had been Mentioned in Despatches, in connection with a little affair, as he described it, which had happened weeks ago, on the Aisne! One of the other two men concerned in it had received the Victoria Cross, and Rose was secretly rather hurt, as was also Lady Blake, that Jervis had not been equally honoured. But that thought did not occur to either his father or himself.

Just now Rose was enjoying half an hour of pleasant solitude with her lover, after what had been a trying morning for him. Sir Jacques Robey had asked down an old friend of his own, a surgeon too, to see Jervis, and they had spent quite a long time pulling the injured foot about.

Sir John Blake had also come down to spend the day at Witanbury. He had been able to get away for a few hours from his work at the War Office to tell his boy how very, very pleased he was at that mention in Sir John French's Despatches. Indeed, all the morning telegraph boys had been bringing to "Robey's" the congratulations of friends and even acquaintances.

Jervis was very tired now—tired because the two surgeons, skilful and careful though they were, had not been able to help hurting him quite a good bit. It was fortunate that Rose Otway, dearly as she loved him, knew little or nothing of pain. She had been sent away during that hour, right out of the house, to take a walk with Mr. Robey. She had been told quite plainly by Sir Jacques that they would rather she were not there while the examination was taking place. It was important that the house should be kept as far as possible absolutely quiet.

Jervis did not talk very much, but there was no need for him to do so. He and Rose would have plenty of time to say everything they wanted to one another, for Sir Jacques had told her, only yesterday night, that a very long time must go by before Jervis would be fit to go back. "Any injury to the foot," he had said casually, "is bound to be a long and a ticklish business." The words had given her a rush of joy of which she felt ashamed.

There came a knock at the door, and then the younger of Jervis's nurses came quietly into the room. "They're asking for you downstairs, Miss Otway," she said quietly. "And I think that perhaps Mr. Blake might now get a little sleep. He's had a rather tiring, exciting morning, you know. Perhaps you could come up and have tea with him about five o'clock? He's sure to be awake by then."

And then the young nurse did a rather odd thing. Instead of going on into the room and up to the bedside, she went out of the door for a moment, and Rose, during that moment, bent down and laid her soft cheek against Jervis's face. "Good-bye, my darling Jervis. I shan't be away long." And then she straightened herself, and went out of the room.

Of course she was happy—happy, and with a heart at rest as it had not been for months and months. But still it would be a great comfort when Jervis was up. She hated to see him lying there, helpless, given over to ministrations other than her own.

As she went through the door, the nurse stopped her and said, "Would you go into Mr. Robey's study, Miss Otway? I think Sir John Blake wants to see you before he goes back to town. Mr. Jenkinson has already gone; he had to be there for a consultation at six."

Rose looked at her, a little surprised. It was as if the kind little nurse was speaking for the sake of speaking.

She went down the quiet house, past the door of the large ward where the four other wounded officers now lay, all going on, she was glad to know, very well, and all having had a visit from Mr. Jenkinson, the London specialist.

She hurried on, smiling a little as she did so. She was no longer afraid of Sir John Blake. In fact she was becoming very fond of him, though it hurt her always to hear how sharply and irritably he spoke to his gentle, yielding wife. Of course Lady Blake was very unreasonable sometimes—but she was so helpless, so clinging, and so fond of Jervis.

And then, as she turned a corner—for "Robey's" consisted of three houses, through each of which an intercommunication had been made—there fell on Rose Otway's ear a very dreadful sound, that of some one crying in wild, unbridled grief. The sound came from Mrs. Robey's little sitting-room, and suddenly Rose heard her own mother's voice raised in expostulation. She was evidently trying to comfort and calm the poor stranger—doubtless the mother or wife of one of the four officers upstairs. Two days ago one of these visitors had had something very like a fit of hysterics after seeing her wounded husband. Rose shrank from the memory. But this was worse—far worse. She hurried on into Mr. Robey's study.

The study, which was a very agreeable room, overlooked the Close. It was panelled with dark old oak, and lined on one side with books, and opposite the centre window hung Mr. Robey's greatest treasure, a watercolour by Turner of Witanbury Cathedral, painted from the meadows behind the town.

To-day Mr. Robey himself was not there, but his brother and Sir John Blake were both waiting for her. Eagerly she walked forward into the room, and as she did so she made a delightful picture—or so those two men, so very different the one from the other, thought—of youth, of happiness, and yes, of young love satisfied.

Sir Jacques took a step forward. The General did not move at all. He was standing with his back to the further window, his face in shadow.

"Now, Miss Rose, I want you to listen very carefully to me for a few minutes."

She looked at him gravely. "Yes?" she said questioningly.

"I have asked you to come," went on the great surgeon, "because I want to impress upon your mind the fact that how you behave at this juncture of his life may make a very great, I might almost say all the difference, to your future husband, to Mr. Jervis Blake."

Rose's senses started up, like sentinels, to attention.

"You will have need of all your courage, and also of all your good sense, to help him along a very rough bit of road," he went on feelingly.

Rose felt a thrill of sudden, unreasonable terror. "What is it?" she exclaimed. "What is going to happen to him? Is he going to die? I don't mind what it is, if only you will tell me!" She instinctively moved over to Sir John Blake's side, and he, as instinctively, put his arm round her shoulder.

"Mr. Jenkinson agrees with me," said Sir Jacques, slowly and deliberately, "that his foot, the foot that was crushed, will have to come off. There is no danger—no reasonable danger, that is—of the operation costing him his life." He waited a moment, and as she said nothing, he went on: "But though there is no danger of his losing his life, there is a very great danger, Miss Otway, of his losing what to such a man as Jervis Blake counts, I think, for more than life—his courage. By that of course I do not mean physical bravery, but that courage, or strength of mind, which enables many men far more afflicted than he will ever be, to retain their normal outlook on life." Speaking more to himself, he added, "I have formed a very good opinion of this young man, and personally I think he will accept this great misfortune with resignation and fortitude. But one can never tell, and it is always best to prepare for the worst."

And then, for the first time, Rose spoke. "I understand what you mean," she said quietly. "And I thank you very much, Sir Jacques, for having spoken to me as you have done."

"And now," he said, "one word more. Sir John Blake does not know what I am going to say, and perhaps my suggestion will not meet with his approval. It had been settled during the last few days, had it not, that you and Jervis were to be married before he went back to the Front? Well, I suggest that you be married now, before the operation takes place. I am of course thinking of the matter solely from his point of view—and from my point of view as his surgeon."

Her heartfelt "Thank you" had hardly reached his ear before Sir John Blake spoke with a kind of harsh directness.

"I don't think anything of the sort can be thought of now. In fact I would not give my consent to an immediate marriage. I feel certain that my son, too, would refuse to take advantage of his position to suggest it."

"I think," said Sir Jacques quietly, "that the suggestion in any case would have to come from Miss Rose."

And then, for the first time, Rose lost control of herself. She became agitated, tearful—in her eagerness she put her hand on Sir John's breast, and looking piteously up into his face, "Of course I want to marry him at once!" she said brokenly. "Every time I have had to leave him in the last few days I have felt miserable. You see, I *feel* married to him already, and if you feel married, it's so very strange not to *be* married."

She began to laugh helplessly, and the more, shocked at what she was doing, she tried to stop, the more she laughed.

Sir Jacques came quickly forward. "Come, come!" he said sharply, and taking her by the arm he shook her violently. "This won't do at all——" he gave a warning look at the other man. "Of course Miss Rose will do exactly what she wishes to do! She's quite right in saying that she's as good as married to him already, Sir John. And it's our business—yours, hers, and mine—to think of Jervis, and of Jervis only just now. But she won't be able to do that if she allows herself to be upset!"

"I'm so sorry—please forgive me!" Rose, to her own measureless relief, had stopped laughing, but she felt oddly faint and queer. Sir Jacques poured out a very small wineglassful of brandy, and made her drink it. How odd to have a bottle of brandy here, in Mr. Robey's study! Mr. Robey was a teetotaller.

"Would you like me to go up to Jervis now?" asked Sir John slowly.

Sir Jacques looked into the speaker's face. It was generally a clear, healthy tan colour; now it had gone quite grey. "No," he said. "Not now. If you will forgive me for making a suggestion, I should advise that you and Miss Rose take Lady Blake out somewhere for an hour's walk. There's nothing like open air and a high road for calming the nerves."

"I would rather not see my wife just now," muttered Sir John frowning.

But Sir Jacques answered sternly, "I'm afraid I must ask you to do so; and once you've got her out of doors for an hour, I'll give her a sleeping draught. She'll be all right to-morrow morning. I don't want any tears round my patient."

It was Rose Otway who led Sir John Blake by the hand down the passage. The dreadful sounds coming from Mrs. Robey's sitting-room had died down a little, but they still pierced one listener's heart.

"Do be kind to her," whispered the girl. "Think what she must be going through. She was so happy about him this morning——"

"Yes, yes! You're quite right," he said hastily. "I've been a brute—I know that. I promise you to do my best. And Rose?"

"Yes," she said.

"What that man said is right—quite right. What we've got to do now is to start the boy on the right way—nothing else matters."

She nodded.

"You and I can do it."

"Yes, I know we can—and will," said Rose; and then she opened the door of Mrs. Robey's sitting-room.

At the sight of her husband, Lady Blake's sobs died down in long, convulsive sighs.

"Come, my dear," he said, in rather cold, measured tones. "This will not do. You must try for our boy's sake to pull yourself together. After all, it might have been much worse. He might have been killed."

"I would much rather he had been killed," she exclaimed vehemently. "Oh, John, you don't know, you don't understand, what this will mean to him!"

"Don't I?" he asked. He set his teeth. And then, "You're acting very wrongly!" he said sternly. "We've got to face this thing out. Remember what Sir Jacques said to you." He waited a moment, then, in a gentler, kinder tone, "Rose and I are going out for a walk, and we want you to come too."

"Oh, I don't think I could do that." She spoke uncertainly, and yet even he could see that she was startled, surprised, and yes, pleased.

"Oh, yes, you can!" Rose came forward with the poor lady's hat and black lace cloak. Very gently, but with the husband's strong arm gripping the wife's rather tightly, they between them led her out of the front door into the Close.

"I think," said Sir John mildly, "that you had better run back and get your hat, Rose."

She left them, and Sir John Blake, letting go of his wife's arm looked down into her poor blurred face for a moment. "That girl," he said hoarsely, "sets us both an example, Janey."

"That's true," she whispered, "But John?"

"Yes."

"Don't you sometimes feel dreadfully *jealous* of her?"

"I? God bless my soul, *no!*" But a very sweet smile, a smile she had not seen shed on her for many, many years, lit up his face. "We'll have to think more of one another, and less of the boy—eh, my dear?"

Lady Blake was too surprised to speak—and so, for once doing the wise thing, she remained silent.

Rose, hurrying out a moment later, saw that the open air had already done them both good.

CHAPTER XXIV

You've got to make him believe that you wish for the marriage to take place now, for your own sake, not for his."

It was with those words, uttered by Sir Jacques Robey, still sounding in her ears, that Rose Otway walked up to the door of the room where Jervis Blake, having just seen his father, was now waiting to see her.

Sir John Blake's brief "He has taken it very well. He has a far greater sense of discipline than I had at his age," had been belied, discounted, by the speaker's own look of suffering and of revolt.

Rose waited outside the door for a few moments. She was torn with conflicting fears and emotions. A strange feeling of oppression and shyness had come over her. It had seemed so easy to say that she would be married at once, to-morrow, to Jervis. But she had not known that she would have to ask Jervis's consent. She had supposed, foolishly, that it would all be settled for her by Sir Jacques....

At last she turned the handle of the door, and walked through into the room. And then, to her unutterable relief, she saw that Jervis looked exactly as usual, except that his face, instead of being pale, as it had been the last few days, was rather flushed.

Words which had been spoken to him less than five minutes ago were also echoing in Jervis's brain, pushing everything else into the background. He had said, "I suppose you think that I ought to offer to release Rose?" and his father had answered slowly: "All I can say is that I should do so—if I were in your place."

But now, when he saw her coming towards him, looking as she always looked, save that something of the light and brightness which had always been in her dear face had faded out of it, he knew that he could say nothing of the sort. This great trouble which had come on him was her trouble as well as his, and he knew she was going to take it and to bear it, as he meant to take it and to bear it.

But Jervis Blake did make up his mind to one thing. There should be no hurrying of Rose into a hasty marriage—the kind of marriage they had planned—the marriage which was to have taken place a week before he went back to the Front. It must be his business to battle through this grim thing alone. It would be time enough to think of marriage when he was up and about again, and when he had taught himself, as much as might be possible, to hide or triumph over his infirmity.

As she came and sat down quietly by the side of his bed, on the chair which his father had just left, he put out his hand and took hers.

"I want to tell you," he said slowly, "that what my father has just told me was not altogether a surprise. I've felt rather—well, rather afraid of it, since Sir Jacques first examined me. There was something in the nurses' manner too—but of course I knew I might be wrong. I'm sorry now that I didn't tell you."

She still said nothing—only gripped his hand more and more tightly.

"And Rose? One thing father said is being such a comfort to me. Father thinks that I shall still be able to be of use—I mean in the way I should like to be, especially if the war goes on a long time. I wonder if he showed you this?" He picked up off his bed a little piece of paper and held it out to her.

Through her bitter tears she read the words: "German thoroughness" — and then a paragraph which explained how the German military authorities were using their disabled officers in the training of recruits.

"Father thinks that in time they'll do something of the sort here—not yet, perhaps, but in some months from now."

And then, as she still did not speak, he grew uneasy. "Come a little nearer," he whispered. "I feel as if you were so far away. We needn't be afraid of any one coming in. Father has promised that no one shall disturb us till you ring."

She did as he asked, and putting his uninjured arm right round her, he held her closely to him.

It was the first time since that strange home-coming of his that Jervis had felt secure against the sudden irruption into the room of some well-meaning person. Of the two it was Jervis who had been silently determined to give the talkative, sentimental nurses no excuse for even the mildest, the kindliest comment.

But now everything was merged in this great ordeal of love and grief they were battling through together—secure from the unwanted presence of others as they had not been since he had last felt her heart fluttering beneath his, in the porch of the cathedral.

"Oh, Rose," he whispered at last, "you don't know what a difference having you makes to me! If it wasn't for you, I don't know how I could face it."

For a moment she clung a little closer to him. He felt her trembling with a wave of emotion to which he had no present clue. "Oh, Jervis—dear Jervis, is that true?" she asked piteously.

"Do you doubt it?" he whispered.

"Then there's something I want you to do for me."

"You know that there isn't anything in the world you could ask me to do that I wouldn't do, Rose."

"I want you to marry me to-morrow," she said. And then, as for a moment he remained silent, she began to cry. "Oh, Jervis, do say yes— unless you very, very much want to say no!"

During the next forty-eight hours Sir Jacques Robey settled what was to be done, when it should be done, and how it was to be done.

Of the people concerned, it was perhaps Lady Blake who seemed the most under his influence. She submitted without a word to his accompanying her into her son's bedroom, and it was in response to his insistent command— for it was no less—that instead of alluding to the tragic thing which filled all her thoughts, she only spoke of the morrow's wedding, and of her happiness in the daughter her son was giving her.

It was Sir Jacques, too, who persuaded Mrs. Otway to agree that an immediate marriage was the best of all possible solutions for Rose as well as for Jervis; and it was he, also, who suggested that Sir John Blake should go over to the Deanery and make all the necessary arrangements with Dr. Haworth. But perhaps the most striking example of Sir Jacques's good sense and thoroughness occurred after Sir John had been to the Deanery.

Dr. Haworth had fallen in with every suggestion with the most eager, ready sympathy; and Sir John, who before coming to Witanbury had regarded him as a pacifist and pro-German, had come really to like and respect him. So it was that now, as he came back from the Deanery, and up to the gate of the Trellis House, he was in a softer, more yielding mood than usual.

Sir Jacques hurried out to meet him. "Is everything all right?"

"Yes—everything's settled. But it's your responsibility, not mine!"

"I've been wondering, Sir John, whether the Dean reminded you that we shall require a wedding ring?"

"No, he did not." Sir John Blake looked rather taken aback. "I wonder what I'd better do?" he muttered helplessly.

"You and Lady Blake had better go into the town and buy one," said Sir Jacques. "I don't feel that we can put *that* job on poor little Rose. She's had quite enough to do as it is—and gallantly she's done it!"

And as Sir John began to look cross and undecided, the other said with a touch of sharpness, "Of course if you'd rather not do it, I'll buy the ring myself. But I've been neglecting my work this morning."

Ashamed of his ungraciousness, as the other had meant him to be, Sir John said hastily, "Of course I'll get it! I was only wondering whether I hadn't better go alone."

"Lady Blake would be of great use in choosing it, and for the matter of that, in trying it on. If you wait here a moment I'll go and fetch her. She's got her hat on, I know."

So it happened that, in three or four minutes, just long enough for Sir John to begin to feel impatient, Jervis's mother came out of the Trellis House. She was smiling up into the great surgeon's face, and her husband told himself that it was an extraordinary thing how this wedding had turned their minds—all their minds—away from Jervis's coming ordeal.

"I wonder if Rose would like a broad or narrow wedding ring?" said Lady Blake thoughtfully. "I'm afraid there won't be very much choice in a place like Witanbury."

Sir Jacques looked after the couple for a few moments, then he turned and went into the Trellis House, and so into the drawing-room.

"Bachelors," he said meditatively, "sometimes have a way of playing the very mischief between married couples—eh, Mrs. Otway? So it's only fair that now and again a bachelor should do something towards bringing a couple together again."

She looked at him, surprised. What odd—and yes, rather improper things—Sir Jacques sometimes said! But—but he was a *very* kind man. Mrs. Otway was a simple woman, though she would have felt a good deal nettled had anyone told her so.

"I rather wonder," she said impulsively, "why *you* never married. You seem to approve of marriage, Sir Jacques?" She was looking into his face with an eager, kindly look.

"If you look at me long enough," he said slowly, "I think you'll be able to answer that question for yourself. The women I wanted—there were three of them——" and then, as he saw that she again looked slightly shocked, he added, "Not altogether, but consecutively, you understand—well, not one of them would have me! The women who might have put up with me—well, I didn't seem to want them! But I should like to say one thing to you, Mrs. Otway. This particular affair in which you and I are interested does seem to me, if you'll allow me to say so, 'a marriage of true minds——'" He stopped abruptly, and to her great surprise left the room without finishing his sentence.

Such trifling, and at the time such seemingly unimportant, little happenings are often those which long afterwards leap out from the past, bringing with them poignant memories of joy, of sorrow, of pain, and of happiness.

Rose Blake will always remember that it was her poor old German nurse, Anna Bauer, who, on her wedding day, made her wear a white dress and a veil. She had meant to be married, in so far as she had given any thought to the matter at all, in her ordinary blue serge skirt and a clean blouse.

Those about her might be able to forget, for a few merciful hours, what lay before Jervis; but she, Rose Otway, could not forget it. She knew that she was marrying him now, not in order that she might be even closer to him than she felt herself to be—that seemed to her impossible—but in order that others might think so. She would have preferred the ceremony to take place only in the presence of his parents and of her mother. But as to that she had been given no say; Sir Jacques and Mr. and Mrs. Robey had announced as a matter of course that they would be present, and so she had assented to her mother's suggestion that Miss Forsyth should be asked. If Mr. and Mrs. Robey and Sir Jacques were to be there, then she did not mind Miss Forsyth, her kind old friend, being there too.

Anna had protested with tearful vehemence against the blue serge skirt and the pretty blouse—nay, more, she had already taken the white gown she intended that her beloved nursling should wear, out of the bag which she, Anna, had made for it last year. It was a very charming frock, a fine exquisitely embroidered India muslin, the only really beautiful day-dress Rose had ever had in her young life. And oddly enough it had been a present from Miss Forsyth.

Miss Forsyth—it was nearly eighteen months ago—had invited Rose to come up to London with her for a day's shopping, and then she had suddenly presented her young friend with this attractive, and yes, expensive gown. There had been a blue sash, but this had now been taken off by Anna, and a bluey-white satin band substituted. As to that Rose now rebelled. "If I *am* to wear this dress to-day, I should like the blue sash put back," she said quickly. "Blue is supposed to bring luck to brides, Anna."

What had really turned the scale in Rose's mind had been Anna's tears, and the fact that Miss Forsyth would be pleased to see her married in that gown.

But over the lace veil there had been something like a tug of war. And this time it was Mrs. Otway who had won the day. "If you wear that muslin dress, then I cannot see why you should not wear your grandmother's wedding veil," she had exclaimed—and again Rose had given in.

Poor old Anna! It was a day of days for her—far more a day of days than had been the marriage of her own daughter. Yet Louisa Bauer's wedding had been a great festival. And the old woman remembered what pains Mrs. Otway had taken to make that marriage of five years ago, as far as was possible in such a very English place as Witanbury, a German bridal. In those days they had none of them guessed what an unsatisfactory fellow George Pollit was going to turn out; and Louisa had gone to her new home with quite a German trousseau—that is, with what would have appeared to English eyes stacks of under-clothing, each article beautifully embroidered with a monogram and lavishly trimmed with fine crochet; each set tied up with a washing band or *Waschebander*, a strip of canvas elaborately embroidered in cross-stitch.

It seemed strangely sad and unnatural that Anna's gracious young lady should have no trousseau at all! But that doubtless would come afterwards, and she, Anna, felt sure that she would be allowed to have a hand in choosing it. This thought was full of consolation, as was also her secret supposition that the future trousseau would be paid for by the bridegroom.

There was certainly cause for satisfaction in that thought, for Anna had become conscious of late that her dear mistress felt anxious about money. Prices were going up, but thanks to her, Anna's, zealous care, the housekeeping bills at the Trellis House were still kept wonderfully low. It was unfortunate that Mrs. Otway, being the kind of gracious lady she was, scarcely gave Anna sufficient credit for this. It was not that she was ungrateful, it was simply that she did not think anything about it—she only remembered that she was short of money when the household books were there, open in front of her.

CHAPTER XXV

And now the small group of men and women who were to be present at the marriage of Rose Otway and Jervis Blake were gathered together in Mrs. Robey's large drawing-room. Seven people in all, for the Dean had not yet arrived.

In addition to the master and mistress of the hospitable house in which they now all found themselves, there were there Sir John and Lady Blake; Miss Forsyth—who, alone of the company, had dressed herself with a certain old-fashioned magnificence; Sir Jacques, who had just come into the room after taking Rose and her mother up to Jervis's room; and lastly good old Anna Bauer, who sat a little apart by herself, staring with a strange, rather wild look at the group of people standing before her.

To Anna's excited mind, they did not look like a wedding party; they looked, with the exception of Miss Forsyth, who wore a light grey silk dress trimmed with white lace, like people waiting to start for a funeral.

No one spoke, with the exception of Lady Blake, who occasionally addressed a nervous question, in an undertone, to Mrs. Robey.

At last there came the sound of the front door opening and shutting. Mr. Robey went out, rather hurriedly, and his wife exclaimed, "I think that must be the Dean. My husband is taking him upstairs——" And then she waited a moment, and glanced anxiously at her brother-in-law, Sir Jacques. It was strange how even she, who had never particularly liked Sir Jacques, looked to him for guidance to-day.

In answer to that look he moved forward a little, and made a queer little sound, as if clearing his throat. Then, very deliberately, he addressed the people before him.

"Before we go upstairs," he began, "I want to say something to you all. I cannot help noticing that you all look very sad. Now of course I don't ask you to try and look gay during the coming half-hour, but I do earnestly beg of you to try and feel happy. Above all—" and he looked directly at Lady Blake as he spoke—"above all," he repeated, "I must beg of you very earnestly indeed to allow yourselves no show of emotion. We not only hope, but we confidently expect, that our young friends are beginning to-day what will be an exceptionally happy, and—and——" he waited for a moment, then apparently found the word he wanted—"an exceptionally harmonious married life. I base that view of what we all believe, not on any exaggerated notion of what life generally brings to the average married couple, but on the knowledge we possess of both these young people's characters. Nothing can take away from Jervis Blake his splendid past, and we may reasonably believe that he is going to have with this sweet, brave young woman, who loves him so well, a contented future."

Again Sir Jacques paused, and then not less earnestly he continued: "I want Jervis Blake to look back on to-day as on a happy and hallowed day. If anyone here feels that they will not be able to command themselves, then I beg him or her most strongly to stay away."

He turned and opened the door behind him, and as he did so, his sister-in-law heard him mutter to himself: "Of course at the great majority of weddings if the people present knew what was going to come afterwards, they would do nothing but cry. But this is not that sort of wedding, thank God!"

Sir Jacques and old Anna came last up the staircase leading to Jervis Blake's room. He and the old German woman were on very friendly terms. Before the War Sir Jacques had been in constant correspondence with two eminent German surgeons, and as a young man he had spent a year of study in Vienna. He now addressed a few cheerful, heartening remarks in German to Rose's old nurse, winding up rather peremptorily with the words: "There must be no tears. There is here only matter for rejoicing." And Anna, in a submissive whisper, had answered, "Ja! Ja!"

And then, as she walked last into the room, Anna uttered a guttural expression of delighted surprise, for it was as if every hothouse flower in Witanbury had been gathered to do honour to the white-clad, veiled figure who now stood, with downcast eyes, by the bridegroom's bedside.

The flowers were Mr. Robey's gift. He had gone out quite early that morning and had pressed all those of his acquaintances who had greenhouses, as well as the flower shops in Witanbury, under contribution; and the delicate, bright colouring with which the room was now filled gave a festive, welcoming air to this bridal chamber.

Rose looked up, and as her eyes met the loving, agitated glance of her nurse, she felt a sudden thrill of warm gratitude to good old Anna, for Jervis had whispered, "How lovely you look, darling! Somehow I thought you would wear an everyday dress—but this is much, much nicer!"

Those present followed the order of the marriage service with very varying emotions, and never had the Dean delivered the familiar, awesome words with more feeling and more grace of diction.

But the only two people in that room whose breasts were stirred to really happy memories were Mr. and Mrs. Robey. They, standing together a little in the background, almost unconsciously clasped each other's hands.

Across the mind of Sir John Blake there flashed a vivid memory of his own wedding day. The marriage had been celebrated in the cantonment church of an up-country station, where, after a long, wearying engagement, and a good deal of what he had even then called "shilly-shallying," his betrothed had come out from England to marry him. He remembered, in a queer jumble of retrospective gratitude and impatience, how certain of the wives of his brother officers had decorated the little plain church; and the mingled scents of the flowers now massed about him recalled that of the orange blossoms and the tuberoses at his own wedding.

But real as that long-vanished scene still was to Jervis's father, what he now remembered best of all the emotions which had filled his heart as he had stood waiting at the chancel steps for his pretty, nervous bride were the good resolutions he had made—made and so soon broken....

As for Sir Jacques, he had never been to a wedding since he had been last forced to do so as a boy by his determined mother. The refusal of all marriage invitations was an eccentricity which friends and patients easily pardoned to the successful and popular surgeon, and so the present ceremony had the curious interest of complete novelty. He had meant to read over the service to see what part he himself had to play, but the morning had slipped away and he had not had time.

Jervis, in answer to perhaps the most solemn and awful question ever put to man, had just answered fervently "I will," and Rose's response had also been uttered very clearly, when suddenly someone gave Sir Jacques a little prod, and the Dean, with the words, "Who giveth this woman to be married to this man?" made him a quiet sign.

Sir Jacques came forward, and in answer, said "I do," in a loud tone. And then he saw the Dean take Jervis's right hand and place it in Rose's left, and utter the solemn words with which even he was acquainted.

"I, Jervis, take thee, Rose, to be my wedded wife, to have and to hold from this day forward, for better for worse, for richer for poorer, in sickness and in health, to love and to cherish, till death us do part, according to God's holy ordinance; and thereto I plight thee my troth."

A series of tremendous promises to make and to keep! But for the moment cynicism had fallen away from Sir Jacques's heart, and somehow he felt sure that, at any rate in this case, those tremendous promises would be kept.

He had been afraid that the Dean would make an address, or at the least would say a few words that would reduce some of the tiny congregation to tears. But Dr. Haworth was too wise for that, and perhaps he knew that nothing he could say could improve on the *Beati omnes*.

And it was then, towards the close of that wedding ceremony, that Sir Jacques suddenly made up his mind what should be the words graven inside what he intended should be his wedding gift to Rose Blake—that gift was a fine old-fashioned ruby ring, the only one of his mother's jewels he possessed, and the words he then chose in his own mind were those of the Psalmist, "O well is thee, and happy shalt thou be."

CHAPTER XXVI

Dear Mrs. Otway,

"I am so very glad to be able to send you the enclosed. Of course I have not read it. In fact I do not know German. But I gather that it contains news of Major Guthrie, and that it is written with a kindly intention. It was probably intended to arrive for Christmas.

"Yours very truly,

"Annabel Gaunt.

"P.S.—Any letters you write in answer must be left open."

The envelope enclosed by Mrs. Gaunt, which bore the Censor's stamp, had come from Switzerland, and had been forwarded by favour of the Geneva Red Cross.

With an indescribable feeling of suspense, of longing, and of relief, Mrs. Otway drew out the sheet of paper. It was closely covered with the cramped German characters with which she was, of course, familiar.

"Minden,

"*15 December, 1914.*

"Dear Madam,

"As Medical Superintendent of the Field Lazarette at Minden, I write on behalf of a British prisoner of war, Major Guthrie, who has now been under my care for fourteen weeks.

"I wish to assure you that he has had the very highest medical skill bestowed on him since he came here. Owing to the exceptional exigencies and strain put on our Medical Service at the Front, he did not perhaps obtain the care to which he was entitled by our merciful and humane usages of war, as soon as would have been well. He received a most serious wound in the shoulder. That wound, I am pleased to tell you, is in as good a state as possible, and will leave no ill-effects.

"But I regret to tell you, Madam, that Major Guthrie has lost his eyesight. He bears this misfortune with remarkable fortitude. As a young man I myself spent a happy year in Edinburgh, and so we have agreeable subjects of conversation. He tells me you are quite familiar with my language, or I should of course have written to you in English.

"Believe me, Madam,

"To remain with the utmost respect,

"Yours faithfully,

"Karl Brecht."

Underneath the signature of the doctor was written in hesitating, strange characters the words in English, "God bless you.—Alexander Guthrie."

And then, under these five words, came another sentence in German:

"I may tell you for your consolation that it is extremely probable that Major Guthrie will be exchanged in the course of the next few weeks. But I have said nothing of that to him, for it will depend on the good-will of the British Government, and it is a good-will which we Germans have now learnt to distrust."

She read the letter through again. There came over her a feeling of agony such as she never imagined any human being could suffer.

During the past weeks of suspense, she had faced in her own mind many awful possibilities, but of this possibility she had not thought.

Now she remembered, with piteous vividness, the straight, kindly gaze in his bright blue eyes—eyes which had had a pleasant play of humour in them. Sight does not mean the same to all men, but she knew that it meant a very great deal to the man she loved. He had always been an out-door man, a man who cared for everything that concerned open-air life—for birds, for trees, for flowers, for shooting, fishing, and gardening.

Ever since she had known that Major Guthrie was alive and wounded, a prisoner in Germany, she had allowed her thoughts to dwell on the letters she would write to him when she received his address. She had composed so many letters in her mind—alternative letters—letters which should somehow make clear to him all that was in her heart, while yet concealing it first from the British Censors and then from his German jailers.

But now she did not give these Censors and jailers a thought. She sat down and wrote quite simply and easily the words which welled up out of her heart:

"My Dearest,

"To-day is New Year's Day, and I have had the great joy of receiving news of you. Also your blessing, which has already done me good. I wish you to get this letter quickly, so I will not make it long.

"I am forbidden to give you any news, so I will only say that Rose and I are well. That I love you and think of you all the time, and look forward to being always with you in God's good time."

She hesitated a moment as to how she would sign herself, and then she wrote:

"Your own
"Mary."

She looked over the letter, wondering if she could say any more, and then a sudden inspiration came to her. She added a postscript:

"I am spending the money you left with me. It is a great comfort."

This was not strictly true, but she made up her mind that it should become true before the day was out.

Far longer did she take over her letter to the German doctor—indeed, she made three drafts of it, being so pitifully anxious to say just the right thing, neither too much nor too little, which might favourably incline him to his prisoner patient.

All the time she was writing this second letter she felt as if the Censors were standing by her, frowning, picking out a sentence here, a sentence there. She would have liked to say something of the time she had spent at Weimar, but she dared not do so; perhaps if she said anything of the kind her letter might not get through.

There was nothing Mrs. Otway desired to say which the sternest Censor could have found fault with in either country, but the poor soul did not know that. Still, even so, she wrote a very charming letter of gratitude— so charming, indeed, and so admirably expressed, that when the Medical Superintendent at last received it, he said to himself, "The gracious lady writer of this letter must be partly German. No Englishwoman could have written like this!"

There was one more letter to write, but Mrs. Otway found no difficulty in expressing in few sentences her warm gratitude to her new friend at Arlington Street.

She put the three letters in a large envelope—the one for the German hospital carefully addressed according to the direction at the top of the Medical Superintendent's letter, but open as she had been told to leave it. On chance, for she was quite ignorant whether the postage should be prepaid, she put a twopenny-halfpenny stamp on the letter, and then, having done that, fastened down the big envelope and addressed it to Mrs. Gaunt, at 20, Arlington Street.

Then she took another envelope out of her drawer—that containing Major Guthrie's bank-notes. There, in with them, was still the postcard he had written to her from France, immediately after the landing of the Expeditionary Force. She looked at the clearly-written French sentence— the sentence in which the writer maybe had tried to convey something of his yearning for her. Taking the india-rubber band off the notes, she put one into her purse. She was very sorry now that she hadn't done as he had asked her—spent this money when, as had happened more than once during the last few weeks, she had been disagreeably short.

And then she went out, walking very quietly through the hall. She did not feel as if she wanted old Anna to know that she had heard from Germany. It would be hard enough to have to tell Rose the dreadful thing which, bringing such anguish to herself, could only give the girl, absorbed in her own painful ordeal, a passing pang of sympathy and regret.

Poor old Anna! Mrs. Otway was well aware that as the days went on Anna became less and less pleasant to live with.

Not for the first time of late, she wondered uneasily if Miss Forsyth had been right, on that August day which now seemed so very long ago. Would it not have been better, even from Anna's point of view, to have sent her back to her own country, to Berlin, to that young couple who seemed to have so high an opinion of her, and with whom she had spent so successful a holiday three years ago? At the time it had seemed unthinkable, a preposterous notion, but now—Mrs. Otway sighed—now it was only too clear that old Anna was not happy, and that she bitterly resented the very slight changes the War had made in her own position.

Anna was even more discontented and unhappy than her mistress knew. True, both Mrs. Otway and Rose had given her their usual Christmas gifts, and one of these gifts had been far more costly than ever before. But there had been no heart for the pretty Tree which, as long as Rose could remember anything, had been the outstanding feature of each twenty-fifth of December in her young life.

Yes, it had indeed been a dull and dreary Christmas for Anna! Last year she had received a number of delightful presents from Berlin. These had included a marzipan sausage, a marzipan turnip, and a wonderful toy Zeppelin made of sausage—a real sausage fitted with a real screw, a rudder, and at each end a flag.

But this autumn, as the weeks had gone by without bringing any answer to her affectionate letters, she had told herself that Minna, or if not Minna then Willi, would surely write for Christmas. And most bitterly disappointed had Anna felt when the Christmas week went by bringing no letter.

In vain Mrs. Otway told her that perhaps Willi and Minna felt, as so many Germans were said to do, such hatred of England that they did not care even to send a letter to someone living there. To Anna this seemed quite impossible. It was far more likely that the cruel English Post Office had kept back the letter because it came from Germany.

Now it was New Year's Day, and after having heard her mistress go out, Anna, sore at heart, reminded herself that were she now in service in Germany she would have already received this morning a really handsome money gift, more a right than a perquisite, from her mistress. She did not remind herself that this yearly benefaction is always demanded back by a German employer of his servant, if that servant is discharged, owing to her own fault, within a year.

Yes, England was indeed an ill-organized country! How often had she longed in the last eighteen years to possess the privilege of a wish-ticket— that delightful *Wunschzettel* which enables so many happy people in the Fatherland to make it quite plain what it is they really want to have given them for a birthday or a Christmas present. Strange to say—but Anna did not stop to think of that now—this wonderful bit of organisation does not always work out quite well. Evil has been known to come from a wish-ticket, for a modest person is apt to ask too little, and then is bitterly disappointed at not getting more than he asks for, while the grasping ask too much, and are angered at getting less!

It would be doing Anna a great injustice to suppose that her sad thoughts were all of herself on this mournful New Year's Day of 1915. Her sentimental heart was pierced with pain every time she looked into the face of her beloved nursling. Not that she often had an opportunity of looking into Rose's face, for Mrs. Jervis Blake (never would Anna get used to that name!) only came home to sleep. She almost always stayed and had supper with the Robeys, then she would rush home for the night, and after an early breakfast—during which, to Anna's thinking, she did not eat nearly enough—be off again to spend with her bridegroom whatever time she was not devoting to war work under Miss Forsyth.

Anna had been curious to know how soon Mr. Blake would be able to walk, but in answer to a very simple, affectionate question, the bride, who had just then been looking so happy—as radiant, indeed, as a German bride looks within a month of her marriage day—had burst into tears, and said hurriedly, "Oh, it won't be very long now, dear Anna, but I'd rather not talk about it, if you don't mind."

Yet another thing added to Anna's deep depression. It seemed to her that Alfred Head no longer enjoyed her company as he used to do. He had ordained that they must always speak English, even when alone; and to her mingled anger and surprise he had told her plainly that, in spite of his solemn assurance, he neither could nor would pay her the fifty shillings which was now owing to her in connection with that little secret matter arranged between herself and Willi three years ago.

About this question of the fifty shillings Mr. Head had behaved very strangely and rudely indeed. He had actually tried to persuade her *that he knew nothing of it*—that it was not he but someone else who had given her the five half-sovereigns on that evening of the 4th of August! Then when she, righteously indignant, had forced the reluctant memory upon him, he had explained that everything was now different, and that the passing of this money from him to her might involve them both in serious trouble.

Anna had never heard so flimsy an excuse. She felt sure that he was keeping her out of the money due to her because business was not quite so flourishing now as it had been.

CHAPTER XXVII

The days went on, and to Mrs. Otway's surprise and bitter disappointment, there came no answer to the letter she had written to the German surgeon. She had felt so sure that he would write again very soon—if not exactly by return, then within a week or ten days.

The only people she told were Major Guthrie's solicitor, Robert Allen, and her daughter. But though both, in their different ways, sympathised with her deeply, neither of them could do anything to help her. Rather against her will, Mr. Allen wrote and informed his client of Mrs. Guthrie's death, asking for instructions concerning certain urgent business matters. But even that letter did not draw any answer from the Field Lazarette.

As for Rose, she soon gave up asking if another letter had come, and to Mrs. Otway's sore heart it was as if the girl, increasingly absorbed in her own not always easy problem of keeping Jervis happy under the painful handicap of his present invalid condition, had no time to spare for that of anyone else. Poor Rose often felt that she would give, as runs the old saying, anything in the world to have her man to herself, as a cottage wife would have had hers by now—with no nurses, no friends, no doctor even, save perhaps for a very occasional visit.

But Mrs. Otway was not fair to Rose; in never mentioning Major Guthrie and the terrible misfortune which had befallen him, she was treating her mother as she herself would have wished to be treated in a like case.

A great trouble overshadows all little troubles. One disagreeable incident which, had life been normal with her then, would have much irritated and annoyed the mistress of the Trellis House, was the arrival of a curt notice stating that her telephone was to be disconnected, owing to the fact that there resided in her house an enemy alien in the person of one Anna Bauer.

Now the telephone had never been as necessary to Mrs. Otway as it was to many of her acquaintances, but lately, since her life had become so lonely, she had fallen into the way of talking over it each morning with Miss Forsyth.

Miss Forsyth, whom the people of Witanbury thought so absurdly old-fashioned, had been one of the very first telephone subscribers in Witanbury. But she had sternly set her face against its frivolous and extravagant use. This being so, it was a little strange that she so willingly spent five minutes or more of her morning work-time in talking over it to Mrs. Otway. But Miss Forsyth had become aware that all was not well with her friend, and this seemed the only way she was able to help in a trouble or state of mental distress to which she had no clue—though sometimes a suspicion which touched on the fringe of the truth came into her mind.

During these morning talks they would sometimes discuss the War. Mrs. Otway never spoke of the War to anyone else, for even now she could not bring herself to share the growing horror and, yes, contempt, all those about her felt for Germany. Miss Forsyth was an intelligent woman, and, as her friend knew, had sources of information denied to the amateur strategists and gossips of Witanbury Close. So it was that the forced discontinuance of the little morning talk, which so often brought comfort to Mrs. Otway's sore heart, was a real pain and loss.

She had made a spirited protest, pointing out that all her neighbours had the telephone, and that by merely asking any of them to allow her servant to send a message, she could circumvent this, to her, absurd and unnecessary rule. But her protest had only brought a formal acknowledgment, and that very day her telephone had been disconnected.

She would have been astonished, even now, had she known with what ever-swelling suspicion some of her neighbours and acquaintances regarded her.

The great rolling uplands round the city were now covered with vast camps, and Witanbury every day was full of soldiers; there was not a family in the Close, and scarce a family in the town, but had more than one near and dear son, husband, brother, lover, in the New Armies, if not yet—as in very many cases—already out at the Front.

In spite of what was still described as Rose Otway's "romantic marriage," Mrs. Otway was regarded as having no connection with the Army, and her old affection for Germany and the Germans was resented, as also the outstanding fact that she still retained in her service an enemy alien.

And, as is almost always the case, there was some ground for this feeling, for it was true that the mistress of the Trellis House took very little interest in the course of the great struggle which was going on in France and in Flanders. She glanced over the paper each morning, and often a name seen in the casualty lists brought her the painful task of writing a letter of condolence to some old friend or acquaintance. But she did not care, as did all the people around her, to talk about the War. It had brought to her, personally, too much hidden pain. How surprised her critics would have been had an angel, or some equally credible witness informed them that of all the women of their acquaintance there was no one whose life had been more altered or affected by the War than Mary Otway's!

She was too unhappy to care much what those about her thought of her. Even so, it did hurt her when she came, slowly, to realise that the Robeys and Mrs. Haworth, who were after all the most intimate of her neighbours in the Close, regarded with surprise, and yes, indignation, what they imagined to be an unpatriotic disinclination on her part to follow intelligently the march of events.

It took her longer to find out that the continued presence of her good old Anna at the Trellis House was rousing a certain amount of disagreeable comment. At first no one had thought it in the least strange that Anna stayed on with her, but now, occasionally, someone said a word indicative of surprise that there should be a German woman living in Witanbury Close.

But what were these foolish, ignorant criticisms but tiny pin-pricks compared with the hidden wound in her heart? The news for which she craved was not news of victory from the Front, but news that at last the negotiations now in progress for the exchange of disabled prisoners of war had been successful. That news, however, seemed as if it would never come.

In one thing Mrs. Otway was fortunate. There was plenty of hard work to do that winter in Witanbury, and, in spite of her supposed lack of interest in the War, Mrs. Otway had a wonderful way with soldiers' wives and mothers, so much so that in time all the more difficult cases were handed over to her. ⇁

"This is to warn you that you are being watched. A friend of England is keeping an eye on you, not ostentatiously, but none the less very closely. Dismiss the German woman who has already been too long in your employment. England can take no risks."

Mrs. Otway had come home, after a long afternoon of visiting, and found this anonymous letter waiting for her. On the envelope her name and address were inscribed in large capitals.

She stared down at the dictatorial message—written of course in a disguised hand—with mingled disgust and amusement. Then, suddenly, she made up her mind to show it to Miss Forsyth before burning it.

Tired though she was, she left the house again, and slowly walked round to see her old friend.

Miss Forsyth smiled over it, but she also frowned, and she frowned more than she smiled when Mrs. Otway exclaimed, "Did you ever see such an extraordinary thing?"

"It is not so extraordinary as you think, Mary! I must honestly tell you that in my opinion the writer of this anonymous letter is right in believing that there is a good deal of spying and of conveying valuable information to the enemy."

She waited a moment, and then went on, deliberately: "I suppose you are quite sure of your old Anna, my dear? Used she not to be in very close touch with Berlin? Has she broken all that off since the War began?"

"Indeed she has!" cried Mrs. Otway eagerly. She was surprised at the turn the conversation had taken. Was it conceivable that Miss Forsyth must be numbered henceforth among the spy maniacs of whom she knew there were a good many in Witanbury? "She made every kind of effort early in the War—for the matter of that I did what I could to help her—to get into touch with her relations there, for she was very anxious and miserable about them. But she failed—absolutely failed!"

"And how about her German friends in England? I suppose she has German friends?"

"To the best of my belief, she hasn't a single German acquaintance!" exclaimed Anna's mistress confidently. "She used to know those unfortunate Fröhlings rather well, but, as I daresay you know, they left Witanbury quite early in the War—in fact during the first week of war. And she certainly hasn't heard from them. I asked her if she had, some time ago. Dear Miss Forsyth, do believe me when I say that, apart from her very German appearance, and her funny way of talking, my poor old Anna is to all intents and purposes an Englishwoman. Why, she has lived in England twenty-two years!"

There came a very curious, dubious, hesitating expression on Miss Forsyth's face. "I daresay that what you say is true," she said at last. "But even so, if I were you, Mary, I should show her that letter. She may be in touch with some of her own people—I mean in all innocence. It would be very disagreeable for you if such turned out to be the case. I happen to know that Witanbury is believed to be—well, what shall I call it?—a spy centre for this part of England. I don't know that it's so much the city, as the neighbourhood. You see, we're not so very far away from one of the beaches which it is thought the Germans, if they did try a landing, would choose as a good place."

Mrs. Otway's extreme astonishment showed in her face.

"You know I never gossip, Mary, so you may take what I say as being true. But I beg you to keep it to yourself. Don't even tell Rose, or the Dean. My information does not come from anyone here, in Witanbury. It comes from London."

Straws show the way the wind is blowing. The anonymous letter sent to the Trellis House was one straw; another was the revelation made to Mrs. Otway by Miss Forsyth.

The wind indicated by these two small straws suddenly developed, on the 25th of March, into a hurricane. Luckily it was not a hurricane which affected Mrs. Otway or her good old Anna at all directly, but it upset them both, in their several ways, very much indeed, for it took the extraordinary shape of a violent attack by a mob armed with pickaxes and crowbars on certain so-called Germans—for they were all naturalised—and their property.

A very successful recruiting meeting had been held in the Market Place. At this meeting the local worthies had been present in force. Thus, on the platform which had been erected in front of the Council House, the Lord Lieutenant of the County, supported by many religious dignitaries, headed by the Dean, had made an excellent speech, followed by other short, stirring addresses, each a trumpet call to the patriotism of Witanbury. Not one of these speeches incited to violence in any form, but reference had naturally been made to some of the terrible things that the Germans had done in Belgium, and one speaker had made it very plain that should a German invasion take place on the British coast, the civilian population must expect that the fate of Belgium would be theirs.

The meeting had come to a peaceful end, and then, an hour later, as soon as the great personages had all gone and night had begun to fall, rioting had suddenly broken out, the rioters being led by two women, both Irish-women, whose husbands were believed to have been cruelly ill-treated when on their way to a prison camp in Germany.

The story had been published in the local paper, on the testimony of a medical orderly who had come back to England after many strange adventures. True, an allusion had been made to the matter in one of the recruiting speeches, but the speaker had not made very much of it; and though what he had said had drawn groans from his large audience, and though the words he had used undoubtedly made it more easy for the magistrate, when he came to deal with the case of these two women, to dismiss them with only a caution, yet no one could reasonably suppose that it was this which led to the riot.

For a few minutes things had looked very ugly. A good deal of damage was done, for instance, to the boot factory, which was still being managed (and very well managed too) by a naturalised German and his son. Then the rioters had turned their attention to the Witanbury Stores. "The Kaiser," as Alfred Head was still called by his less kindly neighbours, had always been disliked in the poorer quarters of the town, and that long before the War. Now was the time for paying off old scores. So the plate-glass windows were shivered with a will, as well as with pickaxes; and all the goods, mostly consisting of bacon, butter, and cheese, which had dressed those windows, had been taken out, thrown among the rioters, and borne off in triumph. It was fortunate that no damage had been done there to life or limb.

Alfred Head had fled at once to the highest room in the building. There he had stayed, locked in, cowering and shivering, till the police, strongly reinforced by soldiers, had driven the rioters off.

Polly at first had stood her ground. "Cowards! Cowards!" she had cried, bravely rushing into the shop; and it was no thanks to the rioters that she had not been very roughly handled indeed. Luckily the police just then had got in by the back of the building, and had dragged her away.

Even into the quiet Close there had penetrated certain ominous sounds indicative of what was going on in the Market Place. And poor old Anna had gone quite white, or rather yellow, with fright.

By the next morning the cold fit had succeeded the hot fit, and all Witanbury was properly ashamed of what had happened. The cells under the Council Chamber were fuller than they had ever been, and no one could be found to say a good word for the rioters.

As for Dr. Haworth, he was cut to the heart by what had occurred, and it became known that he had actually offered the hospitality of the Deanery to Mr. and Mrs. Alfred Head, even to sending his own carriage for them — or so it was averred. Gratefully had they accepted his kindness; and though Alfred Head was now back in his place of business, trying to estimate the damage and to arrange for its being made good, Polly was remaining on at the Deanery for a few hours.

But those two days, which will be always remembered by the people of the cathedral city as having witnessed the one War riot of Witanbury, were to have very different associations for Mrs. Otway and her daughter, Rose Blake. For on the morning of the 26th a telegram arrived at the Trellis House containing the news that at last the exchange of disabled prisoners had been arranged, and that Major Guthrie's name was in the list of those British officers who might be expected back from Germany, *via* Holland, within the next forty-eight hours.

And, as if this was not joy enough, Sir Jacques, on the same day, told his young friends that now at last the time had come when they might go off, alone together, to the little house, within sound of the sea, which an old friend of Lady Blake had offered to lend them for Jervis's convalescence — and honeymoon.

CHAPTER XXVIII

Anna was hurrying through the quiet streets of Witanbury on her way to Mr. Head's Stores.

As she walked along, looking neither to the right nor to the left, for she had of late become unpleasantly conscious of her alien nationality, she pondered with astonishment and resentment the events of the last two days—the receipt of a telegram by Mrs. Otway, and its destruction, or at any rate its disappearance, before she, Anna, could learn its contents; and, evidently in consequence of the telegram, her mistress's hurried packing and departure for London.

Then had followed a long, empty day, the old woman's feelings of uneasiness and curiosity being but little relieved by Rose's eager words, uttered late on the same evening: "Oh, Anna, didn't mother tell you the great news? Major Guthrie is coming home. She has gone up to meet him!" The next morning Mrs. Jervis Blake herself had gone to London, this being the first time she had left her husband since their marriage.

There had come another day of trying silence for Anna, and then a letter from Rose to her old nurse. It was a letter which contained astounding news. Mrs. Otway was coming back late to-night, and was to be married— *married*, to-morrow morning in the Cathedral, to Major Guthrie!

The bride-elect sent good old Anna her love, and bade her not worry.

Of all the injunctions people are apt to give one another, perhaps the most cruel and the most futile is that of not to worry. Mrs. Otway had really meant to be kind, but her message gave Anna Bauer a most unhappy day. The old German woman had long ago made up her mind that when it suited herself she would leave the Trellis House, but never, never had it occurred to her that anything could happen which might compel her to do so.

At last, when evening fell, she felt she could no longer bear her loneliness and depression. Also she longed to tell her surprising news to sympathetic ears.

All through that long day Anna Bauer had been making up her mind to go back to Germany. She knew that there would be no difficulty about it, for something Mrs. Otway had told her a few weeks ago showed that many German women were going home, helped thereto by the British Government. As for Willi and Minna, however bitterly they might feel towards England, they would certainly welcome her when they realised how much money, all her savings, she was bringing with her.

As she walked quickly along—getting very puffy, for she was stout and short of breath—it seemed to her as if the kindly old city, where she had lived in happiness and amity for so many years, had changed in character. She felt as if the windows of the houses were frowning down at her, and as if cruel pitfalls yawned in her way.

Her depression was increased by her first sight of the building for which she was bound, for, as she walked across the Market Place, she saw the boarded up shop-front of the Stores. "Mr. Head hoped to get the plate-glass to-morrow"—so the boy who had brought the butter and eggs that morning had exclaimed—"but just now there was a great shortage of that particular kind of shop-front glass, as it was mostly made in Belgium."

Meanwhile the Witanbury Stores presented a very sorry appearance—the more so that some evilly disposed person had gone in the dark, after the boarding had been put up, and splashed across the boards a quantity of horrid black stuff!

Anna hurried round to the back door. In answer to her ring, the door was opened at last a little way, and Polly's pretty, anxious face looked out cautiously. But when she saw who it was, she smiled pleasantly.

"Oh, come in, Mrs. Bauer! I'm glad to see you. You'll help me cheer poor Alfred up a bit. Not but what he ought to be happy now—for what d'you think happened at three o'clock to-day? Why, the Dean himself came along and left a beautiful letter with us—an Address, *he* called it." She was walking down the passage as she spoke, and when she opened the parlour door she called out cheerfully, "Here's Mrs. Bauer come to see us! I tell her she'll have to help cheer you up a bit."

And truth to tell Alfred Head did look both ill and haggard—but no, not unhappy. Even Anna noticed that there was a gleam of triumph in his eyes. "Very pleased to see you, I'm sure!" he exclaimed cordially. "Yes, it is as Polly says—out of evil good has come to us. See here, my dear friend!"

Anna came forward. She already felt better, less despondent, but it was to Polly she addressed her condolences. "What wicked folk in this city there are!" she exclaimed. "Even Mr. Robey to me says, 'Dastardly conduct!'"

"Yes, yes," said Polly hastily. "It was *dreadful*! But look at this, Mrs. Bauer——" She held towards Anna a large sheet of thick, fine cream-laid paper. Across the top was typed—

"TO ALFRED HEAD,
CITY COUNCILLOR OF WITANBURY."

Then underneath, also in typewriting, the following words:

> We the undersigned, your fellow-countrymen and fellow-citizens of Witanbury, wish to express to you our utter abhorrence and sense of personal shame in the dastardly attack which was made on your house and property on March 25, 1915. As a small token of regard we desire to inform you that we have started a fund for compensating you for any material loss you may have incurred which is not covered by your plate-glass insurance."

There followed, written in ink, a considerable number of signatures. These were headed by the Dean, and included the names of most of the canons and minor canons, four Dissenting ministers, and about a hundred others belonging to all classes in and near the cathedral city.

True, there were certain regrettable omissions, but fortunately neither Mr. and Mrs. Head nor Anna seemed aware of it. One such omission was that of the Catholic priest. Great pressure had been brought to bear on him, but perhaps because there was little doubt that members of his congregation had been concerned in the outrage, he had obstinately refused to sign the Address. More strange and regrettable was the fact that Miss Forsyth's name was also omitted from the list. In answer to a personal appeal made to her by the Dean, who had himself gone to the trouble of calling in order to obtain her signature, she had explained that she never did give her signature. She had made the rule thirty years ago, and she saw no reason for breaking it to-day.

Anna looked up from the paper, and her pale blue, now red-rimmed, eyes sparkled with congratulation. "This is good!" she exclaimed in German. "Very, very good!"

Her host answered in English, "Truly I am gratified. It is a compensation to me for all I have gone through these last few days."

"Yes," said Polly quickly. "And as you see, Mrs. Bauer, we are to be really compensated. We were thinking only yesterday that the damage done—I mean the damage by which we should be out of pocket—was at least £15. But, as Alfred says, that was putting it very low. He thinks, and

I quite agree—don't you, Mrs. Bauer?—that it would be fair to put the damage down at—let me see, what did you say, Alfred?"

"According to my calculation," he said cautiously, "I think we may truly call it twenty-seven pounds ten shillings and ninepence."

"That," said Polly, "is allowing for the profit we should certainly have made on the articles those wretches stole out of the windows. I think it's fair to do that, don't you, Mrs. Bauer?"

"Indeed yes—that thoroughly to agree I do!" exclaimed Anna.

And then rather sharply, perhaps a trifle anxiously, Alfred Head leant over to his visitor, and looking at her very straight, he said, "And do you bring any news to-night? Not that there ever seems any good news now—and the other sort we can do without."

She understood that this was Mr. Head's polite way of asking why she had come this evening, without an invitation. Hurriedly she answered, "No news of any special kind I have—though much that me concerns. Along to ask your advice I came. Supper require I do not."

"Oh, but you must stop and have supper with us—with me I mean," said Polly eagerly, "for Alfred is going out—aren't you, Alfred?"

He hesitated a moment. "I shall see about doing that. There is no hurry. Well, what is it you want to ask me, Mrs. Bauer?"

At once Anna plunged into her woes, disappointment, and fears. Now that the excitement and pride induced by the Address had gone from his face, Alfred Head looked anxious and uneasy; but on hearing Anna's great piece of news he looked up eagerly.

"Mrs. Otway and this Major Guthrie to be married at the Cathedral to-morrow? But this is very exciting news!" he exclaimed. "D'you hear that, Polly? I think we must go to this ceremony. It will be very interesting——" his eyes gleamed; there was a rather wolfish light in them. "The poor gentleman is blind, is he? It is lucky he will not see how old his bride looks——" he added a word or two in German.

Anna shrank back, and, speaking German too, she answered, "Mrs. Otway has a very young face, and when not unhappy, she is very bright and lively. For my part, I think this Major a very-much-to-be-envied man!" Her loyalty to the woman who had been kind and good to her over so many years awakened, tardily.

"No doubt, no doubt," said Alfred Head carelessly. "But now I suppose you are thinking of yourself, Frau Bauer?"

Polly broke in: "Do talk in English," she said pettishly. "You can't think how tiresome it is to hear that rook's language going on all the time!"

Her husband laughed. "Well, I suppose this marriage will make a difference to you?" he said in English.

"A difference?" exclaimed Anna ruefully. "Why, my good situation me it loses. Home to the Fatherland my present idea is——" her eyes filled with big tears.

Her host looked at her thoughtfully. What an old fool she was! But that, from his point of view, was certainly not to be regretted. She had served his purpose well—and more than once.

"Mrs. Otway she a friend has who a German maid had. The maid last week to Holland was sent, so no trouble can there be. However, one thing there is——" she looked dubiously at Polly. "Mrs. Head here knows, does she, about my——?"

And then at once between Alfred Head's teeth came the angry command, in her own language, to speak German.

She went on eagerly, fluently now: "You will understand, Mr. Head, that I cannot behave wrongly to my dear nephew Willi's superior. I have been wondering to-night whether I could hand the affair over to you. After all, a hundred marks a year are not to be despised in these times. You yourself say that after the War the money will be made up——" she looked at him expectantly.

He said rather quickly to his wife, "Look here, Polly! Never mind this—it's business you wouldn't understand!" And his wife shrugged her shoulders. She didn't care what the old woman was saying to Alfred. She supposed it was something about the War—the War of which she was so heartily sick, and which had brought them, personally, such bad luck.

"It is difficult to decide such a thing in a hurry," said Alfred Head slowly.

"But it will have to be decided in a hurry," said Anna firmly. "What is to happen if to-morrow Mrs. Otway comes and tells me that I am to go away to London, to Louisa? English people are very funny, as you know well, Herr Hegner!" In her excitement she forgot his new name, and he winced a little when he heard the old appellation, but he did not rebuke her, and she went on: "Willi told me, and so did the gentleman, that on *no* account must I move that which was confided to me."

"Attend to me, Frau Bauer!" he said imperiously. "This matter is perhaps more important than even you know, especially at such a time as this."

"Ach, yes!" she said. "I have often said that to myself. Willi's friend may be interned by now in one of those horrible camps—it is indeed a difficult question!"

"I do not say I shall be able to do it, but I will make a big effort to have the whole business settled for you to-morrow morning. What do you say to that?"

"Splendid!" she exclaimed. "You are in truth a good friend to poor old Anna Bauer!"

"I wish to be," he said. "And you understand, do you not, Frau Bauer, that under no conceivable circumstances are you to bring me into the affair? Have I your word—your oath—on that?"

"Certainly," she said soberly. "You have my word, my oath, on it."

"You see it does not do for me to be mixed up with any Germans," he went on quickly. "I am an Englishman now—as this gratifying Address truly says— —" he waited a moment. "What would be the best time for the person who will come to call?"

Anna hesitated. "I don't know," she said helplessly. "The marriage is to be at twelve, and before then there will be a great deal of coming and going at the Trellis House."

"Is it necessary for you to attend the bridal?" he asked.

Anna shook her head. "No," she said, "I do not think so; I shall not be missed." There was a tone of bitterness in her voice.

"Then the best thing will be for your visitor to come during the marriage ceremony. That marriage will draw away all the busybodies. And it is not as if your visitor need stay long— —"

"Not more than a very few minutes," she said eagerly, and then, "Will it be the same gentleman who came three years ago?"

"Oh, no; it will be someone quite different. He will come in a motor, and I expect a Boy Scout will be with him."

A gleam of light shot across Anna's mind. But she made no remark, and her host went on:

"You realise that great care must be taken of those things. In fact, you had better leave it all to him."

"Oh, yes," she nodded understandingly. "I know they are fragile. I was told so."

It was extraordinary the relief she felt—more than relief, positive joy.

"As to the other matter—the matter of your returning to Germany," he said musingly, still speaking in his and her native language, "I think, yes, on the whole your idea is a good one, Frau Bauer. It is shameful that it should be so, but England is no place at present for an honest German woman who has not taken out her certificate. I wonder if you are aware that you will only be allowed to take away a very little money? You had better perhaps confide the rest of your savings to me. I will take care of them for you till the end of the War."

"Very little money?" repeated Anna, in a horrified, bewildered tone. "What do you mean, Herr Hegner? I do not understand."

"And yet it is clear enough," he said calmly. "The British Government will not allow anyone going to the Fatherland to take more than a very few pounds—just enough to get them where they want to go, and a mark or two over. But that need not distress you, Frau Bauer."

"But it does distress me very much!" exclaimed Anna. "In fact, I do not see now how I can go——" She began to cry. "Are you sure—quite sure—of what you say?"

"Yes, I am quite sure," he spoke rather grimly. "Well, if you feel in that way, there is nothing more to be said. You will either stay with your present lady, or you will have to go to the Pollits."

She looked up at him quickly; she was surprised that he remembered her daughter's married name, but it had slipped off his tongue quite easily.

"Never will I do that!" she exclaimed.

"Then you had better arrange to stop here. There are plenty of people in Witanbury who would be only too glad to have such an excellent help as you are, Frau Bauer."

"I shall not be compelled to look out for a new situation," she said quickly. "My young lady would never allow that—neither would Mrs. Otway!"

But even so, poor Anna felt disturbed—disturbed and terribly disheartened. The money she had saved was her own money! She could not understand by what right the British Government could prevent her taking it with her. It was this money alone that would ensure a welcome from the Warshauers. Willi and Minna could not be expected to want her unless she brought with her enough, not only to feed herself, but to give them a little help in these hard times. But soon she began to feel more cheerful. Mrs. Otway and the Dean would surely obtain permission for her to take her money back to Germany. It was a great deal of money—over three hundred pounds altogether.

Within an hour of her return to the Trellis House Anna heard the fly which had been ordered to meet Mrs. Otway at the station drive into the Close. For the first time, the very first time in over eighteen years, Anna did not long to welcome her two ladies home. Indeed, her heart now felt so hurt and sore that when she heard the familiar rumble she would have liked to run away and hide herself, instead of going to the front door.

And yet, when the two came through into the hall, Rose with something of her old happy look back again, and Mrs. Otway's face radiant as Anna had never seen it during all the peaceful years they two had dwelt so near to one another, the poor old woman's heart softened. "Welcome!" she said, in German. "Welcome, my dear mistress, and all happiness be yours!"

And then, after Rose had hurried off to Robey's, Mrs. Otway, while taking off her things, and watching Anna unpack her bag, told of Major Guthrie's home-coming.

In simple words she described the little group of people—of mothers, of wives, of sweethearts and of friends—who had waited at the London Docks for that precious argosy, the ship from Holland, to come in. And Anna furtively wiped away her tears as she heard of the piteous case of all those who thus returned home, and of the glowing joy of certain of the reunions which had then taken place. "Even those who had no friends there to greet them—only kind strangers—seemed happier than anyone I had ever seen."

Anna nodded understandingly. So she herself would feel, even if maimed and blind, to be once more in her own dear Fatherland. But she kept her thoughts to herself....

At last, after she had a little supper, Mrs. Otway came into the kitchen, and motioning to Anna to do likewise, she sat down.

"Anna?" she asked rather nervously, "do you know what is going to happen to-morrow?"

Anna nodded, and Mrs. Otway went on, almost as if speaking to herself rather than to the woman who was now watching her with strangely conflicting feelings: "It seems the only thing to do. I could not bear for him to go and live alone—even for only a short time—in that big house where he left his mother. But it was all settled very hurriedly, partly by telephone to the Deanery." She paused, for what she felt to be the hardest part of her task lay before her, and before she could go on, Anna spoke.

"I think," she said slowly, "I think, dear honoured lady, that it will be best for me to go to Germany, to stay with Minna and Willi till the War is over."

Mrs. Otway's eyes filled with tears, yet she felt as if a load of real anxiety had suddenly been lifted from her heart.

"Perhaps that will be best," she said. "But of course there is no hurry about it. There will be certain formalities to go through, and meanwhile——" Again she stopped speaking for a moment, then went on steadily: "A friend of Major Guthrie's—one of his brother officers who has just come home from the Front—is also to be married to-morrow. His name is Captain Pechell, and the lady also is known to Major Guthrie; her name is Miss Trepell. I have arranged to let the Trellis House to them for six weeks, and I have to tell you, Anna, that they will bring their own servants. Before I knew of this new plan of yours, I arranged for you to go to Miss Forsyth while this house is let. However, the matter will now be very much simpler to arrange, and you will only stay with Miss Forsyth till arrangements have been made for your comfortable return to Germany."

The colour rushed to Anna's face. Then she was being turned out—after all these years of devoted service!

Perhaps something of what Anna was feeling betrayed itself, for Mrs. Otway went on, nervously and conciliatingly: "I did try to arrange for you to go and spend the time with your daughter, but apparently they will not allow Germans to be transferred from one town to another without a great deal of fuss, and I knew, Anna, that you would not really want to go to the Pollits. I felt sure you would rather stay in Witanbury. But if you dislike the idea of going to Miss Forsyth, then I think I can arrange for you to come out to Dorycote——" But even as she said the words she knew that such an arrangement would never work.

"No, no," said Anna, in German. "It does not matter where I go for a few days. If I am in Miss Forsyth's house I can see my gracious young lady from time to time. She will ever be kind to her poor old nurse." And Mrs. Otway could not find it in her heart to tell Anna that Rose was also going away.

CHAPTER XXIX

Anna stood peeping behind the pretty muslin curtain of her kitchen window. She was standing in exactly the same place and attitude she had stood in eight months before, on the first day of war. But oh, how different were the sensations and the thoughts with which she now looked out on the familiar scene! She had then been anxious and disturbed, but not as she was disturbed and anxious to-day.

The Trellis House had become so entirely her home that she resented bitterly being forced to leave it against her will. Also, she dreaded the thought of the days she would have to spend under Miss Forsyth's roof.

Anna had never liked Miss Forsyth. Miss Forsyth had a rather short, sharp way with her, or so the old German woman considered—and her house was always full of such queer folk below and above stairs. Just now there was the Belgian family, and also, as Anna had managed to discover, three odd-come-shorts in the kitchen.

Anna's general unease had not been lessened by a mysterious letter which she had received from her daughter this morning. In it the writer hinted that her husband was getting into some fresh trouble. Louisa had ended with a very disturbing sentence: "I feel as if I can't bear my life!"—that was what Louisa had written.

The minutes dragged by, and Anna, staring out into the now deserted Close—deserted, save for a number of carriages and motors which were waiting by the little gate leading into the Cathedral enclosure—became very worried and impatient.

From her point of view it was much to be wished that the visitor she was expecting should be come and gone before the marriage party came out of the Cathedral; yet when she had seen how surprised, and even hurt, both her dear ladies had been on learning of her intention to stay at home this morning, she had nearly told them the truth! Everything was different now—Willi would not, could not, mind!

What had restrained her was the memory of how strongly Alfred Head had impressed on her the importance of secrecy—of secrecy as concerned himself. If she began telling anything, she might find herself telling everything. Also, Mrs. Otway might think it very strange, what English people call "sly," that Anna had not told her before.

And yet this matter she had kept so closely hidden within herself for three years was a very simple thing, after all! Only the taking charge of a number of parcels—four, as a matter of fact—for a gentleman who was incidentally one of Willi Warshauer's chiefs.

The person who had brought them to the Trellis House had come in the March of 1912, and she remembered him very distinctly. He had arrived in a motor, and had only stayed a very few minutes. Anna would have liked to have given him a little supper, but he had been in a great hurry, and in fact had hardly spoken to her at all.

From something which he had said when himself carefully bringing the parcels through the kitchen into her bedroom, and also from a word Willi had let fall, she knew that what had been left with her was connected with some new, secret process in the chemical business. In that special branch of trade, as Anna was aware, the Germans were far, far ahead of the British.

And as she stood there by the window, waiting, staring across the now deserted green, at the group of carriages which stood over near the gate leading to the Cathedral, she began to wonder uneasily if she had made it quite clear to Mr. Head that the man who was coming on this still secret business must be sure to come to-day! The lady and gentleman to whom the house had been let were arriving at six, and their maids two hours before.

Suddenly the bells rang out a joyous peal, and Anna felt a thrill of exasperation and sharp regret. If she had known that her visitor would be late, then she, too, could have been present in the Cathedral. It had been a bitter disappointment to her not to see her gracious lady married to Major Guthrie.

Letting the curtain fall, she went quickly upstairs into what had been Miss Rose's bedroom. From there she knew she could get a better view.

Yes, there they all were—streaming out of the great porch. She could now see the bride and bridegroom, arm-in-arm, walking down the path. They were walking more slowly than most newly married couples walked after a wedding. As a rule, wedding parties hurried rather quickly across the open space leading from the porch to the gate.

She lost sight of them while they were getting into the motor which had been lent to them for the occasion, but she did catch a glimpse of Mrs.

Otway's flushed face as the car sped along to the left, towards the gate house.

The path round the green was gradually filling up with people, for the congregation had been far larger than anyone had thought it would be. News in such a place as Witanbury spreads quickly, and though the number of invited guests had been very, very few, the number of uninvited sympathisers and interested spectators had been many.

Suddenly Anna caught sight of her young lady and of Mr. Jervis Blake. As she did so the tears welled up into her eyes, and rolled down her cheeks. She could never get used to the sight of this young bridegroom with his crutch, and that though he managed it very cleverly, and would soon—so Rose had declared—be able to do with only a stick.

Anna hoped that the two would come in and see her for a minute, but instead they joined Mr. and Mrs. Robey, and were now walking round the other side of the Close.

Anna went downstairs again. In a moment, Mr. Hayley, whom she had never liked, and who she felt sure did not like her, would be coming in to have his luncheon, with another gentleman from London.

Yes, there was the ring. She went to the front door and opened it with an unsmiling face. The two young men walked through into the hall. It would have been very easy for James Hayley to have said a kind word to the old German woman he had known so long, but it did not occur to him to do so; had anyone suggested it, he would certainly have done it.

"We've plenty of time," she heard him say to the other gentleman. "Your train doesn't go till two o'clock. As for me, I'm very hungry! I made a very early start, you know!" and he led his guest into the dining-room, calling out as he did so: "It's all right, Anna! We can wait on ourselves."

Anna went back into her kitchen. She reminded herself that Mr. Hayley was one of those gentlemen who give a great deal of trouble and never a tip—unless, that is, they are absolutely forced to do so by common custom.

In Germany a gentleman who was always lunching and dining at a house would, by that common custom, have been compelled to tip the servants—not so in this hospitable but foolish, ill-regulated England. Here people only tip when they sleep. Anna had always thought it an extremely unfair arrangement. Now Major Guthrie, though he was an Englishman, had lived enough in Germany to know what was right and usual, and several times, in the last few years, he had presented Anna with half a sovereign. This had naturally made her like him more than she would otherwise have done.

There came another ring at the door. This time it was Miss Forsyth, and there was quite a kindly smile on her face. "Well," she said, "well, Mrs. Bauer?" (she had never been as familiar with Anna as were most of Mrs. Otway's friends). "I have come to find something for Mrs. Ot—— I mean Mrs. Guthrie. She has given me the key of her desk." And she went through into the drawing-room.

Anna began moving about restlessly. Her tin trunk was packed, and all ready to be moved to Miss Forsyth's. And Mrs. Otway, busy as she had been and absorbed in her own affairs while in town, had yet remembered to stipulate that one of the large cupboards in Anna's bedroom should remain locked, and full of Anna's things.

It was now nearly one o'clock. What could have happened to her business visitor? And then, just as she was thinking this for the hundredth time, she heard the unmistakable sound of a motor coming slowly down the road outside. Quickly she went out to the back door.

The motor was a small, low, open car, and without surprise she saw that the man who now was getting out of it was the same person whom she had seen in the autumn leaving Alfred Head's house. But this time there was no Boy Scout—the stranger was alone.

He hurried towards her. "Am I speaking to Mrs. Bauer?" he asked, in a sharp, quick tone. And then, as she said "Yes," and dropped a little curtsey, he went on: "I had a breakdown—a most tiresome thing! But I suppose it makes no difference? You have the house to yourself?"

She hesitated—was she bound to tell him of the two gentlemen who were having their luncheon in the dining-room which overlooked the garden, and of Miss Forsyth in the drawing-room? She decided that no— she was not obliged to tell him anything of the sort. If she did, he might want to go away and come back another time. Then everything would have to be begun over again.

"The parcels all ready are," she said. "Shall I them bring?"

"No, no! I will come with you. We will make two journeys, each taking one. That will make the business less long."

He followed her through the kitchen, the scullery, and so into her bedroom.

There were two corded tin boxes, as well as a number of other packages, standing ready for removal.

"Surely I have not to take all this away?" he exclaimed. "I thought there were only four small parcels!"

Anna smiled. "Most of it my luggage is," she said. "These yours are— — " she pointed to four peculiar-shaped packages, which might have been old-fashioned bandboxes. They were done up in grey paper, the kind grocers use, and stoutly corded. Through each cord was fixed a small strong, iron handle. "They very heavy are," observed Anna thoughtfully.

And the man muttered something—it sounded like an oath. "I think you had better leave the moving of them to me," he said. "Stand aside, will you?"

He took up two of them; then once more uttered an exclamation, and let them gently down again. "I shall have to take one at a time," he said. "I'm not an over-strong man, Mrs. Bauer, and as you seem to have managed to move them, no doubt you can help me with this one."

Anna, perhaps because her nerves were somewhat on edge to-day, resented the stranger's manner. It was so short, so rude, and he had such a funny accent. Yet she felt sure, in spite of the excellent German she had overheard him speak to Mr. Head, that he was not a fellow-countryman of hers. Then, suddenly, looking at his queerly trimmed beard, she told herself that he might be an American. Alfred Head had lived for a long time in America, and this probably was one of his American friends.

After they had taken out two of the parcels and placed them at the back of the motor, Anna suddenly bethought herself of what Alfred Head had said to her. "Give me, please," she said, "the money which to me since January 1st owing has been. Fifty shillings—two pound ten it is."

"I know nothing of that," said the man curtly. "I have had no instructions to pay you any money, Mrs. Bauer."

Anna felt a rush of anger come over her. She was not afraid of this weasel-faced little man. "Then the other two parcels take away you will not," she exclaimed. "To that money a right I have!"

They were facing each other in the low-ceilinged, dim, badly-lit bedroom. The stranger grew very red.

"Look here!" he said conciliatingly; he was really in a great hurry to get away. "I promise to send you this money to-night, Mrs. Bauer. You can trust me. I have not got it on me, truly. You may search me if you like." He smiled a little nervously, and advancing towards her opened his big motor coat.

Anna shrank back. "You truly send it will?" she asked doubtfully.

"I will send it to Hegner for you. Nay, more— — I will give you a piece of paper, and then Hegner will pay you at once." He tore a page out of his pocket-book, and scribbled on it a few words.

She took the bit of paper, folded it, and put it in her purse.

As they were conveying the third oddly-shaped parcel through the kitchen, she said conciliatingly, "Curious it is to have charge of luggage so long and not exactly what it is to know!"

He made no answer to this remark. But suddenly, in a startled, suppressed whisper, he exclaimed, *"Who's that?"*

Anna looked round. "Eh?" she said.

"You told me there was no one in the house, but someone has just come out of the gate, and is standing by my motor!" He added sternly, "Was heisst das?" (What does this mean?)

Anna hurried to the window and looked through the muslin curtain hanging in front of it. Yes, the stranger had spoken truly. There was Mr. Hayley, standing between the little motor-car and the back door.

"Do not yourself worry," she said quickly. "It is only a gentleman who luncheon here has eaten. Go out and explain to him everything I will."

But the man had turned a greenish-white colour. "How d'you mean 'explain'?" he said roughly, in English.

"Explain that they are things of mine—luggage—that taking away you are," said Anna.

The old woman could not imagine why the stranger showed such agitation. Mr. Hayley had no kind of right to interfere with her and her concerns, and she had no fear that he would do so.

"If you are so sure you can make it all right," the man whispered low in German, "I will leave the house by some other way—there is surely some back way of leaving the house? I will walk away, and stop at Hegner's till I know the coast is clear."

"There is no back way out," whispered Anna, also in German. She was beginning to feel vaguely alarmed. "But no one can stop you. Walk straight out, while I stay and explain. I can make it all right."

In a gingerly way he moved to one side the heavy object he had been carrying, and then, as if taking shelter behind her, he followed the old woman out through the door.

"What's this you're taking out of the house, Anna?" Mr. Hayley's tone was not very pleasant. "You mustn't mind my asking you. My aunt, as you know, told me to remain here to-day to look after things."

"Only my luggage it is," stammered Anna. "I had hoped to have cleared out my room while the wedding in progress was."

"Your luggage?" repeated James Hayley uncomfortably. He was now feeling rather foolish, and it was to him a very disturbing because an unusual sensation.

"Yes, my luggage," repeated Anna. "And this"—she hesitated a moment—"this person here is going to look for a man to help carry out my heavy boxes. There are two. He cannot manage them himself."

James Hayley looked surprised, but to her great relief, he allowed the stranger to slip by, and Anna for a moment watched the little man walking off at a smart pace towards the gate house. She wondered how she could manage to send him a message when the tiresome, inquisitive Mr. Hayley had gone.

"But whose motor is that?" Mr. Hayley went on, in a puzzled tone. "You must forgive me for asking you, Anna, but you know we live in odd times." He had followed her into the kitchen, and was now standing there with her. As she made no answer, he suddenly espied the odd-looking parcel which stood close to his feet, where the stranger had put it down.

Mr. Hayley stooped, really with the innocent intention of moving the parcel out of the way. "Good gracious!" he cried. "This is a tremendous weight, Anna. What on earth have you got in there?" He was now dragging it along the floor.

"Don't do that, sir," she exclaimed involuntarily. "It's fragile."

"Fragile?" he repeated. "Nonsense! It must be iron or copper. What is it, Anna?"

She shook her head helplessly. "I do not know. It is something I have been keeping for a friend."

His face changed. He took a penknife out of his pocket, and ripped off the stout paper covering.

Then, before the astonished Anna could make a movement, he very quietly pinioned her elbows and walked her towards the door giving into the hall.

"Captain Joddrell?" he called out. And with a bewildered feeling of abject fear, Anna heard the quick steps of the soldier echoing down the hall.

"Yes; what is it?"

"I want your help over something."

They were now in the hall, and Miss Forsyth, standing in the doorway of the drawing-room, called out suddenly, "Oh, Mr. Hayley, you are hurting her!"

"No, I'm not. Will you please lock the front door?"

Then he let go of Anna's arms. He came round and gazed for a moment into her terrified face. There was a dreadful look of contempt and loathing in his eyes. "You'd better say nothing," he muttered. "Anything you say now may be used in evidence against you!"

He drew the other man aside and whispered something; then they came back to where Anna stood, and she felt herself pushed—not exactly roughly, but certainly very firmly—by the two gentlemen into the room where were the remains of the good cold luncheon which she had set out there some two hours before.

She heard the key turned on her, and then a quick colloquy outside. She heard Mr. Hayley exclaim, "Now we'd better telephone to the police." And then, a moment later: "But the telephone's gone! What an extraordinary thing! This becomes, as in 'Alice in Wonderland,' curiouser and curiouser——" There was a tone of rising excitement in his quiet, rather mincing voice. Then came the words, "Look here! You'd better go outside and see that no one comes near that motor-car, while I hurry along to the place they call 'Robey's.' There's sure to be a telephone there."

Anna felt her legs giving way, and a sensation of most horrible fear came over her. She bitterly repented now that she had not told Mr. Hayley the truth—that these parcels which she had now kept for three years were only harmless chemicals, connected with an invention which was going to make the fortune of a great many people, including her nephew, Willi Warshauer, once this terrible war was over.

The police? Anna had a great fear of the police, and that though she knew herself to be absolutely innocent of any wrong-doing. She felt sure that the fact that she was German would cause suspicion. The worst would be believed of her. She remembered with dismay the letter some wicked, spiteful person had written to her mistress—and then, with infinite comfort, she suddenly remembered that this same dear mistress was only a little over two miles off. She, Anna, would not wish to disturb her on her wedding day, but if very hard pressed she could always do so. And Miss Rose—Miss Rose and Mr. Blake—they too were close by; they certainly would take her part!

She sat down, still sadly frightened, but reassured by the comfortable knowledge that her dear, gracious ladies would see her through any trouble, however much the fact that her country was at war with England might prejudice the police against her.

CHAPTER XXX

It was late afternoon in the same day, a bright, sunny golden afternoon, more like a warm May day than a day in March.

The bride and bridegroom, each feeling more than a little shy, had enjoyed their late luncheon, the first they had ever taken alone together. And Major Guthrie had been perhaps rather absurdly touched to learn, from a word dropped by Howse, that the new mistress had herself carefully arranged that this first meal should consist of dishes which Howse had told her his master particularly liked. And as they sat there, side by side, in their pleasant dining-room—for he had not cared to take the head of the table—the bridegroom hoped his bride would never know that since his blindness he had retained very little sense of taste.

After luncheon they had gone out into the garden, and she had guided his footsteps along every once familiar path. Considering how long he had been away, everything was in very fair order, and she was surprised to find how keen he was about everything. He seemed to know every shrub and plant there, and she felt as if in that hour he taught her more of practical gardening than she had ever known.

And then, at last, they made their way to the avenue which was the chief glory of the domain, and which had certainly been there in the days when the house had stood in a park, before the village of which it was the Manor had grown to be something like a suburb of Witanbury.

There they had paced up and down, talking of many things; and it was he who, suggesting that she must be tired, at last made her sit down on the broad wooden bench, from where she could see without being seen the long, low house and wide lawn.

They both, in their very different ways, felt exquisitely at peace. To his proud, reticent nature, the last few days had proved disagreeable—sometimes acutely unpleasant. He had felt grateful for, but he had not enjoyed, the marks of sympathy which had been so freely lavished on him and on his companions in Holland, on the boat, and since his landing in England.

In those old days which now seemed to have belonged to another existence, Major Guthrie had thought his friend, Mrs. Otway, if wonderfully kind, not always very tactful. It is a mistake to think that love is blind as to those matters. But of all the kind women he had seen since he had left Germany, she was the only one who had not spoken to him of his blindness, who had made no allusion to it, and who had not pressed on him painful, unsought sympathy. From the moment they had been left alone for a little while in that unknown London house, where he had first been taken, she had made him feel that he was indeed the natural protector and helper of the woman he loved; and of the things she had said to him, in those first moments of emotion, what had touched and pleased him most was her artless cry, "Oh, you don't know how I have missed you! Even quite at first I felt so miserable without you!"

It was Rose who had suggested an immediate marriage; Rose who had—well, yes, there was no other word for it—coaxed them both into realizing that it was the only thing to do.

Even now, on this their wedding day, they felt awkward, and yes, very shy the one with the other. And as he sat there by her side, wearing a rough grey suit he had often worn last winter when calling on her in the Trellis House, her cheeks grew hot when she remembered the letter she had written to him. Perhaps he had thought it an absurdly sentimental letter for a woman of her age to write.

The only thing that reassured her was the fact that once, at luncheon, he had clasped her hand under the table; but the door had opened, and quickly he had taken his hand away, and even moved his chair a little farther off. It was true that Howse had put the chairs very close together.

Now she was telling him of all that had happened since he had gone away, and he was listening with the eager sympathy and interest he had always shown her, that no one else had ever shown her in the same degree, in those days that now seemed so long ago, before the War.

So she went on, pouring it all out to him, till she came to the amazing story of her daughter Rose, and of Jervis Blake. She described the strange, moving little marriage ceremony; and the man sitting by her side sought and found the soft hand which was very close to his, and said feelingly, "That must have been very trying for *you*."

Yes, it had been trying for her, though no one had seemed to think so at the time. But he, the speaker of these kind understanding words, had always known how she felt, and sympathised with her.

She wished he would call her "Mary"—if only he would begin, she would soon find it quite easy to call him "Alick...."

Suddenly there came on his sightless face a slight change. He had heard something which her duller ears had failed to hear.

"What's that?" he asked uneasily.

"It's only a motor-car coming round to the front door. I hope they will send whoever it is away," the colour rushed into her face.

"Oh, surely Howse will do that to-day——"

And then she saw the man-servant come out of the house and advance towards them. There was a salver in his hand, and on the salver a note.

"The gentleman who brought this is waiting, ma'am, to see you."

She took up the envelope and glanced down at it. Her new name looked so odd in Dr. Haworth's familiar writing—it evoked a woman who had been so very different from herself, and yet for whom she now felt a curious kind of retrospective tenderness.

She opened the note with curiosity.

> "Dear Mrs. Guthrie,
>
> "The bearer of this, Mr. Reynolds of the Home Office, will explain to you why we are anxious that you should come into Witanbury for an hour this afternoon. I am sure Major Guthrie would willingly spare you if he knew how very important and how delicate is the business in question. Please tell him that we will keep you as short a time as possible. In fact, it is quite probable that you will be back within an hour.
>
> "Very truly yours,
> "Edmund Haworth."

She looked down at the letter with feelings of surprise and of annoyance. Uncaring of Howse's discreet presence, she read it aloud. "It's very mysterious and queer, isn't it? But I'm afraid I shall have to go."

"Yes, of course you will. It would have been better under the circumstances for the Dean to have told you what they want to see you about."

In the old days, Major Guthrie had never shared Mrs. Otway's admiration for Dr. Haworth, and now he felt rather sharply disturbed. The Home Office? The words bore a more ominous sound to him than they did, fortunately, to her. Was it possible that she had been communicating, in secret, with some of her German friends? He rose from the bench on which they had been sitting: "Is the gentleman in the motor, Howse?"

"Yes, sir. He wouldn't come in."

"Go and tell him that we are coming at once."

And then, after a moment, he said quietly, "I'm coming, too."

"Oh, but——" she exclaimed.

"I don't choose to have my wife's presence commanded by the Dean of Witanbury, or even, if it comes to that, by the Home Office."

She seized his arm, and pressed close to him. "I do believe," she cried, "that you suspect me of having got into a scrape! Indeed, indeed I have done nothing!" She was smiling, though moved almost to tears by the way he had just spoken. It was a new thing to her to be taken care of, to feel that there was someone ready, aye, determined, to protect her, and take her part. Also, it was the first time he had called her his wife.

A few minutes later they were sitting side by side in a large, open motor-car. Mr. Reynolds was a pleasant, good-looking man of about thirty, and he had insisted on giving up his seat to Major Guthrie. There would have been plenty of room for the three of them leaning back, but he had preferred to sit opposite to them, and now he was looking, with a good deal of sympathy, interest, and respect at the blind soldier, and with equal interest, but with less liking and respect, at Major Guthrie's wife.

Mr. Reynolds disliked pro-Germans and spy-maniacs with almost equal fervour; his work brought him in contact with both. From what he had been able to learn, the lady sitting opposite to him was to be numbered among the first category.

"And now," said Major Guthrie, leaning his sightless face forward, "will you kindly inform me for what reason my wife has been summoned to Witanbury this afternoon? The Dean's letter—I do not know if you have read it—is expressed in rather mysterious and alarming language."

The man he addressed waited for a moment. He knew that the two people before him had only been married that morning.

"Yes, that is so," he said frankly. "I suppose the Dean thought it best that I should inform Mrs. Guthrie of the business which brought me to Witanbury three hours ago. It chanced that I was in the neighbourhood, so when the Witanbury police telephoned to London, I, being known to be close here, was asked to go over."

"The police?" repeated both his hearers together.

"Yes, for I'm sorry to tell you"—he looked searchingly at the lady as he spoke—"I'm sorry to tell you, Mrs. Guthrie, that a considerable number of bombs have been found in your house. I believe it to be the fact that you hold the lease of the Trellis House in Witanbury Close?"

She looked at him too much surprised and too much bewildered to speak. Then, "Bombs?" she echoed incredulously. "There must be some mistake! There has never been any gunpowder in my possession. I might almost go so far as to say that I have never seen a gun or a pistol at close quarters——"

She felt a hand groping towards her, and at last find and cover in a tight grip her fingers. "You do not fire bombs from a gun or from a pistol, my dearest." There was a great tenderness in Major Guthrie's voice.

Even in the midst of her surprise and disarray at the extraordinary thing she had just heard, Mrs. Guthrie blushed so deeply that Mr. Reynolds noticed it, and felt rather puzzled. He told himself that she was a younger woman than he had at first taken her to be.

In a very different tone Major Guthrie next addressed the man he knew to be sitting opposite to him: "May I ask how and where and when bombs were found in the Trellis House?" To himself he was saying, with anguished iteration, "Oh, God, if only I could see! Oh, God, if only I could see!" But he spoke, if sternly, yet in a quiet, courteous tone, his hand still clasping closely that of his wife.

"They were found this morning within half an hour, I understand, of your wedding. And it was only owing to the quickness of a lady named Miss Forsyth—assisted, I am bound to say, by Mr. Hayley of the Foreign Office, who is, I believe, a relation of Mrs. Guthrie—that they were found at all. The man who came to fetch them away did get off scot free—luckily leaving them, and his motor, behind him."

"The man who came to fetch them away?" The woman sitting opposite to the speaker repeated the words in a wondering tone—then, very decidedly, "There has been some extraordinary mistake!" she exclaimed. "I know every inch of my house, and so I can assure you"—she bent forward a little in her earnestness and excitement—"I can assure you that it's quite *impossible* that there was anything of the sort in the Trellis House without my knowing it!"

"Did you ever go into your servant's bedroom?" asked Mr. Reynolds quietly.

Major Guthrie felt the hand he was holding in his suddenly tremble, and his wife made a nervous movement, as if she wanted to draw it away from his protecting grasp.

A feeling of terror—of sheer, unreasoning terror—had swept over her. *Anna?*

"No," she faltered, but her voice was woefully changed. "No, I never had occasion to go into my old servant's bedroom. But oh, I cannot believe— —" and then she stopped. She had remembered Anna's curious unwillingness to leave the Trellis House this morning, even to attend her beloved mistress's wedding. She, and Rose too, had been hurt, and had shown that they were hurt, at old Anna's obstinacy.

"We have reason to suppose," said Mr. Reynolds slowly, "that the explosives in question have been stored for some considerable time in a large roomy cupboard which is situated behind your servant's bed. As a matter of fact, the man who had come to fetch them away was already under observation by the police. He has spent all the winter in a village not far from Southampton, and he is registered as a Spaniard, though he came to England from America just before the War broke out. Of course, these facts have only just come to my knowledge. But both this Miss Forsyth and your cousin, Mr. Hayley, declare that they have long suspected your servant of being a spy."

"Suspected my servant? Suspected Anna Bauer?" repeated Mrs. Guthrie, in a bewildered tone.

"Then you," went on Mr. Reynolds, "have never suspected her at all, Mrs. Guthrie? I understand that but for the accidental fact that Witanbury is just, so to speak, over the border of the prohibited area for aliens, she would have *had* to leave you?"

"Yes, I know that. But she has been with me nearly twenty years, and I regarded her as being to all intents and purposes an Englishwoman."

"Did you really?" he observed drily.

"Her daughter is married to an Englishman."

Mr. Reynolds, in answer to that statement, remained silent, but a very peculiar expression came over his face. It was an expression which would perchance have given a clue to Major Guthrie had Major Guthrie been able to see.

Mrs. Guthrie's face had gone grey with pain and fear; her eyes had filled with tears, which were now rolling down her cheeks. She looked indeed different from the still pretty, happy, charming-looking woman who had stepped into the car a few minutes ago.

"I should not have ventured to disturb you to-day—to-morrow would have been quite time enough——" said Mr. Reynolds, speaking this time really kindly, "were it not that we attach the very greatest importance to discovering whether this woman, your ex-servant, forms part of a widespread conspiracy. We suspect that she does. But she is in such a state of pretended or real agitation—in fact, she seems almost distraught—that none of us can get anything out of her. I myself have questioned her both in English and in German. All she keeps repeating is that she is innocent, quite innocent, and that she was unaware of the nature of the goods—she describes them always as goods, when she speaks in English—that she was harbouring in your house. She declares she knows nothing about the man who came for them, though that is false on the face of it, for she was evidently expecting him. We think that he has terrorised her. She even refuses to say where she obtained these 'goods' of hers, or how long she has had them. You see, we have reason to believe"—he slightly lowered his voice in the rushing wind—"we have reason to believe," he repeated, "that the Germans may be going to try their famous plan of invasion within the next few days. If so, it is clear that these bombs were meant to play a certain part in the business, and thus it is extremely important that we should know if there are any further stores of them in or about Witanbury."

CHAPTER XXXI

They were now in the streets of the cathedral city, and Mrs. Guthrie, agitated though she was, could see that there was a curious air of animation and bustle. A great many people were out of doors on this late March afternoon.

As a matter of fact something of the facts, greatly exaggerated as is always the way, had leaked out, and the whole city was in a ferment.

Slowly the motor made its way round the Market Place to the Council House, and as it drew up at the bottom of the steps, a crowd of idlers surged forward.

There was a minute or two of waiting, then a man whom Mrs. Guthrie knew to be the head inspector of the local police came forward, with a very grave face, and helped her out of the car. He wished to hurry her up the steps out of the way of the people there, but she heard her husband's voice, "Mary, where are you?" and obediently she turned with an eager, "Here I am, waiting for you!" She took his arm, and he pressed it reassuringly. She was glad he could not see the inquisitive faces of the now swelling crowd which were being but ill kept back by the few local police.

But her ordeal did not last long; in a very few moments they were safe in the Council House, and Mr. Reynolds, who already knew his way about there, had shown them into a stately room where hung the portraits of certain long dead Witanbury worthies.

"Am I going to see Anna now?" asked Mrs. Guthrie nervously.

"Yes, I must ask you to do that as soon as possible. And, Mrs. Guthrie? Please remember that all we want to know now are two definite facts. The first of these is how long she has had these bombs in her possession, and how she procured them? She may possibly be willing to tell you how long she has had them, even if she still remains obstinately silent as to where she got them. The second question, and of course much the more important from our point of view, is whether she knows of any other similar stores in Witanbury or elsewhere? That, I need hardly tell you, is of very vital moment to us, and I appeal to you as an Englishwoman to help us in the matter."

"I will do as you wish," said Mrs. Guthrie in a low voice. "But, Mr. Reynolds? Please forgive me for asking you one thing. What will be done to my poor old Anna? Will the fact that she is a German make it better for her—or worse? Of course I realise that she has been wicked—very, very wicked if what you say is true——"

"And most treacherous to you!" interposed the young man quickly. "You don't seem to realise, Mrs. Guthrie, the danger in which she put you;" and as she looked at him uncomprehendingly, he went on, "Putting everything else aside, she ran the most appalling danger of killing you—you and every member of your household. Of course I don't know what you mean to say to her——" he hesitated. "I understand that your relations with her have been much closer and more kindly than are often those between a servant and her employer," and as she nodded, he went on: "The Dean was afraid that it would give you a terrible shock—in fact, he himself seems extremely surprised and distressed; he had evidently quite a personal feeling of affection and respect for this old German woman, Anna Bauer!"

"And I am sure that if you had known her you would have had it too, Mr. Reynolds," she answered naïvely. Somehow the fact that the Dean had taken this strange and dreadful thing as he had done, made her feel less miserable.

"Ah! One thing more before I take you to her. Anything incriminating she may say to you will *not* be brought as evidence against her. The point you have to remember is that it is vitally important to us to obtain information as to this local spy conspiracy or system, to which we believe we already hold certain clues."

The police cell into which Mrs. Guthrie was introduced was in the half-basement of the ancient Council House. The walls of the cell were whitewashed with a peculiar, dusty whitewash that came off upon the occupant's clothes at the slightest touch. There was a bench fixed to the wall, and in a corner a bed, also fixed to the ground. A little light came in from the window high out of reach, and in the middle of the ceiling hung a disused gas bracket.

Those of Anna Bauer's personal possessions she had been allowed to bring with her were lying on the bed.

The old woman was sitting on the bench, her head bowed in an abandonment of stupor, and of misery. She did not even move as the door opened. But when she heard the kind, familiar voice exclaim, "Anna? My poor old Anna!—it is terrible to find you here, like this!" she drew a convulsive breath of relief, and lifted her tear-stained, swollen face.

"I am innocent!" she cried wildly, in German. "Oh, gracious lady, I am innocent! I have done no wrong. I can accuse myself of no sin."

Mr. Reynolds brought in a chair. Then he went out, and quietly closed the door.

Anna's mistress came and sat on the bench close to her servant. It was almost as if an unconscious woman, spent with the extremity of physical suffering, crouched beside her.

"Anna, listen to me!" she said at last, and there was a touch of salutary command in her voice—a touch of command that poor Anna knew, and always responded to, though it was very seldom used towards her. "I have left Major Guthrie on our marriage day in order to try and help you in this awful disgrace and trouble you have brought, not only on yourself, but on me. All I ask you to do is to tell me the truth. Anna?"—she touched the fat arm close to her—"look up, and talk to me like a reasonable woman. If you are innocent, if you can accuse yourself of no sin—then why are you in such a state?"

Anna looked up eagerly. She was feeling much better now.

"Every reason have I in a state to be! A respectable woman to such a place brought! Roughly by two policemen treated. I nothing did that ashamed of I am!"

"What is it you *did* do?" said Mrs. Guthrie patiently. "Try and collect your thoughts, Anna. Explain to me where you got"—she hesitated painfully—"where you got the bombs."

"No bombs there were," exclaimed Anna confidently. "Chemicals, yes—bombs, no."

"You are mistaken, Anna," said Mrs. Guthrie quietly. She rose from the bench on which she had been sitting, and drew up the chair opposite to Anna. "There were certainly bombs found in your room. It is a mercy they did not explode; if they had done, we should all have been killed!"

Anna stared at her in dumb astonishment. "Herr Gott!" she exclaimed. "No one has told me that, gracious lady. Again and again they have asked me questions they should not—questions I to answer promised not. To you, speak I will——"

Anna looked round, as if to satisfy herself that they were indeed alone, and Mrs. Guthrie suddenly grew afraid. Was poor old Anna going to reveal something of a very serious self-incriminating kind?

"It was Willi!" exclaimed the old woman at last. She now spoke in a whisper, and in German. "It was to Willi that I gave my promise to say nothing. You see, gracious lady, it was a friend of Willi's who was making a chemical invention. It was he who left these goods with me. I will now confess"—she began to sob bitterly—"I will now confess that I did keep it a secret from the gracious lady that these parcels had been confided to me. But the bedroom was mine. You know, gracious lady, how often you said to me, 'I should have liked you to have a nicer bedroom, Anna—but still, it is your room, so I hope you make it as comfortable as you can.' As it was my room, gracious lady, it concerned no one what I kept there."

"A friend of Willi's?" repeated Mrs. Guthrie incredulously. "But I don't understand—Willi is in Berlin. Surely you have not seen Willi since you went to Germany three years ago?"

"No, indeed not. But he told me about this matter when he took me to the station. He said that a friend would call on me some time after my return here, and that to keep these goods would be to my advantage——" she stopped awkwardly.

"You mean," said Mrs. Guthrie slowly, "that you were paid for keeping these things, Anna?" Somehow she felt a strange sinking of the heart.

"Yes," Anna spoke in a shamed, embarrassed tone. "Yes, that is quite true. I was given a little present each year. But it was no one's business but mine."

"And how long did you have them?" Mrs. Guthrie had remembered suddenly that that was an important point.

Anna waited a moment, but she was only counting. "Exactly three years," she answered. "Three years this month."

Mrs. Guthrie also made a rapid calculation. "You mean that they were brought to the Trellis House in the March of 1912?"

Anna nodded. "Yes, gracious lady. When you and Miss Rose were in London. Do you remember?"

The other shook her head.

Anna felt almost cheerful now. She had told the whole truth, and her gracious lady did not seem so very angry after all.

"They were brought," she went on eagerly, "by a very nice gentleman. He asked me for a safe place to keep them, and I showed him the cupboard behind my bed. He helped me to bring them in."

"Was that the man who came for them this morning?" asked Mrs. Guthrie.

Anna shook her head. "Oh no!" she exclaimed. "The other gentleman was a gentleman. He wrote me a letter first, but when he came he asked me to give it him back. So of course I did so."

"Did he give you any idea of what he had brought you to keep?" asked Mrs. Guthrie. "Now, Anna, I beg—I implore you to tell me the truth!"

"The truth will I willingly tell!" Yes, Anna was feeling really better now. She had confessed the one thing which had always been on her conscience—her deceit towards her kind mistress. "He said they were chemicals, a new wonderful invention, which I must take great care of as they were fragile."

"I suppose he was a German?" said Mrs. Guthrie slowly.

"Yes, he was a German, naturally, being the superior of Willi. But the man who came to-day was no German."

"And during all that time—three years is a long time, Anna—did you never hear from him?" asked Mrs. Guthrie slowly.

It had suddenly come over her with a feeling of repugnance and pain, that old Anna had kept her secret very closely.

"I never heard—no, never, till last night," cried the old woman eagerly.

"But even now," said Mrs. Guthrie, "I can't understand, Anna, what made you do it. Was it to please Willi?"

"Yes," said Anna in an embarrassed tone. "It was to please my good nephew, gracious lady."

CHAPTER XXXII

And now," said Mrs. Guthrie, looking at the little group of people who sat round her in the Council Chamber, "and now I have told you, almost I think word for word, everything my poor old Anna told me."

As Mr. Reynolds remained silent, she added, with a touch of defiance, "And I am quite, quite sure that she told me the truth!"

Her eyes instinctively sought the Dean's face. Yes, there she found sympathy,—sympathy and belief. It was impossible to tell what her husband was thinking. His face was not altered—it was set in stern lines of discomfort and endurance. The Government official looked sceptical.

"I have no doubt that the woman has told you a good deal of the truth, Mrs. Guthrie, but I do not think she has told you *all* the truth, or the most important part of it. According to your belief, she accepted this very strange deposit without the smallest suspicion of the truth. Now, is it conceivable that an intelligent, sensible, elderly woman of the kind she has been described to me, could be such a fool?"

And then, for the first time since his wife had returned there from her interview with Anna, Major Guthrie intervened.

"I think you forget, Mr. Reynolds, that this took place long before the war. In fact, if I may recall certain dates to your memory, this must have been a little tiny cog in the machine which Germany began fashioning after the Agadir crisis. It was that very autumn that Anna Bauer went to visit her nephew and niece in Berlin, and it was soon after she came back that, according to her story, a stranger, with some kind of introduction from her nephew, who is, I believe, connected with the German police——"

"Is he indeed?" exclaimed Mr. Reynolds. "You never told me that!" he looked at Mrs. Guthrie.

"Didn't I?" she said. "Yes, it's quite true, Wilhelm Warshauer is a sub-inspector of police in Berlin. But I feel sure he is a perfectly respectable man."

She fortunately did not see the expression which flashed across her questioner's face. Not so the Dean. Mr. Reynolds' look stirred Dr. Haworth to a certain indignation. He had known Anna Bauer as long as her mistress had, and he had become quite fond of the poor old woman with whom he had so often exchanged pleasant greetings in German.

"Look here!" he began, in a pleasant, persuasive voice. "I have a suggestion to make, Mr. Reynolds. We have here in Witanbury a most excellent fellow, one of our city councillors. He is of German birth, but was naturalised long ago. As I expect you know, there was a little riot here last week, and this man—Alfred Head is his name—had all his windows broken. He refused to prosecute, and behaved with the greatest sense and dignity. Now I suggest that we set Alfred Head on to old Anna Bauer! I believe she would tell him things that she would not even tell her very kind and considerate mistress. I feel sure that he would find out the real truth. As a matter of fact I met him just now when I was coming down here. He was full of regret and concern, and he spoke very kindly and very sensibly of this poor old woman. He said he knew her—that she was a friend of his wife's, and he asked me if he could be of any assistance to her."

Thinking he saw a trace of hesitation on the London official's face, he added, "After all, such an interview could do no harm, and might do good. Yes, I strongly do advise that we take Alfred Head into our counsels, and explain to him exactly what it is we wish to know."

"I am quite sure," exclaimed Mrs. Guthrie impulsively, "that Anna would not tell him any more than she told me. I am convinced, not only that she told me the truth, but that she told me nothing but the truth—I don't believe she kept *anything* back!"

Mr. Reynolds looked straight at the speaker of these impetuous words. He smiled. It was a kindly, albeit a satiric smile. He was getting quite fond of Mrs. Guthrie! And though his duties often brought him in contact with strange and unusual little groups of people, this was the first time he had ever had to bring into his official work a bride on her wedding day. This was the first time also that a dean had ever been mixed up in any of the difficult and dangerous affairs with which he was now concerned. It was, too, the first time that he had been brought into personal contact with one of his own countrymen "broken in the war."

"I hope that you are right," he said soothingly. "Still, as Mr. Dean kindly suggests, it may be worth while allowing this man—Head is his name, is it?—to see the woman. It generally happens that a person of the class to which Anna Bauer belongs will talk much more freely to some one of their own sort than to an employer, however kind. In fact, it often happens that after having remained quite silent and refused to say anything to, say, a solicitor, such a person will come out with the whole truth to an old friend, or to a relation. We will hope that this will be the case this time. And now

I don't think that we need detain you and Major Guthrie any longer. Of course you shall be kept fully informed of any developments."

"If there is any question, as I suppose there will be, of Anna Bauer being sent for trial," said Major Guthrie, "then I should wish, Mr. Reynolds, that my own solicitor undertakes her defence. My wife feels that she is under a great debt of gratitude to this German woman. Anna has not only been her servant for over eighteen years, but she was nurse to Mrs. Guthrie's only child. We neither of us feel in the least inclined to abandon Anna Bauer because of what has happened. I also wish to associate myself very strongly with what Mrs. Guthrie said just now. I believe the woman to be substantially innocent, and I think she has almost certainly told my wife the truth, as far as she knows it."

He held out his hand, and the other man grasped it warmly. Then Mr. Reynolds shook hands with Mrs. Guthrie. She looked happy now—happy if a little tearful. "I hope," he said eagerly, "that you will make use of my car to take you home."

Somehow he felt interested in, and drawn to, this middle-aged couple. He was quite sorry to know that, after to-day, he would probably never see them again. The type of man who is engaged in the sort of work which Mr. Reynolds was now doing for his country has to be very human underneath his cloak of official reserve, or he would not be able to carry out his often delicate, as well as difficult, duties.

He followed them outside the Council House. Clouds had gathered, and it was beginning to rain, so he ordered his car to be closed.

"Mr. Reynolds," cried Mrs. Guthrie suddenly, "you won't let them be *too* unkind to my poor old Anna, will you?"

"Indeed, no one will be unkind to her," he said. "She's only been a tool after all—poor old woman. No doubt there will be a deportation order, and she will be sent back to Germany."

"Remember that you are to draw on me if any money is required on her behalf," cried out Major Guthrie, fixing his sightless eyes on the place where he supposed the other man to be.

"Yes, yes—I quite understand that! But we've found out that the old woman has plenty of money. It is one of the things that make us believe that she knows more than she pretends to do."

He waved his hand as they drove off. Somehow he felt a better man, a better Englishman, for having met these two people.

There was very little light in the closed motor, but if it had been open for all the world to see, Mary Guthrie would not have minded, so happy, so secure did she feel now that her husband's arm was round her.

She put up her face close to his ear: "Oh, Alick," she whispered, "I am afraid that you've married a very foolish woman——"

He turned and drew her into his strong arms. "I've married the sweetest, the most generous, and—and, Mary, the dearest of women."

"At any rate you can always say to yourself, 'A poor thing, but mine own—'" she said, half laughing, half crying. And then their lips met and clung together, for the first time.

CHAPTER XXXIII

Mr. Reynolds walked back up the steps of the Council House of Witanbury. He felt as if he had just had a pleasant glimpse of that Kingdom of Romance which so many seek and so few find, and that now he was returning into the everyday world. Sure enough, when he reached the Council Chamber, he found Dr. Haworth there with a prosaic-looking person. This was evidently the man to whom the Dean thought Anna would be more likely to reveal the truth than to her kind, impulsive employer.

Mr. Reynolds had not expected to see so intelligent and young-looking a man. He was familiar with the type of German who has for long made his career in England. But this naturalised German was not true to type at all! Though probably over fifty, he still had an alert, active figure, and he was extraordinarily like someone Mr. Reynolds had seen. In fact, for a few moments the likeness quite haunted him. Who on earth could it be that this man so strongly resembled? But soon he gave up the likeness as a bad job— it didn't matter, after all!

"Well, Mr. Head, I expect that Dr. Haworth has already told you what it is we hope from you."

"Yes, sir, I think I understand."

"Are you an American?" asked the other abruptly.

The Witanbury City Councillor looked slightly embarrassed. "No," he said at last. "But I was in the United States for some years."

"You were never connected, I suppose, with the New York Police?"

"Oh no, sir!" There was no mistaking the man's genuine surprise at the question.

"I only asked you," said Mr. Reynolds hastily, "because I feel as if we had met before. But I suppose I made a mistake. By the way, do you know Anna Bauer well?"

Alfred Head waited a moment; he looked instinctively to the Dean for guidance, but the Dean made no sign.

"I know Anna Bauer pretty well," he said at last. "But she's more a friend of my wife than of mine. She used sometimes to come and spend the evening with us."

He was feeling exceedingly uncomfortable. Had Anna mentioned him? He thought not. He hoped not. "What is it exactly you want me to get out of her?" he asked, cringingly.

Mr. Reynolds hesitated. Somehow he did not at all like the man standing before him. Shortly he explained how much the old woman had already admitted; and then, "Perhaps you could ascertain whether she has received any money since the outbreak of war, and if so, by what method. I may tell you in confidence, Mr. Head, there has been a good deal of German money going about in this part of the world. We hold certain clues, but up to the present time we have not been able to trace this money to its source."

"I think I quite understand what it is you require to know, sir," said Alfred Head respectfully.

There came a knock at the door. "Mr. Reynolds in there? You are wanted, sir, on the telephone. A London call from Scotland Yard."

"All right," he said quietly. "Tell them they must wait a moment. Will you please take Mr. Head to the cell where Anna Bauer is confined?"

Then he hurried off to the telephone, well aware that he might now be about to hear the real solution of the mystery. Some of his best people had been a long time on this Witanbury job.

Terrified and bewildered as she had been by the events of midday, Anna, when putting her few things together, had not forgotten her work. True, she had been too much agitated and upset to crochet or knit during the long hours which had elapsed since the morning. But the conversation she had had with her mistress had reassured her. How good that dear, gracious lady had been! How kindly she had accepted the confession of deceit!

Yes, but it was very, very wrong of her, Anna Bauer, to have done what she had done. She knew that now. What was the money she had earned—a few paltry pounds—compared with all this fearful trouble? Still, she felt now sure the trouble would soon be over. She had a pathetic faith, not only in her mistress, but also in Mrs. Jervis Blake and in the Dean. They would see her through this strange, shameful business. So she took her workbag off the bed, and brought out her crochet.

She had just begun working when she heard the door open, and there came across her face a sudden look of apprehension. She was weary of being questioned, and of parrying questions. But now she had told all she knew. There was great comfort in that thought.

Her face cleared, became quite cheerful and smiling, when she saw Alfred Head. He, too, was a kind friend; he, too, would help her as much as he could—if indeed any more help were needed. But the Dean and her own lady would certainly be far more powerful than Alfred Head.

Poor Old Anna was not in a condition to be very observant. She did not see that there was anything but a cordial expression on her friend's face, and that he looked indeed very stern and disagreeable.

The door was soon shut behind him, and instead of advancing with hand outstretched, he crossed his arms and looked down at her, silently, for a few moments.

At last, speaking between his teeth, and in German, he exclaimed, "This is a pretty state of things, Frau Bauer. You have made more trouble than you know!"

She stared up at him, uncomprehendingly. "I don't understand," she faltered. "I did nothing. What do you mean?"

"I mean that you have brought us all within sight of the gallows. Yourself quite as much as your friends."

"The gallows?" exclaimed old Anna, in an agitated whisper. "Explain yourself, Mr. Head——" She was trembling now. "What is it you mean?"

"I do not know what it is you have told," he spoke in a less savage tone. "And I know as a matter of fact that there is very little you *could* say, for you have been kept in the dark. But one thing I may tell you. If you say one word, Frau Bauer, of where you received your blood money just after the War broke out, then I, too, will say what *I* know. If I do that, instead of being deported—that is, instead of being sent comfortably back to Berlin, to your niece and her husband, who surely will look after you and make your old age comfortable—then I swear to you before God *that you will hang!*"

"Hang? But I have done nothing!"

Anna was now almost in a state of collapse, and he saw his mistake.

"You are in no real danger at all if you will only do exactly what I tell you," he declared, impressively.

"Yes," she faltered. "Yes, Herr Hegner, indeed I will obey you."

He looked round him hastily. "Never, never call me that!" he exclaimed. "And now listen quite quietly to what I have to say. Remember you are in no danger—no danger at all—if you follow my orders."

She looked at him dumbly.

"You are to say that the parcels came to you from your nephew in Germany. It will do him no harm. The English police cannot reach him."

"But I've already said," she confessed, distractedly, "that they were brought to me by a friend of his."

"It is a pity you said that, but it does not much matter. The one thing you must conceal at all hazards is that you received any money from me. Do you understand that, Frau Bauer? Have you said anything of that?"

"No," she said slowly. "No, I have said nothing of that."

He fancied there was a look of hesitation on her face. As a matter of fact we know that Anna had not betrayed Alfred Head. But that she had not done so was an accident, only caused by her unwillingness to dwell on the money she had received when telling her story to Mrs. Guthrie.

The old woman turned a mottled red and yellow colour, in the poor light of the cell.

"Please try and remember," he said sternly, "if you mentioned me at all."

"I swear I did not!" she cried.

"Did you say that you had received money?"

And Anna answered, truthfully, "Yes, Herr Head; I did say that."

"Fool! Fool indeed—when it would have been so easy for you to pretend you had done it to please your nephew!"

"But Mrs. Otway, she has forgiven me. My gracious lady does not think I did anything so very wrong," cried Anna.

"Mrs. Otway? What does she matter! They will do all they can to get out of you how you received this money. You must say—— Are you attending, Frau Bauer?"

She had sunk down again on her bench; she felt her legs turning to cotton-wool. "Yes," she muttered. "Yes, I am attending——"

"You must say," he commanded, "that you always received the money from your nephew. That since the war you have had none. Do I make myself clear?"

"Yes," she murmured—"quite clear, Herr Head."

"If you do not say that, if you bring me into this dirty business, then I, too, will say what I know about you."

She looked at him uncomprehendingly. What did he mean?

"Ah, you do not know perhaps what I can tell about you!"

He came nearer to her, and in a hissing whisper went on: "I can tell how it was through you that a certain factory in Flanders was shelled, and eighty Englishmen were killed. And if I tell that, they will hang you!"

"But that is not true," said Anna stoutly. "So you could not say that!"

"It *is* true." He spoke with a kind of ferocious energy that carried conviction, even to her. "It is absolutely true, and easily proved. You showed a letter—a letter from Mr. Jervis Blake. In that letter was information which led directly to the killing of those eighty English soldiers, and to the injury to Mr. Jervis Blake which lost him his foot."

"What is that you say?" Anna's voice rose to a scream of horror—of incredulous, protesting horror. "Unsay, do unsay what you have just said, kind Mr. Head!"

"How can I unsay what is the fact?" he answered savagely. "Do not be a stupid fool! You ought to be glad you performed such a deed for the Fatherland."

"Not Mr. Jervis Blake," she wailed out. "Not the bridegroom of my child!"

"The bridegroom of your child was engaged in killing good Germans; and now he will never kill any Germans any more. And it is *you*, Frau Bauer, who shot off his foot. If you betray me, all that will be known, and they will not deport you, they will hang you!"

To this she said nothing, and he touched her roughly on the shoulder. "Look up, Frau Bauer! Look up, and tell me that you understand! It is important!"

She looked up, and even he was shocked, taken aback, by the strange look on her face. It was a look of dreadful understanding, of fear, and of pain. "I do understand," she said in a low voice.

"If you do what I tell you, nothing will happen to you," he exclaimed impatiently, but more kindly than he had yet spoken. "You will only be sent home, deported, as they call it. If you are thinking of your money in the Savings Bank, that they will not allow you to take. But without doubt your ladies will take care of it for you till this cursed war is over. So you see you have nothing to fear if you do what I tell you. So now good-bye, Frau Bauer. I'll go and tell them that you know nothing, that I have been not able to get anything out of you. Is that so?"

"Yes," she answered apathetically.

Giving one more quick look at her bowed head, he went across and knocked loudly at the cell door.

There was a little pause, and then the door opened. It opened just wide enough to let him out.

And then, just for a moment, Alfred Head felt a slight tremor of discomfort, for the end of the passage, that is, farther down, some way past Anna's cell, now seemed full of men. There stood the chief local police inspector and three or four policemen, as well as the gentleman from London.

It was the latter who first spoke. He came forward, towards Alfred Head. "Well," he said rather sternly, "I presume that you've been able to get nothing from the old woman?"

And Mr. Head answered glibly enough, "That's quite correct, sir. There is evidently nothing to be got out of her. As you yourself said, sir, not long ago, this old woman has only been a tool."

The two policemen were now walking one each side of him, and it seemed to Alfred Head as if he were being hustled along towards the hall where there generally stood, widely open, the doors leading out on to the steps to the Market Place.

He told himself that he would be very glad to get out into the open air and collect his thoughts. He did not believe that his old fellow-countrywoman would, to use a vulgar English colloquialism, "give him away." But still, he would not feel quite at ease till she was safely deported and out of the way.

The passage was rather a long one, and he began to feel a curious, nervous craving to reach the end of it—to be, that is, out in the hall.

But just before they reached the end of the passage the men about him closed round Alfred Head. He felt himself seized, it seemed to him from every side, not roughly, but with a terribly strong muscular grip.

"What is this?" he cried in a loud voice. Even as he spoke, he wondered if he could be dreaming—if this was the horrible after effect of the strain he had just gone through.

For a moment only he struggled, and then, suddenly, he submitted. He knew what it was he wished to save; it was the watch chain to which were attached the two keys of the safe in his bedroom. He wore them among a bunch of old-fashioned Georgian seals which he had acquired in the way of business, and he had had the keys gilt, turned to a dull gold colour, to match the seals. It was possible, just possible, that they might escape the notice of these thick-witted men about him.

"What does this mean?" he demanded; and then he stopped, for there rose a distant sound of crying and screaming in the quiet place.

"What is that?" he cried, startled.

The police inspector came forward; he cleared his throat. "I'm sorry to tell you, Head"—he spoke quite civilly, even kindly—"that we've had to arrest your wife, too."

"This is too much! She is a child—a mere child! Innocent as a baby unborn. An Englishwoman, too, as you know well, Mr. Watkins. They must be all mad in this town—it is quite mad to suspect my poor little Polly!"

The inspector was a kindly man, naturally humane, and he had known the prisoner for a considerable number of years. As for poor Polly, he had always been acquainted with her family, and had seen her grow up from a lovely child into a very pretty girl.

"Look here!" he said. "It's no good kicking up a row. Unluckily for her, they found the key with which they opened your safe in her possession. D'you take my meaning?"

Alfred Head grew rather white. "That's impossible!" he said confidently. "There are but two keys, and I have them both."

The other looked at him with a touch of pity. "There must have been a third key," he said slowly. "I've got it here myself. It was hidden away in an old-fashioned dressing-case. Besides, Mrs. Head didn't put up any fight. But if she can prove, as she says, that she knows no German, and that you didn't know she had a key of the safe—for that's what she says—well, that'll help her, of course."

"But there's nothing *in* the safe," Head objected, quickly, "nothing of what might be called an incriminating nature, Mr. Watkins. Only business letters and papers, and all of them sent me before the War."

The other man looked at him, and hesitated. He had gone quite as far as old friendship allowed. "That's as may be," he said cautiously. "I know nothing of all that. They've been sealed up, and are going off to London. What caused you to be arrested, Mr. Head—this much I may tell you—is information which was telephoned down to that London gentleman half an hour ago. But it was just an accident that the key Mrs. Head had hidden away was found so quickly—just a bit of bad luck for her, if I may say so."

"Then I suppose I shan't be allowed to see Polly?" There was a tone of extreme dejection in the voice.

"Well, we'll see about that! I'll see what I can do for you. You're not to be charged till to-morrow morning. Then you'll be charged along with that man—the man who came to the Trellis House this morning. He's been found too. He went straight to those Pollits—you follow my meaning? Mrs. Pollit is the daughter of that old German woman. I never could abide *her*! Often and often I said to my missis, as I see her go crawling about, 'There's a German as is taking away a good job from an English woman.' So she was. Well, I must now tell them where to take you. And I'm afraid you'll have to be stripped and searched—that's the order in these kind of cases."

Alfred Head nodded. "I don't mind," he said stoutly. "I'm an innocent man." But he had clenched his teeth together when he had heard the name of Pollit uttered so casually. If Pollit told all he knew, then the game was indeed up.

CHAPTER XXXIV

After the door had shut behind Alfred Head, Anna Bauer sat on, quite motionless, awhile. What mind was left to her, after the terrifying and agonising interview she had just had, was absorbed in the statement made to her concerning Jervis Blake.

She remembered, with blinding clearness, the afternoon that Rose had come into her kitchen to say in a quiet, toneless voice, "They think, Anna, that they will have to take off his foot." She saw, as clearly as if her nursling were there in this whitewashed little cell, the look of desolate, dry-eyed anguish which had filled Rose's face.

But that false quietude had only lasted a few moments, for, in response to her poor old Anna's exclamation of horror and of sympathy, Rose Otway had flung herself into her nurse's arms, and had lain there shivering and crying till the sound of the front door opening to admit her mother had forced her to control herself.

Anna's mind travelled wearily on, guided by reproachful memory through a maze of painful recollections. Once more she stood watching the strange marriage ceremony—trying hard, aye, and succeeding, to obey Sir Jacques's strict injunction. More than one of those present had glanced over at her, Anna, very kindly during that trying half-hour. How would they then have looked at her if they had known what she knew now?

She lived again as in long drawn-out throbs of pain the piteous days which had followed Mr. Blake's operation.

Rose had not allowed herself one word of fret or of repining; but on three different nights during that first week, she had got out of bed and wandered about the house, till Anna, hearing the quiet, stuffless sounds of bare feet, had come out, and leading the girl into the still warm kitchen, had comforted her.

It was Anna who had spoken to Sir Jacques, and suggested the sleeping draught which had finally broken that evil waking spell—Anna who, far more than Rose's own mother, had sustained and heartened the poor child during those dreadful days of reaction which followed on the brave front she had shown at the crisis of the operation.

And now Anna had to face the horrible fact that it was she who had brought this dreadful suffering, this—this lifelong misfortune, on the being she loved more than she had ever loved anything in the world. If this was true, and in her heart she knew it to be true, then she did indeed deserve to hang. A shameful death would be nothing in comparison to the agony of fearing that her darling might come to learn the truth.

The door of the cell suddenly opened, and a man came in, carrying a tray in his hands. On it were a jug of coffee, some milk, sugar, bread and butter, and a plateful of cold meat.

He put it down by the old woman's side. "Look here!" he said. "Your lady, Mrs. Guthrie as she is now, thought you'd rather have coffee than tea—so we've managed to get some for you."

And, as Anna burst into loud sobs, "There, there!" he said good-naturedly. "I daresay you'll be all right—don't you be worrying yourself." He lowered his voice: "Though there are some as says that what they found in your back kitchen this morning was enough to have blown up all Witanbury sky high! Quite a good few don't think you knew anything about it—and if you didn't, you've nothing to fear. You'll be treated quite fair; so now you sit up, and make a good supper!"

She stared at him without speaking, and he went on: "You won't be having this sort of grub in Darneford Gaol, you know!" As she again looked at him with no understanding, he added by way of explanation: "After you've been charged to-morrow, it's there they'll send you, I expect, to wait for the Assizes."

"So?" she said stupidly.

"You just sit up and enjoy your supper! You needn't hurry over it. I shan't be this way again for an hour or so." And then he went out and shut the door.

For almost the first time in her life, Anna Bauer did not feel as if she wanted to eat good food set before her. But she poured out a cup of coffee, and drank it just as it was, black and bitter, without putting either milk or sugar to it.

Then she stood up. The coffee had revived her, cleared her brain, and she looked about her with awakened, keener perceptions.

It was beginning to get dark, but it was a fine evening, and there was still light enough to see by. She looked up consideringly at the old-fashioned iron gas bracket, placed in the middle of the ceiling, just above the wooden chair on which her gracious lady had sat during the last part of their conversation.

Anna took from the bench where she had been sitting the crochet in which she had been interrupted.

She had lately been happily engaged in making a beautiful band of crochet lace which was destined to serve as trimming for Mrs. Jervis Blake's dressing-table. The band was now very nearly finished; there were over three yards of it done. Worked in the best and strongest linen thread, it was the kind of thing which would last, even if it were cleaned very frequently, for years and years, and which would grow finer with cleaning.

The band was neatly rolled up and pinned, to keep it clean and nice; but now Anna slowly unpinned and unrolled it.

Yes, it was a beautiful piece of work; rather coarser than what she was accustomed to do, but then she knew that Miss Rose preferred the coarser to the very fine crochet.

She tested a length of it with a sharp pull, and the result was wonderful—from her point of view most gratifying! It hardly gave at all. She remembered how ill her mistress had succeeded when she, Anna, had tried to teach her to do this kind of work some sixteen to seventeen years ago. After a very little while Mrs. Otway had given up trying to do it, knowing that she could never rival her good old Anna. Mrs. Otway's lace had been so rough, so uneven; a tiny pull, and it became all stringy and out of shape.

Yes, whatever strain were put on this band, it would surely recover—recover, that is, if it were dealt with as she, Anna, would deal with such a piece of work. It would have to be damped and stretched out on a piece of oiled silk, and each point fastened down with a pin. Then an almost cold iron would have to be passed over it, with a piece of clean flannel in between....

—

CHAPTER XXXV

At eight o'clock the same evening, Mr. Reynolds and Mr. Hayley were eating a hasty meal in the Trellis House. James Hayley had been compelled to stay on till the last train back to town, for on him the untoward events of the day had entailed a good deal of trouble. He had had to put off his cousin's tenants, find lodgings for their two servants, and arrange quarters for the policeman who, pending inquiries, was guarding the contents of Anna's bedroom.

A charwoman had been found with the help of Mrs. Haworth. But when this woman had been asked—her name was Bent, and she was a verger's wife—to provide a little supper for two gentlemen, she had demurred, and said it was impossible. Then, at last, she had volunteered to cook two chops and boil some potatoes. But she had explained that nothing further must be expected of her; she was not used to waiting at table.

The two young men were thus looking after themselves in the pretty dining-room. Mr. Reynolds, who was not as particular as his companion, and who, as a matter of fact, had had no luncheon, thought the chop quite decent. In fact, he was heartily enjoying his supper, for he was very hungry.

"I daresay all you say concerning Anna Bauer's powers of cooking, of saving, of mending, and of cleaning, are quite true!" he exclaimed, with a laugh. "But believe me, Mr. Hayley, she's a wicked old woman! Of course I shall know a great deal more about her to-morrow morning. But I've already been able to gather a good deal to-day. There's been a regular nest of spies in this town, with antennæ stretching out over the whole of this part of the southwest coast. Would you be surprised to learn that your cousin's good old Anna has a married daughter in the business—a daughter married to an Englishman?"

"You don't mean George Pollit?" asked James Hayley eagerly.

"Yes—that's the man's name! Why, d'you know him?"

"I should think I do! I helped to get him out of a scrape last year. He's a regular rascal."

"Aye, that he is indeed. He's acted as post office to this man Hegner. It's he, the fellow they call Alfred Head, the Dean's friend, the city councillor, who has been the master spy." Again he laughed, this time rather unkindly. "I think we've got the threads of it all in our hands by now. You see, we found this man Pollit's address among the very few papers which were discovered at that Spaniard's place near Southampton. A sharp fellow went to Pollit's shop, and the man didn't put up any fight at all. They're fools to employ that particular Cockney type. I suppose they chose him because his wife is German——"

There came a loud ring at the front door, and James Hayley jumped up. "I'd better see what that is," he said. "The woman we've got here is such a fool!"

He went out into the hall, and found Rose Blake.

"We heard about Anna just after we got to London," she said breathlessly. "A man in the train mentioned it to Jervis quite casually, while speaking of mother's wedding. So we came back at once to hear what had really happened and to see if we could do anything. Oh, James, what a dreadful thing! Of course she's innocent—it's absurd to think anything else. Where is she? Can I go and see her now, at once? She must be in a dreadful state. I do feel so miserable about her!"

"You'd better come in here," he said quietly. It was odd what a sharp little stab at the heart it gave him to see Rose looking so like herself—so like the girl he had hoped in time to make his wife. And yet so different too—so much softer, sweeter, and with a new radiance in her face.

He asked sharply, "By the way, where's your husband?"

"He's with the Robeys. I preferred to come here alone."

She followed him into the dining-room.

"This is Mr. Reynolds,—Mr. Reynolds, my cousin Mrs. Blake!" He waited uncomfortably, impatiently, while they shook hands, and then: "I'm afraid you're going to have a shock——" he exclaimed, and, suddenly softening, looked at her with a good deal of concern in his face. "There's very little doubt, Rose, that Anna Bauer is guilty."

"I'm sure she's not," said Rose stoutly. She looked across at the stranger. "You must forgive me for speaking like this," she said, "but you see old Anna was my nurse, and I really do know her very well."

As she glanced from the one grave face to the other, her own shadowed. "Is it very very serious?" she asked, with a catch in her clear voice.

"Yes, I'm afraid it is."

"Oh, James, do try and get leave for me to see her to-night—even for only a moment."

She turned to the other man; somehow she felt that she had a better chance there. "I have been in great trouble lately," she said, in a low tone, "and but for Anna Bauer I don't know how I should have got through it. That is why I feel I *must* go to her now in her trouble."

"We'll see what can be done," said Mr. Reynolds kindly. "It may be easier to arrange for you to see her to-night than it would be to-morrow, after she has been charged."

When they reached the Market Place they saw that there were a good many idlers still standing about near the steps leading up to the now closed door of the Council House.

"You had better wait down here while I go and see about it," said James Hayley quickly. He did not like the thought of Rose standing among the sort of people who were lingering, like noisome flies round a honey-pot, under the great portico.

And when he had left them standing together in the great space under the stars, Rose turned to the stranger with whom she somehow felt in closer sympathy than with her own cousin.

"What makes you think our old servant was a— —" she broke off. She could not bear to use the word "spy."

"I'll tell you," he said slowly, "what has convinced me. But keep this for the present to yourself, Mrs. Blake, for I have said nothing of it to Mr. Hayley. Quite at the beginning of the War, it was arranged that all telegrams addressed to the Continent should be sent to the head telegraph office in London for examination. Now within the first ten days one hundred and four messages, sent, I should add, to a hundred and four different addresses, were worded as follows— —" He waited a moment. "Are you following what I say, Mrs. Blake?"

"Yes," she said quickly. "I think I understand. You are telling me about some telegrams—a great many telegrams— —"

But she was asking herself how this complicated story could be connected with Anna Bauer.

"Well, I repeat that a hundred and four telegrams were worded almost exactly alike: 'Father can come back on about 14th. Boutet is expecting him.'"

Rose looked up at him. "Yes?" she said hesitatingly. She was completely at a loss.

"Well, your old German servant, Mrs. Blake, sent one of these telegrams on Monday, August 10th. She explained that a stranger she met in the street had asked her to send it off. She was, it seems, kept under observation for a little while, after her connection with this telegram had been discovered, but in all the circumstances, the fact she was in your mother's service, and so on, she was given the benefit of the doubt."

"But—but I don't understand even now?" said Rose slowly.

"I'll explain. All these messages were from German agents in this country, who wished to tell their employers about the secret despatch of our Expeditionary Force. 'Boutet' meant Boulogne. Of course we have no clue at all as to how your old servant got the information."

Rose suddenly remembered the day when Major Guthrie had come to say good-bye. A confused feeling of horror, of pity, and of vicarious shame swept over her. For the first time in her young life she was glad of the darkness which hid her face from her companion.

The thought of seeing Anna now filled her with repugnance and shrinking pain. "I—I understand what you mean," she said slowly.

"You must remember that she is a German. She probably regards herself in the light of a heroine!"

The minutes dragged by, and it seemed to Mr. Reynolds that they had been waiting there at least half an hour, when at last he saw with relief the tall slim figure emerge through the great door of the Council House. Very deliberately James Hayley walked down the stone steps, and came towards them. When he reached the place where the other two were standing, waiting for him, he looked round as if to make sure that there was no one within earshot.

"Rose," he said huskily—and he also was consciously glad of the darkness, for he had just gone through what had been, to one of his highly civilised and fastidious temperament, a most trying ordeal—"Rose, I'm sorry to bring you bad news. Anna Bauer is dead. The poor old woman has hanged herself. As a matter of fact, it was I—I and the inspector of police—who found her. We managed to get a doctor in through one of the side entrances—but it was of no use."

Rose said no word. She stood quite still, overwhelmed, bewildered with the horror, and, to her, the pain, of the thing she had just heard.

And then, suddenly, there fell, shaft-like, athwart the still, dark air, the sound of muffled thuds, falling quickly in rhythmical sequence, on the brick-paved space which melted away into the darkness to their left.

"What's that?" exclaimed Mr. Reynolds. His nerves also were shaken by the news which he had just heard; but even as he spoke he saw that the sound which seemed so strange, so—so sinister, was caused by a tall figure only now coming out of the shadows away across the Market Place. What puzzled Mr. Reynolds was the man's very peculiar gait. He seemed, if one can use such a contradiction in terms, to be at once crawling and swinging along.

"It's my husband!"

Rose Blake raised her head. A wavering gleam of light fell on her pale, tear-stained face, and showed it suddenly as if illumined, glowing from within: "He's never been so far by himself before—I must go to him!"

She began walking swiftly—almost running—to meet that strangely slow yet leaping figure, which was becoming more and more clearly defined among the deeply shaded gas lamps which stood at wide intervals in the great space round them.

Then, all at once, they heard the eager, homing cry, "Rose?" and the answering cry, "Jervis?" and the two figures seemed to become merged till they formed one, together.